BEHOOVED

BEHOOVED

M. STEVENSON

HODDERSCAPE

First published in Great Britain in 2025 by Hodderscape
An imprint ofHodder & Stoughton Limited
An Hachette UK company

1

A CIP catalogue record for this title is available from the British Library

Hardback ISBN 978 1 399 73848 4
Trade Paperback ISBN 978 1 399 73849 1
ebook ISBN 978 1 399 73850 7

Printed and bound in Great Britain by Clays Ltd, Elcograf S.p.A.

Hodder & Stoughton policy is to use papers that are natural, renewable and recyclable products and made from wood grown in sustainable forests. The logging and manufacturing processes are expected to conform to the environmental regulations of the country of origin.

Hodder & Stoughton Limited
Carmelite House
50 Victoria Embankment
London EC4Y 0DZ

The authorised representative in the EEA is Hachette Ireland, 8 Castlecourt Centre, Dublin 15, D15 XTP3, Ireland (email: info@hbgi.ie)

www.hodderscape.co.uk

TO MY HUSBAND, WHOM I HAVE YET
TO TURN INTO A HORSE

BEHOOVED

I stood at the door to my parents' chambers, staring at the metal sigil adorning the dark wood and willing my stomach to settle. The enameled insignia, crafted by a master Adept's hand, depicted a riot of lilies with thorn-bearing vines woven between. Gilt paint coated the petals, shimmering in the pale light from the magically forged lanterns lining the walls.

I lifted my hand to the sigil, then paused before my touch could activate it, my resolve faltering. Like most things in the palace, the insignia served a double function—a lock as well as a symbol, emphasizing both my family's position and the magical resources at their fingertips. Even its motif was about as subtle as a horse dressed up in a ball gown. Lilies bristling with thorns to represent the power of House Liliana: my family, one of the nine noble Houses that ruled Damaria.

The family, according to my parents, that my very existence disappointed.

I let my hand fall back to my side. I wanted to believe the roiling in my gut was only my condition flaring, nothing to do with nerves. But I knew better. Discussions with my parents had never been something I relished. And this time, the summons was unexpected—I could only guess what I'd done to fail them now.

Maybe they just wanted to discuss the plans for my next birthday dance. It was still almost two months away, but my parents would want to be heavily prepared after the disaster of Tatiana's most recent celebration. My sister's latest unauthorized magical invention, something she delightedly called a tempest in a teacup, had escaped its saucer and spun around the ballroom for nearly half an hour—scandalizing everyone but Tatiana herself, who could barely breathe for laughing. My parents still hadn't forgiven her—not for the expense of paying the Adept Guild to overlook yet another transgression, but for the embarrassment.

I could hardly do worse. Could I?

In the next room, one of the Adept-crafted clocks started to chime. Delaying longer would only make things worse. I tucked a loose wisp of hair behind my ear, settled my shoulders, and arranged my expression to conceal the nausea churning through my stomach. My condition had flared again this morning, but I'd taken a double dose of tonic before answering my parents' summons. For this conversation, I needed to at least appear strong.

Keep your guard up, Nita always told me on the training grounds. *Give them no opening. That's how you win.*

Surely discussing the details of a birthday celebration couldn't be worse than a fencing match, much as I'd prefer the latter. I took a deep breath and pressed my palm to the sigil. A pale light glowed between my fingers, and the bolts retracted with a series of clicks. I pushed open the door with hands kept steady by force of will.

My parents sat at the small table they used for the rare occasions when they dined in private—a sight that stirred the anticipation of rebuke in my already troubled stomach. They were bent close together over a stack of parchment, conversing in lowered voices. Both glanced up as I entered—my mother impassive, my father with lips pinched, giving him an owlish look. Their rich clothes echoed the oil paintings adorning the walls: depictions of the Virtues that founded the core of the Adepts' magical training, detailed in glowing colors. Silence, serenity, strength. Unsubtle reminders of the expectations I never quite managed to meet.

No servants attended them tonight. The matter at hand was too private to risk any gossip getting out. My stomach turned again.

"Bianca. Good, you're here." My mother's tone gave nothing away. I'd learned the art of hiding my emotions under her tutelage. She nodded at the seat to her left—the place I usually occupied.

I sank into the chair, relieved that I wouldn't have to devote energy to standing during this conversation; it would be impossible to maintain the facade of strength my parents valued while leaning on the walls for support.

My mother turned towards me. "Have you been following the situation in Gildenheim?"

I blinked, uncertain where this conversation was heading. "Of course."

It would be difficult not to. A week ago, the queen of Gildenheim, our neighbor to the north, had suddenly passed away—leaving a sole heir, a man around my age about whom I knew little except that he was famously reclusive.

"Good." My mother's lips compressed. "Gildenheim is threatening war."

That jolted me out of my attempt at calm. I sat forward, my eyes widening. "What? Since when?"

Gildenheim had long prodded at our northern border, but no true conflict had broken out between our countries in several centuries. Both sides knew Damaria commanded the resources to rebuff an invasion—at a steep price to all involved. Had our neighbor gone mad?

My father rubbed the place on his brow where fine lines had started to collect, like the surface of a cloth stretched too tight. "The new king is hungry for power. The Council of Nine received a missive this past week demanding a new treaty with radically different terms. Increased trade between our countries. An expanded market for Gilden iron and lumber—he plans to significantly develop their logging and mining industries." My father counted each item off on one bejeweled finger after another. "And an exclusive market for the latest Adept technology."

At that, I couldn't stop my eyebrows from lifting. The Adept Guild that trained all Damarians with magical potential held its technological advances almost as close as its secrets. Adept-crafted magical devices—firearms, clockwork, explosives—were second only to Damaria's oceanic trade in cementing our country's place as a world power. It wasn't difficult to understand why Gildenheim would want them; the country's ungoverned magic was only one example of its backwardness. Gildenheim still had a *monarchy*, for ocean's sake. But the Council of Nine would rather sink Damaria into the seas than agree to these terms.

"We countered, of course," my mother said. "Our ambassador persuaded the king to agree to the treaty sans that particular demand, so long as we provide . . . insurance."

She pushed the stack of papers towards me. A seal at the top—deep green wax with a silver stamp of a winged horse wearing a crown, Gildenheim's royal emblem—identified the missive's origin beyond a doubt.

I ran my eyes over the document, reading its points—written once in Damarian, again in Gilden. The terms of the treaty were much as my father had described. Until I reached the end, where a sharp, slanting hand—most likely the Gilden heir's writing, since I didn't recognize it—had struck out the portion about Adept devices and replaced it with—

I read the section twice more.

A noble hand in marriage.

Surely not.

I looked up at my parents, my eyebrows raised. My voice was

steady, betraying none of the shock and misgiving coursing through my veins. "You want me to marry the new king of Gildenheim?"

My mother steepled her fingers, leaning back in her chair. "Better than wasting resources in a pointless war. You're unattached and close to his age. It would give House Liliana a significant advantage to have one of our daughters on the Gilden throne."

My mouth was dry. With my gifted older sister the more likely heir, I'd always expected an arranged marriage. But not as *insurance* against warfare. Not sprung on me without warning, without months of negotiation.

"But it's Tatiana that everyone loves," I protested. "She can get in anyone's good graces."

"And her preferences in the bedchamber are incompatible for this union." My mother brushed my objection aside impatiently—it was an obvious obstacle, large enough that I shouldn't have tripped over it. I was flexible about the gender of my partners. My sister was not. "This treaty is a delicate matter. Any source of friction could upset it."

And Tatiana was not one to be delicate. Despite how much we resembled each other, sometimes it was hard to believe we were sisters. Tatiana cared for no one's opinion save her own. I could never manage to do the same.

I struggled to keep the turmoil of my thoughts from both my face and my voice. To regain my footing on solid ground. "But even so, Tatiana's the one with magical ability. Isn't that exactly what this new king wants?" My parents might chafe at paying the Adept Guild to look the other way, but Tatiana's talents were a point of pride for them nonetheless—and another area in which I was at a deficit.

"Precisely why it would be foolish to send her." My father had started reading through a separate stack of papers. I was tiring my parents, taking too long to grasp the situation.

My mother tapped one neatly trimmed fingernail on the table. Her eyes met mine, and despite their rich brown color, they were as cold as a rare winter storm. "Are you refusing this match, Bianca?"

My mind stuttered. My stomach gave another nauseating twist, and I swallowed against the threat of bile.

"No, I—of course not." The words rushed out, as if they could close the long-standing rift between us. I might let my parents down in other ways, but never in doing my duty. "But . . . what about my condition?"

My parents exchanged a glance laden with meaning.

Oh. My condition wasn't a sticking point. It was the reason they had volunteered me for this marriage.

Bitterness burned in my throat, mingling with nausea from the very condition in question. I knew my parents believed I wasn't strong enough to represent House Liliana. It was the reason Tatiana was set to inherit despite her intractability, though Damarian law allowed any living descendant to take up the succession. Of the two of us, I was the dependable one.

But only when I wasn't sick.

Keep your mask in place. Let no one see your weakness. My parents had driven in those words since my condition first started to trouble me, and by now they overlaid my mind like scars: no longer painful, but impossible to overlook. I must hide my ailment at all costs. Other daughters, common-born daughters—they could break and bend, but House Liliana demanded untarnished steel from its descendants. Let my weakness show, allow our noble rivals to think my lineage's power was susceptible, and I let my family down.

But it was impossible to hide an illness that could flare at any moment forever. I drank my tonics without complaint and gritted my teeth through dances and dinners, trying to force at least the semblance of health whenever politics demanded it. But despite my best efforts, despite my parents' attempts to quash even the quietest whisper, I had missed enough public appearances, retired abruptly from enough negotiations, that rumors had started to seep through the palace walls like a cold draft. It was only a matter of time before the other noble Houses of the court put the pieces together and forged them into a weapon against House Liliana.

"You'll hide your condition, at least until after the wedding," my mother said firmly. "You've managed before. And you'll bring your apothecary with you. If your husband asks about the tonics, tell him they're for your cycle."

The move was logical. Utilitarian. It was obvious, from an objective standpoint, that I was the more suitable choice. My value in the Damarian court was limited, especially since a marriage here would reveal my ailment eventually; in Gildenheim, my illness wouldn't threaten House Liliana's influence even if it were discovered. This was a solution that cemented my parents' power in more ways than one—removing me from the scrutiny of their closest rivals, while simultaneously establishing a link to the Gilden throne.

And it wasn't as if I wished Tatiana to go in my stead. Marrying a king she didn't know—she would hate it, just as she had always hated our parents' many strictures. Whereas I had always clung to my duty like a lifeline, doing exactly as my parents expected, part of me still hoping it would earn me their love long past when the evidence showed otherwise. Even now, I couldn't quite bury that hope entirely.

"Will you accept what your House requires?" my father asked.

I glanced between my parents, willing myself to look strong. To *be* strong. Whatever my feelings about the matter, someone needed to marry the man, and it might as well be me. Better a marriage than a war—or a future sitting on the outskirts at dances I was too nauseated to attend, watching the court whisper about House Liliana's sick daughter.

If my parents deemed marriage my only use, perhaps I could turn this alliance into an opportunity. Hope flickered through me at the thought. I would still have responsibilities—most likely more than ever before. But instead of forcing myself to attend dinners and speeches at my parents' instruction, instead of smiling at would-be allies through gritted teeth when my stomach burned like a coal and I could barely keep my meals down . . . as a queen, I could choose my own appointments. Keep to my rooms, or my bed, when I was too sick to stand instead of making myself more ill by pushing through, and do so without dreading the rebuke I knew was coming at the first private moment. I would still have my flares to contend with, but in Gildenheim, I might be able to decide what shape I wanted my life to take rather than continue along the grooves worn deep by tradition.

And more than that—this was a chance to prove myself. A chance to do my duty as Duchess Liliana. To finally have my parents deem me *enough* instead of merely *expendable*.

I lifted my chin, meeting my parents' eyes.

"I am a daughter of Damaria," I said. "It's my responsibility to protect our people. Of course I accept."

My mother straightened the stack of treaty papers. "You'll leave in seven days."

Which meant they had started preparing for the alliance before they'd even asked me. I kept my face blank as fresh vellum, giving none of my feelings away.

"Give me a pen," I said, my voice steady. "I'll sign the papers now."

I dipped the pen in deep blue ink, the color of Damaria. As I lifted the nib above the treaty, a single drop of ink fell, spattering the parchment beside my newly betrothed's name. Aric of Gild-enheim.

Tatiana would have said it was a poor omen. But my sister saw a possible future in each ocean wave, and I knew there was only one that counted: the firm road set out by duty. Responsibility called me, looming at the northern border, and I would answer.

I blotted the errant mark away and signed my name. There. A line of ink, and now I was engaged.

"Bianca." My mother touched my elbow as I stood to leave. When I faced her, I saw a trace of worry in her eyes for the first time since I'd entered the room. "You'll have to pretend you're strong for this to succeed. Don't show anyone your flaws. Don't let them see your failures. If they learn of your weakness, they'll use it against you, and then they'll cut you down."

I met her eyes, willing her to see a strength that wasn't there. "I won't."

This was my duty. And at that, I'd never failed.

I wasn't about to start now.

2

Back in my room, I went straight to the Adept-forged box on my bureau and pressed my thumb to the metal lock until it glowed. The small chest sprang open to reveal a row of glass bottles of tonic. Snatching one up, I sank into my chair, pulled the cork with unsteady hands, and downed the entire flask. My mouth flooded with the familiar, bitter taste even the tonic's generous portion of honey couldn't override. I closed my eyes and swallowed it down. The tonics weren't a cure for my condition—nothing was—but they eased its symptoms, and they were more palatable than the countless treatments various apothecaries had forced on me before it became clear that my ailment was intermittent but permanent.

"You shouldn't be taking so much in one day. It isn't safe."

I choked, nearly inhaling tonic, and twisted in my chair. Julieta had come in without my notice, her steps nearly silent on the rug. After years of my apothecary's service, I ought not to be startled by her discreet movements, but I still jumped every time she appeared from the shadows without warning.

I grimaced at my reflection in the polished silver mirror. "I know. I'll take less if my condition's still flaring tomorrow."

"You'd better. Too many doses at once, and you'll make yourself unwell." Julieta plucked the empty bottle from my hands and replaced it with a cobalt glass brimming with water.

"How? By giving myself stomach pains?" I sipped at the water, clearing the tonic's acrid taste from the roof of my mouth.

"Very funny, your Grace." Julieta moved to stand behind my chair. I watched her in the mirror as she took the pins from my hair and laid them on the polished wood one by one, neat as a row of infantry. Everything about her was precise: the coif of her hair, the sharp lines of her livery, the economy of her words. "I mean it. It's my job to keep you safe. Including preventing you from poisoning yourself."

"I know. Thank you." I set down the water, repentant. Meeting with my parents had put me in a dour mood as always, but I didn't need to take it out on my staff. Julieta was a friend as well as a servant. Sometimes, though she was only fifteen years my senior, Julieta felt like more of a mother to me than my own. She was certainly more affectionate.

"Julieta," I said. "How would you feel about accompanying me to Gildenheim?"

Her hands stilled for the briefest moment. I watched her face in the mirror, but the only change in her expression was a slight tightening around the corners of her eyes.

"I take it my lady is marrying the new king."

My brows drew together. "How did you know? My parents only informed me of the treaty this afternoon."

Julieta hesitated for the span of a heartbeat. "The palace gossips, your Grace, and I have ears." She removed the last of the pins, freeing the dark length of my hair to tumble around my shoulders.

Of course the palace gossiped. I ought to know that better than anyone, after my own mistake a decade ago. I grimaced.

"You don't have to decide now," I said. "I wouldn't ask you to give up your life here if you don't want to."

"Of course I'll go, your Grace," Julieta said quietly. "You know I would do anything for you."

A knot of emotion swelled in my throat, threatening to choke me. I worked to keep my face blank. Emotion was not one of the nine Virtues; and revealing my feelings, as my mother had recited endless times, was a vulnerability anyone could exploit.

"Thank you," I said, my voice level.

Without warning, a fist thundered on the door to my chambers, loud as a warhorse's hooves. Julieta and I both flinched. An instant later the door flew open and Tatiana stormed in, a whirlwind of rose-colored skirts.

"I'll finish this, Julieta," she said, swiping the comb from my apothecary's hand. "You can take the rest of the evening off."

Julieta shot me a glance. I nodded, resigned. Arguing with my sister was, at best, a waste of breath.

As my attendant slipped out the servants' door, Tatiana stationed herself behind me, brandishing the comb like a weapon. My scalp already stung in anticipation.

I watched my sister in the mirror, bracing myself as she tackled my hair with alarming zeal. Although I'd been born nearly a year after Tatiana, we were often mistaken for twins: we shared the same soft features, olive-toned skin that bronzed easily in summer, dark waves of hair, and umber eyes—although her irises, unlike mine, were spangled with the gold flecks that identified those who had manifested the ability to channel magic. At the moment, her eyes were bright with anger, and her jaw was set with a determination I knew all too well.

I winced as the comb snagged on a knot. "Since when do you have any interest in combing my hair?"

"Since when do you agree to marry a foreign king without even talking to me first?"

"So our parents told you already."

"Of course they did. Why didn't *you* tell me first?"

"Ow!" I ducked away from her. "Virtue of Restraint, Tatiana. You're going to make me bald."

"Maybe your fiancé will like that."

I twisted to face her, nearly getting a comb to the eye for my efforts. "Why are you so angry? It's not as if *you* wanted to marry him."

Tatiana set the comb down on the bureau with an aggressive click. "Maybe because I don't want my sister going off to marry a man she doesn't want?"

I stiffened. "It's my choice, Tatiana. Gildenheim is threatening war. It's my duty to—"

"Yes. Your precious *duty*." My sister's tone torqued towards mockery. "You don't always have to do what's expected of you, you know. You're allowed to choose things for yourself, not just because our parents decide they benefit our House."

Now annoyance simmered in my chest, stirring old resentment. It was easy enough for Tatiana to warp my decision into something I'd done wrong when our parents were happy to ignore the aspects of *her* that didn't serve them, in favor of the parts that did. As if she weren't perfectly aware that in the absence of magic or health, duty was all I had to offer.

"Duty is not a choice." My voice was level, though I knew my sister would detect the heat below its surface. "But if it were, I would choose it anyway."

"Of course you would, little bee. And do you think our parents don't know that? That they don't take advantage of your sense of duty?"

Now I didn't bother to hide my scowl. Tatiana knew I hated that particular nickname. A good little bee, she liked to call me, a dutiful worker in the hive. She'd used that taunt since I was fifteen years old and had my heart broken for the first and only time.

"This isn't the same as what happened with Catalina," I retorted. "And why would you care, anyway? It's not *you* they asked to marry him."

All at once, Tatiana's anger vanished like a candle snuffed out. She leaned against the bureau, scattering Julieta's neat array of pins.

"I know," she said. "And I know you're not being forced into this at knifepoint. But our parents are still pressing this marriage on you, Bianca. And they would have sent me instead without hesitation if they thought I was better suited for the role. They don't give a horse's ass about us as daughters. We're just pieces to be moved around a board."

I didn't contradict her. "So you think I should refuse, and let the treaty fall apart?"

Tatiana fidgeted with one of my hairpins, her face a summer storm. "No," she said sharply. "And that's why I'm angry. Because this isn't right, but there's no refusing it anyway."

I took the pin from her fingers before she could bend it out of shape. "It's all right, Tatiana. I'll be a *queen*. And the new king is only twenty-eight. I've seen his portraits—he's even moderately handsome."

Not that this meant I would have any attraction to him in person. Portrait artists were paid to craft flattering lies, and pictures said little about what lay beneath the surface. It was entirely possible that in reality, Aric was both hideous and cruel. But sharing those thoughts with Tatiana wasn't going to alleviate her fears, and it was only serving to worsen mine.

"It will be fine," I said again, for both our benefits. "I'm marrying him to broker a peace treaty, after all. And I'll have a retinue of guards and Julieta with me."

Not Tatiana. The thought was a sudden twist in my abdomen, like the start of one of my flares. True, my sister and I fought viciously and often. But we'd spent almost every day of our lives together, and there was no one who knew me better—no one else with whom I could speak the fullness of my thoughts without restraint. This marriage meant I would truly be separated from her for the first time in my life. Not just for a few weeks while she accompanied one of our parents on an ambassadorial foray, or the single month she'd lasted in Adept training before all parties quietly agreed to exempt her from the mandated nine years of instruction in exchange for House Liliana's generous support of the Guild. With the exception of occasional visits, this separation was forever.

Tatiana was looking at me like I'd grown an extra pair of legs. I dredged up a smile to quash both of our misgivings. "The change of scenery will be good for me. No one in Gildenheim knows about my condition, and I intend to keep it that way. Consider it a fresh start." I raised my eyebrows meaningfully. "And no one says a marriage can't have benefits."

Seas knew I would like a partner I could afford to sleep with more than once. I was tired of selecting my rare bedmates not only for their lack of attachment, but for their discretion.

"Hmph. Well, at least it will be harder for our parents to nag at you from the other side of the mountains." My sister sighed, her doubts still obvious. "I'm not going to change your mind about this, am I?"

"No."

Tatiana smirked. "Then it's a good thing I already finished your birthday present."

My sister dug a hand into her pocket. My brows drew together in confusion.

"I'm not leaving yet. And my birthday isn't for another two months." I would be married by then. Only an hour ago, I hadn't yet been betrothed. The thought was dizzying.

"I know. But you need it more now, so you're welcome."

From her pocket, Tatiana pulled out a small bag crafted from imported Zhei silk—a product of the oceanic trade that, alongside Adept magic, had lifted Damaria to power. She upended it to spill its contents into her palm: a silver pendant on a delicate chain. Even from this distance, it emanated a subtle hum of power.

I reached for the pendant, but she held it away from my grasp. "Not so fast. You mustn't set it off by accident."

I narrowed my eyes at her, suspicious. "Explain."

Tatiana came behind me to fasten the chain around my neck. The pendant fell below my collarbones, as refreshingly cool as late spring rain. A locket, I saw now—an oval piece of silver, worked in delicate filigree. The design on the front was a single lily, evoking the emblem of our House.

"It's a protection charm," Tatiana explained. "Well . . . protection of sorts. It's a bit experimental." In the mirror, I watched her gaze become evasive. "Don't open it unless you're in grave danger."

I brushed my fingers against the rapidly warming silver. Cautiously. "This isn't illegal, is it?" Even Tatiana wouldn't dabble in something as dangerous as working with living beings—a practice the Adept Guild had outlawed over a century ago—but her creations often strayed from the approved applications of light, heat, and metal.

Tatiana shrugged, all innocence. "Legal is a matter of perspective."

"Tatiana."

She sighed. I was spoiling her game. "No, it's not strictly legal, but the best spells aren't."

My hand sprang away from the locket. Rolling her eyes, Tatiana moved my hand back into place.

"Relax, little bee. I made sure to give it limits. It's a device to defend yourself against an attacker."

"I'm going to Gildenheim to keep the peace. There's no reason I'd be attacked." Still, the possibility sent a frisson of fear through me. The late queen's death had been so sudden. The Council's spies reported that some of the royal family's more distant branches had discussed attempting a coup following her demise. And come to think of it, hadn't the queen's spouse died surprisingly young, when my betrothed was still a child?

My *betrothed*. Seas, I was an engaged woman now.

"Well, you can't be too careful. They say their royal family can cast spells with blood—it can't hurt to have a little magic of your own." Tatiana lifted my hair free of the chain, so that it fell in waves down my back. "But truly, don't open it unless you need it. It only works once."

I folded my hand around the locket, mindful to keep it closed.

"Thank you," I said, the words thick in my throat. "I hope I never have to use it."

Against my will, my eyes felt tight, hot with tears I had no desire to shed. I shouldn't be so emotional. It wasn't as if I were riding off to my death. It was just a marriage.

Tatiana wrapped her arms around me from behind, resting her chin on my head.

"If you ever need me," she said, "I'll come, and blast our parents to the bottom of the sea if they try to stop me. Even if you just need someone to argue with."

I crossed my hands over Tatiana's, while my chest rose and fell within the circle of her arms. We sat in silence as our breathing slowly synchronized. We fought more than we expressed our love, but I never doubted it was there.

"This isn't goodbye," I said finally. "You know I'm not leaving yet."

"I know." Tatiana rolled her eyes. "So don't you dare get all sentimental on me."

I choked out a laugh. But despite the assurance I'd just given her that this wasn't the end, I couldn't help the feeling that it was.

3

One week later I stood at the rail of the *Gilded Lily*, my hands white-knuckled on the polished wood. Salt spray kissed my face, stinging my cracked lips, and the wind tried to steal my hair from its pins. I closed my eyes against the sickening motion of the ship. I felt as if I were riding an unbroken stallion and coming out the worse for it. Each wave was a fresh surge of nausea, twisting my gut into knots.

The galleon plunged, sending my stomach swooping towards my chest. I bent over the rail and retched again. Nothing came out except unappealing noises. I'd already voided my stomach into the sea enough times that my abdominal muscles ached. Some opportunity this was starting out to be.

Julieta, standing carefully upwind of me, rubbed comforting circles on my back. "Only three more days to Arnhelm, my lady. At least you're not having a flare."

I released an eloquent groan.

I knew why the Council of Nine had chosen to send me by ship: the massive galleon, one of the ships that made up Damaria's fleet, was impressive. Every inch of the *Gilded Lily*'s considerable length was built to catch the eye: gleaming bulwarks; crisp sails bearing a massive rendition of Damaria's blue ninefold star; the Adept-forged cannons set along the gun deck. The ship was a message, and not a subtle one. Gildenheim had threatened war; Damaria reciprocated with peace offerings, but they were offerings set with sharp teeth. An armed conflict would cost our neighbor dearly.

I had liked the idea of an ocean voyage. Unlike Tatiana, I'd never ventured far enough from home to merit one before, but nautical adventures featured heavily in the romantic tales that my sister and I had devoured as children—stories of warriors defending villages from vicious monsters with dauntless blades, of curses broken with true love's kiss, of brave adventurers with enchanted boots that crossed seven leagues in a single stride. I'd spent enough time in a carriage to know I loathed the way they jolted my stomach—especially when I was in the midst of a flare—and the journey was too long for horseback, my preferred means of travel, to be practical. A ship had seemed an appealing alternative—at least in theory.

In practice, apparently, I was violently seasick. Thank the Virtue of Mercy my future husband was not aboard; the sight of his betrothed puking over the rail for hours was not exactly the show of strength the Council, or my parents, desired. Nor, for that matter, how I wanted to meet Aric. I somehow doubted my intended would be charmed by vomiting.

The ship rolled. I bent over the rail again, retching.

Something wet and slimy slapped me across the face.

I leaped back with a yelp, stumbling as the deck rolled beneath my feet. Julieta grabbed me with one arm, a knife appearing in her other hand to fend off an attack. Regaining my balance, I looked around, baffled. There was no sign of an assailant.

"My lady?" Julieta asked.

I touched a hand to my cheek. My fingers came away wet and salty. "I believe the sea just slapped me in the face."

Julieta's brow furrowed. Then she snorted and sheathed her dagger, pointing to the deck. "Your attacker, your Grace."

I looked down and yelped again. A rainbow-sheened creature the length of my palm was flapping across the wet boards. At first glance, it was a fish. Except I had never seen a fish with a set of feathered wings and a pointed beak.

"What is *that*?" I demanded.

"I believe, my lady, that would be a birdfish."

My brows lifted towards my hairline. "Those still exist? I thought they were extinct."

Curiosity overcoming my nausea, I pulled out a handkerchief and stooped. The birdfish jackknifed across the deck, tail flapping feebly. Gingerly, mindful not to crush its wings, I caught it in the handkerchief to examine it.

The birdfish stared back at me, eyes bulging, beak opening and closing soundlessly. Its wings fluttered against the handkerchief. Up close, they were not feathered as I'd thought, but sheathed in iridescent, plume-like scales coated by protective slime.

I'd heard of such unnatural creatures—as examples in a cautionary tale. An illustration of why magic's uses should be limited to unliving metal and stone. The birdfish was strangely lovely, but a shimmer of apprehension ran through me. The folktales sprang to my memory again, bristling with legendary beasts: firedrakes that spat bilious green flame; wyrdwolves that hunted the souls of the dying; trees that walked on their roots beneath the full moon, wandering in search of human flesh. If the birdfish was real, what more dangerous beings might exist in a country with unregulated magic?

"Your Grace. May I have a word?"

A woman's low voice spoke behind me, close enough that I flinched in surprise. Not Julieta. Absorbed in examining the birdfish, I hadn't been aware of her approach. I drew a bracing breath and turned to face the newcomer, keeping one hand on the rail for support.

My hand tightened on the wood as I laid eyes on the speaker: a woman of Damarian heritage near my own age, her olive skin tanned by hours of martial practice under the peninsula's constant sun. The wind plucked at her dark curls as if it cherished them for its own. Hands folded behind her back in a soldier's wide-legged stance, she watched me with a caution I had planted in her myself.

Virtue of Serenity. Of all the people I wanted to talk to between bouts of vomiting up my guts, Catalina Espada, the captain of my appointed retinue of guards and formerly my closest friend, was exceptionally low on the list.

I forced a polite smile onto my face, ignoring the guilt doing its best to contort my mouth in the opposite direction.

"If it's quick," I conceded. "I'm somewhat preoccupied."

Catalina's eyes flitted from my face to my hand, just as the birdfish gave a vigorous twitch. "With your . . . fish?"

Heat rose to my cheeks. Sink me to the depths—I'd forgotten I was holding it. I looked a fool, addressing her with a winged fish in hand.

I thrust the handkerchief-wrapped birdfish at Julieta. "Um. If you would . . ."

She took it from me as naturally as if I'd passed her a glass of water. "I'll put it back over the rail, my lady."

Julieta turned away, her steps enviably steady despite the heaving deck. I looked back at Catalina, my heart sinking towards my long-suffering stomach as I realized I'd unintentionally granted her a private audience. By all the Virtues, I was not prepared for this. I hadn't spent the last ten years avoiding looking her in the eye only to have an intimate conversation en route to my wedding. In truth, I'd thought I was leaving her behind for good—I'd never expected her to volunteer for this mission, much less to captain the retinue of guards that would attend me in my new home. She deserved better.

Through my sleeve, I touched the outlines of the dagger strapped to my wrist—a new precaution, though one I'd readily agreed to. Maybe Catalina just wanted to talk about our security measures. We'd been over them extensively before setting sail, and every night since as well. But when it came to my safety, Catalina was clearly . . . dedicated.

Better to get this over with.

"Well?" I asked, working to keep all inflection from my voice. "You have your word."

Catalina glanced after Julieta, who was now out of earshot and showed no intention of rescuing me from this conversation, drown her. My captain of the guard rocked from toe to heel, a nervous gesture I recognized from countless hours spent training together. Nita, our fencing instructor, would have smacked her. Not that Nita had trained her in years. Now Catalina trained with the palace guards, and I went to my daily weapons practice alone.

"May I speak freely, your Grace?" Catalina asked.

"If you must."

She shifted her weight again. "I wanted to talk to you about . . ." Her eyes searched the deck as if she hoped to find the right words inscribed on the planks.

"Yes?" I prompted. The ship surged, and I fought down another wave of bile.

"About your marriage," Catalina said, in a tone that suggested each syllable pained her like acid.

My stomach roiled. Please let her mean the security measures. "We've already discussed this. I trust your precautions. I'll be safe enough with the plans we've put in—"

"I don't mean the plans." Any other one of my guards would have been appalled at cutting me off, but Catalina didn't stop or apologize. She carried on without pause as if dragged full tilt by a team of horses. "No amount of planning will ensure your safety if the threat is the man you're marrying."

I swallowed back nausea that wasn't entirely due to the ship's motion. "I don't know what you mean."

"Bianca, I'm not oblivious to the rumors. People are saying he killed his own mother to ascend the throne. That he's cold and arrogant—everyone's beneath him, he hardly talks to anyone if he can avoid it. I'm concerned for you. As the captain of your guard." Her eyes finally lifted to mine, and a flicker of their old warmth showed beneath the ice glazing their surface. "And as . . . a friend."

I kept my face impassive. The rumors weren't reassuring, but my betrothed wasn't the only partner in this match who generated gossip; I knew how whispers spread. And while Catalina might be correct, she overlooked the relevant point.

"My marital happiness has nothing to do with this arrangement." Years of practice at hiding my thoughts kept my face untroubled and my tone even. "My wedding to King Aric is a political arrangement to ease tensions between Gildenheim and Damaria."

"And that's why I'm concerned for you." Catalina's gaze darkened. "Did *you* agree to this marriage? Or did House Liliana?"

I looked away from her, afraid of what she might think she read in my expression. Sunlight speared between scattered clouds and shimmered on the waves, leaving a bright afterimage across my gaze.

"I'm not being forced. This is my choice, Cata."

A muscle in her jaw flickered at the childhood nickname. Curse my careless tongue. Now more than ever, I needed to maintain the distance I'd so carefully laid out.

"Are you certain?" Her voice dropped, low enough that I could barely hear it. "This wouldn't be the first time you were forced into something you called a choice."

Against my will, memories sped past like leaves caught on a strong breeze. Lingering glances before weapons training. The brush of a hand against mine as we passed in the hallway. A kiss beneath the ripe fruits of an apricot tree, sweetness on my tongue. Those sensations were a decade old, but they had been my firsts. Despite my best efforts, I couldn't purge them from my memory.

But those feelings were only a flame that had flared briefly and died out years before. Despite what Catalina believed, it *had* been my choice to end things between us. It was for the best. I'd laid those embers to rest and done my best to forget they'd ever burned, and Catalina had done the same. The last I'd heard, she was betrothed to a court tailor—a good woman. One who wouldn't cast her aside when politics required it.

Not that I'd been paying attention to Catalina's personal affairs, of course.

"You're mistaken," I said stiffly.

"I know we've both moved on. I'm not speaking from a place of jealousy." Catalina looked up at me, her gaze snaring mine. "But I know that what you believe and what you *say* you believe haven't always aligned, Bianca. If you're being forced into this marriage—if this isn't truly your choice—"

I raised my hand sharply, cutting her off. Like the good soldier she was, Catalina fell silent.

"You're overreacting, Captain Espada." I did my best to banish all emotion from my voice. My mother would have been proud for once. "I'm marrying the man, not joining his kitchen staff."

Catalina's fingers closed around the hilt of her rapier. "If you don't want this marriage . . . I could help you. I volunteered for this voyage to protect you—*you*, not House Liliana. There are other countries. Other continents, even."

And in all of them, Damaria's ships made port. Besides, there was the treaty to think of. Didn't Catalina realize what would happen if war broke out? While the concept of Damaria at war felt as distant as the bottom of the sea—something I knew was real but couldn't truly picture—I'd read enough history to know its cost. War, even one we could win, meant sacrifice, and commoners like her—*soldiers* like her—would be the first to fall.

I put the ring of Adept-forged steel into my voice, cutting off any further protests. "I've agreed to this marriage. My decision is final. We won't speak of this again."

Catalina's mouth flattened into a narrow line. I could see her disagreement, her hesitation. But her current concerns were only proof that I'd been right to cut things off when we were younger—I would always have hurt her. At least now she grappled with worry for my safety rather than heartbreak.

"Please leave," I said, my words gentler this time. "Nothing you say is going to change my mind. Discussing this further will only make it worse for us both."

Catalina gathered herself. Returned her shoulders to the upright posture of a soldier.

"I understand, your Grace." She bowed politely, the space between us suddenly leagues wider. "I'll speak no more of this matter. Is there anything else I can do for you?"

I turned my gaze away from the disapproval clouding her eyes. "Send Julieta back to me, please."

Catalina bowed again and turned away, her steps rigid. A soldier's gait, dutifully battling the ocean's churning.

I turned back to the open sea, so I didn't have to watch her go. And then vomited again, retching out the bile I'd been keeping at bay during our conversation.

Empty, I hung over the rail. The sun dazzled from the sea into my eyes, half blinding me. In the distance a school of birdfish flashed in and out of the waves, each leap a miniature rainbow.

But I was in no state to appreciate the ocean's beauty. Weariness hung heavy on me, as if the ship's anchor had been slung over my shoulders. I wiped my mouth, the acid taste of my own stomach contents stinging my palate. I was in the public eye. I needed to appear strong, even if on the inside my bones had turned to eggshells. Bracing myself against the rail, I forced my shoulders to square instead of slumping as they wanted to.

At least the seasickness was understandable—something I didn't have to hide. Julieta was right. It could have been worse. But not by much. Even without the galleon's roll, my own thoughts would have made me nauseated.

My parents. My sister. Now Catalina, who apparently could still cut me even through the walls I'd built between us. Each said they supported me while questioning all my decisions. I knew they wanted the best for me, but I wished they trusted me to decide what that meant for myself.

I was almost twenty-six, a woman grown. I wasn't a child, deluding myself with the glitter of a golden crown, unaware of the sharpness beneath its bright gleam. I knew what this decision entailed. And I had made it anyway.

A husband or a war. The choice was simple.

I touched the hidden dagger again, tracing the outlines of its sheath.

Perhaps Catalina was right about my future husband's character. I knew hardly anything of the man; no one had expected him to ascend the throne before reaching the age of thirty, so he hadn't been the subject of intense surveillance, and he'd largely hidden himself from the public eye. His father had died young, and his mother, the widowed queen, had been in excellent health until her sudden demise—or at least, so our ambassador reported. A monarchy that used blood for magic, if the rumors Tatiana had told me were correct, must be a ruthless lineage. Perhaps Aric really *had* killed his mother to gain the throne.

The thought sent a shiver down my back, but I brushed it aside. There was no guarantee that the rumors were true—or that they weren't an exaggeration of something far more benign. Even if Aric and I weren't ultimately a good match, this marriage was still an opportunity to unfold my life from the rigid shape it had always hewed. Already I'd seen more of the world in the past few days than I had in my entire lifetime—complete with birdfishes to the face. Perhaps my future husband would be equally surprising.

In any case, whoever my betrothed proved to be, I would learn soon enough, and I would match him. Blade for blade. Move for move. Perhaps even heart for heart—though I knew better than to count on the last.

It didn't matter. Noble marriages were built on necessity, not love. And this was the right choice. The only one.

I had to see it through.

4

When the *Gilded Lily* reached Arnhelm, the capital of Gildenheim, we hove into port under clouds heavy with the threat of rain.

I stood on the quarterdeck and watched the city swallow the ship. Where Damarian towns boasted clusters of whitewashed buildings with terra-cotta roofs, the houses here were the muted grey of old limestone and hunkered low to the ground. Arnhelm's streets were twisting and narrow, as if each had been wrested with great effort from a land reluctant to be tamed. As we coasted into the harbor mouth, wharves extended towards us like fangs. I followed the line of the city up from the docks, where it clawed its way towards the mountains before becoming engulfed by mist. I knew the castle rested there, at Arnhelm's highest point, poised between mountains and sea. But thanks to the cloud-thick skies, I couldn't see my future home.

Home. The word felt as foreign as the Gilden tongue. Another thing I would have to grow accustomed to.

I shivered and pulled my embroidered shawl closer around my shoulders. In Damaria, spring was already dancing through the hills, flowers springing abundant like courtiers in brightly colored ball gowns. But I wouldn't be surprised if snow still veiled the earth of Gildenheim. Grey stone under grey skies. It felt like the entire country was devoid of color.

Julieta touched my shoulder, her hand warmer than the air by a wide margin. "Is your condition flaring again, your Grace?"

I shook my head, resisting the urge to lean into the comfort of her touch. I did feel somewhat lightheaded. But I suspected that was due to vomiting most of the way to Gildenheim rather than my illness.

"It's nothing. Only the breeze."

Julieta's dubious look told me she didn't believe my words, but she didn't question them. There was nothing she could change about the circumstances anyway. We were almost at the docks, close enough to count the soldiers awaiting us should I care to do so. I'd already taken a preemptive dose of tonic this morning, and I wasn't about to gulp another in front of my betrothed. I had only one opportunity to make a first impression. I couldn't squander it on a moment of weakness.

I let out my breath. There was nothing to be concerned about. I was perfectly fine. I was here of my own volition, accompanied by the blessing of the entire Council of Nine, a half dozen well-trained soldiers, and my personal apothecary. Diplomacy had prevented the Council from sending a fully trained Adept as well, but it wouldn't have been necessary. I was as safe as I could be.

With a thud of weathered wood, the gangway connected with the wharf. I scanned the quay, searching for my betrothed. The banner of Gildenheim—a green field, with a winged white horse wearing a crown—flew over a double line of soldiers stretching along the pier. They were dressed in forest green coats, long in the Gilden style and reaching to the knee, rather than the gleaming armor and deep blue adornments I was accustomed to. The points of their halberds glittered like icicles in the wan sunlight as the soldiers angled their weapons forward, creating a tunnel that gave the impression of a gauntlet rather than an honor guard. Instead of a pistol and powder kit at one hip, they bore heavy sabers. I'd known firearms were uncommon in Gildenheim since Damarian imports were their only source, but I hadn't realized they were so scarce even the castle guard didn't wear them. The reminder of Gildenheim's backwardness should have been comforting, but somehow the lack of pistols only made the soldiers more imposing.

I resisted the urge to touch my hidden dagger. This was only an honor guard, I reminded myself, as my heart sped faster. They were here to welcome me to Gildenheim. I'd expected to be greeted by a group of courtiers, not a show of military force, but the customs of our northern neighbor were different. This wasn't a threat. We'd signed the treaty, after all. There was no need for hostilities. That was the entire point of being here.

"Your Grace?" Julieta prompted, her voice pitched for my ears alone. "Everyone is waiting."

Of course. As the most important member of the delegation, I was to disembark first.

I sent a silent prayer to the Virtue of Strength that my legs would be steady and descended the stairs from the quarterdeck, making my way to the rail. Up close, the gangway was terrifyingly narrow. Its angle changed every second as the *Gilded Lily* lifted on the water and then dropped again. A small movement that would have meant little to someone with steadier legs.

My vision swam, and I gritted my teeth. Oceans drown the cumbersome skirts of the formal dress I'd chosen. I could have worn trousers, but I'd wanted to make a strong first impression, and yards of expensive imported silk were a means to that end. At least my skirts would hide the wobble in my knees.

I took a deep breath and stepped onto the gangway. It was steeper than I'd expected, but there were raised slats of wood set into it for traction. This wouldn't be so bad.

Ahead of me, a carriage door thudded closed. I looked up as a man stepped into the midst of the soldiers. Tall, pale, with hair the faded color of old wheat, tied back into a queue in the northern style. He didn't match the portraits I'd been studying, but that was to be expected.

This must be him. My betrothed. Aric of Gildenheim.

I summoned a smile, lifting my hand in greeting.

Only to step on the hem of my own skirts, windmill frantically, and topple face-first into the harbor.

It was a short drop from the gangway. I didn't even have time to scream before I plunged into the frigid water, bubbles fizzing around me like champagne. My skirts—my ornate, cumbersome skirts—billowed around me, far heavier than any fabric had the right to be. The harbor's cold hit me like a physical blow. I fought off my shock and kicked towards the surface, salt burning my eyes—

Hands closed around my arms and hauled me out of the water. My feet landed on the solid planks of the wharf, my knees buckling under me at the impact. I wiped my eyes, coughing and spluttering. When I managed to clear my vision, I found myself flanked by two soldiers dressed in Gilden green, the sleeves of their uniforms darkened by salt water. Aric's soldiers. Already on the quay, they'd been closer than my own guards.

Ocean take me to the depths. So much for making a first impression: this was one the entire Gilden court would remember for perpetuity. Only force of habit kept me from curling into a sodden ball of mortification.

"My lady!"

Julieta pushed past the soldiers. Shrugging off her own shawl, she wrapped it around my shoulders. Mine must be sinking towards the bottom of the harbor.

"Th-thank you," I managed through chattering teeth. I hugged the shawl closer and turned to the soldiers who had pulled me ashore. "Thank y-you as w-well for your s-swift action."

The two women exchanged a blank look. They probably didn't even understand Damarian. I should have addressed them in Gilden instead.

"Duchess Liliana?"

I looked up, and my stomach curled with embarrassment. The man from the carriage stood only a few steps away, watching water drip from my skirts and form a slowly spreading stain on the docks. The curve of his mouth tiptoed the border between amusement and mockery.

Dismay rippled through me. Up close, he matched the portraits even less. And he was much older than I'd expected—he looked closer to forty than thirty, though the mourning grey he wore could have aged him. Still, this had to be my betrothed.

"Y-your Majesty?" I ventured.

He shook his head. "No, your Grace. I am Lord Varin of Gildenheim, merely a humble courtier at your service. I've been sent to escort you to the castle."

Anger sparked in my chest, hot and bright. A *humble courtier*—Aric hadn't even sent someone important to greet me?

I was shivering hard, and being cold, wet, and humiliated only soured my mood. My tone sharpened to a razor edge. "I had expected King Aric to meet me."

Lord Varin's mouth tightened ever so slightly. Displeasure, annoyance, regret—I wasn't certain which his expression indicated, or who it was aimed at. "The heir apparent has many other pressing duties, my lady. But he greatly anticipates meeting you at a mutually convenient time." He placed just enough emphasis on Aric's title to make my error clear—my betrothed had yet to be crowned.

Years of practice kept my face free of emotion, even while

indignation burned in my chest. I bit my tongue, preventing myself from unleashing my outrage on Varin. He was only here on Aric's orders. But Aric himself . . . when I saw him face-to-face, he should be prepared to get on his knees and grovel.

I lifted my chin, my anger giving me warmth. "In that case, Lord Varin, let us proceed to the castle. I will be sure to thank the heir apparent for his warm welcome when I see him."

Varin offered me his arm, and I took it, touching him as little as possible. We proceeded between the line of guards, my skirts dripping a trail down the wharf. Other than the two who had pulled me out, the soldiers had maintained their formation with perfect discipline, although a few of them appeared to be holding back smirks.

I allowed an attendant to hand me into the waiting carriage, Julieta and Varin at my heels. As the door slammed shut and the driver slapped the reins, my anger tempered into icy resolve. I couldn't afford to show emotion now, to allow Aric to learn how deep his barb had pierced. But that didn't mean I would let this offense go unanswered.

I didn't know what game my intended was playing, but I was not a woman he could insult with impunity. I was her Grace, Duchess Bianca Liliana, flower of Damaria and scion of my House. I was not some petitioner to be addressed at his leisure and granted the boon of his attention when he felt it *convenient*. I was the representative of the Council of Nine. His future wife. His equal. And if Aric thought he could insult me without consequence, I would soon show him otherwise.

Just let him wait until our first private moment. I would knock him off his high horse so hard he would never mount it again. He greatly anticipated meeting me? Well, I could say the same for myself. I really *would* make an impression on Aric. One that my betrothed would be certain not to forget.

Put them on the defensive. Nita's reminder whispered in my head. *That's how you win.*

I folded my hands in my lap and narrowed my eyes. Soon, Aric of Gildenheim would learn exactly how badly he'd misjudged.

5

Though I was half expecting it by the time we rolled through the castle gates, the lack of a royal reception there, too, hardened my anger into a stone sitting below my breastbone. I allowed Lord Varin to hand me from the carriage and swept through the double doors of the castle entrance with as much grace as I could muster. A small crowd of courtiers had gathered in the entryway. It was impossible to miss the whispers that sizzled through their ranks as they took in the sight of me—silken skirts plastered to my legs, hair a sodden mess—but I kept my mask firmly in place, refusing to let any embarrassment show. I merely nodded, acknowledging them with a tight-lipped smile as if I were dragged out of a harbor on a daily basis.

On second thought, perhaps it was to my advantage that Aric hadn't turned out a full royal welcome. This way the entire Gilden court didn't witness my bedraggled arrival—although I didn't doubt the whole castle would know of it within the hour.

At least if my welcome to Arnhelm was less than desired, my rooms made up for the lack. Varin departed, and a palace official showed me to a full royal suite on the castle's second floor with tall windows that overlooked an arboretum, rooms for my personal attendants, and brightly colored tapestries to help ward off the northern chill. A large bureau took up much of one wall. To my immense relief, a fire crackled in the hearth—the trip from the wharves had done little to dry my clothes, and the harbor's cold was beginning to set in deep. I started eagerly towards the fire, only for Catalina's arm to descend, blocking my path.

"Wait here, please, your Grace." Any trace of the familiarity she'd shown on the *Gilded Lily* was gone, leaving a woman as professionally cold as a marble fountain. "We must ensure your rooms are safe."

A retort hovered at my tongue—I was freezing, and I doubted Aric would risk the treaty by doing anything as obvious as booby-trapping the chambers he assigned me. But Catalina and I were no longer familiar enough for me to say so, and I was too tired to argue anyway. I waited, trying not to visibly shiver, while Catalina and my guards turned the suite upside down searching for any possible threat. I winced as a pair of guards prodded the pillows on the canopy bed and heaved aside the mattress. Another rammed a poker up the chimney, scattering a shower of soot across the rug. I appreciated their enthusiasm for my safety, but was being quite so thorough really necessary? My fingers were practically blue with cold.

I cast a longing glance at the hearth—and blinked. The flames glowed oddly green—nearly the color of leaves in spring. Perhaps it was a peculiarity of the wood? But Gildenheim was known for its pines and firs—the same wood we built our ships from, the same wood we burned. And I had never seen it burn this color.

"All clear, your Grace," Catalina said, jolting me out of my thoughts.

Virtue of Mercy. It appeared as if Tatiana had unleashed her tempest in a teacup on the suite. I didn't envy the servants tasked with cleaning the rooms—especially since Catalina would undoubtedly have their persons searched with equal thoroughness.

I glanced back at the fire. The color had vanished, the flames an ordinary palette once again. I must have been imagining things.

"Thank you," I said, and headed for the hearth. The mess could wait for later.

To my immense relief, the suite included a personal washroom, with hot water at the ready. Once I had warmed enough for my hands to function again and had washed the harbor's mildewed stench out of my hair, Julieta helped me into my most striking gown—blue and gold and ornate, like Damaria itself. I sat at the bureau so she could brush color onto my salt-chapped lips and work my damp hair into something presentable. Varin had informed me there would be a welcome ball this evening—my first formal public appearance as Aric's betrothed. I did not intend to waste it.

A few volumes in the Damarian language were neatly stacked on the bureau's polished surface. My brows drew together as I read their titles. *A History of Conflict on the Peninsula*. *Tales for Sleepless Children*. And, most confusingly, what appeared to be a pamphlet on Damarian fashion, almost two decades out of date.

Clearly, they were intended to send a message, but its substance confused me. Did Aric mean to warn me with my own country's history of war? Suggest that I was childish? Take a jibe at my fashion sense? Whatever he meant by the books, it didn't bode well.

I supposed I could ask him myself soon enough. Surely he didn't intend to hide until our wedding night.

In the mirror, I glanced involuntarily at the far wall of the suite. Reflected in the glass was a door that led directly to what I'd been told were the king's chambers. It was firmly closed. For now.

I forced my eyes away from the door. I didn't care to think about what lay on the other side. Not yet. I would consider Aric's bedchamber and all it entailed after I had actually met the man.

I shifted my attention to the tapestries instead. Their wool was dyed in jewel tones—pigments likely imported from the Zhei Empire through Damarian trading routes. At home, such decorations would have borne representations of the Virtues. Instead, these tapestries depicted people and animals in scenes of nature, mixed with fantastical creatures whose melding of body parts reminded me of the birdfish.

My gaze stilled on a tapestry depicting a pale woman with dark hair and golden eyes. She stood beside a winged horse with a crown perched between its ears—the same creature rampant on the flag of Gildenheim, though here it stood on four legs instead of rearing on two. The bright color of the woman's eyes, picked out with gilt thread, suggested she could channel magic with the strength of a high-level Adept. Confusion brought a frown to my face. I'd known Gildenheim had magic users, of course—unlike in Damaria, where everyone with magical potential was required to complete nine years of Adept training and have their subsequent careers monitored by the Guild, untrained wielders of wild magic were not only tolerated but encouraged here. But I'd been taught that greenwitches, as Gildenheim called such individuals, were weak at best, dangerous at worst. The tapestry must be an exaggeration.

A soft knock sounded at the door. Not the door to Aric's chambers, thank the seas. The main door to my suite.

I turned sharply, causing Julieta to mutter a curse as her careful work twisted out of place. My hand slid to the hilt of the knife strapped to my forearm. Tatiana's locket was warm in the hollow beneath my collarbones.

One of the guards posted at the door gave me a questioning look. His hand hovered near the hilt of his rapier. The woman beside him rested a hand on her own weapon.

I nodded, silently ordering them to admit the visitor. Their caution was merited, but if I were to live in Gildenheim, I couldn't expect every visit to be an attack. Still, a trickle of unease slid down my spine like a drop of the harbor's cold water.

The door opened to reveal a reedy man somewhere between my own age and my parents'. His dark hair, olive complexion, and clothing in the Damarian style—an embroidered doublet with slashed sleeves, hair cut short—identified him as a citizen of my own country.

"Ambassador Dapaz?" I guessed. I'd never seen Evito Dapaz's portrait, but there were only a handful of Damarian courtiers in Gildenheim. My retinue's arrival had at least doubled their number.

The ambassador gave me a bow of precisely the correct depth, confirming my suspicions. His brown eyes were keen over a hawkish nose.

"Your Grace. I don't believe we've yet had the pleasure of meeting."

He was correct. His features were familiar—I'd probably met members of his family at balls or dinners—but I'd been too young to attend court functions regularly when he took up his ambassadorial role abroad.

"It's an honor to finally make your acquaintance, ambassador. I've heard much about you." Ambiguous flattery couldn't hurt. "You've been in Gildenheim how many years now?"

"Twelve."

Julieta had moved on to tightening the laces of my dress. I suppressed a grimace as she tugged harder than usual. "Damaria thanks you for your service. What can I assist you with, ambassador?"

"Actually, your Grace, I believe I can assist you. I came to see how you are settling into your quarters and whether they suit your needs. And also to escort you to the welcome ball." His mouth pressed into a thin smile. "I imagine you have not had adequate time to learn your way around the castle."

Was this another one of Aric's attempts to insult me? Had he meant for me to blunder around the castle on my own, making even more of a spectacle of myself? My jaw tightened with renewed anger at my betrothed. Thank the seas for Dapaz's foresight. At least someone in this wretched country was on my side.

"Thank you," I told Evito. "My quarters are proving satisfactory so far, though I admit I've not fully explored them." Though Catalina and my guards had done so more than adequately. I winced internally as Evito's gaze followed mine, sweeping over the mess, but he was a trained courtier. His expression didn't change.

"Of course, my lady." The ambassador inclined his head.

"But I do have a question." I gestured to the tapestry that had caught my eye, trying to keep my torso still for Julieta's sake. "What does this image portray?"

A flicker of surprise crossed Evito's face. Whether it stemmed from my lack of knowledge or my topic of interest, I couldn't determine. "It's from one of the local folktales, your Grace. The story of the Lady of the Wilds. The Gilden people say she was the first queen of this land—she made a pact with the local deities, who gave her the crown in exchange for a promise to protect the wild places. Such superstition is why Gildenheim refuses to open more iron mines or log the forests, despite the immense potential for profit."

Interesting, especially since those two things were specifically outlined in the treaty. I would have to ask Aric about this. Whenever he showed his face. "Was she real? The Lady?"

"By all accounts, your Grace, the woman was real. The legends . . . well." Evito gave a condescending smile. "I'm sure your Grace can draw your own conclusions."

I studied the image of the first Gilden queen, more intrigued than before. Rather than satisfy my curiosity, Evito's answer had piqued it.

"If your Grace is almost ready?" Evito prompted.

"Of course." I shouldn't be late to a ball held in my own honor. "Julieta?"

My attendant gave a final tug on my laces. "Finished, my lady." Her words were clipped.

When I glanced in the mirror, her lips were pressed together so firmly they had paled. Perhaps she regretted accompanying me to Gildenheim after all. I would have to discuss it with her when I had a spare moment. If she wanted to go home, I wouldn't make her stay.

I caught her hand and pressed it in silent gratitude, hoping the gesture conveyed my thoughts, then rose to my feet. "Ambassador, I would appreciate it if you directed me to the ballroom."

I followed him, two of my guards only steps behind. A headache pulsed faintly at my temples, but at least I wasn't having a flare, and the water and fruit Julieta had forced me to consume before we disembarked were helping me recover from the voyage. Thank the seas. I needed all my strength tonight.

Within minutes of leaving the suite I was grateful for Dapaz's guidance. I had never gotten lost in any Damarian hall of state; the bright mosaics, stained glass frescoes, and individualized depictions of the Virtues served as waypoints, every room unique. The castle of Arnhelm was hall after hall of grey limestone. Narrow windows let in glimpses of a sunset the color of ripe plums, blurred by rain that had begun to fall without my notice, but those hints at the outside world didn't orient me to the castle's twists and turns. This was a place built for defense, not beauty. My parents would have liked it.

Dapaz led the way to a pair of tall double doors reinforced with spiked iron bands. Even the courtrooms here were equipped for battle. At least their handles had a touch of artistry: each was fashioned into the semblance of an open-mouthed predator. Not particularly welcoming, but at least it was more subtle. Slightly.

Evito nodded to the two soldiers stationed beside the doors. Gilden troops, wearing the same forest green uniforms, a silver sash across their chests. They bore ceremonial halberds hung with the flag of Gildenheim: the green field, the winged white horse. The same image from the tapestry in my room. Unease stirred behind my sternum. Were the guards merely for show? To send me a message? Or were they truly here to defend—but against what? I thought again of the rumors of royal relatives angling for the throne. Surely they wouldn't dare strike so publicly.

As we approached, the guards threw open the doors, revealing a grand ballroom with a polished marble floor and arched ceilings. A dozen sparkling chandeliers cascaded light over a crowd of well-dressed courtiers. At the far end, two thrones occupied a raised dais. Both were empty. Was Aric really going to refuse to meet me again?

The two soldiers thudded the base of their pikes onto the floor. I managed not to flinch at the booming sound.

"Announcing her Grace," Dapaz called, "Duchess Bianca Liliana, flower of Damaria, betrothed of Aric of Gildenheim."

Gazes swung to meet me, accompanied by whispers. A smattering of polite applause rose from the crowd. Like the court at home, the guests here were a varied group—mixed in with the predominant pale complexions and muted attire of Gildenheim's people, I spotted the boldly patterned fabrics and ranging brown skin tones of the Mobolan Alliance's member states; the shining silks and sleek black hair of the Zhei Empire's representatives; the richly embroidered doublets, flowing skirts, and olive-toned countenances of fellow Damarians, though I recognized none of them aside from Evito. All of them united in staring at me.

I donned a smile, masking my nerves behind it. This, at least, I was accustomed to. I could navigate a courtly dance as easily as I could breathe.

A ripple went through the crowd, a scythe parting a field of wheat. Through the gap walked a man dressed in the dark grey of Gilden mourning, a circlet resting on his golden hair. He stopped a sword's reach from me but did not bow.

Our eyes locked, his the cold blue of a winter sky. The air went static between us, like the feeling just before lightning strikes.

I needed no introduction. I would have known this man even had I not perused his portrait for hours on the journey from Damaria, reading meaning in every brushstroke. Aric of Gildenheim, heir apparent to the throne.

My betrothed. At last.

6

I swept Aric an exaggerated curtsy, my nerves thrumming with tension. "We finally meet," I said in Gilden. "Husband."

Aric's eyes narrowed. He bowed in return, just deep enough to be polite, and held his hand out stiffly. I stared at it for a beat before realizing he meant me to take it.

So this was how he wanted to play the game. Pretending he hadn't slighted me twice over.

"It is customary for the betrothed couple to share the first dance." He answered me in the same language. His voice was softer than I'd expected, mellifluous, like the notes of a viola. I'd imagined a harsh commander to go with his coldness and insults.

Still, not even a pretense at a welcome speech. No inquiry as to how I'd found my rooms or the journey, nor acknowledgment that he'd failed to greet me. Clearly, I was engaged to a man of scarce words and scarcer manners.

I smiled at him, wide enough to show my teeth, and placed my hand in his. A shock of static jumped between us when we touched, and we both flinched. But neither of us pulled back. Aric closed his fingers around mine as reluctantly as if my hand were a used handkerchief. He led me to the center of the floor.

Music began, a slow three-count air. Aric placed his free

hand on my waist, his palm barely skimming my bodice as if he couldn't bear to touch me. In reply, I draped my left arm along his shoulder with more force than necessary. His arm was rigid beneath mine, as unwelcoming as the castle itself. We were poorly suited. Our tension would make the dance awkward. This boded ill for the bedchamber.

"Do you know the waltz?" Aric asked.

I smiled at him again, my jaw beginning to hurt from clenching my teeth. "Of course. We do not lack for manners in Damaria." I put just the slightest emphasis on my country's name.

Aric, snubbing me yet again, didn't reply. Instead, his jaw tight, he swung me into the first steps of the dance. One-two-three. One-two-three. I was reminded of fencing practice. If only I could hit Aric with a foil—it would have been more agreeable than this charade of courtesy.

At least Aric proved to be a competent dancer, if not a gracious one. He performed the steps as flawlessly and rigidly as an Adept-made clock. His muscles were hard beneath my arm, his hand stiff on my waist. He said nothing, dancing in stubborn silence.

Well, two could play that game.

I studied him while I waited for him to speak. Aric's portrait had not done him justice. The artist's paints had captured his handsomeness, but softened him into something as ordinary as a field of golden grain. He was not beautiful like that. His beauty was like a dagger: sharp, narrow, best admired from a distance. The dark grey of his coat echoed the circles under his eyes. Now that I was closer, their color was more like steel than sky.

Those eyes were fixed on my face. I realized he was studying me, too, and warmth rushed to my cheeks at the thought that he might mistakenly believe I was doing something so inane as admiring him.

"Tell me," Aric said abruptly, "do you always wear a dagger in your sleeve?"

I nearly missed a step of the waltz. The loose lines of my dress hid the weapon from sight, but he must feel its outline where my forearm rested on his shoulder—I'd practically ground it into him in my irritation.

My mind raced, trying to think of an excuse. Hidden weapons were a poor start to a relationship.

But then, so was slighting your future wife before the entire court.

I smiled, poison sweet. If he would not apologize, neither would I. "Not at all. I find that some dresses pair much better with a rapier. But that would interfere with dancing, don't you think?"

Surprise flashed across his face, brief as lightning. For a moment he looked unbalanced, his facade cracking. Satisfaction settled in my chest, purring like a cat.

"I see. I've heard of your prowess with weapons." Aric's voice was as carefully blank as scraped vellum, his surprise locked away again—and with it that small glimpse of his humanity. "I hope you're not planning to use that dagger in the bedchamber."

I gazed up at him innocently. "I thought the bedchamber was exactly the place for—how do you say it? *Swords?*"

Twin spots of color flamed in Aric's cheeks. The word I'd used, a less than courtly term, had other meanings besides the weaponry sense. My Gilden wasn't perfect, but like any young person learning a foreign language, I'd acquired as many lascivious phrases as possible early on.

I smiled, pretending to miss his embarrassment. "I couldn't help but notice that you failed to meet me at the wharf when I arrived. I do hope this doesn't indicate a lack of attention to your other . . . duties?" I shifted my posture, ensuring the swoop of my neckline was well within his field of view. Trade agreements were not the only assets I brought to this arrangement.

His eyes dipped to my chest, then skittered away as his flush deepened and spread. So he *did* like women—the treaty hadn't specified otherwise, but his hostility had made me start to wonder.

"I was occupied with other matters," Aric said, his voice now emerging slightly hoarse. "A newly crowned king has much to attend."

My triumph yawed back towards irritation. I'd given him the perfect opening—was he really so determined not to apologize? I resisted the urge to stomp on his foot. Barely. "As the humble courtier you sent to greet me pointed out, you're not crowned yet."

A muscle ticked in his jaw. "No. Nor did I expect to be for many years. My mother's passing was . . . untimely."

Oh. My anger ebbed towards empathy. The former queen had died barely a month ago; the somber grey of Aric's jacket was a reminder. Perhaps I ought to extend the man more leniency. As rude as he'd been so far, people were never at their best while grieving.

Assuming he actually *was* grieving, and hadn't murdered the queen himself to take the throne as the rumors suggested. After all, he'd wasted no time threatening war with his neighbors. My anger returned, bolstered by indignation.

"When *is* the coronation?" I asked, an earnest question this time. Events had been in motion during the weeks I prepared and traveled, and news was scarce on a galleon. Obviously the wedding had to wait for my arrival, but I hadn't been sure until we docked that he hadn't already assumed the throne.

Aric's eyes narrowed, a sky darkening before a storm. Physically, he was not intimidating, narrow-shouldered and not much taller than me. But his expression made me want to draw back. Only the tense circle of his arm around my waist prevented me from missing a step in the waltz. Suddenly I was grateful for Catalina's overzealous precautions—this man had murder in his eyes.

"You seem eager to assume the crown of Gildenheim." His voice hummed low, with the resonance of a garotte.

I forced myself to keep my eyes locked on his. *He* was the one who had demanded a spouse to sit beside him; he could hardly fault me for taking up the task.

Abandoning my play at flirtation, I poured ice into my voice, matching the chill in his.

"Assuming the crown is part of the duties I'm here to fulfill. Unless you've changed your mind about our marriage."

His hand tightened around mine, verging on painful. I stared at him and held steady, refusing to flinch.

"I haven't," Aric said coldly. "Our wedding will take place tomorrow evening, and the coronation on the spring equinox—a week from now. You can tell your Council I keep my promises, *wife.*"

Tomorrow? Shock slowed my steps, nearly making me stumble. I'd thought I would have at least a little more time to orient myself before we were bound in marriage.

Aric had stopped moving. It took me a moment to realize the music had ended. We stepped away from each other at the same moment.

Aric bowed to me, the movement a cut. "I'll leave you to dance with whomever you feel like ingratiating yourself with for the remainder of the night. Welcome to Gildenheim, Duchess Liliana."

He turned on his heel and stalked away, the other dancers parting before him. I stared after him, anger simmering in my stomach.

Beneath my anger, though, lurked a cold as deep as a northern winter night. I hadn't even been in Gildenheim a full day. I'd spoken with Aric for only a single dance. Yet I was already certain of one terrible fact.

My future husband hated me.

7

A hand touched my elbow, making me startle. I turned and found myself looking up at Lord Varin, the courtier who had witnessed my humiliation at the docks.

"Might I have the honor of this next dance, your Grace?" A smile touched his lips. "Or perhaps I should say your Majesty?"

"Of course." I struggled to comb through my thoughts, tangled from Aric's frigid reception and the shock of learning my wedding was in less than twenty-four hours. "I mean, of course you may have this dance. Just Bianca will do."

"Bianca," Lord Varin said, stretching my name out syllable by syllable as if it were a foreign taste. "How delightfully informal."

Had I made another blunder? I'd studied as much as I could of Gildenheim's customs, but this was my first direct experience with its court. I kept my eyes on Varin's, wearing a polite smile like armor. "We are not so concerned with differences of rank in Damaria, my lord."

The next air began—a waltz slower than the first—and Varin stepped closer, his hand moving to my waist. This time, I turned my wrist so my dagger would not press against his shoulder. I didn't need the entire court knowing I'd worn a hidden blade to my own welcome ball.

The floor had filled now, but eyes still turned to us from every corner, prickling my skin like freshly cut grass. Dancing with Aric, I'd been aware of little outside the intensity of his attention. But now it was impossible to miss that I occupied the center of the court's focus along with the center of the room. A few whispers touched my ears as Varin swept us past a cluster of courtiers—*so unsuitable—pity her—if only their positions were reversed, it's such a shame that—*

"I've heard inheritance and rank work differently in your country," Varin said, before I could piece together what the courtiers were whispering about. "The peninsula hasn't had a monarch in quite some time, has it?"

"No, my lord." I bit back the impulse to mention that Damaria had moved beyond such relics of the past. I didn't need to begin by insulting everyone I met. I would be better than my betrothed.

In fact, if Aric was already determined to despise me, I should make my own allies—and I might as well begin now. I studied Varin with greater interest. Having seen Aric in person, it was evident why I'd thought my current dance partner might be my betrothed. Their resemblance was unmistakable, though Varin was older, broader in the shoulders, his features harder.

"Excuse my ignorance," I said, hiding my bluntness behind my most innocent smile, "but are you somehow related to the heir apparent?"

It was brief, but unmistakable: with a flash like a discharged cannon, livid anger flared behind Varin's eyes. Then it was gone again, snuffed by the quick hand of practice.

"I forget you have yet to be steeped in the gossip of this court," Varin said. "I am a bastard, your Grace. Born out of wedlock with a nobody for a father before the late queen was married."

Ah. I'd forgotten that such details mattered here. I could recite

Aric's entire lineage back ten generations, along with the dates of every political development between Damaria and Gildenheim. But apparently I'd memorized the wrong facts.

"My apologies," I said. "I didn't mean to touch on a tender subject."

"It's nothing," Varin said. "The matter is common knowledge."

Common knowledge, perhaps, but evidently sensitive nonetheless. In Damaria, Varin would have been considered a viable candidate to inherit—likely the *more* viable candidate of the two, given his greater age and experience. I didn't doubt a courtier like him was perfectly aware of the fact.

Though my condition was a closely guarded secret, I could empathize. I knew the sting of being deemed unworthy for something outside your control. I doubted my betrothed had ever known that experience.

Unintentionally, my gaze drifted to Aric. He was hard to miss. He leaned against one of the thrones on the raised dais and—of all things—he was *reading.* A thick leather-bound book partially obscured his face, though it didn't disguise the displeased slant of his brows. I almost laughed aloud with incredulity. He was so determined to spite me, he had decided to disdain his entire court in the effort. *This* was the man I was to marry tomorrow?

Beside Aric stood a short woman with inky hair and dark monolid eyes denoting Zhei heritage, muscles a bear would have envied, and a scowl as sour as turned wine. Her glare was fixed on me without the slightest attempt to hide it.

Caught unawares by the stranger's radiating hatred, I missed a step of the dance. Varin gracefully made up for my mistake, catching me around the waist and sweeping me into a turn.

I resisted the urge to look back at the dais. "Who is that woman standing beside Aric?"

Varin glanced in her direction, and a grimace darkened his

features. "Captain Marya Dai. The commander of the heir apparent's personal guard."

I snuck a glance over my shoulder. The woman—Marya—was still glaring openly. Her gaze tracked me like a hunter sighting her prey. I noted the practical knot of her hair, crisp lines of her uniform—forest green, like the other soldiers', but embroidered with silver accents—and the saber hanging at her hip. Unlike the halberds at the door, it was definitely not for ceremonial purposes.

"Do balls not agree with her?"

Varin leaned in closer, so that his breath warmed my ear. "Careful what you say, your Grace. The court has means of listening to private conversations. But you should know that Marya and Aric are . . . extremely close, if you catch my meaning. She did not take well to your arrival."

A bitter taste rose to my tongue. I caught his meaning all too well. My betrothed had a lover. No wonder he'd been so cold to me.

"I see." I managed to keep my tone even. "Thank you for the warning."

The music ended. Lord Varin bowed, and I swept a curtsy.

"Would you care to dance again, my lady?" he asked, still holding my hand.

I withdrew, shaking my head with an apologetic smile. I couldn't afford to dance with him twice, not without knowing what signal it would send. "My thanks for your generosity. But I've not yet had a chance to meet the rest of the court."

"I understand." Varin bowed again. "I'm certain your Grace will have no lack of partners."

The courtiers were already descending like pigeons eager for crumbs. I could feel their beady eyes on me, bright with curiosity.

I would have to be careful here. Every dance mattered. Every song was an alliance. And I was practically alone in a foreign court. I couldn't afford to make any enemies.

I glanced towards the dais. Aric was still reading, glowering at the page as if the book had personally offended him. But his captain was watching me, her face a storm.

Never mind that. I couldn't afford to make any *more* enemies. I already had two—and all I had done was arrive.

Back in my chambers, hours that felt like an eternity later, I dismissed Julieta the moment she finished helping me undress. Normally I might have asked her to stay, to talk over the disaster of this entire day. But the hour was late, and I was too exhausted to do anything but brood. I watched the door close behind her, swept the room with my gaze to confirm I was alone, and dropped my head into my hands with a groan.

The bureau's polished wood pressed hard against my elbows. I closed my eyes, a fledgling headache fluttering at my temples. Outside, the rain had intensified; drops pattered against the windows, obscuring the dark woods beyond.

Three hours of dancing with courtiers whose names and faces blurred together. I'd kept my careful mask in place the entire time, spoken polite inanities until the words threatened to blend into nonsense, made certain not to dance with anyone twice. As far as balls went, it had been a success. Most of the courtiers were far easier to talk to than Aric; the majority were friendly enough, some outright welcoming. One lady had expressed delight that Damaria and Gildenheim had finally agreed on a formal alliance; another lord had offered the hope that the court might see more of both myself and my betrothed after the marriage, leading me to wonder again at how Aric had spent most of the evening ignoring the court—perhaps I wasn't the only one he'd snubbed in this manner in the past. In short, I'd done well for myself and had successfully laid the groundwork to secure alliances.

And yet the first dance, the one that mattered most—at that, I had somehow failed.

Aric clearly resented me. He'd angered me, too, it was true, but that was because he'd openly insulted me. I had ample reason to nurse a grudge; his outright coldness was a different breed of distaste. It made no sense to me. *He* was the one who had demanded a treaty with Damaria. *He* was the reason this match was arranged. And yet now that I'd arrived, he acted as if I were an imposition. As if I'd offended him, when the offense was all on his part. I'd done nothing but perform my duty.

Well—that, and hidden a dagger up my sleeve. But self-defense in a strange land was understandable. Surely he'd have done the same had our situations been reversed. Although the close-fitting style of Gilden sleeves would make it more difficult—

I cut myself off. My thoughts were rambling to hide my fears: that my sister and Catalina's concerns had been well placed. That Aric was a cruel king and would prove a cruel husband. That I should never have agreed to this marriage in the first place.

I raised my head to look at myself in the mirror. Released from its pins, my hair curled around my face in dark waves. I looked strained, tired, but I was no monster from a children's tale. I wasn't renowned for my beauty—as if that really mattered anyway—but I couldn't find anything about my features that should offend Aric.

They certainly hadn't offended Catalina.

For a moment, I allowed myself to think of Catalina's calloused hands and warm skin, calling up the old memories. Though almost ten years had passed, though I'd tried to forget, I vividly remembered the way our mouths fit together. The idea of physical pleasure, of just feeling *wanted,* was alluring, especially after Aric's coldness.

If Aric had a lover, why shouldn't I? The thought was a bitter flash of rage, quick and violent as lightning. For a moment, vindictiveness coursed through me.

But rationality intervened almost as soon as the notion crystallized. Even if attempting to remake what I'd broken was anything other than the most foolish, selfish impulse, I couldn't sleep with someone else to punish Aric. No—I would be better than my betrothed. I would uphold my end of our agreement, regardless of what Aric decided to do. If he chose dishonor, he could choose it alone.

Besides, Catalina was engaged herself, and happier without me—of that I was certain. There was no going back, and it would be cruel to try.

I sighed. Tatiana's locket glinted in the mirror, and I ran a finger over its filigreed surface.

Only two weeks ago, when I'd signed my name to the treaty, I'd been so certain it was the right decision. I hadn't counted on a husband who hated me at first sight. Even worse, a husband who already had a lover.

But then why had he wanted a wife to begin with, if he already had a lover at court? Why rush into wedlock with someone he'd never met before he'd even been crowned? And it *was* a rush—couldn't he at least allow a few days for us to get to know one another?

It must be a show of power. That was the only explanation I could think of. After all, our betrothal had been part of the treaty negotiations; Aric had laid out his demand for a Damarian spouse in the same document that called for expanding the lumber trade. He had never wanted to love me, or even to give me a chance. He'd only wanted to expand his power. It explained why everything had been so hasty, why he hadn't even requested to meet me before the treaty was signed and didn't care to even pretend at courtship now.

Maybe it didn't even matter who I was because he'd never intended to go through with the wedding.

For the first time, I wondered if that had been his plan. Perhaps his intention all along had been to provoke war and lay claim to as much of Damaria's assets as he could seize. It would explain his dislike of me: he'd never intended to marry me, yet I'd shown up anyway. Now I was an obstacle.

Fear rose in my throat, as familiar as bile. I hadn't counted on this complication. What if my parents were right, and I wasn't strong enough to see this through?

I took a deep breath and closed my fingers around Tatiana's locket. I could do this. I had to. If I was right about the reason for Aric's hostility, then it was even more important that I go through with the wedding. I couldn't back down and give him an excuse for war. I couldn't let him win.

I must marry him. Whatever the cost.

8

I woke late on the day of my wedding to persistent rain and the worst flare I'd had in months. The ceremony itself would take place at dusk, and I'd intended to make the most of the day before then. I had plans to meet with Evito this morning to review the treaty and begin discussions on how to enact its provisions, as well as be briefed on other pressing matters of the Gilden court. But nausea gripped me too hard to let me stay on my feet, even after I'd swallowed a dose of tonic. I was barely able to perform my toilette before I fell back into bed, curled on my side with my fist pressed into the churning knot of my stomach.

Shame washed through me along with the nausea. Bitter experience had taught me that forcing myself through the flare would only make it worse, but this was an ocean away from how I'd wanted my new life to begin. The only mercy was that my parents weren't at the door demanding to know why I wasn't up and at my duties.

"Here, my lady." Julieta appeared beside me, proffering an earthenware mug wreathed with steam. "Drink this."

I forced myself to sit up and accept the drink. The first sip carried the spice of imported ginger root and the bright taste of mint, along with the generous sweetness of honey. I closed my eyes in relief. "I don't know what I'd do without you, Julieta."

"You'd be absolutely fine, my lady. You're stronger than you give yourself credit for." She smiled, but it was a distant look, not a happy one.

Which reminded me of my earlier resolve to ask Julieta about remaining here. I lowered the mug, looking at her through the steam. "Julieta . . . if you would rather return to Damaria, I wouldn't stop you. I want what's best for you."

Julieta was silent for a moment, her expression inscrutable. "My lady," she said finally, "I hope this isn't too bold, but I have long viewed you as more than an employer. I care for you as deeply as a daughter, your Grace, and I will do whatever is required to keep you safe and well."

My heart filled, relieving some of my nausea. Julieta rarely spoke about the family she'd lost before joining my staff. I had never presumed to replace them, though I'd often secretly, traitorously wished she could replace certain members of mine.

I reached out and clasped her hand. "I feel the same. Which is why I ask again whether you would be happier at home."

Julieta shook her head firmly. "My home is where you are. I'm staying." She squeezed my hand and stood, the set of her jaw offering no room for further protest. "Now drink the rest of that tea. Every drop. I'll bring you your correspondence."

My correspondence, it soon became clear, was no small matter. Apparently half the Gilden court had written to me in the scant hours since the welcome ball, all eager to position themselves for my favor. I paged through the teetering pile of sealed letters, trying to determine which to open first. My eye fell on a deep green seal, stamped with the silver insignia of a winged horse wearing a crown. The same seal I'd seen on the treaty. Aric's.

I broke the wax without delicacy, both eager and apprehensive to learn what the man I was marrying in a few hours thought important enough to send me on our wedding day. An apology, perhaps? A retraction of his hand in marriage?

The parchment held a single line, written in a rounded, infuriatingly flawless hand.

The heir apparent wishes to know whether her Grace will deign to appear at breakfast.

My brows rose. So now he was ordering me about with thinly veiled insults, attempting to dictate the terms of my life here. As if I hadn't already moved to a different *country* for this marriage.

I reached for a pen before I could think it through and dashed off a quick answer.

If the heir apparent wishes her Grace's presence, her Grace suggests he might deign to ask her in person.

I sent my reply off with a courier and returned to the rest of my letters. But my mind was only partly on the task. Aric's note lay on the bed beside me, a taunt I could ignore no more easily than a pebble in my shoe. Would he write back to me? Show up at the door demanding I come down to dine?

Oh seas, I should have thought my reply through. The last thing I needed was for Aric to burst into my bedchamber and realize I wasn't well. I cast a look at the door dividing our suites, wondering if Aric was on the other side. Likely not, if he was missing me at breakfast. But it was all too easy to picture him storming through and . . . what? Thrusting a pastry into my face?

I was being ludicrous.

His reply came late enough that I'd half given up on receiving one. This time it was not only a note, but a parcel wrapped in silk.

I opened the latter first, stopping in confusion as the fabric fell back to reveal a silver circlet.

First he insulted me, and then he sent me a gift?

I opened the accompanying letter. Like the first, it was brief.

The heir apparent hopes her Grace will deign to wear this for the ceremony tonight.

Underneath, as if it were an afterthought:

It is customary.

Now I did wish Aric had shown up in person, if only so I could give him a scathing look. I turned the circlet in my hands. So that was all. No apology. No change. Barely even an acknowledgment that we were to be married in just a few hours. He had merely wanted to hand over a ceremonial object.

I put the circlet and letter aside with a faint and unplaceable feeling of disappointment. Perhaps it was only the nausea; it wasn't as if Aric handing me the crown himself would have been an improvement. In fact, his rudeness might be for the best: the less I saw of the man, the better. It prevented me from saying something I might regret.

I spent the rest of the day in bed, drinking teas and tonics and answering letters—and trying hard not to think about this evening. But as the arboretum darkened towards dusk outside my window, I could put off neither the event itself nor the thought of it any longer.

My wedding was at hand.

Julieta helped me into my dress just before dusk. I breathed through waves of nausea as she fastened the pearl buttons at the cuffs of my sleeves. The silk was as cold as Aric's reception, in both temperature and hue. In Damaria, weddings were as jubilantly colorful as spring. But I'd bowed to Gilden traditions: my dress was winter white. A barren color. Its only sparks of brightness were the golden lilies embroidered on the skirt and bodice, a concession to my House and family.

A family who wouldn't even witness my wedding. I was almost grateful that my parents couldn't leave their duties with the Council, so I wouldn't have to endure the sting of their judgment. But I wished they'd allowed Tatiana to come. I would have given anything to have my sister teasing me now, distracting me from my dread by raising my ire.

My fingers closed around the locket at my neck. She'd made me a protection charm. I could have used a spell for a happy marriage, or at least a cordial one, instead.

"You don't need to be afraid, my lady," Julieta said. Jolted out of my dark reverie, I glanced at her in the mirror. She stood behind me, putting the final touches on my hair. I held still as she settled the circlet on my head.

"I'm not afraid." My denial was a reflex. But it occurred to me, now that she'd suggested it, that perhaps I was. That the roiling sensation in my abdomen was not merely my condition flaring, but also my nerves at play.

I didn't have the luxury to be afraid. I'd agreed to this match, and I would see it through. This marriage must take place—for the sake of the peace between our nations, and the thousands of lives that would not fall to cannon fire or saber's edge. They would not fall, because I would not let them. This was my duty: first and foremost, to my people. Not to my heart.

I touched the locket one more time, lifted my chin, and turned towards the door.

The procession to the throne room felt like a waking dream. Distantly, I knew that I was flanked by my own retinue of guards. That both courtiers and commoners lined the way, watching me with looks as delving as needles. That the great hall from the night before had been redecorated: rows of seats set up for spectators, banners hung from the walls, lanterns arrayed every few feet so that the room dazzled with light. But it all felt indistinct, as faded as the details of a nightmare come morning. I passed through my environs feeling as slow and buoyant as if I were underwater, barely taking any of it in. Perhaps it was the pain that washed through me in waves, making it difficult to concentrate on any-thing besides remaining upright. Perhaps it was an enchantment, a folly of light or atmosphere.

When I reached the dais, however, my surroundings cut abruptly into focus. Aric stood at the dais's edge, dressed in white as I was and freshly shaven. A circlet adorned his head—the same one he'd worn last night, gold to contrast my silver. He held his hand out to me, a gesture as sharp as broken glass.

I took it and stepped onto the dais. We turned towards one another, and our gazes locked. Today his eyes were the dark blue of a stormy winter sea. They held mine for only a moment before sliding away.

I followed his gaze. At the entrance to the throne room, an older woman with steely coils of hair had appeared between the open doors. All eyes trailed her as she made her way down the aisle. Silver robes hung from her shoulders, embroidered with green tendrils that snaked like living vines. In one hand, she bore a chalice brim-ming with red liquid. In the other, a knife.

The room tilted around me. I hadn't been prepared for blood-shed.

Aric flexed his fingers, and I realized I was still holding his hand, far too tight. I loosened my fingers, expecting him to pull away, but he didn't. This must be another part of the ceremony, since judging by the tension in his grip, he certainly wasn't holding my hand for his own comfort.

The woman reached the edge of the dais and stopped.

"We gather tonight by the Lady's grace to witness these two hearts bind together in marriage." Her words—spoken in Gilden—echoed throughout the entire chamber. Perhaps it was the effect of a spell, though her brown eyes didn't bear the gold flecks of a magic wielder. "Aric of Gildenheim. Bianca Liliana of Damaria. Do both of you agree to this union, of your own free volition, and without any prior ties?"

I lifted my chin, willing my voice to be steady. "Yes."

Both of us looked to Aric. His gaze flickered for an instant.

"Yes," he said, the word barely audible.

"Then with the Lady's blessing, you may recite your vows."

My tongue felt suddenly numb. I looked at Aric, panic speeding my breath. I didn't know the Gilden wedding ceremony by heart. Only that it involved the chalice the dignitary was holding—and, apparently, a knife.

Aric held my gaze this time. His eyes were chips of ice.

"I, Aric of Gildenheim, promise to take you as my wife. I swear to protect you, honor you, and stand by you. To hold you first and care for you as long as this union binds us."

His gaze didn't waver from mine. The entire hall was waiting. I swallowed.

"I, Bianca Liliana of Damaria, promise to take you as my husband." Each word burned like a paper cut dipped in lemon. "I swear to protect you, honor you, and stand by you. To hold you first and care for you as long as this union binds us."

Aric's hand tightened on mine, his fingers a vise, and then released me.

"I seal these vows," he said, "with my blood."

My heartbeat rushed in my own ears. I should flee, as Catalina had urged me on the ship. Seize the knife and fight my way out of this trap before its jaws closed fully.

I couldn't.

The dignitary handed Aric the knife. Did he mean to stab me? Was armed combat part of Gilden marriage ceremonies? Seas have mercy on me, I should have worn my wrist dagger after all.

Aric took the knife in his right hand and held out his left. He braced himself, failing to conceal a grimace, and then pressed the knife to the tip of his fourth finger. A line of blood welled up, shockingly red.

The dignitary proffered the chalice. Aric let a single drop of blood fall into the vessel's liquid, which glowed momentarily white.

My heart sped with fear—and the stirrings of anger. This ceremony wasn't mere symbolism—this was *magic*.

They say their royal family can cast spells with blood. The rumors Tatiana had mentioned were true. I forced away the urge to grasp my locket. What spell was Aric casting? What had he tricked me into?

Aric handed the knife to me. My hands shook with fine tremors. I should stop now. End this madness, despite the cost.

"I seal these vows with my blood." My voice was steady, years of practice coming to my aid. My pulse thudded as loudly as a warhorse's hooves. At least only I could hear it.

I pressed the knife to my fingertip. It was sharp, the cut almost painless. Blood welled immediately. I shook a drop into the waiting chalice, which flared white once more.

The dignitary passed the chalice to me. I looked at Aric over the heavy vessel, unsure what to do with it. I was tempted to throw its contents in his face.

Aric gestured, indicating that I should offer it to him. Grabbing for the remaining shreds of my poise, I held the chalice to

Aric's mouth so he could drink. His eyes fluttered closed as he swallowed.

Aric took the cup from me. He lifted it towards my mouth, watching me over the rim with a challenge in his eyes. As if he dared me to refuse to drink.

I met his gaze with a challenging look of my own. Virtues guide me, I would not back down now.

Aric put the chalice to my lips. The cup shook slightly, as if he wanted it to spill. I caught his wrist, his bones pressing sharp into my palm, and held him steady. The rich taste of the wine flooded my mouth, too sweet, with an undertone of iron.

A shock buzzed through my veins, overriding the nausea of my flare. The fine hairs stood up along my arms.

Whatever this spell was, it was cast on us. On *me*.

I nearly knocked over the chalice. My eyes met Aric's over the vessel.

"By the grace of the Lady," the dignitary proclaimed, "you are now pledged in marriage."

A roar of applause rose like distant thunder, shaking the room. It was done. A cut, a sip, a spell, and now, for better or for worse, Aric and I were wed.

The roaring turned into a whine in my ears. My knees folded, and the dais rushed towards me.

9

I didn't fall. An arm wrapped around my waist, holding me upright.

"Breathe," Aric said into my ear. "It will pass."

His arm tightened, keeping me pinned against his side. To the audience, we looked like newlyweds sharing an intimate moment. Only I could feel the tension running through Aric's entire body like a crossbow ready to fire. Why was he helping me? Watching me fall should satisfy him no end.

I drew in a shaky breath. The roaring in my ears subsided.

"That was blood magic." My voice sounded faint, as though I had spoken from far away.

"Yes." Aric's tone was clipped. "I thought you knew beforehand."

I took another, deeper breath. My condition was still flaring, pain wreathing my abdomen, but at least the spell's immediate effects were fading. In its place rose anger. Once again, this man—now my husband, by magic whose effects I could only guess—had completely disregarded basic manners, lacking even the courtesy to inform me of what I was agreeing to.

Fury gave my voice an edge, overriding my restraint. "If you had deigned to meet with me in person, I would have been forewarned."

"If you had deigned to come to breakfast, I would have ensured you were." Aric's arm was hard as steel around my ribs. Not crushing me, not even close, but I could tell he wanted to.

I opened my mouth, a scathing retort on my tongue.

"Sit," Aric said, before I could unleash the full brunt of my anger on him. "It's not over yet."

He guided me towards the thrones. Remembering our audience, I bit down on my harsh words. Shock and the magic's effects had caught me off guard, but I couldn't afford to lose control now. Not with the entire Gilden court bearing witness. I forced my feet to move so that I didn't trip us both.

"Please tell me there isn't more bleeding," I muttered. "I would have brought my own dagger."

Aric made a startled sound. When I glanced at him, for the barest moment his mouth twitched towards amusement.

An instant later, however, the smile was gone, making me wonder if I'd imagined it. He looked at the pair of thrones with a shuttered expression, his arm tightening around me again—viselike, inadvertent. The ornate seats were identical to me, but evidently not to Aric. He came to a decision and let me down onto the left-hand throne, surprisingly gentle.

Before I could ask what was next, he had withdrawn, seating himself on the second throne. The pair was close enough that we could have bridged the space between them with our hands. Too close. After the way he'd not only insulted me, but tricked me into a magical binding, I wished I could shove Aric's seat to the opposite side of the room. Or even better, straight into the sea.

At least the cut from the ceremony had numbed. I turned my hand palm up, and another shock jolted through me. The wound had entirely closed, leaving in its place a thin golden mark like a line of gilt embroidery. When I ran my thumb over it, the skin was smooth to the touch, indistinguishable from the rest of my flesh.

My eyes widened. What in the ocean's hundred names had he done?

I glanced at Aric, apprehension and fresh fury curdling in my chest, but he was determinedly looking anywhere but at me. His fingers drummed on the armrest as he surveyed the grand hall and the people in it. People who were now flowing towards us like a current.

Ah. So that was what came next. Reluctantly, I set aside my questions and my anger. I straightened my shoulders and braced myself to meet what felt like every citizen of Gildenheim.

The ambassadors were the first to approach—representatives from each of Gildenheim's neighbors and allies, all murmuring congratulations along with a few words referencing their countries' commitment to a continued peace; it occurred to me as they spoke that Damaria might not be the only nation on which Gildenheim had threatened war, though my parents hadn't spoken of any other rising tensions. Evito was one of their number, bowing precisely to first me, then Aric.

"Your Grace," he said smoothly. "Your Majesty. I speak for the entire Council when I say Damaria greatly anticipates a brighter future for both our countries, steered by the reins of much-needed progress."

Aric said nothing, but his fingers curled tight on the armrest of his throne. I thanked Evito without looking at Aric, all too conscious of the tension radiating from my new husband's direction.

Next came the highest-ranking members of the Gilden court, starting with a lady with a net of jewels adorning her blond hair. Her dark gown glittered with silver thread as she swept a low curtsy. I recalled meeting her last night—she'd offered the hope that there would be more balls in the near future.

"Majesties," she said. "Congratulations on your marriage. It is a delight to see a true courtier on the throne once more."

This time I did glance at Aric, puzzled by the statement. Did she mean the throne had been empty since the late queen's death? But that couldn't be right—not to judge by the way Aric's hands had tightened again, a muscle in his jaw ticking. There was a current to her words too deep for me to read. I wondered if this was one of the relatives the Council's spies had reported as having private designs on the throne.

"Your opinions are noted, Countess Signa," Aric said tightly. "As always."

I looked back at the countess and smiled, hoping neither my confusion nor my nausea was evident. The countess curtsied again, the corner of her own smile sharp and knowing, and retreated to make way for the next supplicant.

I did my best to note each arrival's rank, to respond appropriately to each greeting. But between my dizziness, exhaustion, and the sheer number of strangers, all too soon I could barely even manage to nod and smile. Time blurred as they came to greet us, a stream of courtiers and commoners as relentless and eroding as a river. Their words flowed over me, each washing away a little more of my strength. Pain roiled in my stomach and pulsed in my skull. The circlet began to pinch my temples. I thought I might be sick.

Virtues help me, this horrid evening refused to end. It must be after midnight, yet the river of people stretched endlessly towards the sea.

"You should eat."

Fogged with pain, I took a moment to realize Aric was speaking to me. I stared at him, not bothering to hide my surprise. He was watching me, his blue eyes narrowed—undoubtedly in distaste. The circles beneath them had returned, or perhaps had never left.

Refreshments had appeared on a small table between the two

thrones. I hadn't even noticed their arrival. From the looks of it, Aric hadn't touched the repast yet. Was this another trap?

I managed to smile, thin as a knife's edge. "I'm not hungry. And I'm perfectly fine."

"You don't look fine." Aric's voice was low, pitched for my ears alone. Had I not known he hated me, it might have felt intimate. "At least drink some water."

I studied him, suspicious. Since when was he solicitous of my needs?

"I don't want you passing out in front of the entire court," Aric said, annoyance limning his syllables now. He pushed his own cup towards me, water nearly sloshing over the silver sides. "Drink."

My eyes had followed the gesture, drawn by the precise movement of his hands. Now I risked another look at his face. Aric's expression was rife with undisguised antipathy. But if there was guile there, I could not find it.

I didn't know what his wedding vows meant to him. But he was sworn to protect me, bound to his promise by the same magic he'd tricked me into. Perhaps he didn't mean me harm after all. Not now, at least.

Of course not. I wasn't thinking clearly. If he wanted an excuse to invade Damaria, poisoning his new wife in full sight of everyone of importance in Gildenheim, not to mention all the foreign dignitaries who were witnessing the occasion, would be an exceptionally bad decision.

Cautiously, keeping my gaze on him, I drank. The cup was heavier than I expected. Or perhaps my flare was worse than I'd realized.

The water made me feel better. Which made my feelings churn with confused emotions about Aric—irritation that he'd been right, gratitude that his actions had helped.

I slid the cup back towards him, but he caught my hand, stopping the chalice's motion. His fingers were warm as they wrapped over mine.

Both of us froze. Then Aric pulled away, sharp as a cut. He hadn't meant to touch me.

"Keep it," he said. "You need it more than I do."

He turned deliberately away, leaving me feeling more conflicted than ever. This evening was an ordeal, but I could survive it. But if the man I'd married couldn't even bear to touch my hand in public, I wasn't sure I could make it through what came when we were alone.

I would. I had to. For the sake of my people.

I curled my hand around Tatiana's locket and prayed I wouldn't need it.

Somehow, hours later, the interminable evening had flowed to its end. I didn't remember returning to my chambers, yet here I was, sitting at the bureau, preparing for the greatest ordeal of the night.

Outside, the sky had turned from deep navy to a dreary grey. On any other day I would be rising at this hour, not steeling myself to go to the bed of a man who despised me. Everything felt backwards, as if I'd been trapped in an inverted version of reality like the reflection in the bowl of a spoon. The weather contributed to the feeling of distortion: dawn's approach and the veil of falling rain blurred the arboretum into an indistinct mass of grey.

Inside, however, everything was as clear and sharp as broken crystal. The way my thin shift hugged my body. The heaviness of the silk dressing gown I wore over it, lily pink. The tug of the brush on my scalp as Julieta loosened my hair from its coif, each golden pin singing against the bureau as she laid it down. My flare had finally subsided, and with it the headache that had blurred my senses for the majority of the evening. But I almost wished for the pain back. Or, even better, I wished to be numb. It would make what came next easier.

"My lady?" Julieta adjusted the collar of my dressing gown. "I think it's time."

Dutifully, I rose. My legs were steady, though it would have been more honest for them to collapse beneath me again. I ran my thumb over the golden mark from the wedding ceremony as I turned towards the door of Aric's chambers.

It looked so ordinary. Just a common wooden door, perhaps in need of a coat of polish. It shouldn't have held so much weight.

I had known this was part of what I agreed to from the beginning. And it wasn't as if the man I'd married was a bane to the eye—rather the opposite, despite his abominable manners. But now that the reality of the marriage bed was only a door's thickness away, it was suddenly hard to keep my breath steady.

My fingers trembled as they brushed the lacquered wood.

I took a deep breath, my pulse fluttering in my throat. I wasn't afraid. Of course I wasn't afraid. I knew what the act entailed; this wouldn't be my first time. Perhaps, if I were lucky, Aric would have some skill. If not, at least it would be over quickly, and I could retire to my own chambers and sleep with the Virtues' blessings, knowing I had kept my country safe.

I touched my sister's locket one more time, let out a deep breath, and turned the handle.

The door opened into a bedchamber, larger than my own. Adept-crafted lights—an import from my own country—rested in wrought iron sconces, casting the room in a soft glow that reminded me of light through shallow water.

Aric stood on the other side of the bed. He had removed his

jacket and circlet; his hair hung in loose golden waves around his pale face. If I considered him as a painting instead of a man, this could almost be enjoyable. One could admire a thing of beauty without loving it, after all.

His gaze swept over me, raking like claws, and I shivered. He had no admiration for me—the open hatred in his eyes burned like acid.

This would not be enjoyable at all.

Without looking away from him, I closed the door behind me. It clicked into place with a note of finality.

"Let's get this over with." Aric spoke in Gilden, his words curt and short. The harsh syllables of the language made it sound like a curse.

Aric drew his shirt over his head in a gesture as fluid and cold as a spring river. The garment dropped to the floor, and his hands slid to the waist of his trousers.

It was too much. Like a chill wind, his cold dismissal blew on the ember smoldering in my chest, making my anger flare to life. This time, I didn't tamp it down; I let it blaze. I could be graceful in the face of his insults in public, but this was our marriage bed. I was not something to be *gotten over with*.

"That's enough," I snapped, answering him in my own tongue. My fists were clenched so tightly my nails bit into my palms. "I will not be insulted like this."

Aric's hands stilled on his waistband. His eyes met mine for the first time since I'd entered his room. To my shock, they burned white-hot with an anger to match my own.

"What more do you want?" His voice was jagged with animosity. "Do you want me on my knees, *wife*? On top of the rest of your demands, do you now require my humiliation?"

"My *demands*?" My voice was rising, but I made no attempt to rein it in. "What are you suggesting? *You're* the one who's made all the demands. I've only done as you asked. And in return, you've publicly insulted me, you've been insufferably rude, and now you're treating bedding me like an ordeal as if this weren't what *you* wanted in the first place!"

Aric's face grew livid. "You continue to mock me. As if you don't know full well that this could never be what I wanted."

His cruelty sank a blade through my chest, but I would not be cut down so easily. *He* was in the wrong here—not me. I'd come to Gildenheim with good intentions. I'd tried to do everything right. And now he was acting as if I should have known from the start that he wouldn't want me, when he'd never even given me a chance.

"Am I not good enough for you?" I seethed. "Well, *husband,* I am sorry for your disappointment, but I will not apologize for being inadequate. If there was something in particular you required in your future spouse, you should have had the foresight to name it before making your threats of war!"

Aric's eyes widened—now he dared pretend to be surprised. His rudeness truly had no end. "What are you talking about?"

"Don't play the innocent. You know exactly why I came here and at whose request." I took a step towards him, teeth gritted. "So tell me, your Majesty, what exactly *did* you want? A fairer face? A fuller figure?" I wasn't making sense—he'd hated me before he'd even seen me. But I had him on the defensive, and I'd been trained too well to concede a fight I could win.

"What? I—"

"You didn't seem to mind my figure when we danced. Is it that I have no magic?"

"Duchess Liliana—"

"So that's it. You wanted a pet Adept to keep on a leash as you wreaked war against—"

"*Bianca!*"

The urgency of his words cut me short. Aric wasn't looking at me any longer. He was looking over my shoulder.

To the door that had flown silently open and the black-clad figure racing towards us, blade glinting in their hand like a predator's fangs.

10

I whirled, my hand going to my waist for my rapier. But I wore only a shift and a dressing gown. My weapons were out of reach in my chambers—behind the armed intruder. I had a scant moment to see the attacker's dark clothing and glinting steel—

Then they were past me, closing in on their target. Not me. Aric.

I'd already scrambled backwards before I realized the assassin's aim. Now they were halfway around the bed, knife raised to strike. Aric's eyes went huge with panic. He threw up his arms to shield his face, as if that would be enough to stop the knife.

No time to think. Only to act. I snatched up a pillow and rolled across the bed, throwing myself between Aric and the assassin. Steel flashed. I thrust the pillow upwards to block the descending blade. Silk ripped and feathers exploded. I drove my knee into my attacker's abdomen. They doubled over with a grunt.

"The lanterns!" I yelled at Aric, who was staring, frozen. "Hand me a lantern!"

The assassin clutched their gut, wheezing. I grabbed a lamp from Aric's fumbling fingers and smashed it over their head. Glass shattered. A viscous white liquid sprayed everywhere, cold as it soaked through my dressing gown.

I shoved the attacker away. They went down hard against the

wall. The remnants of the lantern dripped from my fingers, mingling with a darker fluid—blood. My hand was burning, a tingling sensation spreading up my arm. I'd cut myself on the glass.

I had no time to tend my wounds. The assassin was already stumbling back to their feet. The knife flashed in their hand as they adjusted their grip. Their face was covered, but their dark eyes darted to Aric, plotting a route around me. My efforts had thwarted them for only a moment, and now I had no defenses.

No weapons. No shields. Even the glass from the lantern had disintegrated into shards too small to use as blades.

It will defend you against an attacker.

My hand flew to the locket at my neck, slicking the silver with my blood.

The assassin darted forward. Aric shoved me aside, stepping in front of me.

"Don't—" he began.

I flipped the locket open.

With a sound like an earthquake, the chamber exploded into blazing white light.

The force of the spell threw me backwards onto the bed. The room spun sickeningly around me. Black sparks chased each other at the edges of my vision.

Get up. I had to get up. The assassin could be anywhere—could be closing in on Aric again at this instant, or deciding to come for me instead. I couldn't lie here in a daze, even if my vision was swimming. I gritted my teeth and pushed myself up on my elbows.

And froze, bewildered.

I was face-to-face with a large, white . . . horse.

I blinked, certain I must be hallucinating. But as my vision cleared, the horse remained. Its large brown eyes rolled back in its head, showing the whites in an expression I recognized as panic.

It blew out a huff of hay-scented air in my face and shied away from me, hooves clattering on the floor.

I didn't have time to deal with magically summoned stallions. I rolled to my feet, nearly colliding with the horse. The floor lurched beneath my bare soles, and I hastily grabbed the bedpost to steady myself. Now of all times, I couldn't afford weakness.

The assassin was slumped against the wall, head lolling. The force of Tatiana's enchantment must have thrown them across the room. I had only a few moments before they recovered. I needed to find Aric and run for help before they could strike again. Where *was* the blasted man?

"Aric?" My voice was raw with fear.

No one answered. He must be hiding behind the horse. Or under the bed. Or perhaps he'd fled. Not exactly commendable, but I could overlook that given the circumstances. Or maybe the spell had stunned him, too?

The horse whinnied and pranced, blocking my view. I shoved at its flank in irritation, cursing again as it refused to budge. The horse's sudden appearance in the bedchamber had to be Tatiana's doing, but this was a very strange sort of protection indeed. What had my sister been *thinking*? Was I supposed to ride out of danger? The beast didn't even have a saddle, and a horse would be useless against an assassin. In fact, it was making things decidedly more difficult.

A groan. My gaze shot towards the sound.

The assassin was stirring. As I watched in dismay, they rolled to their hands and knees, groping across the floor for their weapon.

"Aric!" I shouted, abandoning subtlety. "Where are you?"

The horse butted me with its nose, nearly knocking me back onto the bed. I shoved it away again with an oath. Virtue of Serenity, now I was being attacked by a horse as well as an assassin.

-Get on my back.-

My mouth fell open. The voice had sounded *inside* my head. Clear. Oddly familiar. And, though I couldn't have said how I knew, unmistakably coming from the horse.

Shock was making me imagine things, because horses simply *did not talk*. Especially not in my head.

The horse stamped a hoof against the floor with a resounding crack. -*Get on my back. Now. Before both of us are killed.*-

Practicality rushed back in. As unnerving as it was to be telepathically addressed by a magically materializing warhorse, the creature was right—I had to get out of here before the assassin recovered. Searching for Aric would only give our assailant time to kill us both.

I made an ungraceful lunge towards the horse, grabbed it by the mane, and scrambled onto its back.

A shudder rippled through the horse's flanks. Drown me, it would be just my luck to have conjured a horse that couldn't stand a rider, especially since I had neither bridle nor saddle. Tatiana could have considered that in her spell. I gripped its mane more tightly.

"Go," I urged. "Get us out of here!"

The horse shuddered again. And then, nearly throwing me from its back, it reared. I shrieked and clung desperately to its neck, my legs sliding down its flanks. Glass chimed, catching the first light of morning, as the horse's hoof smashed through the nearest window. My steed dropped to all fours and gathered itself, muscles bunching beneath me. I barely had time to finish screaming before it leaped straight through the shattered second-story window.

Broken glass snagged my dressing gown, ripping my sleeve. Fabric billowed around me. For a terrible moment, I was airborne. And then the horse's hooves hit the ground, bone-shatteringly hard, and it was galloping into the dawn, leaving the castle behind.

We plunged through the trees of the arboretum I'd seen from my window. A cold, wet wind whipped my face, tangling my hair into knots and squeezing tears from my eyes. Frigid rain soaked through my dressing gown in an instant. I clung to the horse's neck, my legs clamped around its sides. The world dissolved into a blur of snow and shadow. Branches loomed around me, bristling with needles. One snatched my hair, and I couldn't stifle a cry of pain as strands ripped from my scalp.

Finally, the horse slowed and came to a standstill, sides heaving. I dared to lift my head and look around. We were alone in the midst of a dense, dark wood. Grey light paled the clouds above the trees; lingering patches of snow dotted the ground beside a few bold green shoots. The earth shone with the wet, chill glint of mud.

A shiver racked through me. I was wearing only a soaked dressing gown and a shift, and a Gilden spring was as cold as the depths of Damarian winter. I'd nearly died and I wasn't yet out of danger. I was alone, weaponless, with only a horse for company—a large, regrettably white horse that glowed against the rain-shrouded trees like a lantern, betraying our location to anyone in pursuit.

And the assassin—who had sent them? Had they followed us out the window? The chill pierced all the way to my heart as I realized: they had come through my chambers. My retinue wouldn't have let them pass without a fight, but I hadn't heard a single warning sound. Julieta—Catalina—were they drugged? Dead? And Aric—what had happened to him?

Virtues, please let him be alive. I might despise the man, but I didn't want him dead. Especially not when the peace between our countries depended on our union.

"Aric," I muttered, talking to myself. "Where in the ocean's hundred names are you?"

The horse shifted beneath me, making me hastily tighten my grip on its mane. And then that voice sounded in my head again. Smooth, melodic, and undeniably annoyed.

-*Right here. Now get off my back.*-

My jaw went slack. I must have hit my head during the fight, for now the horse was not only talking, but doing so in the voice of the man I'd just married.

-*Did you not hear me? Get off my back.*- The horse stamped a hoof. Earth splattered, and it shook itself, nearly unseating me again. -*Ugh. I despise mud.*-

I closed my mouth with an audible click. "A-Aric? Are you—a *horse?*"

The horse turned its head to glare at me over its shoulder. *His* shoulder. The expression dissipated my doubt, though not my shock. That cold annoyance was definitely Aric's, bizarre though it was to see it on an equine face.

-*What do you think I look like? A chicken?*- the horse demanded. -*Now for the last time, get off my back before I buck you into this rotted mud.*-

"Virtue of Patience. You could at least give me a moment to process the circumstances."

I slid from the horse's—*Aric's*—back, wincing as my bare feet hit the frigid ground with a splash. Icy mud slid between my toes. My knees nearly gave way under me and, without thinking, I caught myself on the horse's side. A shiver ran through his flanks, and I snatched my hand away.

I turned to look at him, my eyes narrowed. "You're really my husband?"

-*Regrettably. Unless you've managed to acquire a divorce in the last few hours without my knowledge?*-

Yes, that was definitely Aric. And transforming him into the emblem of his own country did seem like exactly the sort of thing

Tatiana would find diverting. I clutched my head in my hands, my fingers tangling in my sodden hair.

"This is impossible." A hysterical laugh bubbled up and spilled out into the early morning air. "I'm married to a horse."

The horse—Aric—stamped a hoof (*a hoof!*) alarmingly near my bare feet. Mud splashed onto the silk of my already ruined dressing gown. *-Control yourself, wife. This is no laughing matter. This situation would be grave even if we weren't fleeing an assassin.-*

Right. The assassin. The thought was a cold bucket of water, dousing the flames of my laughter. "Who were they? Why did they try to kill you?"

Aric gave me a look that showed the whites of his eyes. *-I think you know that better than I.-*

It took me a moment to understand the implication. "Wait. You think *I* sent the assassin? I nearly got myself killed *protecting* you from them!"

-How very convenient.-

I was nearly speechless with rage. "It was hardly convenient! I'm cut, bruised, soaked, and I nearly lost my life. And besides, *I* entered this marriage in good faith. I'm not the sort of person who would have my husband murdered on my wedding night!"

-You wore a dagger to your own welcome ball.-

"For self-defense! Which was clearly well merited! How do I know that wasn't *your* assassin?"

Aric snorted, indignant. *-I would never assassinate my spouse in my bedchamber. Even one who forced me to marry them. It would ruin the sheets.-*

"It would—" I sputtered. "Wait, what do you mean, forced you to marry—"

A cacophony of bells broke out in the distance, cutting my protest short. An alarm. Someone had discovered the assassination attempt.

Both our heads turned sharply in the direction of the noise. Lights were bobbing through the trees—the dull flickering orange of torches struggling against the rain, mixed with the paler glow of Adept-forged lanterns. A search party. And I would wager my life that the assassin had slithered into the searchers' ranks, passing themselves off as part of the castle household.

Aric's head swung back to face me, though his ears remained turned towards the alarm bells.

-We don't have time for this discussion now. Undo your spell before the assassin finds us.-

I winced. "I . . . don't know how."

Aric's nostrils flared. They were really quite large nostrils. *-What do you mean, you don't know how? It was your spell!-*

"It wasn't my spell, actually." I touched my hand to my throat. Miraculously, the locket had survived the breakneck journey through the woods. It hung from its chain, still open. "My sister made it for me. It was meant to be a protection device. I don't really know how it works. I'm not the one with magical abilities, remember?"

Aric might have been a horse, but apparently he could still give me an entirely withering look.

"Fine. I'll try my best to—to unhorse you." I fumbled with the rain-slick locket. Since opening it had activated the spell, perhaps closing it would reverse the enchantment. My fingers were clumsy from the cold, but I managed to pinch the pendant between them.

-Wait——- Aric started.

I squeezed my eyes closed and clicked the locket shut.

No rush of air. No burst of light.

I cautiously opened my eyes to find myself still face-to-face with a large, annoyed, and entirely untransformed white stallion.

"One moment. I'll try again." With increasing urgency, I clicked the locket open and shut, open and shut.

Aric pawed impatiently at the muddy earth. *-We have no time for this. Get on my back.-*

"A moment ago you wanted me to get off—"

-Archives and indices, wife, just stop arguing and do as I say. Do you really want to explain to my guards why I'm a horse and you have blood on your shift? Assuming it's my guards who find us first, and not the assassin.-

I had no argument. I shut my mouth. Aric lowered himself to his knees, muttering irritably about the mud all the while. I swung a leg over his back. Mounting him felt entirely different now that I knew he wasn't an ordinary horse. My bare thighs touched his sides, and I wore nothing beneath my shift.

Heat rushed to my face. Thank the seas he couldn't see my face. Or could he? His eyes were on the sides of his head. What was a horse's vision like?

Virtue of Mercy. I was married to a horse.

Hysterical laughter threatened to spill out again. I clamped my lips closed on it. Aric was right: this wasn't something to laugh about. It was only the exhaustion and shock making me react in unhinged ways.

Aric jolted to his feet. I gripped his mane, and we plunged deeper into the forest's embrace.

"Where are we going?"

-You'll see. Somewhere safe.- He paused. *-I hope.-*

11

Aric said nothing further, and I didn't press. Behind us, the woods echoed with shouts and the ceaseless tolling of the alarm bells. A dog began to bark, and my heart clenched. The sky was brightening now that the sun had cleared the horizon, adding urgency to our flight—the daylight was against us, making it harder to hide.

I knew the arboretum was contained within the castle walls, yet as Aric forged on it seemed endless, a spiraling scape of trees and rain and shadow. Surely we'd seen those same clumps of fir and spruce multiple times.

"Do you even know where we're going?" I hissed at Aric through chattering teeth.

-Hush. You'll draw attention.-

"That wasn't an answer."

Behind us, a groaning creak of wood. I twisted to look over my shoulder and bit back a gasp. From among the trees—no, *from* the trees themselves—peered faces with burls for noses and bristling bark eyebrows.

"Aric," I whispered. "Are the trees . . . looking at us?"

-I did say you'd draw attention.-

Unnerved, I gripped his mane more tightly. Horses weren't supposed to talk. Trees weren't supposed to literally watch you. What had the magic in this country been drinking?

Finally, Aric stopped beside a pair of massive firs that looked older than the castle itself. This time I slid from his back without being prompted. My feet were so cold that hitting the ground was a shock of pain. I swayed, nearly fell, grabbed his mane for balance.

Aric's flanks rippled in annoyance. He shook me off. -*In there. Between those two firs.*-

I stared at the trees in puzzlement—they looked no different from any other patch of forest. Then I blinked and looked again. What at first glance seemed like just a darker area of shadow was, on closer inspection, a narrow, derelict building. Half the wood-shingled roof had fallen away, revealing the edifice's bones. As shelters went, it wasn't promising.

I looked at Aric skeptically. "Won't it be obvious we're hiding out here?"

He shook his head impatiently, tail flicking. -*To find this place, you have to have been here first.*-

More irregular magic. Just what I needed. "And we're assuming the assassin hasn't paid this charming abode a visit before?"

-*Only three people alive have been here, including you and me. And the third would never try to kill me.*-

I ignored the implication—I *hadn't* arranged the assassin, whether he believed me or not. I had only his word that this unknown third party was equally innocent. But I didn't feel like arguing the point. A light wind had sprung up, driving rain into my face. I was trembling with cold and didn't fancy being stared at by hostile trees. The hut wouldn't be comfortable, but at least it was out of the rain.

I started forward. For a moment I felt as if I pushed against a great wind. Then, with a *pop* like pressure releasing in my ears, the entire building suddenly came into clear focus. My breath hitched. An unsettling magic indeed.

The building's single wooden door hung askew from its hinges. I shoved it open with both hands and stepped inside cautiously. The scents of damp straw and mildew assailed my nose. Rain poured steadily in where the roof had given way, and elsewhere a chorus of drips plunked out a lugubrious hymn. A cold drop found the back of my neck, and I shivered as it scurried down my spine.

My eyes ran over rows of thin walls fronted by half doors, most nearly rotted away. "Is this . . . a barn?"

-It was a stable for the realm's finest mounts before the arboretum grew up. Now it's a last retreat for the royal family if the castle falls. Move aside before I step on you.-

I stepped out of the way as Aric pushed through the door, muttering again about the rain and mud. The doorway was a tight fit—his sides rubbed off flakes of lichen that had taken the opportunity to bedeck the frame. Inside, he shook himself with a disgruntled shudder, shedding bits of plant matter and mud. I shielded my eyes from the spray.

-Look in the stalls.- His words were curt. Still hostile, but at least we weren't outright arguing. *-There are supplies. Blankets and such.-*

"Probably wet and mouse eaten," I muttered, but I complied.

This place may have housed the realm's finest mounts once, but now it would be better fit for a troop of toads. The weak morning sunlight revealed that the roof's collapse had exposed all but two of the stalls to the open sky; most of the building was wet and reeked of mildew and rot. The two surviving stalls were in only marginally better shape. One was stacked with wooden crates; the other held a scattering of moldy straw. At least it was sheltered from the rain.

I wrestled the lid off the nearest crate with difficulty; my fingers had numbed almost to uselessness. I could have cried with relief at what I found inside: the rough weave of heavy woolen fabric. A length of cloth spilled out when I pulled. A blanket.

There were two: thick, coarse—and, thank the seas, *warm*. I wrapped one around myself like a shawl.

-Give me one of those.-

I flung the second blanket at Aric, hoping it hit him in the face—until he apologized, I was determined to make him wish he had. "Since you asked so kindly. Good luck getting that on without hands."

Aric huffed in annoyance. Ignoring him, I headed towards the other sheltered stall, eager to lie down somewhere dry.

Only to find Aric blocking my way.

"Move," I snapped, in no mood to pretend at courtesy. "I need to sit down."

He flared his nostrils at me, ears twitching. *-Find somewhere else. I'm taking this stall.-*

I set my jaw. "You're a horse. Horses stand out in the rain all the time. You don't need it."

-I deserve it. Because, as you astutely pointed out, I am indeed a horse, a state which is entirely your fault. Find your own stall.-

My teeth hurt from being gritted so hard. "There's only one that's suitable."

-Another astute observation.-

Drown the man—the horse—whatever he was. I hugged the blanket more tightly around my shoulders as a gust of wind attempted to pry it away.

"Let's compromise," I said, exasperated. "We share the stall, and I will put the other blanket on you. Since, as we have *both* astutely observed, you are a horse."

Aric considered, his tail flicking irritably.- *Fine. But you'd better put it on properly, or I will kick you out.-* He blew out a huff of air. *-Archives and indices. Couldn't you have turned me into something with opposable thumbs?-*

We wedged ourselves into the narrow stall, as far from each other as humanly—or equinely—possible. I draped the second blanket over Aric's flanks far more charitably than I felt, then curled into a ball in the far corner and tucked my own around myself. Gradually, my shudders ebbed. Everything hurt, and the straw I sat on smelled strongly of mildew, but at least I wouldn't freeze to death.

No—actually, everything *didn't* hurt. Not as much as it should. My body ached with developing bruises and my legs still stung with cuts from the window. But my hands, where I'd sliced myself on the smashed lantern, hurt only from the cold.

I extracted one of my hands from the blanket and held it towards the light from the collapsed roof. Even in the dimness of a rain-shrouded morning, my skin was unmistakably whole. My wounds were gone. But golden lines crossed my palm like gilt scars, echoing the mark from the wedding ceremony.

A chill swept through me that had nothing to do with the cold.

-Are you hurt? Did the assassin wound you?- Aric sounded hopeful.

"Sorry to disappoint you, but I'll live." I tucked my hand back into the blanket. Should I tell him about the marks? Ask him what they meant? For all I knew, they were a sign he'd placed a curse on *me*.

-Incredible as it may seem to you, I would prefer you remain among the living.-

"Incredible as it may seem to *you*, I would prefer that you do the same."

-Naturally. Which is why you sent an assassin into my bedchamber and transformed me into a horse.-

Irritation flared. "I told you, I didn't send the assassin. And the spell wasn't meant for you—I was trying to *save* both of us. None of this is how I anticipated our wedding night unfolding."

-I've yet to grasp how exactly you did *expect it to go. After the assassin and the curse, what was the next stage of your plan?-*

If only Tatiana's spell had included a provision of silence. I gritted my teeth. "Also as I told you, I had no plan. My only intention was to fulfill the terms of the treaty. And had I known how insufferably rude you would turn out to be, I would have insisted the Council renegotiate those terms."

-So you continue to deny orchestrating this marriage in the first place?-

That was thrice he'd said something to that effect, and this time I was in a better state to pay attention to it. I sat up straighter, frowning, to focus on him fully.

"I had nothing at all to do with arranging this marriage. I was selected by the Council of Nine as the most suitable candidate to satisfy your thinly veiled threats of war."

-My threats? *I've never threatened Damaria. Your Council was the one making all the demands.-*

This made no sense. I'd seen the treaty draft myself, complete with Aric's seal. "What demands, exactly, do you think the Council has made?"

I could practically picture him ticking them off on his fingers. If he'd still had fingers.

-Expanding the trade agreement. Committing to an annual quota of purchases of Adept technology. Increasing our lumber and iron exports. Agreeing to wed a partner of the Council's choice before the coronation, without even meeting you first—-

"Wait," I interrupted. If my head spun any harder, it would roll right off my shoulders. "The Council didn't demand any of that. *I* didn't demand any of that. The insistence on marriage was all from *you*!"

Aric's nostrils flared. *-Why in the Lady's name would I insist on marriage?-*

My brows rose incredulously. "To make a statement as a new king? To test your power by claiming a tithe from Damaria?"

-You are a woman, not a tithe.- Aric snorted. *-And if I wanted a tithe, why would I demand to marry* you?-

I'd just been insulted again, but he didn't give me room to retaliate. *-I'm not even crowned yet. Why would my first move be to aggravate my closest neighbor with a list of demands that could easily spark a war?-*

I opened my mouth, then closed it again. I could think of counterarguments, but they were all as limp as wet silk.

He was right. Now that I'd heard it from his perspective, forcing the treaty wasn't a logical move at all. I hardly knew Aric, not yet. But from what I'd seen of him, aside from his personal grudge against me, he didn't seem like the sort of man eager to start a fight. He had literally hidden behind a book at the welcome ball. Not the sort of action a king bent on war would take.

Yet if he was telling the truth, that left a problem even more salient than Aric's new form.

"But if neither of us asked for this marriage . . . who did?"

12

Neither Aric nor I had answers, and both of us were too exhausted to continue the conversation with any fruitfulness. I was cold, damp, and aching; we'd barely survived an assassination attempt; and someone wanted Aric, me, or both of us dead. I feared for my retinue's safety, but I was all too aware that I could do nothing for them now. Showing up with a bloodied shift and a horse for a husband could only make things worse.

So instead, since there was nothing more productive to be done at the moment, I curled up in the corner of the stall and attempted to get warm. It rapidly proved a futile gesture, despite the blanket. Though the building was marginally warmer than the air outside, the ground and my wet clothes sapped the heat straight from my bones. Intermittent shivers coursed through me, making my muscles cramp. Between my earlier flare, the cold, and the fact that I'd been up all night, I wouldn't be able to function even if I figured out what in the ocean's hundred names I was supposed to do about all this.

-Bianca.-

Aric's voice in my head sent my pulse spiking again. I closed my eyes, too tired for another argument.

-We should share each other's warmth.-

My eyes flew open with surprise. My face heated. Yes, we were married—if the assassin hadn't shown up, we would already be intimately acquainted with each other's bodies. But the idea of sharing his warmth felt strangely . . . personal.

Also, he was a horse.

Aric sighed, with what felt like both irritation and embarrassment. *-You won't be much use if you make yourself sick with the chill. And . . . you're not the only one who's cold.-*

I turned his suggestion over in my mind, weighing my reluctance like a new blade. There was no particular reason to refuse—other than the awkwardness of the situation. If he planned to hurt me, he'd had ample opportunity already. I was shivering, he was a large warm animal, and we couldn't risk a fire, even if we'd had the materials to make one.

I was too practical, and too cold, to be stubborn about it. He'd invited me. I lost nothing by accepting, not even my dignity—it was far too late to salvage that.

"Fine," I said shortly. "If you roll over on me, I will make you regret it profoundly."

Aric huffed out a breath. *-I already regret this profoundly.-*

Still, he lowered to his knees. I scooted over to lean against him. As my shoulder brushed his side, I paused, frowning.

"You're shivering."

-As I mentioned, I'm cold.-

But I'd seen enough of horses to know that this wasn't just the cold at work. Now that I was paying attention, I noticed how the whites of his eyes showed, how every line of his body was rigid. Temperature alone didn't cause that sort of response.

"Aric," I said quietly. "Are you all right?"

His voice was thick with disdain. *-All right? Of course I'm not all right. I'm a horse.-*

I winced. "You're taking it surprisingly well."

-I am not taking it well.- His voice sharpened. *-I'm barely staving*

off panic. I have no idea whether this spell is reversible, since apparently you don't understand its workings. I can't do something as simple as open a door or pick up a blanket. I am covered in mud. Sleeping in the cold is an indignity. And on top of that, I've just learned there's a plot to force us to marry and another plot, or perhaps the same, to have me killed. The only reason I'm holding myself together at all is that if I didn't, we'd both be dead.-

I bit my lip. It was true—without his quick thinking, and quick response, we'd still be in the bedchamber with the assassin. I'd taken his apparent calmness at face value, but now that his facade had cracked, it was all too easy to see what lay beneath. I knew firsthand that one could appear collected while falling to pieces inside.

I leaned into his side, taking advantage of the warmth he'd offered. Aric flinched, his muscles rippling. Then, obviously forcing himself, he relaxed. Marginally.

"I'm sorry about the enchantment," I said, hoping he could hear my sincerity. "I didn't mean for any of this to happen."

Aric released a heavy sigh. *-I'm struggling to accept that as true.-*

Stubborn ass. No, horse. "I'll swear it by any of the Virtues you like."

-That's . . . that's not what I meant.- I could feel him considering. Reluctant to speak his mind. *-It's that . . . if you're telling the truth, then I'm afraid I've misjudged you rather badly.-*

"Yes. Yes, you have. And you've been horribly rude about it, too."

-I concede my manners have been . . . somewhat lacking.-

I eyed him suspiciously. Why was he suddenly agreeing with me? This must be another trap. "If you are attempting to find a reason to continue lacking manners, I refuse to assist in your endeavors."

-Actually, Bianca, I am attempting to suggest a truce.-

I blinked, disoriented. I'd thought we were exchanging the opening blows to another sparring match, and instead . . . he was extending a—a hoof? "A truce?"

-Yes.- I could practically feel Aric rolling his eyes. *-It's a mutually beneficial arrangement in which we agree to stop fighting each other, at least until our lives are out of immediate danger.-*

"I *know* what a truce is," I retorted, in a decidedly belligerent tone. Then I checked myself, reconsidering.

I was still suspicious of Aric—and begrudging. Even if his suggestion wasn't underlined by nefarious motives, after how he'd treated me, I was reluctant to let him move past his rudeness so easily.

But then again, I *had* accidentally turned him into a horse. Perhaps that was retribution enough. For now. A truce, after all, was temporary. And it would be easier to resolve the rest of this disaster and figure out who was behind the assassination attempt if Aric and I weren't sparring the entire time.

"Very well," I said finally. "In that case, I will attempt to agree to your truce whenever you manage to actually offer one. Provided you don't take my acceptance as permission to resume said lack of manners."

Aric snorted. *-I offer you a truce,* wife. *We work together until we've lifted the curse and determined who wants us dead.-*

"I accept your truce, *husband.*" I was still wary, but I was too tired to keep fighting. And despite his boorish behavior, it was becoming clear that he wasn't the enemy I'd taken him for. I folded my arms. "I would suggest we shake on it, but your hooves are filthy."

-That is not *my fault.-*

"Never mind whose fault it is. Are we agreed?"

-Fine. Agreed.-

A beam of morning sun filtered through the clouds, illuminating the floor of the stable; the rain was finally petering out. The air was warming—no, *I* was warming, thanks to Aric's heat. My shivering had subsided, and between his warm bulk and the blanket, I could almost pretend to be comfortable.

I should make a plan. Figure out how to reverse Tatiana's spell, get safely back into the castle, and determine who had sent the assassin and how they had slipped past Julieta and my guards—and whether my retinue was all right. Please, *please* let them be all right.

But the warmth was compelling, and my exhaustion bone-deep. I allowed myself to lean against Aric and close my eyes. Just for a moment.

"Hey. Wake up."

A boot was nudging my leg, quite insistently. I mumbled a protest and pulled the blanket closer. Surely it wasn't time for Julieta to rouse me yet. I'd barely slept at all.

Steel scraped. The sound brought me fully awake in an instant. I sat up in a rush, my eyes flying open.

Noon sun shafted into the stables. Its diffuse beam illuminated a human figure standing over me, drawn sword in hand.

The assassin. They'd found us.

I was moving before my thoughts caught up with my actions. I rolled away from Aric, leaving the blankets behind in a rush of cold. My hand scrabbled through the rotting straw for a fistful of dirt, which I flung at my attacker's eyes.

My opponent stumbled back, cursing roundly in one of the Zhei dialects. My training in foreign tongues hadn't included the common terminology of overseas tavern brawls, but to judge by how vehemently the person was swearing, some of the dirt had gotten into their eyes.

I scuttled out of range, scanning my surroundings for a

weapon. Perhaps a rock. Or if I could get behind the assassin and twist the blanket around their throat—

-Stop.- Aric surged to his feet. One hoof slammed down scant inches from my bare foot. *-Don't fight her. It's Marya.-*

"Marya?" It took me a moment to place the name: the woman Lord Varin had pointed out at the welcome ball. Aric's captain of the guard. His lover.

"That's Captain Dai to you," the woman spat in Gilden, rubbing fiercely at her eyes. Tears streamed down her cheeks. She didn't sheath her saber. "Where's Aric? No one else could have shown you this place."

-Marya.- The horse took a careful step towards her. More carefully than he'd moved around me. *-It's me. I know this is a shock, but—-*

"Answer me," Marya demanded, cutting him off. "Or I swear I'll run you through, duchess or not."

She looked more than capable of following through on her threats. And I didn't have a blade of my own at hand.

"Aric's right here," I said, answering her in Gilden. I kept my voice cool, collected, as if this were an ordinary appointment at court. "Didn't you hear him?"

Her dark eyes narrowed. They were bloodshot from the dust. "Don't try my patience. The only reason I haven't run you through yet is because Aric is the only one who could have led you here. You'd better tell me where he is if you value keeping your guts intact."

I addressed Aric without looking at him, wary of the sword in Marya's hand. "Tell her. *Husband.*"

-Marya,- Aric began again. *-I'm right here. I'm the horse.-*

"There you have it," I told Marya. "From the horse's mouth."

Her saber slid up to point at my throat. "I won't stand for mockery. Not when Aric is missing. *Where is he?*"

-Bianca,- said Aric, *-I don't think she can hear me.-*

I didn't dare look at him, not with a sword only one move away from my jugular. "I was coming to that same conclusion myself."

"What conclusion?" Marya demanded. "Tell me what you've done with Aric, or I'll—"

"—run me through. Yes, I gathered that distinct impression." It hadn't escaped me that she'd used Aric's first name. Not his title. If I'd needed proof of Lord Varin's ballroom insinuations, I had it now.

I examined the woman's face, trying to decide which approach to take. She seemed approximately as flexible, and persuadable, as a granite boulder. Courtly manners would get me nowhere except the business end of her blade. Which, as she'd already informed me, she was zealously eager to use.

"Aric is the horse," I said, opting for bluntness. "He's been trying to tell you so himself, but apparently you can't hear him."

Marya's eyes narrowed to a blade's edge. "You expect me to believe that this horse is the king of Gildenheim."

"Well, he's not officially the king yet. But he *is* my husband, as of last night. When is the coronation again? In a week?"

-Six days,- Aric corrected. *-At the equinox. Keep your facts in order, wife.-*

Marya's blade lowered ever so slightly. She stared at me as if she couldn't decide whether I was addled, dishonest, or both.

"I swear it's the truth," I said. "By—by archives and indices, or whatever it is you swear by around here."

Marya's eyes widened. "That's Aric's phrase." She glanced at the horse and then back at me. "But—if *that* is really Aric, then why is he a *horse*?"

"It was the assassin's fault, really," I said. "They broke in and tried to kill us both. A spell went awry. Here we are."

-You are leaving out a stupendous amount of detail,- Aric reprimanded me.

"Hush. She's pointing a sword at my throat. I'm a bit distracted."

Marya said, incredulous, "And I'm supposed to believe you're talking to him now."

"Believe whatever you like," I countered. "But I certainly wasn't talking to *you*. In fact, I'd rather not. You're quite welcome to leave."

-Don't offend her,- Aric said. *-She's here to help us.-*

"To help *you*, maybe. Not me. Unless her idea of helping me constitutes putting a hole in my throat. Which, for the record, I would not regard as *help*."

Marya finally lowered her blade. Her free hand came up to rub at her brow, as though she were trying to erase a headache. "I'm getting dizzy trying to follow this. Fine—let's say I believe you, and Aric has been turned into this horse." She gestured skeptically at Aric. "Prove it. Have him tell you something nobody else would know. No one except Aric and me."

I sighed. I was not particularly keen on knowing what secrets the man I'd married shared with his lover.

"Well?" I asked Aric.

-Her favorite tale is the story of the Wildwood Crown. Tell her we used to read it together behind the drapes in the library. She'd pinch her nose so she didn't sneeze and get us caught.-

At least it wasn't an anecdote about her preferences in bed.

When I relayed this information to Marya, the tension finally went out of her sword arm. She looked wide-eyed at Aric, as if seeing the massive horse for the first time. It would have been the perfect opportunity to attack, if only I had a blade at hand.

"Well. Rot it to the roots." She rubbed her brow again, then turned on me so sharply that I flinched. "Turn him back, then. Whatever it takes."

"I can't," I said, exasperated. "We've already been over this."

"Tell him—wait, he can understand me?"

"*Yes*," Aric and I said at the same time. Though of course Marya could only hear one of us.

She turned back to Aric. "You're needed at the castle immediately. It's a disaster. Half the court is convinced you've been murdered, the other half that you've been kidnapped. It took me this long just to get away without anyone noticing." She paused, pinching her nose exactly as Aric had described. "By the Lady, I can't believe I'm talking to a horse. This had better not be a joke at my expense."

"Murdered?" I cut in. "They found the assassin, then?"

"Not exactly." Marya grimaced. "From what I've gathered, there was a commotion, and someone alerted the night watch. When they gained entry to Aric's chambers they found a broken window, a knife of Damarian make, and blood staining the bed and floor. Lots of it."

I frowned, trying to parse the events in Aric's bedchamber. "Well, we broke the window getting out, and I suppose the assassin could have dropped the knife. But the blood—that doesn't make sense. I cut my hand, but it was only a few scratches—"

-*It's a setup,*- Aric cut in. -*Someone wants to make it appear that the assassination attempt succeeded.*-

I turned on him. "You're saying that someone wants to make it look like you're dead."

-*Exactly.*-

"Then they must have a reason." I grasped on to the politics of the situation as something I could comprehend. "Claiming the throne, perhaps, or pinning the blame on someone—"

"You," Marya interrupted. She'd apparently managed to follow the conversation's turns, despite being unable to hear Aric.

I turned back to her. "What about me?"

"You did it," she repeated. "That's the general conclusion. Most of the castle thinks that you murdered Aric."

The earth swayed under me. I didn't want to believe Marya, but it made perfect sense. As far as anyone knew, I was the last person to have seen Aric alive. A wedding night was the perfect opportunity for a would-be assassin—or a regicidal wife—to get him alone and unarmed. Especially if the Gilden court believed, as Aric had, that the Council of Nine had demanded our marriage and a number of other concessions besides . . . the evidence began to pile into mountainous proportions. The irony—to my parents, I was a weakling excuse for a daughter, but to the Gilden court I'd become a queen ruthless enough to murder my own husband.

I hadn't killed Aric. He wasn't even dead. But no one knew that—no one aside from Aric, me, and now Marya. And maybe the assassin, if they had seen Aric transform. But I somehow doubted they were going to come forth and say so publicly.

I struggled to focus my thoughts. "So I'm being framed for a murder that didn't happen. Where does everyone think I am?"

"The most popular theory is that you've fled back to Damaria," Marya said. "No one knows for sure. Aside from me, of course. Your retinue has been taken in for questioning."

Catalina. Julieta. My throat tightened at the thought of them thrown into a prison cell, perhaps even tortured for information. Especially after how cold I'd been to Catalina the last time we spoke. "We have to get them out. We'll go back to the castle, explain what happened—tell them that Aric isn't dead, he's just . . . a horse . . ."

I trailed off. I'd had enough difficulty convincing Marya—Aric's own lover—of his identity. If I showed up in a bloodstained dressing gown claiming that I'd turned my husband into a horse, the court would think me insane at best. At worst, I would confirm their suspicions that I had actually murdered their king. I would be an invader trying to claim the Gilden throne after dispatching its rightful heir on my own wedding night.

-*It won't work,*- Aric said, echoing my thoughts. -*They won't believe I'm alive unless you can turn me back into a man. They'll just arrest you, too. Or worse.*-

I set my jaw. "Then we have to turn you back. Immediately."

-*Be my guest,*- Aric said, sardonic. -*Anytime you like.*-

"Isn't there something you can do?" Marya asked. She was toying with the hilt of her saber again, in a manner that made me itch to take it out of her hands. Not that I would be foolish enough to try. "Anything you haven't attempted?"

There were plenty of things I hadn't attempted—as many as stars in the sky. Turning cartwheels, for instance. Beating on pots and pans while chanting hymns to the Virtues. Dressing Aric in human clothing, sticking a crown on his head, and pretending everything was normal until, perhaps, it was. All of those seemed equally as likely to succeed as me continuing to try magic—since, after all, I knew how this curse worked as well as a birdfish knew the waltz.

But I knew someone who did understand it. Someone who had crafted the spell in the first place.

I closed my hand around the locket.

"Marya. I have an idea, but I need your help. I have to get a message to my sister."

13

I hunched my shoulders, keeping my head down, as I followed Marya through the castle halls. I should have been glad to have some distance from Aric—we'd left him in the arboretum's derelict stable half an hour or so before—but my relief was tempered both by Marya's ill-humored presence and the risk of being caught. I'd changed from my bloodstained dressing gown into a shirt, jacket, and trousers Marya had unearthed from another box in the stable, so at least my attire didn't draw attention. But my visage was all too exposed for anyone to see. And the entire court had gotten a long look at my face during the wedding yesterday.

Hard to believe it was only yesterday. The alarms had mercifully ceased along with the rain, and the afternoon bells for three o'clock were chiming now. Less than twenty-four hours since I'd married Aric, but it felt like an eternity.

Marya stopped, so suddenly I almost ran into her, and held out a warning hand. I peered over her shoulder in time to see a duo of castle guards march by, halberds braced across their chests. No doubt searching for me, Gildenheim's evil queen-to-be. I hastily ducked behind Marya, wishing she were taller.

The guards walked past without looking in our direction. I let out a sigh of relief as the echo of their footsteps faded.

"Ludicrous," Marya muttered. "I'm hiding from my own soldiers like some sort of criminal."

She scanned the corridor and waved me on. I scuttled after her, clinging to the shadows as tightly as a spider to her web.

We passed three more patrols on our way to our destination, and I was grateful for Marya, even though the feeling clearly wasn't mutual: without her quick reactions, we would undoubtedly have been caught. I didn't even know my way through the castle's halls. I could all too easily have walked straight into the guards' ready hands.

The ambassadors' suites were on a separate wing, in a part of the castle I hadn't yet seen. The hallways here were decorated to pay homage to other nations, hung with ceremonial banners and artwork in the bold and colorful styles of the Mobolan Alliance, the flowing lines of the Zhei Empire's many member states, and the jewel tones of my own country. My steps slowed as we passed an image depicting the Virtue of Strength—in this version, a woman with her hand resting on her chest and a knowing smile on her face.

My hand drifted to my own chest, where the locket rested above my heart. I sent a quick prayer to the Virtue to bless me with that same quality. I certainly needed it now.

"Keep up," Marya hissed. "Before I change my mind about all this."

I'd expected Marya to lead me directly to Ambassador Dapaz's door. Instead, she abruptly veered into an alcove, ducked behind the Damarian flag hung on the wall, and disappeared.

I followed, and found a hidden passageway behind the banner. Marya pressed herself flat so I could slip past her, then slid a panel shut, concealing the entrance. The narrow aisle was barely wide enough to walk through without my shoulders brushing against the walls. It was clear of dust and cobwebs, indicating frequent use.

Intrigue and anger wrestled for dominance at the revelation that the Gilden castle had spy passages leading to its ambassadors' chambers. Would Aric have ever informed me of their existence if the assassin hadn't forced matters?

Marya made a preemptive shushing gesture and slid past me. Her footsteps were as quiet as a still night. She'd clearly used this spyway before.

Murmurs of conversation drifted from both sides as we moved down the passage, sometimes accompanied by pinpricks of light from spyholes. I caught a few words in one of the Mobolan languages, a snatch of Zhei in the formal register. It wasn't just the Damarian ambassador the court was spying on—it was all the diplomats. Perhaps that should have made me feel better. I wasn't certain it did. Though perhaps my indignation was hypocritical: while I'd never engaged in espionage myself, Damaria's noble Houses were infamous for their private networks of intelligence. Knowledge was power, my mother liked to say, and blackmail was control.

I wondered what she would have made of the assassination attempt. Knowing my parents, they would already be fully confident of who was behind it had they been in my place.

Finally, Marya stopped and pressed her ear to the wall. She listened in absolute stillness for several long moments. Then she peered through one of the peepholes, her eyes narrowed against the brightness of the room beyond. A thin sliver of light illuminated her iris, making it glow like dark amber.

Apparently satisfied, she twisted a small lever in the wall. A panel slid aside, dropping a shaft of light into the spyway. Marya stepped through the opening, and I followed.

I emerged into a sitting room stuffed to the brim with an eclectic array of ornaments, vases, and statuary, much of it infused with the deep blue of Damaria. In the midst of the clutter, Ambassador Evito Dapaz sat at a writing desk overflowing with papers, quill in hand. He rose to greet us, looking rather less surprised than I'd expect him to be at the sight of two women emerging from the wall of his private chambers.

"Your Grace," he greeted me in Damarian, bowing. "Thank the seas you're safe. Are you well?"

My thoughts went straight to my condition, but for once it wasn't my primary complaint. Lacerations from the window glass burned on my shins. A dozen bruises were making themselves known, some in inconvenient places. I curled my hands, remembering the strange golden marks from the shattered lantern.

"I'm well enough," I hedged.

Evito's shoulders relaxed ever so slightly. "Virtues' mercy. I'm afraid I don't have proper refreshments to offer you, but perhaps you'd care for some wine or hothouse oranges?"

Marya glowered at him before I could answer. "You knew about this passageway."

"I'd surmised its existence, yes." If Marya was a brewing storm, Evito was a torpid summer day. "Some of your people are less discreet than others, and I always know exactly where I left my things. Would you like to sit?"

"We can't stay long," I cut in before Marya could offer to impale Evito, too. "Ambassador, I need your help to get a message to my sister."

He raised his brows slightly, inviting me to go on.

"I take it you're aware of what happened this morning?"

Evito's lips thinned. He flicked a look at Marya. "I've heard rumors, but there are guards posted at the door of these chambers. They dissuaded me from investigating the matter in as much depth as I desired."

Marya and I both glanced at the door. I lowered my voice.

"I'll be brief," I said. "There was an assassination attempt in the royal chambers at dawn. I fought the attacker off, but they evaded capture. The heir apparent and I escaped out the window and found a safe place to hide, but he is now . . . in an unfortunate condition."

Evito's eyes focused on my face, as intent as a scholar reading a rare text. "The heir apparent? Is his life in danger?"

I hesitated, considering how much to tell him. Despite Evito's position, and my reliance on his help, I didn't want to explain the full situation. If word of what I'd done got out—even if it became common knowledge only after the spell was reversed, which, Virtues help me, Tatiana could accomplish quickly—it could wreak considerable damage. I knew how rumors spread, whispers of flame that appeared as harmless as candles but turned into an all-consuming blaze. And if the news reached the wrong ears, especially while the assassin was still at large and whoever had sent them could all too easily dispatch another . . .

No. I would not tell the ambassador, or anyone who didn't absolutely need to know, that I had accidentally turned my husband into a horse.

"He's in no more danger than I am," I said. "But we'll both be in hiding for a few days, until the assassin is caught and we learn who they're working for. In the meantime, I need to send a message to my sister. One that won't be intercepted by Gilden intelligence. I believe this is something you can help with, ambassador."

"Of course," Evito said at once. He'd been sending sensitive messages to the Council for years, including the terms of the treaty that brought me here; my request was simple by comparison. He slid another glance towards Marya. "Would you like me to encrypt it?"

Though Marya wasn't who I was worried about, the offer was

tempting—another assurance that my message would not be read by the wrong eyes. But it would mean letting Evito read the message in full, as I didn't know the codes well enough to write an encrypted message myself, and it would take too much time. We'd already dallied long enough.

"That won't be necessary," I said. "I'll use my personal seal. I trust you to take the greatest care of it."

There was a warning in my words. If Evito heard it, it didn't affect his composure. He stepped back, gesturing to his desk. "Everything I have to offer is at your disposal."

I chose a piece of vellum, worn thin from multiple scrapings, and penned a quick note to Tatiana, explaining in brief that her defensive spell had gone awry and I needed her help to reverse it. I would meet her at the border and tell her the rest in person. There was an inn commonly used by messengers ferrying international correspondence only a few miles from the actual boundary; she would know the one.

I paused before signing the note, wondering whether to be more detailed. If I told her I was bringing Aric in horse form, she might be better prepared to help me.

A droplet of ink fell and splattered on the vellum. I set the pen aside and blotted my message. I'd taken long enough already. It was Tatiana's spell. My sister was as clever as she was unconventional; she would figure it out. She had to.

I folded the note over, dripped blue wax over it from the stick Evito had ready, and sealed it with Tatiana's locket. The impression gleamed up at me from the cooling wax: a blooming lily, a simplified version of my House's sigil. Something my sister would recognize.

I handed the letter to Evito. "I'm going to be leaving the castle for a few days for my personal safety. Can I count on you to keep me updated of any developments here?"

The ambassador took the missive, inclining his head. "As always, your Grace, I am at House Liliana's disposal."

"The castle correspondence will be watched," Marya cut in, scowling. "They'll check all the outbound messengers, and they have hawks for the pigeons. How precisely are you intending to send it?"

Evito gave her a withering look. "My dear. I was handling sensitive messages before you could even talk."

Marya glared. Judging by her expression, she would have been glad to skewer the ambassador right then and there. "I'm not the one who will be monitoring outgoing messages, you pomp bucket. My king's life is at stake here. I deserve to know how you're planning to—"

"Damarian secrets and magic are both proprietary," Evito said, his own composure unblemished. "Look to your own jurisdiction, captain."

"I'm sure Ambassador Dapaz can be trusted to handle the correspondence," I said hastily, trying to smooth things over before Marya erupted. "You could even give him messages yourself, Captain Dai."

A look passed between Evito and Marya that told me, without a single word being uttered, that she would rather cut off her own thumbs and hand them to him on a string.

"It will be taken care of," Evito said. "Your Grace, will the heir apparent be accompanying you?"

I hesitated. As ambassador, Evito ought to be my closest ally in the castle. But he was also deeply immersed in the Gilden court, which meant he had his own interests and alliances. I trusted him to send a discreet message, but I wasn't sure how much I trusted him to keep his mouth shut. Relations between Gildenheim and Damaria had been anything but tranquil of late, and a single wrong word could wreak more damage than a cannonball.

"No," I said. "He's staying hidden on the castle grounds."

"We should go," Marya said. "Before someone thinks to search these chambers."

"Already done," Evito said, his lip twisting.

If his room had been searched already, we had a little more leeway than I'd thought. But Marya was right—time was not a luxury we had to spare. "Thank you, ambassador. For everything. I must be on my way."

Marya was already heading back towards the spyway entrance. Evito took my hand and bowed over it.

"Be careful, your Grace." His eyes held a warning. "Don't let your guard down."

Marya made an impatient sound. I withdrew my hand from Evito's.

"I never do," I said, and followed the captain of the guard into the darkness.

14

The bells were chiming five when Marya and I finally left the ambassadorial wing, after several tense moments of lurking around corners while castle guards marched past.

"I'll drop you off in the arboretum while I gather provisions," she said brusquely, peering around the corner of the alcove where we were currently hiding. "You can hide in a shrubbery or something until I come get you."

My stomach churned—a reminder both that I hadn't eaten the entire day, and that my condition could flare again at any time. "I need to stop by my chambers first."

Marya looked at me as if I were the one with hooves. "Have you lost your mind? The royal suites are crawling with guards."

"It's important," I insisted. "There's something there I can't leave without." Not to mention returning to my chambers might give me an opportunity to find out what had happened to my retinue during the attack—and potentially gather more clues about who had sent the assassin.

"Well, you'll have to leave without it anyway. I'd rather lick the bottoms of that pompous ambassador's boots than sashay in there so you can fetch your underthings. Are you trying to get me arrested, too?"

"Then I'll go by myself. And I wouldn't take such a risk for my *underthings*."

Marya snorted. "By yourself, my ass."

I folded my arms. "I won't be able to make the journey without it."

Marya eyed me suspiciously for a long moment. Then she blew out an irritated breath. "Fine. I'll go get it. What is this critical item, anyway?"

"It's a personal matter, and I have to go with you," I insisted, though I didn't relish the thought any more than she did. "It's in a chest with an Adept-forged lock that opens only to my touch." And Julieta's, but Marya didn't need to know that.

The captain of the guard thumbed her saber hilt with an alarmingly speculative expression. "Well, maybe if I took just a portion of you . . ."

Removing body parts was out of the question, but . . . I flexed my hands, recalling the newly formed golden marks. If I'd learned anything since arriving in Gildenheim, it was that magic didn't always work the way I expected.

"A toe, perhaps?" Marya was musing. "Or maybe an ear?"

"Do you have a handkerchief?" I asked her.

Her brows rose. "I didn't expect you to actually agree to this."

"I'm not. Give me a cloth. I have a better idea."

"Precedent suggests otherwise," Marya grumbled, but she handed me a handkerchief. I dropped to one knee and rolled up the leg of my trousers.

The cuts on my hand had healed instantly, leaving those strange scars, but the scratches on my shins from the window glass had clotted over like a wound was supposed to do. I picked off one of the larger scabs, wincing a little as I did so, and pressed Marya's handkerchief to it until it darkened.

Marya's nose wrinkled as I held the bloody cloth in her direction. "I think I would have preferred a toe."

I thrust it at her face. "Do you want to help Aric or not?"

It was the right thing to say. Marya gave me a disgruntled look, but shoved the handkerchief into her pocket.

"Fine," she grumbled. "But if this doesn't work, I absolutely insist on a toe. And I haven't changed my mind about the shrubbery."

No shrubberies were involved after all, but I did spend an undignified hour or so sitting in a broom closet and trying not to sneeze before Marya returned from her mission. To my dismay, she'd managed to grab only three bottles of tonic—barely enough to get me through a single flare, let alone multiple. But it was better than none, and she'd taken a considerable risk to get them, so I didn't voice my disappointment.

We threaded our way through the arboretum, making our way back to the derelict stable loaded with two saddlebags of provisions, a sword, and a saddle—Marya carrying most of it, to my relief. At the edges of the world, the sky was turning the rich, fiery hue of the hothouse oranges Evito had offered. Nearly sunset. Marya had explained that at dusk the guard would change, leaving a narrow window in which we could flee the castle grounds. We had to hurry.

When we reached the stable, Marya dropped the saddle on the cold earth outside the yawning doorway. Her brow shone with sweat, despite the chill. The rain had given way to scattered clouds and a brisk breeze, promising a frigid ride.

"I'll make certain the side gate isn't watched, but you'll have to move quickly. The guards will be on high alert." She glanced into the building, where Aric was a slash of white against the darkness. When she turned back to me, her scowl had returned.

"Aric's a good man." She'd lowered her voice so only I would hear. "Or horse. Whatever he is now. On two legs or four, he's worth more than you take him for."

"I'm not sure what exactly you think I take him for," I said coolly. "Except my husband. Which he is, for better or worse."

Marya's eyes narrowed.

I sighed, reining in my irritation. It wasn't her fault I'd married her lover. She was only someone who cared about Aric and was trying to keep him safe. She probably thought I'd forced him into marrying me, just as Aric had believed until this morning. Her hostility was understandable.

"I swore to protect him, Captain Dai," I said. "I stand by my promises."

Marya studied me suspiciously, then gave a curt nod. "You'd better take care of him. If anything happens to Aric . . ."

"Yes," I said dryly, "you'll run me through. I know."

She eyed me warily, suspecting me of mocking her. I looked back, unflinching.

Then, unexpectedly, Marya flashed a smile, quick and brash as lightning. "Good. Don't forget it." She cast another look towards the stable. "Aric?"

He emerged cautiously, testing each step as if he expected the mud to swallow him whole. As the light caught him, he glowed like a beacon. Of course he had to be a *white* horse.

Marya hesitated, clearly struggling with what to say. She fidgeted with the hilt of her saber.

"You'd better come back safe, you muckhead." Her voice was rougher than usual. "I wish I were going with you."

Aric turned his head towards me. *-Tell her to be careful.*

And . . .- He swished his tail, his hesitation roiling through our mental bond. *-Never mind. Just tell her that.-*

I conveyed the message, selfishly relieved that neither of them had said more. For all that Marya wished she could come with us—and for all that her skills would have been useful—I didn't relish the prospect of translating for my husband and his lover all the way to the Damarian border.

"You know me," Marya said, shrugging.

-Exactly why I'm worried,- Aric muttered. He didn't ask me to relay that to Marya, and I didn't offer.

"I should go," Marya said reluctantly. "I can delay the guards to give you a little more time. Wait a few minutes, and then head to the gate." Abruptly, she barked a laugh. "By the Lady, part of me still thinks you're having me on and this is all some elaborate prank."

Before I could answer, she turned her back with one more look at Aric and was gone into the slant of late afternoon sunlight. I watched her vanish among the trees. Had we met under other circumstances, I suspected I might have liked her quite a bit.

-I see you've acquired a weapon.- Aric was eyeing the rapier at my waist suspiciously.

"And supplies." I gestured at the provisions Marya had obtained. I also had a new dagger strapped inside my sleeve, a little heavier than the one I'd brought from home. But given Aric's earlier pique about my concealed blade, I wasn't about to tell him of its existence, even with our newly established truce.

Aric caught sight of the saddle. He took a step backwards, nostrils flaring. *-I am not subjecting myself to that device.-*

"Well, I can't ride bareback," I retorted. "Not if we want to make any headway." Only the strength of fear had let me cling to him during our flight from the castle, and my muscles were feeling the aftereffects of that effort. If I tried riding bareback to the Damarian border, I would spend more time falling off than actually riding.

-I don't recall agreeing to let you ride me at all. Why is this necessary? Are you not able to walk?-

I folded my arms. No, sometimes I *wasn't* well enough to walk, but I wasn't going to reveal such a vulnerability to Aric. "We need to reach the border quickly. Which means riding. Now. Before we miss our chance and I'm arrested for murdering you."

Not to mention the urgency of clearing my name before I ran out of tonic—or the Council and my parents got wind of the situation and decided to get involved, which would only precipitate the threat of war. Speed was desirable on all fronts.

Aric pawed a hoof at the damp earth, only to recoil as muddy water splattered. I could *feel* his reluctance, like a pin pricking at the back of my mind. It was a strange sensation.

"Besides," I added, "the coronation is supposed to take place in six days. Unless you're willing to delay it . . ."

-Five days now, since this one's almost over. And the coronation cannot be delayed.- He huffed his annoyance. *-Fine. You may ride. But I absolutely refuse to wear a bridle.-*

It took longer than it should have to ready our gear and saddle Aric. I was clumsy from fatigue and nerves, and he kept flinching every time I fumbled. I clenched my teeth, willing myself not to snap at him—he'd been a horse for less than a day, after all; I couldn't expect him to be comfortable with being saddled. Finally, after several false starts, the tack was on, the bags hung. I scrambled onto Aric's back, settled myself in the saddle, and we were off.

It was strange to ride without reins. My hands didn't know what to do with themselves, and it didn't help that I was reluctant to touch Aric any more than strictly necessary. I settled for clutching the pommel with both fists, as if I were a child just learning to ride.

Aric moved at a steady pace, covering ground much faster than I could have on foot—even though he twitched and flinched each time a branch brushed his sides. In a startlingly short time, the castle wall peeked between the arboretum's firs, bathed a bloody red in the waning light.

I gripped the pommel more tightly. My hands were clammy, despite the breeze's pervasive chill. If we were stopped now, recognized now, everything would be lost. My rendezvous with Tatiana. My chance to reverse the spell. My retinue, and my chance of securing their freedom.

My heart constricted. I was leaving Julieta and my guards behind in prison. I knew I didn't have a better choice. Even with Marya's help, I didn't stand a chance of breaking them out. The best way to win their freedom was to return with Aric in human form.

And yet it felt like I was abandoning the people who mattered most to me. The people who relied on me. The people who had given up their own lives to protect mine. Once again, as my parents had anticipated, I was failing.

I tried to shrug away my guilt. I couldn't afford to think of Catalina or Julieta now. I was making the right choice. The only choice. There was only ever one.

They would understand.

Aric paused at the edge of the trees, assessing the route ahead. His tail swished, the end of it brushing against my shins. I flinched like a startled horse myself at the contact. At least now I was wearing trousers—thank the seas for that admittedly thin layer between us.

I leaned forward, peering at the empty courtyard ahead. Earth strewn with fir needles gave way to the bare sod of a training ground. The castle loomed to our left, its defensive ramparts to our right. A narrow stairway led up the outer wall towards the battlements, where two human figures, rendered anonymous by distance, patrolled the fortifications.

Guards. But they were moving away from us, and looking over the castle walls—not inwards, in our direction. All we had to worry about for now was the gate.

I swallowed my fear. "Let's go," I urged Aric in a whisper. "Before anyone else comes."

He scanned the courtyard once more, nostrils flaring wide. Then he moved, so suddenly I grabbed for the pommel. We were out in the open before I had fully recovered my balance, the distance between us and the wall closing fast. Hostile eyes— *imagined, please let them be imagined*—prickled my back. And then we were at the wall. The gate was unguarded, as Marya had promised.

I half slid, half fell from Aric's back. My hands shook, clumsy with haste, as I struggled to slide the bolt free. Rust coated the iron; this gate must be rarely used. The bolt grated, resisting. For one terrifying moment, it stuck.

And then it slid free, with a groan of metal that was surely as loud as an avalanche. I pushed the gate open, Aric surged through, and I followed. We stood in the red light of a day preparing to depart. We had made it out of the castle.

Aric was waiting, his tail flicking in discomfort at a bold fly circling his hindquarters. I shoved the gate closed, managed to get my foot into the stirrup, and heaved myself inelegantly onto his back. Thank the ocean there was no one to see. I settled myself in the saddle, flushed and disheveled from the effort. At least I wasn't wearing nightclothes this time.

I tightened my legs around Aric's sides, instinctively, as if he were an ordinary horse and not the man I'd married.

"Let's ride," I said, and this time, he didn't argue. He broke into a trot, then a canter, and soon we were flying along the road, away from the gloaming city.

Towards Damaria. Towards home. Towards, Virtues guide me, a way to set this right.

15

Aric's hooves struck the earth in musical cadence as we bolted along the road. The way was steep, the thoroughfare twining away from the coast and towards the southern mountains. Trees closed their ranks around us, making it feel like we were already in a different world entirely. Snowy peaks reared above their crowns, sheer and cold and beautiful as they glowed in the roseate light preceding dusk.

The sunset colors cast the scenery as something magical, fleshing the world with color like an artist painting over a sketch. My first impression of Gildenheim had been grey and grim, but I realized now that I had seen only an unfinished portrait. The palette of this land wasn't ugly, merely different. It was a place of contrasts and sharp edges, a land pared down to stark essentials. After a lifetime of wearing a golden mask, I found it as shocking and refreshing as the early springtime air.

The vault overhead was deepest blue now, the western skyline red as flames. I glanced over my shoulder in time to see a final sliver of sun, molten gold and every bit as burning, slip below the horizon.

Suddenly I was falling.

Momentum carried me forwards. Training saved me from serious injury. I hit the ground and rolled, head and limbs tucked in close. Pain burst bright as scattered embers across my shoulder as I struck the packed earth of the road. I somersaulted once and came to a stop just before the ditch.

The breath had been knocked out of me. I lay half stunned while I caught it again, my mind as dazed as my body. The shoulder that had struck the ground was a hot map of future bruises. Nothing felt broken, but the shallow cuts on my legs from the shattered window had opened up again—

The window. The assassin. *Aric.*

I rolled over and pushed myself upright, wincing as grit bit into my palms.

What I saw made no sense. The saddle, now cinched around empty air instead of a horse's ribs, lay overturned with saddlebags askew. A few yards down the road was Aric. No longer a horse—a man, grimacing as he dragged himself to hands and knees. A completely *naked* man.

"What in the Virtues' names—" I started.

At the sound of my voice, Aric flinched and drew in on himself. He turned away, leaving me facing the sharp ridge of his spine.

Of all the things to be concerned about. Virtue of Patience, we were *married*. Still, I grabbed the corner of the quilted saddle pad crumpled in the road. I limped over to Aric and draped it around his shoulders.

He stiffened with surprise. Then his shoulders relaxed infinitesimally. He turned his head to look at me. His eyes were wide, their blue matching the darkening sky.

"Are you hurt?" He spoke in Damarian. His voice was graveled with exhaustion and confusion, harsher than I remembered it, but human. Definitely human. And, thank the seas, he wasn't in my head.

"Bruised, but fine. Are *you*? What happened? Is the curse broken?" Seas have mercy, let it be broken. I hadn't exactly missed the man, but being married to a horse was awkward at best. If Aric was human again, we could return to the castle. Clear my name. Find the assassin, and consequently who had sent them. Our journey would be over before it had properly begun, all of this nothing more than a story to laugh over some future evening when we were thoroughly drunk.

"I'm not sure." Aric's tone was cautious. I wasn't sure which of my questions he was answering. I'd asked too many at once.

I tried again. "Are you all right?"

Aric hesitated. "I'm not injured."

Still not a proper answer, but at least more precise.

Aric held up his hand, rotating it for inspection. I swallowed hard as the saddle pad shifted, revealing a swath of lean and muscled thigh. The saddle pad was generous, but not in relation to a full-grown man; it almost called more attention to what it *didn't* cover.

Aric caught the saddle pad, pulling it back into place, and I hastily shifted my gaze to his face. I'd expected him to be elated by the transformation, but his brow was creased into a frown.

"You don't look particularly pleased about being human again," I noted. "Or convinced."

He lowered his hand and looked at me again. "It seems too easy. A few hours and suddenly gone . . . that's not how magic like this works."

I raised one brow. "No? What would *you* know about magic?" I'd observed his eyes more closely than I cared to admit—I wouldn't have missed it if they contained any golden flecks.

"Quite a lot, actually," Aric said, his tone shifting towards annoyance. "I'm not a greenwitch or an Adept, but I've made a study of the theory of magic. It's highly relevant to the crown of Gildenheim."

I held up my hands, open-palmed. I didn't need to argue with

Aric over this, too—not while he was sitting naked in the middle of the road. I took no pleasure in an unfair advantage. "Fine. Tell me how it works, then."

Aric eyed me suspiciously, as if he expected me to try to curse him again.

"Perhaps we could get out of the road first," he suggested after a moment. "I would rather not explain our situation to any passersby."

He had a point. The naked heir to the Gilden throne, the foreign wife wanted for his murder, and a saddle with no horse—the sight of us would raise a lot of questions.

Without thinking, I held my hand out to Aric to help him up. His eyes narrowed in suspicion. I flushed with both annoyance and embarrassment.

"Virtue of Patience. I'm not trying to kill you. We're *married*."

"That didn't stop you from wearing a dagger to our first dance."

"By the oceans' hundred names, would you let that go? I had good reasons. And we've agreed on a truce now, remember? But if you'd rather I didn't help you up, go ahead and do it on your own."

I started to draw my hand back. Unexpectedly, Aric reached out and clasped it. The lengths of our forearms pressed together. His skin was warm, his muscles more pronounced than I'd expected. He met my eyes, and one brow lifted challengingly. My stomach curled—not the symptoms of my condition this time, but an unexpected heat.

I pulled. Aric pushed off—too hard, perhaps unbalanced by the change back from horse to man. He came to his feet in a rush, faster than either of us anticipated, nearly crashing into me. Both of us froze, eye to eye. We were close enough to kiss—or, as Aric seemed to think, to kill. My heart pounded in my ears. I was suddenly all too aware of how near our bodies were and how little he was wearing. I hadn't noticed his scent before—ink and paper, with a hint of something headier I couldn't name.

Abruptly, his hand dropped away from mine, reminding me that he found me repellent.

It was a welcome reminder, for all its sour taste, jolting me back to my senses. I was standing in the middle of the open road with the man I'd supposedly murdered—the mostly *naked* man—thinking about the way he smelled like an utter fool. I cleared my throat and stepped back.

"We should get into the trees."

"Exactly what I just suggested," Aric said, and stalked past me. I swung back to get the saddle.

Across the ditch, the forested land sloped upwards, dotted with boulders that pushed through the earth like fists. Despite the steep climb, by the time we were out of sight of the road Aric was shivering. I was wearing sturdy shoes and a woolen jacket fit for a Gilden winter—warm clothes were one thing this country apparently got right. But Aric had only the saddle pad, which was meager at best. He stood clutching it around his waist, huddled into himself and looking utterly miserable.

I dug through one of the fallen saddlebags, taking advantage of the fading light before it vanished entirely. My three bottles of tonic were unbroken, cushioned in a spare set of clothes. I breathed a sigh of relief. My condition wasn't flaring now, but it was only a matter of time before the symptoms returned. At home, I might go over a week with only mild symptoms if I was lucky, but with how disastrously events had unfolded since my arrival in Gildenheim I wasn't about to count on luck.

I set the bottles carefully aside and drew out the clothes they'd been padded in. Trousers, a linen undergarment, a green woolen shirt cut long in the Gilden style, a thick pair of socks. No shoes, but there was nothing I could do about that now. I folded the clothes into a bundle and held them out to Aric.

"Here. If you're going to be human, you should probably get dressed."

"I don't think it's going to last." But he took the clothes and turned his back to me. I looked away to give him some privacy, studying the trees. These ones, fortunately, didn't seem inclined to stare back.

"So you implied. You were going to explain why." I wasn't certain he had actually intended to do so, but I deserved answers.

A soft thud of cloth against the earth, followed by the rustle of thinner fabric. He'd dropped the saddle pad. My face heated as, involuntarily, I pictured what was underneath. I'd seen enough in the bedchamber to know his face was not the only part of him that was pleasant to look at, despite its resident expression of disdain.

"In its simplest terms, magic is an exchange," Aric said. His voice was slightly muffled; he was pulling the shirt over his head. "Power for something else—change, light, growth. The stronger the spell, the harder to reverse it. A transformation like this shouldn't just vanish after a few hours. It should take an equal act of power to make it undone."

"But you're human again."

"Yes. For now. You can turn around."

I turned to face him. He was fully dressed; the clothes fit him better than me, although the trousers were a touch short. Green suited him much better than mourning grey, bringing out the flush in his cheeks and the color of his hair, minimizing the dark circles under his eyes.

Stop it, Bianca. He was in mourning. He hated me. He was also a horse. Or had been, until a few minutes ago.

I wrestled my distraction into submission. "You think you'll turn back?"

Aric grimaced. "Or worse."

"What could be worse than transforming into a horse?"

Aric gave me a long look. I managed to hold it, but my face heated. There were a thousand things worse than being turned into a horse. "Right. Well. How long do you think we have?"

"I transformed back at sunset," Aric said. "It's possible the spell has a cyclical link. Horse by day, man by night, or something of that nature."

I glanced at the horizon, deep purple and darkening fast. A few brazen stars were peeking out overhead. "That's not how magic works."

"Maybe not in Damaria," Aric said. "Though I believe that's more a result of how your country has chosen to use it than anything inherent to magic itself."

"What do you mean?"

He ran a hand through his hair. The motion drew my eyes to his face, weary but no less beautiful. "Your Adepts are fond of channeling magic into physical constraints—lamps and clockwork and such. But magic tends to run a bit wilder here in the north. And our spells are most powerful when linked to the world's natural cycles." He was warming to the topic, despite his fatigue, and it was unexpectedly riveting. Passion brought color and life to Aric's face. "The coronation, for instance. That's why it must take place at the spring equinox. Balance of day and night. Balance of power. Otherwise, the magic here grows . . . difficult."

He made an open-palmed gesture, like a set of scales, that showed a scattering of gilt marks on his fingertips.

"Wait," I said, my thoughts reeling. "The coronation is a *spell*?" So his insistence that we had to return by the equinox wasn't a matter of bureaucracy, but of magic?

"Of course. Just like the marriage ceremony. Isn't yours?"

"Perhaps it used to be." I turned over the thought, considering the implications. Did the Council of Nine know about this? Did the Adept Guild? "But we haven't had monarchs since the noble Houses united and formed the Council. Ergo, no coronations." Now the Council's transfers of power were by appointment, largely lacking ceremony. If magic had any role in my country's inheritance, this was the first I'd heard of it.

My mind caught on something else he'd said. "Wait. What do you mean by magic growing *difficult*?"

"The woods walking. New creatures forming. Spells going unpredictably awry," Aric said. "It hasn't happened in centuries, so I'm not entirely certain what's exaggeration and what is myth. But the Wildwood Crown—the crown of Gildenheim—is more than just a fable; it's a precaution. The coronation ensures the realm's stability."

Wonderful. So not only did we risk our countries dissolving into war—perhaps civil war, on Gildenheim's part; I wasn't even certain who stood to inherit in the case of Aric's death—if we didn't return by the equinox, but we would also be dealing with a magical catastrophe if we failed to resolve this in time. Walking forests—Virtues, even more of the legends about Gildenheim had a grain of truth to them than I'd realized.

I drew my thoughts back to the relevant point. "In that case, we should return to the castle while you're still recognizably a man. We can't miss the coronation if we don't leave Arnhelm." And I would have an opportunity to obtain more of my tonic before it became critical.

Aric shifted his weight uncomfortably. The ground was frigid; I realized with a surge of guilt that it must be burning his feet, even through the socks. "Much as I would like to get out of the mud and cold, I don't think that's the best idea."

"Why not? We should take the chance to assure the castle you're alive and clear my name while we can. I don't need the entire court of Gildenheim believing I murdered my husband."

"Actually," Aric said, "that belief could work to our advantage."

I stared at him, not trying to hide my incredulity. "Have you lost your mind?"

"Someone sent that assassin. If it wasn't either of us—"

"Well, it certainly wasn't *me*—"

"—then someone else must be responsible. And what happens next will reveal who it is."

I closed my mouth on my half-formed protests. As much as I wished to be exonerated, this . . . actually wasn't a bad idea. Someone wanted Aric dead badly enough to try to kill him once; if he returned, there was nothing preventing that person from trying again—and perhaps taking me out along with him. Allowing our enemies to reveal themselves helped us both.

"If we wait, Marya can find proof of who's behind this," Aric continued. "I trust her to get to the root of it. If we stay clear, she's free to work without the assassin having another opportunity to strike."

I didn't know the captain of the guard well enough to share his confidence, but I had no desire to step in front of an assassin's blade again. And I wasn't without my own resources. "Ambassador Dapaz could keep us updated of her findings."

Aric nodded, a curt gesture. "Exactly."

"Who do *you* think sent the assassin?" I asked. Aric must know his own court far better than me; we had struck a truce, so I might as well take advantage of his insight.

His gaze darkened. "I don't know. Damaria would have been my first guess."

I had to admit—at least to myself—that in other circumstances, it would have been a fair assumption. Tensions between our countries were long-standing, and with Aric dead . . . "Would the crown have gone to me, if they had succeeded?"

Aric nodded, taut.

"And if I were also killed?"

A shadow passed behind his eyes. "It would be contested," he said shortly. "There are at least half a dozen relatives who all believe they have a claim. But there's an old law that in the absence of a legitimate successor, the crown may pass to a bastard with the approval of the court."

Lord Varin. I remembered the rage that had passed across his face when I danced with him—it had been brief, but I was certain I hadn't imagined it. Was his resentment deep enough to want Aric dead? "Would your half brother have the approval he needs?"

Aric hugged his arms around himself, a gesture that didn't seem to be entirely due to the cold.

"It's likely." His voice stung like nettles. "Varin has generally been considered the better of the two of us in all but blood."

If only their positions were reversed. Had the courtiers been whispering not about me, but Aric and Varin?

"We need to go back, then." I looked in the direction of the castle, although of course the distance and the darkness rendered Arnhelm long invisible. "We can confront him while you're still a man, force him to confess that—"

"No," Aric said, more forcefully than I'd heard him speak yet. I turned back to him, my brows raising. He hugged himself tighter, shook his head firmly. "No. I—I don't believe Varin's behind this. We've never been close, but I don't believe he would try to have me killed. Besides, he wouldn't dare anything that would risk his reputation. He would need the court's support to have a chance of inheriting. Anyone who thought they had a strong claim to the throne might be responsible—Countess Signa, for example."

The blond-haired noblewoman who'd greeted us after the wedding had been calculating, but that didn't mean she was plotting murder. The Council's spies had reported discussions among Aric's more distant relatives about seizing the throne, but no actual plans that I knew of. "Varin has the most to gain from your death."

"Less than Damaria," Aric countered. "And only if the court determines he has the strongest claim."

"Damaria gains nothing if I'm blamed for your murder." Anger heated my core—how many times would I have to convince him I'd had nothing to do with the attack?

"Without proof, we're merely throwing accusations at each other," Aric pointed out, interrupting my swirling doubt. "This gets us nowhere."

I sighed, unsettled, and reluctantly checked my irritation. As loath as I was to admit it, he was right. Varin, any other nobles whose veins carried royal blood, perhaps even one of Gildenheim's other neighbors who would benefit from seeing the country thrown into disarray . . . There were too many possibilities to deduce the perpetrator from our private suspicions without more evidence. I wanted the answers to be simple, but that was exhaustion speaking, not logic.

"Fine," I conceded. "We'll wait to hear from Marya and Ambassador Dapaz. But what do you expect us to do in the meantime? We can't skulk about in the woods waiting for messages."

"I think we should continue to Damaria and meet your sister."

My brows lifted. He'd argued against this plan before I visited Evito for so long I'd thought I would never get him out the castle gates. "Even though you're no longer a horse?"

"I gave this some thought while you were off with Marya," Aric said. "The court is already in chaos. It won't make much difference if I allow them to believe I'm dead for a few more days. If we want answers, I can't show up in person or whoever sent the assassin will only go back into hiding and wait for their next chance. It's two days' ride to the border on the main road. The coronation is at dawn on the fifth day from now. We have time to get there and back again." He shrugged. "And besides . . . if this isn't going to last . . . it makes sense to be closer to the person who has the best chance of reversing the spell for good."

I sifted through his points and couldn't find a good reason to refute them. The timing was tight, but we could hire a carriage and drive through the night if we must. Besides, a treacherous part of me *wanted* to continue to Damaria, despite the journey's dangers. I missed Tatiana—I yearned to talk to someone I could trust absolutely, even if she would tease me mercilessly about turning my husband into a horse. And Damaria was still my home.

It was dangerous, but this could work to both our advantages. Provided we survived the journey.

"To Damaria," I agreed. "But if we're going to the border, we should start by finding you some shoes."

16

"I can't believe I'm stealing from my own citizens," Aric muttered. He was bent over his newly acquired pair of boots, tightening the laces.

"You can pay for them once we return to court," I said firmly. "Which we can't do without taking the shoes in the first place."

Aric stared at the boots, his expression clouded. Despite my confident tone, I shared his guilt. Commoners were already struggling. Taking their meager possessions might be his right as king, but it still rested uneasily against my conscience.

Under other circumstances, I would have simply bought the shoes—we had money, after all; Marya's packing had included a purse of Gilden regals. But if Gildenheim was anything like my own country, gossip spread faster than pollen on the wind, and we were only a few miles from the castle. Aric's face was known, and my description would have spread by now, too. If we showed up in the dead of night bartering for a man's shoes with royal coin, the court would know about our escape within the hour. Theft was the only viable option.

And, I admitted, I'd done pretty well at that. The shoes I'd snatched from the first homestead we passed were a yeoman's work boots, not the suede Aric was probably used to, but the fit was better than expected. And they would hold up for the journey.

I was more worried about how Aric and I would fare. My condition was quiescent for now, and I was fit enough from regular rides and weapons practice at home. But the mountains of Gildenheim were considerably colder than even the deepest winter night in Damaria, and the chill was setting in hard now that the sun had set. I was strong enough on the training grounds, but the toll travel extorted was a different sort, especially if we were trekking to the border on foot. And it occurred to me how little I knew about the man I'd married. Could he wield a sword? Shoot a bow? Under pressure, would he fight, bend, or break?

I snuck another sidelong look at Aric. He'd finished tying the laces of the first shoe and was doing up the second. The skies had cleared; now the half-moon's light turned his hair to silver as it cascaded over his head and shoulders, gentled the sharp lines of his jaw. I had the improbable impulse to lay my hand there.

"You're staring." Aric was watching me, his brows drawn together in the slightest frown.

I clasped my hands firmly behind my back, even though I hadn't actually reached towards him. As if I would be so foolish.

"I'm not."

Aric raised one brow. It was a feeble attempt at falsehood, and we both knew it.

I flushed. "I wasn't staring. I was . . . assessing."

"Assessing what? How best to attack me next?"

This man was impossible. "For the last time, that wasn't my assassin."

"I was referring to the horse fiasco, actually." A pause. He looked down at his newly acquired boots. "And I know it wasn't your assassin. I've actually been meaning to thank you."

Now I *was* staring. "Who are you, and what have you done with the surly man I married?"

Aric's flush was visible even in the moonlight. He rose to his feet, and his gaze caught mine. Something stirred behind his eyes.

Perhaps it was anger. This disaster wasn't entirely my fault, but I hadn't exactly made things better.

"I am trying to be better than him," he said, his words clipped. "I know we didn't get off to the best start—"

I snorted, as if I were the one who was periodically equine.

"—but I also realize you were not to blame for my personal misunderstandings. So. Thank you."

I stared at him, startled beyond words by his blunt honesty. I'd been raised to believe that no concession, no expression of gratitude, came without a debt to be collected later. There was something about the way Aric spoke that eschewed guile, but could he truly be offering me his thanks without the expectation of something in return?

After a moment, I said carefully, "What precisely are you thanking me for?"

"For trying to save me. When the assassin attacked, you threw yourself in front of me. You could have been killed."

It was the right thing to do; I hadn't even questioned it. I hadn't had time to think. My mind flew back to the flash of steel. The lantern exploding in my hands. Aric, stepping between me and the assassin as they struck again—the moment before I'd opened the locket.

He'd been terrified. He clearly was hopeless in combat. And yet he'd tried to save me, too.

"You did the same," I said, surprised by the realization.

Aric flushed. "I promised to protect you."

I'd made the same promise. "So your marriage vows *do* mean something to you?"

"Of course they do. If they didn't, I wouldn't have sealed them with magic."

Once again, he'd left me without a ready response. I didn't know what to make of this man. He'd thought I was forcing him into marriage, and so he'd been intolerably rude—that, I could understand. Yet while believing the worst of me, he'd also . . . sworn to protect and care for me? And, more confusingly, meant it?

I'd been silent too long. Aric was watching me, his expression rendered unreadable by shadows. Now he was the one staring—or assessing. I looked away from him, not ready to consider what judgments he was making behind those stormy eyes.

"We should keep moving," I said.

Aric studied me a moment longer. I could feel his gaze like a physical touch, both arousing and unsettling. I couldn't shake the sense that I had somehow given him the wrong response. If I'd answered him some other way, would he have stepped closer? Followed the trail his eyes took over my face with his hand, cupping my chin to tilt my face towards—

I shook myself, face heating. Virtues, fatigue must be addling my wits. Aric had already made it abundantly clear that he harbored no such thoughts about me.

I shouldered the saddlebags, grateful that the nighttime hid my flush. "The border isn't getting any closer."

Without meeting his eyes, I moved past Aric, heading for the moon-gilded road.

Despite my best intentions, we hadn't made much distance down the road before our pace flagged to a crawl. The saddlebags were impossibly heavy, and the way they thumped against my thighs with every step soon bordered on painful. Aric, struggling with the saddle, wasn't faring much better. With his longer legs, I'd expected him to outpace me, but instead he kept pausing to adjust its weight.

"Bianca," he said finally. "We should stop."

I turned to face him. The moon had slipped towards the horizon, taking with it much of the light. The stars wheeled overhead against a cold and crystalline sky.

"We're both exhausted," Aric said. "And if I'm right about the spell, we'll make much better speed in the morning anyway. We should save our strength."

I glanced back along the road, although of course Arnhelm was too distant and the night too dark to see the castle. It would be humiliating to be caught such a short ways into our journey, but I had neither the will nor the strength to argue. Every part of my body ached. I wouldn't have suggested stopping myself, not wanting Aric to find any weakness in me, but I was so tired I could have slept in the middle of the road.

"All right."

Evergreen forest embraced the roadsides, providing convenient cover. We crossed the ditch with its muddy trickle of water and were soon out of sight of the path. So far we'd encountered no other travelers, but it was better to take precautions.

My stomach was curling with hunger, but I was too tired to eat. Aric pulled blankets out of the saddlebags and handed one to me. Despite the cold and the hard ground, I was asleep the moment my head touched the earth.

I woke to the blue light of early dawn and a hand on my shoulder. Aric's. His breath brushed my ear.

"Don't move."

I was fully awake in an instant. My hand crept towards my dagger.

"You'll scare them," Aric whispered.

I stopped, confused. Scare . . . who? Or what?

There was just enough brightness to see Aric's face, cast in grey scale. Keeping one hand on my shoulder, he pressed a finger to his lips and pointed.

At first I didn't know what I was seeing. Near the saddlebags, something was glowing—a pale, glaucous tint like the luminescent tides that sometimes lapped Damaria's shores. I blinked, and the glow came into focus as a serpentine shape about the length of my forearm. It looked rather like a salamander, four-limbed and sinuous, but I'd never seen a salamander glowing like an Adept lantern.

A slight snuffling sound, and another shape appeared—popping right out of one of the saddlebags.

I stifled a startled gasp—not fast enough. Both glowing figures froze. I had a moment to glimpse tiny claws and triangular faces with curious eyes. Then two sets of wings unfurled. A flash of light zipping upwards towards the trees, and they were gone.

Aric let out a breath. I realized his hand was still on my shoulder just as he removed it, leaving the imprint of his warmth behind.

"What *were* they?" I whispered.

"Glow wyrms." Aric, astonishingly, was smiling. I hadn't realized he was capable of the expression. "A rare sight these days—they've been decimated by the logging trade."

The trade that floated Damaria's ships. The trade that the treaty we'd signed would exponentially expand. No, Aric definitely hadn't authored those documents.

Which left the question of who had. Countess Signa or another of Aric's distant relations, hoping to gain a trade advantage along with the throne? Someone within the Council of Nine? But that made no sense—for all my shortcomings, my parents wouldn't rig this marriage agreement only to have me framed for my husband's murder.

"I've never heard of glow wyrms," I said, putting those questions aside to consider later.

"I believe in Damarian the word is *firedrake*."

That word I did recognize, but I shook my head. "That can't be right. Firedrakes were . . ."

I paused, uncertain. I'd been going to say *monsters*. But the word didn't fit what I'd just seen.

"They were large," I settled on instead. "Dangerous. A threat to civilization."

Aric gave me a wry look. His smile had dimmed, like a cloud drawn over the sun. I wanted, foolishly, to bring it back.

"My apologies," he said dryly. "I forgot you were an expert on Gilden magic."

The sky had lightened while we talked; sunrise must be imminent, which meant we were about to test Aric's theory. I stood up, biting back a hiss as my sore muscles screamed in protest. I'd never realized how uncomfortable it was to sleep on the ground. All the heroes did it in the epic tales I'd loved as a child, so it had always sounded romantic to bed down on the earth. In practice, though, I'd woken up with my bruises multiplied by rocks and roots, my neck so stiff I could barely turn my head. If I hadn't been so exhausted, I doubted I would have slept at all.

I hobbled towards the saddlebags. The glow wyrms, or firedrakes, or whatever they were, had made a mess of them. Perhaps they *were* a threat to civilization. I began unpacking the bags to assess the damage.

"Well, if they weren't a threat to civilization," I asked Aric over my shoulder, "then why were they hunted?"

"Perhaps labeling them as such was an excuse. Damaria once boasted extensive forestland, did it not?"

I saw his point, and it did not reflect well on my country. But Damaria needed lumber. Our soil was poor—we hadn't truly prospered until we began to sail. "Would you have the people go hungry instead?"

Speaking of going hungry, the glow wyrms seemed to have

homed straight in on our already scant food supply. I pulled out a loaf of bread hard enough to pass for cast iron, followed by a packet of dried apples. The little beasts had taken a bite out of each. Thank the seas they hadn't decided to sample my tonic, too.

"I would have a balance, if possible," Aric said. "Would you have the glow wyrms vanish altogether for the sake of expanding your fleet?"

I hesitated. Yesterday, I might have said yes. But today, having seen them, I couldn't. Even if the little terrors *had* eaten some of our food.

"I think there's room for compromise," I said carefully.

"At last. Something on which we agree."

I dared another look at him. Aric had tilted his head back to rest against the trunk of the tree, exposing the arch of his throat and the hollow between his collarbones. Our gazes met, and something fluttered in my stomach. My condition must be flaring again.

Aric cleared his throat. "It's almost sunrise."

I closed my hand around the locket and glanced at the eastern horizon. Swathes of clouds blanketed the sky, dyed rose and gold by the waxing light. I hoped the clouds didn't foretell more rain.

"Right. Almost time for me to ride you." Blast it, I was probably turning the same hue as the dawn itself. "I mean . . . that is, I . . . What are you *doing*?"

While I was busy putting my foot in my mouth, Aric had stood up and stripped off his shirt. Color warmed his cheeks as he caught my gaze. At least I wasn't the only one flushing now.

"I'm not sure what happens to my clothing if I transform," he said. "I thought it prudent not to waste a perfectly good set of trousers."

How could my face feel this hot on a morning cold enough to see my breath? "Right. Of course. Please continue being prudent."

Aric gave me a pointed look. It took me entirely too long to grasp its meaning. When I did, I hastily turned around and, determined not to listen to the rustle of clothing being removed, took advantage of his distraction to compose my expression and regain control of my breathing. I put a hand to my stomach, willing the flutter to settle.

Focus, Bianca. Exhaustion and irritation had worn down my usual careful facade. I'd let my mask slip—showing Aric too much of myself. There was something about him that found all the chinks in my armor—worse, made me wonder what it would be like to set it aside.

But that would be the worst sort of mistake. Just because we had a truce didn't mean I could trust him. Not with my self, and certainly not with my weaknesses.

All things considered, it was probably better if he *did* turn back into a horse. He would still be able to talk to me, confound him— but if I was on his back, I couldn't be distracted by the storm of his eyes, or thoughts of how it might feel to have my legs around him as a man—

Virtues help me. This place, this *situation* was making me lose my mind. How long could sunrise possibly take to arrive?

I stared resolutely into the trees and absolutely did *not* think of Aric getting naked behind me until the sun had lifted safely above the horizon.

17

Aric was right about sunrise. I was facing away from him, so I didn't witness the precise moment of his transformation. But a flash of light, a sound like wind rushing through the trees, and when I turned around a tall white stallion had taken his place.

Part of me was relieved, even though Aric—twitching and snorting at insects, muttering irritably about the mud and his lack of hands again—clearly didn't share the sentiment. At least this way I could ride. Every part of my body ached from my earlier fall and sleeping on the cold ground. I was sorely tempted to drink one of my bottles of tonic, but I knew it would do me no good—Julieta's mixture eased the symptoms of my condition, but not of a bruised body.

Or a bruised heart. As the morning unfurled, my mood darkened along with the clouds subsuming the sky. I'd had no word from Evito yet—which was to be expected, since I'd left the castle not even a full day ago—but I couldn't banish the fear threading through my veins when it stemmed from so many sources. I had only three bottles of tonic to get me to the border and back, and my condition could flare at any time. Aric's words about the coronation and its link to Gildenheim's magic unsettled me to the core. By now the Council—and, worse, my parents—could have learned what a mess I'd made of my marriage and be making countermoves, which couldn't possibly improve political tensions; if Evito had the means to contact me securely, there was nothing preventing him from informing my family as well. And that was assuming the Council had nothing to do with the assassination attempt in the first place, as Aric seemed to believe.

And then there was my retinue. Julieta, and Catalina, and the other five guards who'd risked their lives to protect me—were they safe? Or were they being subjected to torture for answers they couldn't possibly know?

-What's on your mind?- Aric's voice sounded in my head, making me startle. *-I can practically* feel *you thinking.-*

I stiffened. I hadn't considered the potential implications of our mental bond. If he could sense my thoughts in turn, I had to be careful. I couldn't let him know about my condition—or, just as mortifying, the way my thoughts kept straying to the color of his eyes, or picturing a thousand more pleasant ways our wedding night could have unfolded, or how badly I'd wanted to turn around when he was undressing at dawn.

"I was just wondering how you take your breakfast," I said quickly. "Since you asked about it so kindly before our wedding."

I didn't need to see his face to sense his skepticism. *-How I take my breakfast? I didn't realize there was much mystery to how a horse eats. Or were you wondering about some function of the spell?-*

Now I sounded like a fool, but I'd successfully rerouted the conversation. "I meant as a man, of course. How do you take your meals? Alone? At the table? In bed? I suppose now that we're married, it could be one of the things we do in bed together. If that's what you like. Eating, that is. I mean—eating breakfast. Not . . . other parts." My face went hot. "Other things, I mean. *Things,* not parts. Things such as . . . draperies?"

Virtue of Silence, what was wrong with me? I was a trained courtier. I shouldn't be gabbling nonsense like an ingenue. What was it about Aric that scattered my composure to the winds?

"Forget I asked," I said, glad that at least I didn't have to look him in the eye. "I just thought we might get to know one another. Since we did just get married."

Aric walked on for a few moments in silence. I could feel him thinking, the quiet churn of his thoughts keeping pace with the fall of his hooves on the road and the occasional irritated swish of his tail.

-If we're to get to know one another, asking how I take my break-fast is a peculiar place to start.- His tone was wary, but not outright hostile. Was he self-conscious? I couldn't read his emotions as readily as his words, but they were present, like currents beneath the surface of deep water. It felt like there was a silent question behind the words. Perhaps even an invitation.

I accepted it. Worrying about my retinue was doing neither me nor my attendants any good.

"Where would you rather start, then?"

-We could talk about things we like to do. What's important to each of us. I believe that's often a place where lovers start courting.-

"We're not lovers. And I think we're a little past courting." We'd been about to get in bed, for ocean's sake. If the assassin hadn't interrupted, I would already know if he felt like the marble statue he resembled, or whether he was capable of being more . . . expressive.

-That doesn't mean it should be omitted entirely,- Aric said. He *was* self-conscious. I wasn't imagining the embarrassment suffusing his words. *-I realize our marriage was founded on a misunderstanding—-*

"Really." I let irony seep through my voice.

-But that doesn't change the fact that we are married. Unless this is your way of telling me you'd rather not be.-

"No, I—that's not what I meant." Truthfully, it hadn't occurred to me that divorce was an option, though it was common enough outside the noble Houses. I hadn't had time to process the implications of learning that neither of us had actually demanded the match. Perhaps this was Aric's way of suggesting we separate.

But even if we did divorce, we would still be neighbors—and, hopefully, allies. Whichever way our relationship went next, I could use what I learned now to Damaria's advantage.

I thought of my fencing lessons with Nita. *Learn your opponent's weaknesses before you engage them,* she always said. I was already far past engagement with Aric. But I could still apply my instructor's principles.

"Very well," I said. "Let's play at courting. We'll take turns posing a question that we both answer. You start, since you took issue with my inquiry about your breakfast habits."

-Your favorite place to spend time,- Aric prompted.

I didn't even need to consider. "The weapons training ground."

Wry amusement flickered through his thoughts. *-Consistent with your choice of dance accessories. What do you like about it?-*

The familiar scents of oil and leather. The weight of a rapier in my hand. The way my muscles burned with hard-earned heat and my focus narrowed to a single point during my daily practice. The satisfaction of scoring a hit against an opponent.

"It's where I feel most myself," I replied. "I don't have to think about politics, or my parents' expectations, or the weight of my duties. Nothing matters except the sword in my hand. Everything is so . . . clear."

Aric was giving me his complete attention—I could feel it, focused on me like a singular beam of sunlight breaking through dark clouds. My cheeks warmed. I was playing him for weaknesses, and I'd already given too many of my own away.

"Your turn," I said briskly. "Tell me your favorite place."

-*The castle library,*- said Aric. Hesitation had crept into his voice again, as if he expected me to judge him harshly.

I waited, tacitly inviting him to go on.

-*It's peaceful there. Quiet. I can lose myself in the pages for hours and not have to worry about fending off irate courtiers who don't like a new policy, or giving an unsatisfactory answer when someone asks me a question. All the answers I need are already in the books, there for the finding.*- He'd softened, like dawn breaking over the sky. Talking of things you loved could do that to a person. -*My tutors often complained that I refused to take my nose out of a book long enough to learn dancing or swordplay. Not that I would ever have excelled at those anyway, not by comparison to . . . well. The library was always more rewarding.*-

"It sounds lovely."

-*It is. I spent most of my hours there, before . . .* - His words faltered.

I could guess what came next. "Before the queen died."

-*Yes. Before fulfilling the duties she left behind consumed my days.*- He'd grown distant again in a heartbeat, retreating to a place I wasn't welcome. I cursed myself for broaching the topic.

"I'm sorry for your loss." The words felt inadequate. He'd probably heard them a thousand times in the last month.

-*Thank you,*- Aric said woodenly.

Every trace of the warmth I'd briefly sensed had vanished. He was the same cold man I'd met in the ballroom, hard and unapproachable. It was hard to believe he'd ever been anything different. Perhaps I'd been wrong about a softer version of the man I'd married. Perhaps it didn't exist.

We rode on in silence for the better part of an hour before I realized our game had stopped. I'd never had the chance to ask my own question.

My condition decided to make itself known midway through the afternoon, an hour or two after we'd paused to eat. Pain flared in my abdomen like a hearth under the bellows, arriving in hot, sharp waves. Along with it came nausea, spiking worse with each pulse of my heart.

As strange as it was to ride without reins, at the moment I was grateful for the lack; otherwise I might have dropped them involuntarily. I pressed my arms to my stomach, regretting every bite of the brick-like loaf I'd forced past my hunger for lunch as it threatened to return the other way. I closed my eyes, my jaw clamped tight.

Send me to the depths. Of all the times for this to happen. I couldn't even take my tonic without Aric noticing and connecting it to my symptoms.

-*Bianca?*- Aric had noticed my distress. He stopped walking, and I could feel his attention focusing on me. -*What's wrong?*-

I gritted my teeth. "I'm fine." I couldn't afford to let Aric see me suffer. Virtues guide me, I'd hoped I could hide my condition at least until we returned to the castle and I could manage it better. The shame was almost as debilitating as the pain.

Another wave of nausea came crashing down. Blackness lapped at the edges of my vision, an encroaching tide. I bit down viciously on a whimper, refusing to let it past my teeth.

-*You're absolutely not fine. You feel like you're about to fall off my back.*-

I'd forgotten he could sense me—physically as well as mentally; my legs had shifted around his sides as I crimped up in pain.

I tried to ease my posture, but another wave of nausea ripped at my abdomen.

"It's nothing," I forced out.

The lie was as flimsy as a cobweb. Aric didn't even bother to acknowledge it. *-Are you injured? Poisoned?-*

I closed my eyes again as dizziness swelled. Ocean take me, I was so drowning *weak*. This wasn't even the worst flare I'd experienced.

"I just get like this sometimes. It will pass."

A moment of consideration. *-Your courses?-*

I flushed. Menstruating was a reasonable assumption; there were plenty of people who needed an apothecary for their pains. But in Damaria, it was typically ignored—not shameful, but an inconvenience no one particularly liked to talk about. Aric's directness startled me.

I shook my head before remembering he couldn't see me. Or could he? I had no real sense of what a horse's vision was like. "Not that. Something . . . something else. It's happened before. Truly, it's nothing."

-You can barely even ride. It's clearly not nothing. Is there anything that helps?- Concern softened Aric's words. If I hadn't known better, I would have thought he cared. But of course he didn't. I was just inconveniencing us both.

Another wash of pain. This time, I let it sweep aside my protests. I'd already revealed my weakness; I might as well just take the tonic. It would help us get moving faster, and perhaps save me from even deeper disgrace. Aric wouldn't think any better of me if I fell off his back thanks to my own stubbornness.

I opened my eyes. "I have a tonic I take for it. There are a few doses in the saddlebags."

Aric held perfectly still as I slid from the saddle. My knees nearly folded when my feet hit the ground, and I gripped the pommel, swaying. By all the Virtues, I was just as weak and useless as my parents had always said.

I focused on my breath and pretended I was folding the pain away like a handkerchief. Tucking it into smaller and smaller squares and sliding it out of sight.

My hands trembled as I uncorked a bottle of tonic and drank it down to the last bitter drop. My body begged for another, but I couldn't afford to run out now. Seas, I yearned to lie down. To curl into a ball in my own bed. I wished I could turn myself to ice, make it all go numb. I wished Tatiana were here to distract me from the pain with an irreverent joke. I wished for Julieta— the only person other than my sister who never castigated me for my physical failures. But I had failed her in other ways, or else I wouldn't be here now.

Aric was waiting—undoubtedly judging my weakness. Wondering when I would get back in the saddle so we could return to more important things. I took the deepest breath I could manage.

"I'm afraid I might need your assistance to mount."

He didn't move. -*We're not going anywhere until you're fit to ride.*-

That stubborn— Another wave of nausea washed through me, cutting off the thought. I braced myself until it passed, then opened my eyes. My knuckles were white where I clutched the saddle, as if the bones showed through.

"Aric," I gritted out, my jaw tight. "I have danced like this. I have fenced like this. I promise you I can ride like this. The tonic will take effect soon, and in the meanwhile we are wasting time we can't afford to lose. Now would you kindly allow me to use my own judgment, or must I grovel at your feet for the honor of mounting you?"

Aric hesitated. I felt his disapproval, his concern, prick at the edges of my consciousness like a rapier. Then he lowered himself to his knees so I could mount.

We continued down the road in silence. Aric's reticence felt as heavy as the clouds looming overhead. I knew he must be judging me. Realizing exactly what manner of woman he had married, weighing possible courses of action. I couldn't bring myself to attempt to pry into his thoughts—I'd heard enough of their ilk from my parents to last me a dozen lifetimes. Instead I kept my eyes on the way ahead and focused on breathing as the waves of pain gradually ebbed, the tonic taking effect.

-*I was thinking,*- Aric said finally, wariness giving his mellow voice an edge. -*This . . . ailment of yours.*-

"I call it my condition." I restrained myself from saying more. He'd already seen too much of a weakness whose existence he was never supposed to suspect.

-*Your condition.*- Aric paused. -*I wish you'd told me.*-

My heart dropped several notches. This was when he would say it. He hadn't known before the marriage. Now that he did, the match was off.

I looked determinedly at the road ahead, over Aric's pointed ears. I was grateful he couldn't see my face—he wouldn't witness how much it hurt to watch my parents' predictions come true. "You're right. I shouldn't have hidden it from you. Now that you know, I'm willing to dissolve the match. But I want to sign a new treaty first. To formalize the peace before we divorce."

Aric's pace faltered, jolting me. -*Before we divorce?*-

Surely he'd heard me the first time. I forced myself to continue. "Yes. Since we've realized that neither you nor the Council is actually threatening war on the other, there's no reason for us to be bound by this arrangement once we've returned to Arnhelm. Especially since you clearly don't want to . . . ah . . . engage in marital duties with me." I felt a renewed flush of shame as I recalled his repulsion in the bedchamber and lifted my chin to hide it. I could hurt later, when I was safely alone. "And now that you know about my condition . . ."

Aric stopped walking. He swung his head to look at me, his expression as unreadable as a stone wall.

-I don't see how your condition has any impact on whether we divorce.-

My heart gave a strange hitch. "You don't?"

-Why should it?-

My parents' voices echoed in my head. The same words I'd heard almost daily since my flares began. *Don't show anyone your flaws. Don't let them see your failure. If they learn of your weakness, they'll use it against you, and then they'll cut you down.*

"Because I'm weak. Too weak to rule by your side." Too weak to be my parents' heir.

His tone darkened. *-Do you think so little of me?-*

"What do you mean?"

-You left your country and family behind for a marriage you never asked for, just to keep the peace. You risked your life to save mine, and now you're risking it again to protect a land that isn't even your home. And on top of that, you're clearly in pain and should be in bed under the care of a greenwitch, not making yourself worse by riding through the cold, but you're determined to push on anyway for the sake of your people. Most people would simply give up, yet you've never wavered. Only a monster would think a woman like that was weak.-

My parents did. And I had never thought of them as monstrous—had always believed the rest of the world would see me and my condition the same way, as a flaw that could be exploited. The other noble Houses of Damaria would certainly think the same if they found out. Why shouldn't everyone else? That was the only reality I'd ever known.

"I *am* weak, though," I protested. "I'm slowing us down."

-Would you say someone with a broken arm was weak for not using it?-

"That's different."

-How?-

I opened my mouth, then closed it again. Part of me insisted that he was wrong, but I couldn't find the words to explain myself. Not when another, smaller part whispered, with a voice I'd never heard before, that perhaps he could be right.

-Strength isn't about what your body can do,- Aric went on. *-It's about how you respond to adversity. And I've never known someone so determined to do the right thing, no matter the personal cost.-*

Heat was creeping up my cheeks. Surely that wasn't admiration in his words—he didn't even like me. "But you said I should have told you about my condition."

-Not so that I could cast you aside, Bianca. So that I could be cognizant of your needs.- His tone was still heightened—with annoyance, but it didn't feel directed at me. *-So that I could* help.-

I stiffened, wary again. "Help how?"

-My hours in the library haven't been spent on storybooks. I've read quite extensively about various ailments of the body, among other things.-

His pace had picked up, mirroring my tension.

"I don't need you to fix me." My words were clipped, as sharp as a horse's shoes striking slate. Memories of a dozen apothecaries endlessly prodding and poking me as if I were a malfunctioning clock. Each of them trying fruitlessly to determine how I was broken. Losing interest when it became clear that while my condition never became worse, it never got better, either.

-I didn't mean to imply otherwise,- Aric said. *-I just thought that if possible, you would prefer not to be in pain.-*

His tail flicked my shins. He'd gone rigid again. If he were in human form, he would be avoiding my eyes and flushing.

But wait. I was the one who should be on edge here. Why would he . . .

Oh. For the first time, I realized his behavior might not stem from arrogance as I'd assumed. The blushing, the stilted words . . . It suddenly occurred to me that Aric wasn't cold, but *nervous.* He'd mentioned his dislike of courtly maneuvering. Perhaps he thought every word he said to me would be misconstrued. And so far I had largely proved him right.

I forced my shoulders to ease their tense line. I'd been treating this marriage like a fencing match, but it was possible that I was the only one holding a weapon.

"I would," I admitted. "I would much prefer that."

Aric relaxed enough that I could feel it, both mentally and physically. Another truce.

I couldn't quite trust it. I'd spent nearly half my life believing that to let my condition show was to fail. But Aric had seen past my defenses, and he'd neither struck me down nor cast me aside. Instead, he'd offered me a hand up.

"If you were to help," I said finally, my throat tight, "what would you need to know?"

Aric's relief felt like drinking Julieta's ginger tea. I realized as I tasted it that we'd both expected me to refuse.

-Well. We could start with the most basic details. When did it begin? Were you born with it?-

I shook my head. "It started when I was about fifteen . . ."

We rode on, Aric questioning and me answering as best I could. The information he sought was diverse in scope: Times of day when my flares arrived. Things that made my symptoms improve or worsen. What precisely the tonics did, and why I could only take so much at a time. Whether my ailment corresponded with the moon, the weather, my cycle, my meals. I hadn't realized

I was paying attention to such things, and yet, as he questioned me, the answers came readily.

And more notably, as Aric questioned me, he relaxed. It was like watching an early spring sunrise, dark and cold at the start, with a slow unfurling into warmth. When he spoke of topics he found interesting instead of making stiff courtesies, Aric felt like a different man altogether from the icy opponent I'd met in the ballroom. A truer, gentler version of himself.

Even though we were clearly incompatible in the physical sense—and not only because he was currently a horse—perhaps this marriage hadn't been a terrible match after all.

The thought caught me by surprise, yet it felt like a truth. A truth, however, that lingered only a few moments, like a butterfly sipping at nectar, before flitting out of my grasp. We weren't on this journey to play at courtship. We were heading to Damaria because I had accidentally turned Aric into a horse on our wedding night and someone had framed me for his murder. We were together for only as long as it took to undo the curse and expose whoever wanted us dead.

And despite Aric's openness, despite the fact that he hadn't struck me down, I couldn't entirely drop my unease. The echoes of my parents' whispers lingered in my ears, telling me that I was only baring my heart to a waiting blade. And though I wanted to ignore them, I'd heard the words too many times to be certain they weren't true, that the sword wasn't ready to fall.

18

By the time the sun hung heavy in the western sky, we'd passed a handful of villages and climbed deep into the mountains. Mixed forest gave way to sparser spruces and firs, bent against the cold like old women, and the peaks' bare slopes were crowned with glittering snow.

A final village, smaller than the rest, clung to the flanks of the mountains in a narrow valley just before a major pass. By unspoken agreement, Aric and I paused in the center of the road, studying it from a distance. The village seemed quiet, no guards in sight. Sturdy sheep dotted its paddocks and smoke drifted serenely from manifold chimneys, blending with the haze of low-hanging clouds. I recognized the pass from my study of Gildenheim's geography, or at least I thought I did.

My heart sank. If I was right about our location, we'd covered less than thirty miles and still had the breadth of the mountains to cross. The journey should have taken two days, but at this rate we'd be lucky to get there before the coronation. We hadn't accounted for Aric being slower than a typical horse—in retrospect, a grave miscalculation.

The already dipping temperature and heavy clouds promised a wet and frigid evening. I pulled my coat tighter to my neck with one hand as a raindrop hit my face.

-The cold will only get worse after sunset,- Aric said, mirroring my thoughts.

I nodded grimly. My body was already weeping at the prospect of another frigid night of sleeping on the ground—especially if it decided to rain in earnest. Along with the cold, fear prickled my spine. The glow wyrms had been harmless enough, but if they and the walking trees were real, what about the rest of Gildenheim's legends? I wasn't keen on taking the chance that the soul-hunting wyrdwolves from the "folktales" Tatiana and I used to scare each other with would turn out to be as harmless as puppies.

-We should see if the village inn has any beds available.-

I hesitated. "You don't think they'd recognize me? Or you, for that matter. Unless you're planning to sleep in the stables?"

-I doubt the news of my assassination has spread this far,- Aric said. *-And no, I don't think they'll recognize either of us. We're not dressed as nobles, and the majority of Gilden citizens can barely even write their own names. I doubt they've been studying my portrait in their spare time.-*

I pulled a face. As far as I was concerned, there was no excuse for illiteracy in a wealthy country.

-It's something I plan to remedy,- Aric said, his tone sharpening as he sensed my disapproval.

"What, having your citizens study your portrait? Do you plan to distribute cameos?"

-Teaching them to read. The knowledge gleaned from books should be available to everyone.-

Annoyance had turned to earnestness in his voice. Interesting. I'd known Gildenheim lacked a system of public schools like those run by the Adepts in Damaria—a worthwhile investment, since any person could potentially manifest magical ability. But I hadn't realized Gildenheim's rulers cared about such things. Perhaps they hadn't, before Aric.

I turned back to the village, scrutinizing its streets. It appeared harmless. Sedate. That didn't mean it was. Smiles and mild manners could hide a weapon just as well as a soldier's uniform.

But I was exhausted. My entire body hurt, both from a night of sleeping on the ground and from the remnants of my earlier flare. The cold already pinched at my skin, threatening a night worse than the last.

"Aric, are wyrdwolves real?"

His words were tinged with confusion at my tangent. -*Why wouldn't they be?*-

That, and another raindrop splattering on my hand, finalized the decision for me. It might be self-indulgent, but I was willing to take Aric's assurances about our safety for my own if it meant a good night's sleep.

"Never mind. Let's ask for a room at the inn."

The sun was already broaching the horizon, so we loitered near the road until Aric transformed back into a man. He shook himself with a full-body shudder as he finished pulling on clothes.

"Archives and indices," he muttered. "Do you have any idea how frustrating it is to not have *hands*? I've been plagued by itches all day."

I managed not to laugh. We made for the village, carrying the saddle and impossibly heavy bags and hurrying to outpace the coming rain.

The village's streets were as quiet as they'd seemed from a distance. A few heads turned to watch us pass, making my shoulders tighten with apprehension. But they soon turned away again, uninterested. I tried to relax. We were on the main road to Damaria, and adjacent to a major mountain pass besides. The villagers here saw travelers every day. We were just two more—albeit two who were carrying an expensive saddle with no horse in sight.

The inn was easy to find. Humble but clean, it had its own small courtyard just off the main road. Inside, the building was dimly lit by tallow candles backed with pewter—they couldn't afford Adept-crafted lanterns; no surprise there—but a hearth spilled warmth and light throughout the interior. I cast a suspicious glance at the fire, remembering the green flames in my chambers at the castle, but this one looked ordinary enough.

The inn's main room was empty aside from a group of three travel-worn customers drinking beside the hearth and an innkeeper behind the bar. I glanced warily at the travelers, who were watching us none too subtly. One of them, a woman, Gilden-pale and dark-haired, didn't even try to pretend she wasn't looking. I didn't like the way her eyes lingered, hungry and intent. It was probably just curiosity on her part. But my nerves prickled, and I was glad of the rapier at my side. The sooner we were out of their sight, the better.

Aric, setting down the heavy saddle, caught my elbow as I started across the room. He lowered his head towards mine, and for a dizzying moment I thought he meant to kiss me.

Instead, his lips brushed against my ear, sending a tingle down my neck. "Let me do the talking." His voice was so low it was almost inaudible.

I pulled my elbow from his grasp. "Why? I can haggle as well as you. Better, probably."

"It's not about haggling. Your accent stands out."

"My accent is *impeccable*," I retorted, deliberately butchering each syllable. Aric winced as if my pronunciation physically pained him, and I hid a smile as I followed him to the bar.

"A room for the night. And a meal." Aric set our purse down on the bar. "We'd prefer to dine in private if possible."

"Of course." The innkeeper's accent, by comparison to Aric's, was like pond water to melted ice. Aric's own pronunciation, of course, was crisp. Flawless. Royal. Too late, I realized that his accent might betray us worse than mine.

I glanced over my shoulder at the other travelers. Still watching. My nape prickled a warning. Did they recognize Aric? Or me?

I leaned around Aric, caring more about speed than hiding my accent. "And a bath, please. As hot as you can make it."

Aric gave me a sharp look. I countered with my most winning smile. "I desire to wash before bed, *husband*. At least one of us smells of horse."

The tips of Aric's ears turned pink. He looked at the bar instead of the innkeeper as the woman named a price.

Aric paid without argument—so much for haggling—and we went upstairs to wash and change. He slotted the key into the lock and turned it.

Then stopped in the open doorway, blocking my view of the room.

"What? Does this room come equipped with assassins, too?" I rose on my toes to look over his shoulder and was treated to a view of a chamber with a washstand, an empty tin tub waiting before the blazing hearth, and a bed with the sheets made up. Smaller than I was accustomed to, but clean. No assassins to be seen, unless they were hiding under the bed.

Oh. The bed. There was only one.

My face warmed. We'd slept together in the arboretum, but the idea of sleeping beside Aric as a man knotted my mind into a much more complicated tangle of conflicting feelings.

The stairs creaked behind us. Someone else was coming up, and we were standing in the hallway for anyone to see. I nudged Aric in the ribs. "Inside. We can discuss inside."

I pushed him into the bedchamber and closed the door behind

us, turning the key in the lock. As the bolt clicked into place, I let out a sigh of relief.

Aric set the saddle he'd been carrying on the ground. "I'll sleep on the floor." His voice was grey with resignation.

I dropped the saddlebags on the bed. I'd managed to go the whole day without thinking of how he'd flinched from me on our wedding night, but it couldn't be avoided forever. "I thought we'd established that I'm not going to stab you during the night. I realize you find me abhorrent, but surely we can manage to occupy the same mattress without touching."

Aric flushed scarlet. "I—ah—I—why do you think I find you abhorrent?"

I folded my arms. "I believe the last time you and I were about to share a bed your words were *Let's get this over with.*"

Aric actually covered his face with his hands. "Bianca. I thought you were planning to kill me and usurp the throne. It had nothing to do with . . . well, you."

Oh. *Oh.* "So your reaction wasn't because you find me abhorrent?" The words slipped out before I could stop them. I wanted to snatch them from the air and stuff them back down my throat where they belonged.

What I could see of Aric's face was the color of sunset. "Abhorrent is not the word I would choose."

I was tempted to ask what word he *would* choose, but I didn't trust my tongue. It seemed determined to tie itself into knots whenever the subject of our relationship came up.

"Well," I managed. "I don't see an issue with sharing the bed, then. We *are* married, after all."

Aric lowered his hands from his face, though he was still flushed. "I'm just . . . not accustomed to sharing a bed."

My brows lifted. He'd caught me by surprise, especially considering that he had a lover at court. Though there were certainly more places than bedchambers in which to engage in such activities. Perhaps he was more adventurous than I'd given him credit for.

I cleared my throat before my mind could run off into the dangerous territory of musing about such adventures. "Well, if you insist on sleeping on the floor, I won't stop you. But if you can tolerate the hardship of lying next to me, I promise not to kill you in the night. Agreed?"

I held out my hand to him, as if we were closing a deal. Instead of taking it, Aric gripped my wrist. His eyes narrowed. He turned my hand palm up, revealing the strange new scars running across my skin: a spiderweb of thin golden lines from the lantern's broken glass.

"When did you perform blood magic?"

I looked up at him sharply. "I haven't, other than our wedding ceremony. This happened when the assassin attacked. I cut myself on the lantern and these marks appeared later. I didn't know what they meant."

Aric cupped my hand in both of his, fitting around mine as if our hands were made for that purpose. His thumb traced the odd scars, warm and gentle. A tingle ran up my arm that had nothing to do with magic.

"These are definitely blood magic marks." His thumb crossed my heart line, following one of the cuts. "See?"

He turned his hand over, showing me his own palm. A handful of golden marks gathered at the tips of his fingers. I picked out the one from our wedding on his fourth finger, which a ring would have graced had we been married in Damaria. They were identical to mine except for the placement and size.

"But I don't even know what blood magic is," I said. "And I'm certainly not an Adept."

Aric released my hand. The heat from his palms lingered on

my skin like the last notes of a song. "You're familiar with witch's eyes, yes?"

We didn't call them the same thing in Damarian, but I gathered the meaning. Each person with magical potential developed golden flecks in their eyes as their power manifested—the same color, I realized, as the marks on our hands. My own eyes were terra-cotta brown, not a hint of gold, but I'd stared into Tatiana's plenty of times—we used to make a contest of seeing which of us would blink first. I nodded.

"Magic always leaves a mark," Aric explained. "Your Adepts are fond of channeling it into physical forms and letting those vessels bear the brunt of it. But there are other ways."

"Greenwitches? But I thought they were just untrained. They can't make weapons or other devices the way Adepts do. Can they?" My concept of Gilden magic was suddenly spinning on its axis.

"No, though we may have to disagree on whether that's a good thing. And greenwitches have their own methods of training— it's just different from Adepts. Most of them apprentice within their communities, so they can better serve as healers or crafters." He caught himself, clearly drawing back from launching into a detailed explanation. "But that's not what I meant. Blood magic is a different method, used only by Gilden royalty. It's an ancient type of spell casting that binds power with pain."

"How charming."

Aric grimaced in agreement. "I prefer to avoid using it if at all possible. But it's required for certain rituals, like the coronation."

"And the wedding ceremony."

"Yes."

I frowned, examining the scars. "But then—what are these from? The only magic I remember is from our marriage."

"Bianca. You turned me into a horse."

"I told you. That wasn't my spell." I tapped the locket. "And besides, I'm not royal. How could I have cast blood magic?"

"Of course you're royal," Aric said. "We're married. Have you forgotten the shared blood?"

I opened my mouth to protest. Closed it again. *Oh.* "That would have been helpful to know."

"I did tell you our vows were sealed with magic."

"Well," I said, "you left out a stupendous amount of detail."

Aric's mouth twitched towards a wry smile.

I curled my hands closed, hiding the marks. So they were the sign of blood magic. If only I knew exactly what that meant. Whatever I had inadvertently done . . . I was almost afraid to guess. At least now I knew why my palms were crisscrossed with golden lines.

Aric was watching me with a pensive expression. A furrow had formed across his brow, and I suppressed the urge to smooth it away with my thumb. I tucked my hands safely behind my back instead, where they couldn't develop a dangerous mind of their own.

"I'll go down and see about that meal we asked for. Let's hope they understand my horrific accent." I flashed Aric an innocent smile and headed for the door.

I was taking the coward's way out, avoiding the dangerous flutter in my chest and what it could possibly mean. But I had always known I was a coward.

The offerings the inn sent up—soup and day-old bread rolls—were better than I'd expected. I devoured two rolls and an entire bowl of soup in a few minutes flat. The broth was enriched with some sort of gamey meat and flavored with dried rosemary and sage. Probably imported from Damaria; I doubted the herbs grew at this altitude.

The inn's girl delivered two steaming pitchers of water when she came to take the empty dishes away. I let out a blissful sigh and started towards the tub, then stopped and turned towards Aric.

"Would you . . ."

He turned around, presenting me with a view of his narrow shoulders. My eyes ran down his back, and I swallowed, trying to quell the unexpected—and unwanted—heat curling in my stomach.

"I was going to ask if you would like to bathe first. You seemed rather upset about the mud."

"Oh." Aric's shoulders were taut. "I . . . that's all right. You're probably worse off than I am."

Not exactly a compliment, but this wasn't an argument I had any desire to win. I headed towards the tub and loosened my hair from its knot. "I'll be quick."

Aric moved to the bed. Straw shifted within the mattress as it settled under his weight. He rummaged through one of the saddlebags, retrieving something from our remaining supplies.

I poured hot water into the tub, unbuckled the dagger at my wrist, and toed out of my shoes. Then paused, my hands on the hem of my undershirt. I glanced over my shoulder. Aric sat with his back to me, bent over something in his lap. The hearth immersed the room in a golden glow. Plenty of light to see by, should he happen to turn around.

Well, even if he did decide to look, I had nothing to be ashamed of. And besides which, we were married. He would have seen it all by now had our wedding night gone according to plan.

I dropped my clothes in a crumpled heap and slid into the bath, biting back a hiss as the hot water found the scabbed-over cuts on my shins. The water lapped at my chin as I sank down as deep as I could. I cupped some in my hands and splashed it over my face, tasting salt as grime washed from my skin.

The tub was already clouded with dirt. Myriad cuts I hadn't even noticed prickled and stung as the water reached them. I should clean them before the bath got cold; Julieta had taught me, among other things, to never ignore a wound—even a small one.

I pushed myself upright, shivering as the cooler air hit my damp skin, and reached for the soap.

Something rapped sharply against the window. I yelped and lunged for my dagger. Water sloshed over the side of the tub. I was halfway to standing before I realized I was still completely naked, and the sound had caught Aric's attention, too.

My eyes locked on his. Both of us froze. Aric was standing, facing me, a book dangling from one hand—when had he acquired *that*? His eyes were a winter sky. They flicked downwards for the briefest instant, then hastily returned to my face. He held my gaze, color in his cheeks and fire in his eyes.

An answering heat kindled low in my stomach. Deliberately, I lifted my chin, challenging him to comment.

Another rap at the window. Both of us flinched, jolted out of whatever impasse we'd fallen into. I twisted towards the window, my dagger half drawn. Outside the panes, a large, wet bird clung to the sill, tapping an oversized orange beak against the glass.

"A . . . puffin?" Aric's voice was huskier than usual.

I sheathed the knife. Not an attack. Just a seabird, confused and very out of place. Perhaps it was disoriented by the rain.

The puffin tapped its beak on the glass again, more insistently. As if it was determined to get in. But why would a bird—

Oh. I grabbed for my towel and, wrapping it hastily around myself, hurried to the window. When I opened the sash, the drumroll of steady rain greeted me.

The puffin thrust out its beak, offering me a tiny vellum scroll. I held out my hand gingerly, wary of being bitten—were puffins friendly? The bird deposited its message into my palm, made a peculiar rattling sound with its bill, and flapped away into the night. I watched it go, incredulous. When Evito assured me he could handle sensitive messages, I'd expected a highly trained spy or a clever spell, not a seabird.

"What was *that*?"

I turned around. Aric was closer than I'd expected—I almost walked straight into him. The towel slipped, and I nearly dropped it. Aric's gaze tracked the movement, and he swallowed hard. Warmth rose to my cheeks, but I didn't step back.

Neither did Aric. His gaze moved to my mouth and stayed there, the blue of his eyes nearly swallowed by the black of his pupils. We stood close enough that I could feel the heat of his body, and it woke an answering warmth in my core. Without conscious thought, I lifted my hand to rest on his chest, feather-light. Aric's heart thumped hard against the splay of my palm.

Scant inches remained between us. It would take only a breath for one of us to close the distance.

Then Aric cleared his throat. He stepped back, far enough that my hand dropped from his chest, and turned deliberately away from me. His knuckles were white on the book in his hand.

Disappointment flared—foolishly, irrationally. I'd been imagining things, my senses eroded by exhaustion. Aric might have been caught by surprise seeing me unclothed, but of course he wasn't actually interested. And neither was I. This wasn't a children's tale where curses were broken by true love's kiss, and even if it had been, we had a truce, not a love match. Thank the seas nothing had actually happened. I couldn't afford another vulnerability, especially one that wasn't returned.

"What did the puffin give you?" Aric asked, still looking firmly away from me.

I dropped my gaze to the scroll, glad of the distraction from my near embarrassment. "A message from Ambassador Dapaz." I scanned the lines of ink, written in a small, neat hand that slanted sharply. The penmanship was familiar, though I couldn't put my finger on why. "He doesn't have much to report. The guards continue to search. He says my retinue is still being detained, but they're unharmed."

Aric frowned. "Nothing about Marya? Or the search for the assassin?"

I shook my head. I'd hoped for some new and useful detail, but Evito's silence on the matter meant nothing. We'd only been gone for one full day—it was likely too soon for the situation to have drastically changed, and Marya might not have trusted the ambassador with anything she'd learned on her own so far. Better no news than word of worsening developments—like a message from my parents. I could only hope they hadn't heard about my wedding night yet.

And that they weren't somehow involved.

"At least you know your people are safe." Aric's shoulders loosened slightly. "I'm sure that's a relief to you."

"It is." I lowered the scroll. "Where did you get a book?"

"Marya included a few key volumes in our provisions."

My brows rose. No wonder the saddlebags had felt like a sack of cannonballs—I'd been unwittingly toting about Aric's personal library. "A *few?* How many is a few?"

"Only six," Aric said. "She limited it to the essentials."

"*Six?* Aric, how were you even planning to read them? Your eyes were on the sides of your head!"

Aric looked down at the book in his hands. "I was optimistic they would be in their normal position for the return trip."

I started getting dressed. I'd had enough of vulnerability for one evening.

"Tell me, then, what books are so essential they needed to accompany us to the border?"

Aric was silent for a long moment. I glanced over my shoulder at him, but he was standing with his back turned, his face hidden. Tension coiled through his frame like an Adept's clockwork device.

"Aric? You can turn around."

He didn't. Instead, he kept his eyes fixed on the book. It was closed, so he couldn't possibly be reading. It occurred to me that silence might be a defense for him, an inverse of how I often concealed my own discomfort with brightly fluttering words.

"I am well aware of my failings," he said at last, his voice as bitter as salt water. "As is most of the Gilden court, for that matter. You needn't parade them before me."

My stomach twisted. He thought I was mocking him.

I walked around to face him. Aric didn't look up.

"Aric. My question was genuine. I want to understand what's important to you. I . . . I want to understand *you*."

Aric, finally, looked up. His eyes were fit to drown in.

"And what if, should you come to understand me, you don't like what you discover?"

My next words could shatter the thin ice we walked on, sinking us both. And while I could tell myself I needed to understand Aric for my country's advantage—the unnerving truth was that I simply wanted to. Because he fascinated me, like the endlessly changing swell of waves on the shore. A current that could all too easily pull me under.

"In our vows, I promised to care for you," I said. "Can you truly care for someone you don't know?"

Aric's gaze flickered. "I would argue it's worse to be truly known and despised than not cared for to begin with."

Virtues, he was as intractable as a statue. I wanted to shatter him.

"Then that's a risk we both take. But *I* would argue we can hardly do worse than how we began our marriage." I picked up one of the other books at random. "Now, I am going to sit by the fire and read about"—I squinted at the title—"a history of agriculture in the Zhei Empire. If you care to join me, I'll be by the hearth."

I sallied over to the fire and settled myself on the flags, doing my best to pretend I was reading and not watching Aric from the corner of my eye.

A long moment passed. Then, hesitantly, as if he suspected me of laying a trap, Aric came to sit beside me, cross-legged.

"It's a volume on alternative logging practices," he said quietly. "After I read the treaty terms, I wanted to learn if there were any means of fulfilling its stipulations without harming Gildenheim's remaining wild places."

This man. How had I ever thought him heartless? My mouth curved.

"How despicable of you."

Aric looked up at me sharply. Our eyes met, and his lips quirked into a wry smile.

"Perhaps not," he admitted. "But there are certainly those who judge the time I spend reading as worthless compared to skills I lack. Compared to . . . certain other people."

His hands had tightened on his book. I was certain he was thinking of Varin. Earlier, I'd thought that Aric must never have known the sting of being deemed unworthy, but I'd been so wrong. *If only their positions were reversed. A true courtier on the throne once more.* If I could go back now, I'd glare the whisperers into silence.

"I think it's admirable," I said, holding his gaze. "And entirely worthy. Knowledge serves a ruler more than fencing, that's for certain."

Aric watched me for another long moment. His smile soft-

ened, deepened, becoming something less careful and more real.
For a moment I thought he might say something further or, Virtues
help me, lean towards me as he had earlier.

Then an ember popped in the fire, and both of us jumped,
startled out of the moment. We looked hastily down at our re-
spective volumes and fell into a silence that was almost comfortable.

Aric read in truth. I let my book lie open on my lap, unable to
focus on the printed words. Aric was absorbed, and unobserved,
I watched the firelight limn his face, tracing his features in gold
and . . . green?

I blinked at the hearth. Yes, the flames burned verdant—just
as they had in the castle.

"Aric," I murmured, "why is the fire green?"

He glanced up from his book. "A greenwitch spell. It makes
the flames last longer to save on wood. You'll see it in every hearth
in Gildenheim, if you look the right way."

I recalled what he'd said earlier about greenwitches apprentic-
ing within and serving their communities. How different from
Damaria, where Adepts not only trained in isolation, but rarely
sold their magics to anyone save nobles or wealthy merchants. It
was a difference I found I didn't mind.

Aric went back to reading. I rested my head against the wall,
the warmth and the deepening night slowly lulling me towards
drowsiness.

The fire shifted and crackled. The rain beat a steady patter on
the roof. The bath had eased the worst of my aches and pains, and
I was warm for the first time in what felt like days. Any inclina-
tion to get up gradually washed away, erased like footprints from
the sand at high tide.

An arm slid beneath my knees. Another around my back. My
eyes fluttered open just enough to see what was happening. Aric had

me in his arms. The ground vanished beneath me as he scooped me up, carrying me to the bed. He eased me onto the mattress. A blanket's weight settled over me. A moment later, the mattress dipped beside me as he slid into bed on the other side, leaving a careful space between us.

I should have protested being tucked in like a child. Instead, exhaustion interfering with my logic, I squirmed towards Aric and nestled myself against the warmth of his side.

Aric stiffened. His muscles were frozen, but his warmth was like a personal hearth, welcome and melting. I sighed and pressed closer, resting my cheek on his chest.

Aric's heart thrummed beneath my ear, a beat as comforting as the familiar swash of the sea. He lay without moving, barely breathing, long enough that he might have turned to stone. Then, just before I crossed into sleep, his arm crept around my waist, so lightly I probably dreamed it.

19

Despite my fatigue, sleep proved fleeting. I woke late in the night to the stirrings of yet another flare. Nausea curdled my stomach, making me regret every bite of dinner.

Beside me, Aric was asleep. He lay on his back, his head turned away from me—I must have imagined pressing up against him, thank the Virtues. The thought alone was enough to make my face heat with embarrassment. He wasn't touching me now, his breaths steady and slow with sleep. A sliver of moonlight trickled through the window and caught his hair, making it shine like molten silver against the pillow; the rain must have finally stopped.

I eased out of bed, wary of waking Aric, and groped my way over to the saddlebags. The tonic bottle's glass was cool against my fingers as I worked it open. I drank half the dose, then put the rest away. I had only one full dose left after this—I couldn't afford to use it now and need it more later.

I slid back into bed, holding my breath so as not to disturb Aric. But now that sleep had escaped me, it was reluctant to return. My cuts and bruises were aching again, and more than the physical discomfort, my mind was restive. I couldn't stop thinking about the events of the past few days. The wedding with its strange magic. The assassin's attack that had started a spiral of disaster. The potential for this crisis to spin into an all-out war, despite everything I'd sacrificed, if we couldn't break the curse before the coronation.

I stared at the rafters, trying not to move, but my mind squirmed mercilessly, prodding me with guilt from every angle. Instead of peace, I'd secured chaos. Half the Gilden court believed I was a murderer, the other half that I was a kidnapper. I had turned the man I married into a part-time horse. And worst of all, I had abandoned my people, the retinue whose only crime was loyalty to the woman who had failed them: me. While I read by a crackling hearth, they shivered in the castle dungeons, subjected to only the seas knew what mistreatments.

Julieta. Catalina. The other soldiers who made up my guard, men and women who'd volunteered to protect my life with their own. What would they think of me now?

Against my will, Catalina's face flashed into my mind. Not as she was now, but as she'd been ten years ago, before I dug a gulf between us and filled it with the bitter salt of regret. Her eyes, soft as she looked into mine, as she brushed her fingers along my jaw. The hurt in them, not much later, when I'd spoken the words I must. She'd volunteered to come to Gildenheim, so perhaps she'd forgiven me. But I couldn't forgive myself, even though by any measure, I'd done the right thing.

I let out a frustrated sigh. Sometimes I wished I could scour unwanted memories from existence. All I did by keeping them was pick at wounds that should have long since scarred over.

"Is your condition bothering you?"

I froze. Drown it. I'd gotten careless again, forgetting that Aric could hear me.

"Sorry," I whispered. "I didn't mean to wake you."

"It's all right." Aric turned onto his side, facing me. "I wasn't sleeping well anyway. I rarely do."

I rolled onto my side, mirroring him. Now our faces were scant inches apart. His lashes cast shadows onto his cheeks.

"It's flaring a little, but the tonic should take effect soon."

"Is that not what's bothering you, then?" Aric's tone was tentative, as if he expected me to lash out in response.

Something about the darkness invited an intimacy I might regret in the morning, but couldn't resist any more than gravity now. "I was thinking about the guards I brought with me to Gildenheim."

Aric waited. I ought to be wary of his patience, but I lacked the strength to muster my defenses.

"I'm worried about them," I confessed. To my horror, my voice cracked, the admission breaking a part of me I'd barely been keeping intact. "They're good people. They've done nothing to deserve being thrown into a dungeon except be loyal to me. Their *job*."

Aric's expression echoed my own guilt. It was his people who had imprisoned my retinue, after all.

"I promise you, Bianca, no one will hurt them in my name. We don't condone torture in Gildenheim."

Maybe so. But even kings didn't know everything that passed within the walls they ruled.

"These guards of yours," Aric said cautiously. "Is one of them . . . more to you?"

I stiffened, then let out another sigh. I had already given too much away. I should make it clear that I wasn't dishonoring my marriage troth before Aric drew the wrong conclusion from my silence. "Yes. No. Both. My captain of the guard—Catalina Espada. We used to be close, but we've never shared a bed. Maybe we could have, once. But I didn't have the choice."

The last spilled out of me before I thought it through. I frowned. No, that wasn't right. I'd *had* the choice. I'd chosen the right thing:

to put Catalina aside before whatever grew between us sank roots deep enough that it would hurt to tear them out. I'd chosen my duty.

"If you would rather keep what lies between you private, I respect your boundaries," Aric said. "But if you're willing to tell me, I would . . . like to know more."

I didn't try to hide my surprise. "Why?"

A wry smile flickered across his face. "Can you truly care for someone you don't know?"

My returning smile was ironic. Of course he would use my own words against me.

I looked down for a moment, considering. My history with Catalina was a vulnerability. But Aric had shared something of himself with me earlier tonight. Maybe a marriage, like magic, was an exchange.

I lifted my gaze to find Aric still watching me. Perhaps it was the moonlight, making everything surreal. Perhaps it was my exhaustion. But in his eyes, I could find no intent to wound—only curiosity, sincere and compelling.

"It started when I was fourteen," I began, and allowed myself to remember.

The connection between Catalina and me had bloomed slow and fragile like a rose in late summer, tempting the frost's bite. Looks exchanged between bouts of weaponry training. Her going too easy on me when we dueled, me going too hard on her. As the months passed, it progressed into more. Touches lasting longer than necessary. Our hands brushing when we passed in the halls.

And then, one spring evening near my sixteenth birthday, our first kiss, in a courtyard beside the training grounds. Catalina shy but eager, I reckless, thinking I was immune. Clumsy and sweet and promising something more, our lips found each other and explored as much as we dared. I thought I was brave. I thought we were alone.

But of course the palace had eyes in every nook and cranny. This was the court of Damaria; futures were made or broken with the power of knowledge, leveraged just so.

My parents called me before them the next morning, as stern and unforgiving as the palace's defensive facades. They understood, they said, that young people had desires. But I represented House Liliana. One day I would marry, not for love, but for advantage. And when I did, I couldn't afford the whispers that my loyalty was compromised because I cared for another.

I was my parents' daughter. I understood. My country, my House, my people all came first. There was no room for anything as small as selfishness. I could want, I could yearn, but I could never *have*. I had to be infallible, to let no one see the cracks in my armor. And love—that was a fatal weakness. One that couldn't be allowed to fester.

I did what was necessary. I told Catalina, unflinching, that we would never be anything more. That what had happened between us was a mistake. I cut my nails into my own palms but showed her no remorse. We'd practically grown up together. For Catalina to believe me, I couldn't give her anything but my utmost resolve.

I watched her heart bleed for long enough to make her think I didn't care. And then I turned away and walked to my room, every bit as sedate and serene as my parents could wish for. I locked the door, refused entrance to anyone save Julieta, and cried until I was empty. Then I rose and made myself forget the feelings I'd briefly entertained, shedding them like snakeskin, until I was a new person and they were no longer true. In their stead, only guilt remained—the guilt of hurting my best friend, a wound time hadn't fully closed.

Aric listened until I was finished. Silence stretched out between us, delicate as gossamer.

"I'm not in love with Catalina," I said. "We've both moved on, and I'm happy for her. She deserves someone who wouldn't hurt her. Someone who would never cast her aside for the sake of politics. But . . ." I swallowed, confessing a truth I rarely admitted even to myself. "I know that's how the world works for people like us. But sometimes, even now, it still hurts. Even though I should be strong enough not to care."

Aric shifted, his brows drawing together. "Caring doesn't make you weak."

I released a raw laugh. "Of course it does. It's a vulnerability that anyone who knows it can exploit."

"Respectfully, I disagree. Caring means you're strong. It means you're brave enough to let yourself feel, even though it puts your heart at risk." Tentatively, Aric reached out, sweeping a lock of hair from my brow. "And you *are* strong, Bianca. Stronger than I think you know."

I caught my breath, not daring to move as his fingers skimmed my cheek. "That isn't true."

Aric's gaze was uncomfortably keen. "Why not?"

It was my turn to hesitate. I was reluctant to let down the walls shielding me from anyone who could do me harm. But Aric had already seen me at my weakest and my worst. It couldn't hurt to tell him what he had surely surmised for himself.

"I'm not brave," I said, the words flat as a blade. "I'm not strong. My whole life, I've done exactly as expected of me: taken the road presented and never strayed from it. If I were brave, I wouldn't have cut Catalina off and avoided her for the past ten years."

I could see Aric thinking, turning his answer over like a pebble rolled across the palm of his hand.

"It takes strength to make a difficult choice," he said.

"Not if it's the only one."

"Was going to a foreign land to marry a man you didn't know the only choice?"

"The only right one," I said. "The only one that counts. It was my duty. That's the only choice that matters."

Aric knew that. It was the choice he had made, too. We were nobles. We did what we had to do, and that didn't take strength or bravery. It took only compliance to follow the roads laid out for us from birth.

Aric was silent for a moment, but he wasn't done. He took my hand by the wrist and turned it over, revealing the gilt scar from our wedding.

"Duty or not, you should have the choice." He touched the thin gold mark, and a shiver thrilled through me despite the bed's warmth. "You ought to decide for yourself who you share your life with."

I shook my head. "We're both born of noble families. You know that isn't how it works."

"But why shouldn't it be?" he countered. "We decide the fates of entire countries—what's stopping us from deciding the course of our own lives?"

I had no answer. The idea was wild, it was ludicrous, it contradicted everything I'd been taught, and yet I wanted it to be true so much it hurt.

Aric folded my fingers closed, hiding the scar from sight.

"You mentioned divorce earlier," he said, resolve steeling his words. "When we return to Arnhelm, I'll give you back your choice. I'll annul the marriage and we'll make a new treaty with our own terms. I want you to choose your life freely."

Shock made me glad I was already lying down. Gradually, our truce had transformed from a necessity to a proper alliance. That our marital arrangement would continue was something I now realized I hadn't questioned. Aric might not want me as a wife, but we were bound together in this nonetheless. Or so I'd assumed.

I hadn't expected him to cast me loose. Much less because he wanted to give me freedom.

The prospect should have made me feel at liberty: the entire ocean before me, any compass direction ready to be made my own. Instead, it unmoored me. I felt lost, adrift with no shore in sight.

Without my marriage to Aric—without a clear and single path to follow—I hardly knew who I was. If I wasn't the daughter unflinchingly fulfilling her duties . . . I wasn't sure I was anyone at all.

Aric was waiting for my answer. I swallowed and forced a smile.

"Thank you," I managed to whisper.

I allowed myself to imagine it. Once we reversed the enchantment and returned to Arnhelm I would be freed from a marriage with a man I didn't love. I could do anything I desired. Marry whomever I chose. Not Catalina—that chance was long gone. But there were countless other options. A woman from the Zhei Empire, who would bring with her silks and spices. A man from Damaria, who would make me always feel at home. The road branched into endless possibilities, a thousand routes whose ends I could not envision.

The choice was mine.

The thought should have been a weight off my shoulders. So why did it feel instead like the weight had doubled, suffocating me?

20

I swam towards consciousness to the sounds of the inn awakening: booted feet in the hallways, the distant clang of pans. I kept my eyes closed, reluctant to rise. The bed was soft, and a full day of travel had as much appeal as taking a bath in ice water. Besides, I was deliciously warm.

Warmer than I should have been. A male body was flush against my back, an arm wrapped around my waist. Moreover, a hard length pressed against my backside. How intriguing.

I nestled closer, rather enjoying the sensation. Aric made a soft sound, and his arm tightened around my waist—

Wait. Aric.

I was rubbing myself against Aric's arousal.

Suddenly I was fully awake. My eyes flew open. I froze, not daring to move. Seas take me, this was even more awkward than turning him into a horse.

Maybe if I extricated myself before he woke up . . . Gingerly, I tried to peel Aric's arm off my waist. Aric made a sound deep in his throat and tightened his grip. Drown the man, he was stronger than he looked. I would have to wrestle my way out, which would unavoidably wake him.

Even worse, I didn't particularly want to. The sound he'd made, and his hardness, were horrifically arousing. I found myself wondering what it would be like to turn to him instead of pulling away.

If he would look up at me with the same intensity he regarded an interesting text, or if he would close his eyes and arch his head back, utterly undone—

This was absolutely not helping. Especially since Aric himself would never have any such thoughts about me. He would be beyond mortified to wake up like this. Knowing him, he would somehow manage to blame me.

I would have to rouse him and hope he woke with no recollection. I eased away from him, trying to create space—not that it succeeded in fully separating certain parts of our bodies—then moistened my lips.

"Aric."

He muttered an unintelligible protest and, to my dismay, adjusted his grip, drawing my backside firmly against him. His hardness twitched. Heat rushed between my legs. Virtues help me, if this kept up . . .

A horse whickered outside the window. Instinctively, I looked in that direction, though I could see nothing beyond the glass but the pale light of dawn. Horror flooded through me, drowning the warmth of arousal in ice water.

It was already dawn. And we were still inside.

"Aric!" I hissed. "We need to get up. It's almost sunrise—"

Aric was wide awake in an instant. He bolted upright in a tangle of sheets, his eyes wide with panic.

Too late. At the same moment, sunlight bloomed in the window.

A blinding white flash. A sound like a hundred candles blowing out at once, followed by the ominous *crack* of breaking wood. I screamed as the bed suddenly dropped under me, rolling me towards the large white horse now occupying the majority of the mattress.

Aric scrambled to his feet, eyes wild and nostrils flaring. Sheets tangled around his legs, nearly sending him crashing to the floor. Beneath his hooves, the boards creaked threateningly. I scrambled away from him, feeling myself in imminent danger of being trampled.

"Blast!" I cursed. "Blast, blast, blast—"

-*Why didn't you wake me?*- Aric demanded. The whites of his eyes were showing. -*This could have easily been avoided*—-

"*You* could have woken *me*!" I snapped back. "And I *did* try to wake you, it's not my fault you were—"

"Gentlefolk?" A rap sounded on the door. "I heard a scream. Is something amiss?"

Both Aric and I froze. We exchanged a mutual look of dismay.

-*Answer her,*- Aric urged. -*Before she comes in.*-

I lurched to my feet, nearly face-planting as the sheets wound around my shins.

"Everything's fine!" Panicked, I barely remembered to respond in Gilden. "Just bedded the horse!"

A confused pause. "Pardon?"

Drown me. Every word of Gilden I knew had apparently chosen that moment to gaily flee my head. "Just . . . uh . . . The horse! I had a big night horse. I'm awake now! Nothing's wrong!"

-*I believe the word you want is "nightmare,"*- Aric put in.

"I *know* that," I hissed at him, then paused. "Wait—that's not helpful at all. I can't tell which language you're speaking. *Are* you even speaking a language?"

"Sorry, milady?"

"Nothing!" I responded hastily. "Just talking to my *husband*."

Aric's admittedly majestic tail gave an irritated swish.

"Shall I bring up your breakfast, then, milady?"

I finally succeeded in untangling myself from the sheets. "No. No thank you. We're all fine here, everything's just fine! The very finest!"

I could practically feel Aric rolling his eyes. *-Convincing.-*

I propped my hands on my hips and glared at him. "You have a go at it, then."

-You know perfectly well why I can't.- He flicked an ear at the door. *-Anyway, she's leaving.-*

I turned to look, although of course I couldn't see the innkeeper through the solid wood. Footsteps were indeed moving away, retreating in the direction of the stairs. I let out a heavy sigh of relief and turned to assess the damage.

The floor seemed to be intact, despite the threatening groans the boards made every time Aric shifted his weight. The same couldn't be said of the bed. The entire frame on the side he'd slept on was bent and splintered. Not quite snapped, but jacked down at an angle that pointed sharply towards the floor. The bed hadn't been built to take the sudden addition of a stallion's full weight.

I grabbed the frame and pulled, as if my efforts could undo the damage. Unsurprisingly, it didn't budge.

"Seas," I groaned. "I don't think we have enough regals left to pay for this." How was I going to explain the destruction to the innkeeper? For that matter, how was I going to explain the appearance of a horse in the bedroom?

-We'll send a bill to the castle,- Aric said.

"What, and let the entire inn know who we are?"

He scuffed a hoof along the floor, making me wince as the boards creaked again. *-They'll be honored.-*

"Of course they will." I rolled my eyes. "I can think of no higher honor in an innkeeper's life than having their king turn into a horse and break their bed."

Aric stared at me, unblinking.

"That was sarcasm. Do you have that in Gildenheim? I don't think they'll be happy at all."

-The castle will compensate them generously.-

"Assuming we can get a message to the castle."

-I thought the ambassador was keeping in contact with you?-

"Yes, but I wasn't foolish enough to tell him you're traveling with me. Besides, I don't know how to send him a return message without risking it being intercepted. I don't have a convenient bird stashed up my sleeve."

-You have room for daggers,- Aric muttered, swishing his tail.

I didn't have the energy to retort. Suddenly, it was all too much. The accidental curse. The attempt on Aric's life—on *our* lives. Now the broken bed. I sat on the edge of the mattress and rested my elbows on my knees, my head in my hands. How in the ocean's hundred names was I going to fix this? Even without the added complication of a horse in the bedroom, we still had at least two full days of travel ahead of us just to reach the border and meet Tatiana, never mind returning in time for the coronation. And the longer we spent on the road, the worse mess I seemed to make of everything.

-Bianca?- Aric's concern tugged at me. *-Are you feeling ill again?-*

I closed my eyes and took a moment to compose myself. In my exhaustion, I had almost lowered my defenses, allowed him to see the fragility of my despair. I couldn't afford that sort of vulnerability. Aric already knew too much of my weakness.

I stood up, forcing an expression of confidence. "Just planning what to do next." I looked between him and the door. "Horses can go down stairs, right?"

A few minutes later, Aric was saddled, I'd buckled on my rapier, and the majority of our coin purse's contents were glinting beside the hearth—we would likely regret their lack down the road, but neither of us could leave in good conscience without paying for the damage. To my immense relief, Aric was able to squeeze through the doorway—though I had to take the saddle off him first, and then resaddle him in the hall. I carried the saddlebags myself, books and all, in an effort to mitigate the weight of a full-sized stallion.

Wood groaned at every step as Aric clopped down the hallway. I gritted my teeth and prayed the boards wouldn't break.

Aric balked at the top of the staircase. *-I can't go down that. The stairs won't hold me.-*

"They will," I whispered, with a surety I didn't feel. "Just . . . don't think about it too hard. Pretend you're very small."

Aric gave me a scathing look. *-And how, precisely, is pretending to be small going to negate the force of my weight against the boards?-*

Before I could retort, a gasp came from below us. One of the inn's staff stood at the bottom of the stairs, a pile of linens about to fall from his arms as he stared open-mouthed at Aric.

I trained my firmest smile on him. "Stand aside, please. We'll be out of the way momentarily."

The man blinked and, shocked into compliance, took a generous step backwards. I prodded Aric's rump, making him snort and flick his tail at me.

"Go," I hissed. "Before he tells the entire village to come and watch."

Aric gave me a final disgruntled look and started down the stairs, testing each one before he put his full weight on it. The boards groaned, a cacophony of squeals reminiscent of a dying herd of pigs. I gritted my teeth so hard my molars threatened to fuse, keeping a smile plastered to my face for the sake of our growing audience. If the boards broke—if Aric fell, and I was stuck with an enchanted horse with a broken leg to boot—

The stairs held. Aric reached the ground floor.

I looked up, releasing a long-held breath. Our audience had multiplied. Now a dozen or so staff and guests stood clustered in doorways, all staring at us with looks ranging from disbelieving to appalled.

I lifted my chin and donned my best expression of courtly hauteur.

"Only the best lodgings for my prize stallion," I declared loftily. "Come, my pet."

I paraded serenely out of the room, head held high and Aric snorting emphatically at my heels.

-My pet?- Aric demanded. *-My* pet?-

Hours down the road, and still he was caught on that single syllable, like a shirt snagged on a nail. Despite our late start, we were making good progress—as far as I could tell. If the rain continued to hold off, we might reach the inn where I'd arranged to meet Tatiana by noon tomorrow.

I rolled my eyes. "I couldn't very well refer to you as my husband, could I?"

-But pet? *The entire Gilden language, and that was the word you chose?-*

I resisted the urge to kick him in the ribs. "Elucidate me, *husband*. Which term of endearment should one use in Gildenheim when referring to a spouse who is currently a horse? My poppet? My stud? My—"

-I will buck you from the saddle.-

I settled my toes more firmly into the stirrups. Just in case. "All right, then. What term of endearment do you prefer?"

A pause. *-I fail to see the need for any such terms.-*

"We're playing at courtship," I said. "Indulge me."

Aric's tone turned dark and dry. *-I haven't found much use—or need—for pillow talk.-*

I arched one brow—not that he could see. "Have your lovers agreed with that assessment?"

I could have kicked myself the moment the words left my lips.

I already knew he had a lover, and it wasn't a subject I was keen to hear more about. Marya—his relationship with Marya—was nothing to me. *Aric* was nothing to me—an ally, a husband, but only in name.

Still, that didn't mean I wanted to learn the details of his affair with someone else. We *were* married, even if neither of us expected it to last.

-*I think you may be putting too much weight on my previous experiences,*- Aric said before I could retract my question. -*I've had enough practice to . . . ah . . . know what I'm doing, but I wouldn't qualify any of those encounters as romantic.*-

I was flushing now. Thank the seas he couldn't see my face—this was a dangerous turn in the conversation, and I'd been a fool to take it. "So they were not . . . repeated experiences? With the same individuals, that is?"

-*No.*- Aric weighed his answer for a moment, as if he expected me to judge him harshly. -*I'm the heir to the Gilden throne. I've taken lovers here and there, but it's better that they don't last. If I don't give anyone the opportunity to pretend they care for me long enough to make me believe them, it won't hurt as much when I realize they were only acting for their own benefit. Keeping people at a distance is . . . less painful.*-

"Wait," I blurted. "I thought . . . What about Marya?"

Blast my impulsive tongue. So much for not wanting to know the details.

Aric snorted with surprise. -Marya? *As if she's ever looked twice at a man that way. And even if she had . . . we're* friends, *Bianca. Childhood friends. She's like the sister I never had. We practically grew up together—the queen thought I might take better to studying weaponry if I had someone to humiliate me by contrast, so she picked the best fencing student to pair me with.*- His tone turned wry. -*It wouldn't have worked even if Marya had been the sort to humiliate another person. But it's the one lesson the queen tried to teach me I'm most grateful for, because it brought us together.-*

"Oh." Well, this was unexpected. How had I ever thought Gildenheim cold? I was melting with embarrassed heat. "I thought . . . I . . . Oh, never mind." I scrambled to return to the previous topic before I could say something even worse. "What about family endearments, then? Varin, perhaps?"

-We've never been close. He's seven years older and we weren't raised together, due to our different . . . statuses.- Aric hesitated. *-We were dissuaded from spending time together as children, and neither of us has ever made much effort to bridge the distance. I know him more as a standard I repeatedly failed to meet than as a—a brother.-*

Sympathy glimmered through me. It sounded like a lonely childhood, and I knew all too well how it felt to be viewed as little more than a disappointment. No wonder he and Marya were close. "And your mother?"

Aric's tone hardened, a shield slipping into place. *-I prefer not to talk about the queen.-*

I bit my lip. I'd forgotten, with everything that happened, that he was still in mourning. Of course he didn't want to talk about his mother—she was barely a full month gone.

It was a harsh reminder of what was at stake. I was wasting time with foolish questions, when I ought to be thinking about how we were going to break the curse and prevent a war. It wasn't as if I would be married to Aric for much longer; this game of courtship didn't matter. We would reach the border soon, and our truce would end.

-Is something wrong?- Aric asked.

I'd stiffened in the saddle. Or perhaps he'd picked up the vinegar flavor that had crept into my thoughts.

"I was just wondering how long we have until dusk."

I twisted in the saddle to observe our surroundings, backing up my falsehood. I had no Adept-forged clock, and the thick clouds made it difficult to tell the sun's location.

A flicker of movement caught my attention on the otherwise empty road. Behind us rode a trio of figures on horseback, distant enough that they were only dark silhouettes where the path met the sky.

My hand crept to my rapier.

"Aric," I said, my mouth going dry as sand. "I think we're being followed."

21

Aric stopped abruptly and turned to survey the road behind us. His tail flicked nervously against my shins.

-It could be couriers,- he said. *-This is the main road through the mountains.-*

"And couriers usually ride in threes?"

Aric didn't answer.

-We should keep moving,- he decided after a moment. *-If they intend to follow us, there's nothing we can do about it here.-*

I swept an evaluating glance across our surroundings. Around us the land had grown wilder still, sparse fir forests clinging to craggy slopes. Just steps off the road, the terrain became too steep for riding—almost too steep for walking. If we wished to leave the road, our only option was to scramble along on foot. I wasn't sure Aric could manage such territory, and even if he could we would soon hit the snow line.

Aric was right. There was nothing we could do but ride on.

I turned to face forward again, adjusting my rapier and the knife strapped to my wrist to ensure both were ready to draw.

Aric and I continued in silence. By unspoken agreement he increased his pace, until his flanks began to steam in the frigid air and my legs burned from the effort of gripping his sides. The sun arched towards the horizon, its path barely visible through the haze of clouds. We passed through one town, then another, without stopping. The hours ticked past.

And every time I glanced behind us, the three riders were still there. Never close enough to make out details. Never far enough to let us out of their sight.

"What are they waiting for?" I asked finally, sharp with nerves.

Aric didn't look back. *-I would assume for a more remote area. Most of the villages have a town guard on call. Or maybe for the cover of darkness.-*

So we were no longer pretending they might be friendly. My hands were white-knuckled on the pommel. "Should we stop at an inn?"

But I knew the answer even before Aric spoke. *-We might not reach the next one before sunset. And . . . I don't think we have enough regals left to pay for a private room.-*

I winced. Accidentally breaking the bed frame was bad enough. The idea of Aric transforming into a horse in the common room of a lodging house was a hundred times worse. And given the state of our finances, I suspected we didn't have enough left to cover even a meal. We had badly miscalculated.

I twisted in the saddle to look behind us. The riders, of course, were still there. Hovering like hawks. And we, the rabbits, could only wait for them to descend.

Our pursuers made their move just before dusk, as the sun skimmed the peaks of the mountains. Between one moment and the next, I looked back and they'd suddenly halved the distance.

I shouted to Aric, but he hardly needed the warning. He broke into a gallop at once. I bent low over his neck, the frigid wind stealing tears from my eyes, and gripped the pommel for dear life. I hadn't the attention to spare for drawing a blade or looking behind us to see if our pursuers were gaining.

Aric was strong, but he was unused to being a horse, and weary from our journey. The drumming sound of our pursuers' steeds grew from a distant patter like spring rain to the roll of thunder. And then they were surrounding us, mud flying from hooves. One pulled ahead and wheeled his horse across the road, blocking the way. Aric shied, half rearing, and nearly threw me from the saddle. The other two riders crowded in on either side, giving us no room to turn around. We were trapped.

One rider put back her hood. A dark-haired woman, her eyes sharp and hungry. A warning tremor of recognition ran through me: I'd seen her at the inn last night, watching us arrive. Now I knew the reason for her interest, and I didn't like the answer.

"And where might you and your prize stallion be headed on this cold evening, milady?" She spoke in Gilden, her syllables running together at the edges. A commoner's accent, unlike the crisp tones of Aric's court.

My hand dropped to the hilt of my rapier. I'd never fought with it in true combat, only in practice. I sent a prayer to the Virtue of Strength that it wouldn't feel different enough from the training grounds to make me falter. Fear swelled in my throat, a bitter taste like wine turned sour. Beneath me, Aric was rigid. His panic melded with my own, turning it choking.

I looked back at the woman, swallowing down my fear for both Aric's sake and my own. "You must have mistaken me for someone else. I'm no noble."

One of her companions snorted—another woman, this one younger with wheat-blond hair, who'd ridden up on my other side. "The finest stallion I've seen this side of the mountains and enough money to spend on the inn's best room. No, of *course* you're not noble."

I turned my gaze on the blond woman, wishing I could cut her with my eyes. "You heard me right."

Aric shifted beneath me. I could feel his hesitation, his frustration at not being able to speak. Seas—what if he bolted and threw me? With this new body, he hardly knew what he was doing.

"Enough pleasantries." The third rider, the one blocking the way, spoke up, his voice a low growl. "Let's make this quick. Hand over your weapons and get down from your horse."

I closed my hand on the hilt of my rapier. "I'll do no such thing."

Metal scraped and clicked, a sound that froze my hand in place: a pistol being cocked. The dark-haired woman's hand was steady, the muzzle of her firearm glinting in the setting sun as she pointed it at my face.

"It wasn't a request."

My hand tightened on my own weapon. We were at close range; any closer and the pistol would be touching my nose. But I knew Adept-made firearms like the one she carried were notorious for missing their targets, and if she wasted her shot it would take her at least a full minute to reload. If I drew fast enough—

-*Bianca. Don't.*- Aric's warning cut through my calculations. -*They'll kill you.*-

I hesitated. Giving up my rapier—and dismounting Aric—also meant giving up any chance at a quick escape. But he was right. Getting myself killed would do nothing to help us.

Reluctantly, I released the hilt of my rapier. The dark-haired woman kept the pistol trained on me as I swung down from Aric's back. Standing beside him in the road, surrounded by mounted enemies, I suddenly felt terribly small. I wished I could talk to him silently in return. Ask him to think of something clever to get us out of this position. All my training in weaponry and negotiations, and yet I was so utterly helpless against raw violence.

Beside me, Aric's hooves danced nervously. I didn't dare reach out to him.

"On your knees, hands in the air," the dark-haired woman snapped. Her eyes fell on the rapier at my side. "And take that off first. Throw it out of reach. Try anything and I'll shoot."

My jaw tight, I unbuckled my sword belt and tossed it to the earth, as close to my reach as I dared. The road's grit bit into my knees as I knelt. Aric was trembling, quivers running through his flanks. I wanted to hiss at him to run, but I wasn't the one who could talk without being overheard.

The blond woman and the man dismounted and began to search through our saddlebags with ruthless efficiency. Our possessions splayed out on the road like the innards of a butchered bird: flasks, food, bedding. The man found the purse and shook it over his open palm, cursing when only a few coins jangled out.

The blond woman had found my tonic. She sniffed the half-drunk dose, tasted it, and spat, throwing the bottle to the road. I clenched my fists as the precious fluid poured into the dust, staining it dark.

She turned away from the empty saddlebags, her expression thunderous. "Where's the rest of it?"

"That's all," I said. "There's nothing more."

"Don't lie to me, you leech." The blond woman strode over to me and, before I could even blink, hit me across the face with ruthless efficiency. I fell forward onto my hands with a muffled cry, my vision sparking with black stars. I had never been struck before, and I hadn't realized how stunning the pain could be.

-Bianca!- Aric whinnied, lifting onto his rear legs, hooves cleaving the air. The two brigands on foot shouted and fell back.

"Secure the horse, you fools!" the leader snapped. "The stallion is the real prize!"

The man snatched up a length of rope from his own saddle

and started towards Aric. I gathered my senses enough to drag in a lungful of air.

"Run!" I cried to him, abandoning caution. "Save yourself!"

Aric pranced in place, dithering. Unwilling, I realized with a jolt, to leave me.

"Go!" I shouted again. "Go, drown you!"

Aric gave me a torn look. Too late. A loop of rope hissed around his neck. Aric shied and screamed. Both brigands on foot threw their weight on the rope until he stopped fighting, shuddering and snorting, his eyes rolling wild.

"Enough of this nonsense," barked the woman with the pistol. "Search her and let's be done with it."

The blond woman spat on the ground, barely missing Aric's hooves, and released her hold on the rope. She strode over to me and jerked me up by one arm, hard enough that my shoulder screamed in its socket.

I bit down on a gasp of pain, reluctant to give her any satisfaction. The woman ran her hands along my sides, searching for hidden wealth. My focus narrowed to the dagger sheathed at my wrist. If I moved quickly, I was close enough to draw the knife and drive it into her chest.

-Don't, Bianca.- Aric met my eyes, his pupils dilated with fear. *-Please.-*

I tasted his panic—sharp with the iron flavor of blood. I was suddenly certain his fear wasn't for himself.

It should have been. The brigands might think they had a prize stallion now, but when he transformed at sunset, they would kill him, too.

Wait. Sunset. Was it possible . . .

My gaze moved to the horizon. The sun had descended below the blanket of clouds. Now it rested in the dip between two mountain peaks, its lower edge just shy of touching the earth.

The woman finished her cursory search and turned back to the other two brigands. "Nothing. That's it."

"Rotting waste of a day," cursed the man. "What is she, the poorest noble in Gildenheim?"

I could almost have laughed. It was so far from the truth, and yet painfully close.

But their leader's next words carved even the thought of laughter out at the root.

"We're done here, then," she said. "Cut her throat and leave her for the wyrdwolves."

22

The blond woman drew her dagger, its steel darkened with old blood.

"Wait!" The plea burst out of me, unplanned, desperate. "I'm worth more alive than dead."

The blond woman lowered the dagger. She glanced at her companions questioningly.

"And why is that?" asked their leader, easing her pistol slightly towards the earth.

-Bianca,- Aric said, his tone sharp with desperation, *-please, whatever you're planning, don't do it. Beg them for mercy. Grovel if you have to. Please, just . . . don't die.-*

I flicked a startled glance at him. I knew he needed me, but . . . the way he spoke, it sounded like he *cared* about me. As a person, not just an ally.

Impossible. It was only our truce talking. And the brigands had made their intentions clear—I had to try. Otherwise we would both end up dead.

"I'm a Damarian Adept," I said, ignoring Aric's warning. "The strongest one alive. You have no idea what the Council of Nine would pay to get me back."

"She does have a Damarian accent," observed the man. "But she doesn't have a witch's eyes."

I smiled viciously at him, showing my teeth. "Care to get a closer look?"

I had the light in my favor. The sun was nearly at the horizon. Shadows stretched long, and the road was swiftly dropping into gloaming.

Any moment now.

The outlaws were looking at each other, their hesitation plain—a weakness I could leverage. I kept talking, the words pouring out in a barrage. "I'll prove it. I can transform matter into any form I like. I'll demonstrate my power on my horse right now." I switched to Damarian, praying the brigands wouldn't know more than a few common phrases of the tongue. "*Asphyxiation, whippersnapper, pulchritude—*"

"Stop that chanting," the leader barked.

"*Indigestion,*" I continued, pouring every ounce of power into my voice that I could, "*discombobulation, fripperies—*"

The dark-haired woman raised her pistol, her face livid.

The sun sank below the mountains.

"*Décolletage!*" I finished desperately.

Light burst across the road. The white horse vanished. The other horses, the real ones, spooked en masse. The two brigands on foot scattered, trying in vain to avoid flailing hooves and surging equine bodies. The dark-haired woman yelled as her own steed reared, throwing her to the ground.

I didn't wait to watch the chaos unfold. I threw myself at the leader's horse, seizing it by the reins, and scrambled onto its back. I reached a hand down for Aric.

"Quick! Get up behind me!"

Desperation lent us both strength. He swung into the saddle and locked his arms around my waist. I kicked my heels into the horse's sides.

"Go," I shouted at it, "go, go, *go*!"

The horse surged beneath me. We were airborne, sailing over the ditch. My teeth came together hard as we landed on the other side.

An explosion. A streak of what felt like fire across my ribs. We plunged away from the road and deep into the trees, Aric's arms so tight around my waist I could barely breathe.

Shouts rose behind us but quickly faded into the distance. I clutched the reins as branches whipped my legs. The forest closed around us, dark and grasping; we crashed onwards, hurdling fallen logs and veering around trunks. If the brigands gave chase, I couldn't hear them over the pounding of the horse's hooves.

My head swam, dizziness washing through me. Something was wrong. I was used to having flares, but not like this—as if the world were peeling itself away in slow layers, everything becoming gradually more distant, the wind roaring louder and louder in my ears until it sounded almost like a lupine howl . . .

I only realized my legs had loosened from the horse's flanks when I slid from its back, landing on my side with an impact that jolted white-hot agony through my entire frame. The world went momentarily black.

"Bianca!" Aric's face filled my vision. He'd turned the horse around, come back for me. He reached for me, then drew back with a hiss. A dark, wet substance covered his palm. "Rot it, you should have told me you were bleeding!"

"Oh," I murmured. "That's why everything hurts."

The fire across my ribs had spread, growing from kindling to all-consuming blaze. I dragged in a shallow breath that stabbed like a dagger. Just enough light remained to see that my shirt was dark with a spreading stain. Oh. That was the blood. I recalled the explosion as the horse bolted. Now I could place the sound: I'd been shot.

"Rot it," Aric hissed. "I need something to stop the bleeding. A shirt, or . . . or . . ."

A manic giggle rose in my throat. He was completely naked.

"It's not funny," Aric snapped. "Get up. We have to find help. You're losing too much blood."

I blinked up at him. His visage spun nauseating circles above me. "Can't." Words came thick and slow as cold honey. "Not strong enough."

"You *are* strong enough." Aric knelt, his knees darkening with dirt as he sank to the earth. "Give me your arm. We have to get you back on the horse."

Dutifully, I tried to push myself upright. My vision swam sickeningly. I dropped my head back to the earth with a moan.

Aric hauled my arm around his shoulders. His hands slipped, slick with my blood. "Get *up*, Bianca! I need you to help me here!"

Pine needles dug into my cheek. The ground didn't feel as cold as I'd expected. "Leave me," I mumbled. "Get to . . . Tatiana."

Aric swore. Then the ground swooped away from me in a dizzying rush. Pain flashed across my vision like a thousand dark stars. He'd picked me up.

I whimpered and turned my face into Aric's bare chest, but he wasn't letting me slip away into peaceful quiet. An agonized blur of movement. A red-hot poker grating across my ribs. Then, somehow—through Aric's sheer force of will—we were both on horseback. Aric gripped the reins with one hand, his other arm holding me against him.

"Don't you dare fall again," Aric ordered, his voice snapping with the force of command. And then we were moving, the forest a blur of grey twilight, the trees dark and skeletal. I buried my face in Aric's neck. He was warm, too warm. Dimly, I realized that I was dangerously cold. The thought was too distant to seem important. The wind was howling—no, it really was a chorus of wolves, their voices on the verge of forming words. *Wyrdwolves.* The horse spooked beneath me, and Aric swore again.

"Stay awake, Bianca," Aric snapped. "They can't have you. You're not allowed to die. I *order* you not to die, understand?"

I lacked the strength to respond, even to release the unexpected laugh that flickered within me like a light in the darkness. As if a king's order could keep me alive. He wasn't even a proper king. Not yet crowned.

Time distilled into sensations. The fire spreading in my side. Wind teasing my hair. Aric's warmth against me. The jolt of a strange horse's stride. And then, in the darkness, an unexpected bloom of firelight from an open window, warm as a lover's embrace.

The horse nickered, the sound splitting the night. A door flew open.

A face peered into mine from below: golden eyes keen as a hawk's, features sharp as if chiseled, hair that gleamed in the firelight.

"Well," a woman's voice said in Gilden, "would you look what the Lady brought us."

I slid from horseback into ready arms, and into darkness.

An owl hooting in the distance. The pungent scent of smoke, laced with the aroma of drying herbs. The heavy weight of wool over my legs. The flicker of greenish firelight playing over whitewashed walls. Pain throbbing in my right side.

I was alive.

I blinked my surroundings into focus. I lay on my back, covered by blankets, surrounded by rough plaster walls. Sunlight shafted through the window, making swirling dust motes glow like stars. A fire burned low in the hearth, embers shifting in a radiant dance. Bundles of drying herbs hung from the rafters. A woven rag rug, a muted spiral of colors, covered the earthen floor. The room held three other beds, all neatly made, all empty.

"You're awake." A girl's voice spoke from somewhere near my feet.

I turned my head towards the sound, the motion washing dizziness through my skull. The speaker was a child of ten or so, her hazel gaze bright with curiosity. Her hands clicked in her lap, busy with knitting needles. When the light caught her eyes, they sparkled with gold flecks like mica.

"Aric," I tried to ask. My voice came out as the faintest whisper.

"Don't be afraid," the girl said. She spoke in Gilden. "You're safe here."

"How—" I tried, in the same language. "Where—"

"You're at a greenhaven," the girl said. When I frowned, not recognizing the word, she tried again. "A place where greenwitches gather. This is the infirmary. My aunt tended your wound."

Cautiously, I lifted my hand to my side. Through the clean shirt I only now realized I was wearing, I traced the outline of bandages.

Memory flooded back in a torrent. The trio of outlaws. Fleeing through the forest. *Aric.*

Urgency surged through me. I had to find Aric and make sure he was all right.

I started to sit up. Immediately, a wave of pain crashed over me, stealing my breath. I fell back onto the pillows with a strangled gasp.

"My aunt said that you're not to move," the girl added belatedly.

I breathed through the pain until it ebbed to the previous dull ache. "But—my husband—I need—"

The door to the hut creaked open. "The only thing you need," a new voice said crisply, "is to lie down and let yourself *heal.*"

A woman who must be a greenwitch stood in the doorway, fists on hips. Eyes keen as spyglasses and speckled with gold, fair hair liberally shot through with grey. I recognized her face. It was the one I'd seen as I slid from the stolen horse's back.

Tattoos like green vines twined up her forearms. Surely it was only the flicker of firelight that made them appear to be moving.

"Try and get up again before that spell's set, and the only place you're going for the next three weeks is the chamber pot." The greenwitch's voice was brisk, no-nonsense, like the sweep of a broom. She cast a look of aspersion at the girl. "You were supposed to keep her from moving."

"I'm sorry, auntie. She only just woke up." The girl who'd been watching me stood up sheepishly. Knitting spilled from her lap, and she made a grab to catch her ball of yarn as it ran a yellow thread towards the corner. I blinked. Were my injuries making me hallucinate, or did the girl's knitting sparkle with the light of an unfinished spell?

The greenwitch scooped up the errant ball as it rolled past her feet and tossed it back to her niece. "Next time, come get one of us immediately. It takes only moments for stitches to tear. Now put your crafts away and get to your luncheon. Your fathers are waiting." Her face softened. "You did well."

The girl bundled up her knitting and ducked out the door with a tiny smile. The greenwitch shut the portal after her and crossed the floor in three steps. She moved the stool to the head of the bed and seated herself on it. Up close, she carried the bitter-sweet scents of soap and burnt sage.

"To answer the questions I'm sure you're burning to ask," the greenwitch said, "yes, your husband is safe. No, he's not hurt. Yes, he's currently a horse. No, he's not in any danger, and no one is going to know you're here. This is a greenhaven. All patients are protected while they're under our care, no matter who they are or what they've done."

My mind was as clouded as a winter day, heavy with waiting snow. I struggled to clear my thoughts. So Aric had transformed again—of course, it was daylight. "Where . . . who . . ."

"I'm a greenwitch. In case you hadn't gathered." It definitely wasn't the firelight: the tattoos really *were* moving, as if they were a living part of the woman's skin. "Your husband is safe. Resting. I promised him we would heal you. Now, don't go disturbing the magic and prove me wrong."

I touched the shirt above my bandage again, feeling the ridges of extra linen. *Disturbing the magic.* Panic flared. She'd cast magic on me. The magic of living things—expressly forbidden by the Adept Guild.

The greenwitch was watching me, her gaze sharp as a scalpel. "Shocking, isn't it? To discover your Adepts could have been healing people all along instead of inventing ways to blow them up? Don't worry, girl, you won't start sprouting hooves or horns. I only sped along what your body already wanted to do."

The greenwitch handed me a tin cup of water. I managed a few sips. It carried the cool taste of peppermint, along with the sharpness of other herbs I didn't recognize. My panic subsided. I didn't *feel* any different—other than the pain, which was mercifully much less than before.

"How bad is it?" My voice felt like a rasp sliding along my throat, but at least it was a full sentence.

"You'll live. The bullet wasn't deep, and it's out now. You have a cracked rib, probably from falling off the horse, but most of the damage was blood loss and shock. You'll be well enough to travel in a day or two—*if* you keep still long enough for the poultice to finish its work."

"And Aric . . ."

"Is perfectly fine. You can see him after sunset. I draw the line at allowing horses into the infirmary."

The greenwitch reached towards a bowl beside the bed and snapped her fingers. Smoke began to rise, herbal and languid. She stood, smoothing down her skirts.

"Now, sleep."

The smoke curled into waves. I wanted to ask the greenwitch more, but the drifting coils lulled me. They carried me away, and all I could do was fall into a slumber laced with verdant dreams.

23

Day slid into dusk, and I slid with it, drifting in and out of sleep. I had no means of ascertaining how much time had passed. But finally, I woke to the soft rush of rain and the warmth of a hand holding mine. Fingers larger than my own laced between my knuckles, a thumb rubbing circles on my palm. It wasn't unpleasant. Actually, rather the contrary.

My eyes fluttered open. The hand snatched away from mine, as quickly as if I'd stung its owner.

A cool breeze whispered in through the half-shuttered windows, bringing with it the cold scent of rainfall. Drops pattered on the roof, striking like musical notes. It was nighttime, and I was in the greenwitch infirmary.

Beside me, perched on the edge of the low stool as if ready to take flight, was Aric. Fully human and dressed in yet another ill-fitting set of clothes, this time too long and rolled up at the wrist. A fine growth of golden stubble shaded his jawline, and the dark circles under his eyes had deepened like inverse moons. I'd slept well, but from the way he looked, he might not have rested since our wedding night.

But he was alive. And here. The greenwitch hadn't lied to me. Relief lightened my chest, taking with it some of my pain and fatigue.

I tried to speak; swallowed; tried again. "Are you hurt?" My voice felt and sounded like the crunch of a footstep on gravel.

Aric shook his head. His hands were on his lap now, fingers running nervously along the spine of a book balanced across his knees—how he'd managed to acquire it, since we'd left our saddlebags stranded on the road, was beyond me. The sensation of a hand in mine . . . surely I'd imagined that. Aric would never hold my hand.

"I'm fine," he said, his voice low and lilting. "How are you feeling?"

I paused to consider. Clean bandages wrapped my side where the bullet had grazed. I pressed gingerly on the area, assessing my injuries. My ribs ached, but it was the dull ache of an old bruise, not the wildfire of last night. I couldn't even tell where the bullet had struck me. Whatever magic the greenwitch had cast, it was potent.

"Better," I said. "What time is it?"

"There are no clocks here, but the sun set perhaps an hour ago. They said you were asleep all day. Do you feel up to eating? The greenwitch said it would help."

I thought wryly of how she'd scolded the girl for letting me move. "If I'm allowed to."

"She said it was fine. Just to be careful when you sit up."

I pushed myself up on my elbows. Aric reached out a hand as if to help me; hesitated; drew it back. He rested his palm on the book instead. I glanced at the title and couldn't read it; the combination of archaic Gilden and overly ornate calligraphy was more than I cared to decipher.

I turned back the blanket and swung my legs over the side of the cot, sitting upright in a single motion. The room swooped beneath me, and Aric hastily set his book aside and reached out to steady me. I reflexively put my hands on his chest, bracing myself. So that was why the greenwitch had said to be careful.

Aric caught my arms. Keeping me from falling, the way he had last night. His scent teased me again, ink and parchment and something headier. His pulse thrummed beneath my palms. My own heart beat faster in response.

Our eyes met. Aric swallowed.

"Are you sure you're feeling well enough to sit up?" he asked.

"Yes," I said, though I'd lost track of precisely what I was agreeing to. It was hard to remember to breathe—definitely due to the bandages around my ribs, not the fact that Aric was so close I could have counted his lashes.

Aric released me, carefully, pausing to make sure I didn't keel over onto my side. The room felt like it had turned from spring all the way around to winter again.

"Lean back against the pillows, at least," Aric said. "You might get dizzy again."

I allowed him to prop them up against the headboard and help me recline at an angle. Normally, I hated being coddled and tended as if I couldn't take care of myself. It was a sign of the weakness I couldn't overcome by force of will. But for whatever reason, with Aric's hands guiding me, I didn't mind nearly as much as usual.

"Here. It's some sort of stew." Aric handed me an earthenware bowl whose contents steamed faintly. I eyed it with suspicion, poking at it with the wooden spoon provided. Potatoes, celery, carrots, and a hearty helping of herbs whose fragrance made my stomach growl in a most uncouth way. Greenwitches did magic with herbs, didn't they?

"I had some already," Aric said, noting my wariness. "It's not poisoned."

I sniffed the pottage again. "Potatoes are a nightshade."

Aric's mouth twitched into a wry smile. "If a bullet didn't kill you, I'm sure you can survive bits of boiled potato."

I took a tentative bite. It was good, and I didn't detect any immediate effects other than the savor flooding my mouth. The best poisons had a delayed effect, though.

Not that I genuinely thought the greenwitch would try to kill me. Yesterday I'd faced people who truly wanted me dead. If not for Aric, and a generous dash of luck, we wouldn't have survived. *I* wouldn't have survived.

I looked up at Aric. "Thank you," I said. "If you hadn't brought me here, I would have died."

He was tracing the edges of the book again. If I hadn't known he was constitutionally incapable of harming a book, I might have worried for its integrity. "I should be thanking you instead," he said quietly. "You saved my life. Both of our lives. That's twice now."

I stabbed at a potato with the tip of the spoon, watched it split. "That's not exactly how I would describe what happened."

"How *would* you describe it, then?"

I stared into the bowl. Now neither of us wanted to meet the other's eyes. The tension between us stretched as taut as a lyre string, every word plucking vibrations along its length.

"As a failure," I said. "I saw the danger coming and should have kept us safe. But I didn't do anything but let it arrive. I didn't even fight. Instead, I got myself injured and lost us time we can't afford, not to mention our remaining supplies. Now we're even worse off than before, thanks to my weakness."

"I don't understand why you persist in calling yourself weak, when you're clearly anything but."

My appetite had vanished. I set the bowl in my lap so my shaking hands wouldn't make it spill. "If you think that, you clearly don't know me at all."

"I know you enough to know your strength. Whatever you think to the contrary."

His gaze was gentle, and that was something I couldn't take.

I was used to keeping up my defenses, holding my ground under attack. But Aric left me with nothing to prove myself against.

I'd spent most of my life keeping everyone at a sword's distance, maintaining my shields so no one could see the weakness within and twist it to their own ends. But Aric had seen past my defenses, and he kept coming back anyway. He hadn't rejected me. Hadn't used me.

What if he was telling the truth? What if I wished he was?

Aric took the bowl from me, setting it aside. Seas, why did he have to be so gentle? I didn't deserve gentle. Once again I had let down my family. My country.

My husband.

Aric was still watching me—brows drawn slightly together as he puzzled me out, like a foreign script he was just on the verge of reading. I turned my hands palm up, remembering the warmth of his hand on mine. The gilt scar from our wedding gleamed in the firelight.

"Aric." My voice emerged as thin as silken thread. "What are we?"

Hesitantly, he touched the mark on my fourth finger. Skin to skin. Scar to scar. "What do you want us to be?"

I swallowed, hard.

"I'm afraid," I said, releasing a truth. Revealing my deepest weakness. "I'm afraid of wanting what I know I can't have."

A muscle flickered in Aric's jaw. "What makes you so certain you can't have it?"

It took every ounce of my remaining strength to not look away. "I'm fairly certain it doesn't want me back."

A flush bloomed pink as dawn on Aric's face, spreading down his neck towards the V of his shirt collar. "Maybe . . . *it* . . . thinks the same about you."

Seas, I was drowning in him. "I don't know why 'it' would have drawn that conclusion."

Aric's flush deepened. His hands tightened on the book on his knees, and I had the treacherous thought that I wondered what they would feel like on me.

"You're my wife," he said, abandoning our feeble pretense that we might be talking about anything else, and my heart stuttered at the word. "But I'm all too aware you were forced into this marriage. I've never expected you to want me, much less love me."

My apprehension seized onto the easier emotion of anger. I flared up, snatching my hand back to my chest. "That's rich, coming from you. I don't understand this game you're playing. You look at me as if you want to kiss me, and then you pull away as if I'm poison. You can hardly even bear to share a bed with me, and yet you hold my hand while saying that I don't want you—"

Aric shook his head sharply, his eyes locking on mine. "It's not a game. It's a weakness. I'm afraid, too."

His words sliced through my protest like broken glass. I stared at him, my thoughts as scattered as summer stars.

"Oh." I could barely manage a whisper.

"Bianca," Aric said. My name was as sharp as a hook from his lips, reeling me towards him whether I willed it or no. He leaned forward, bracing himself on the headboard so that he hovered over me. "There's never been any question that I wanted you. I wanted you even when I thought you intended to kill me, even though I knew I should be running as far from you as I could get. I wanted you to my own humiliation."

I stared up at him, speechless.

"You terrify me, Bianca." Aric was close enough that I could feel the whisper of his breath. "I can't stop wanting you, even if it breaks me."

Heat rushed to my face, my stomach, bloomed between my

legs. The way he looked at me, hungry and tentative and tender all at once, he couldn't be telling anything but the truth.

"Aric," I whispered, a confession for us both, "I've wanted you from the first moment I saw you."

Aric's eyes went wide. He lifted a hand towards my face as he had in the inn, hesitated before making contact.

I made an impatient sound. Before I could lose my nerve, I seized him by the collar with both hands, pulled him in close, and kissed him.

Aric froze, his entire body rigid with surprise. Then, all at once, he softened into me, his mouth matching perfectly to mine.

I'd thought Aric cold, like stone or steel. Now I realized how wrong I was. He burned like untamed magic, like the slice of a blade against skin. His kiss sang through my veins, lighting every nerve in my body with a cascade of sparks.

Aric made a low sound that sent heat rushing through my core. His hands claimed the curve of my waist, his thumb digging into the jut of my hip. He slid one hand to my stomach, finding the hem of my shirt and slipping beneath it. Cool air touched my skin; by contrast, Aric's hands blazed where they traced my ribs, skirting over the bandages. Too light. Too gentle. I arched into him, the ache in my ribs going unheeded against my need to close the distance.

Only for Aric to stop. Pull back. He withdrew his hands, leaving me hot and craving with need.

"Bianca." He bit his lip, sending a frustrated pulse of yearning through me. "We don't have to do this. I—I don't expect—"

Doubt speared through me, cooling my desire. I remembered our wedding night, just before everything had gone so disastrously wrong. *Let's get this over with.* The visible strain in his trousers' fabric suggested Aric didn't feel the same reluctance now, at least not physically, but his hesitation wasn't something I could ignore.

I swallowed hard. To want and not be wanted in return felt

like laying my heart bare to the blade. But we'd started this, and it was too late to pretend I hadn't opened myself to the possibility of being hurt. Whatever damage happened next was something I had to survive.

"Aric," I said softly. "Do *you* not want to do this?"

He shook his head, once, sharply. "That's not what I meant. I just—I don't—I know you value your duty. And I don't want you to feel like consummating our marriage is something you have to do, if it isn't what you truly want for yourself."

So that was why he'd drawn away at the inn—he *had* wanted to kiss me, but he'd read my own desire as stemming from obligation. For once, however, duty was the furthest thing from my mind.

I met his eyes. "Aric. I don't know how to make it any clearer that I want you. All of you. In every sense of the word. In a way that has nothing at all to do with duty."

Aric swallowed. He sat beside me on the bed, putting us eye to eye. I lifted my hand, letting my fingertips trail along his jaw, rough with a trace of golden stubble.

"Say it again." His voice was hoarse. "That you want me."

"I want you, Aric." I drove my gaze into his, showing him the truth. "I want you even if it breaks me, too."

Aric caught my hand and pressed it to his mouth. His eyes were soft, pupils blown wide with desire. It gratified me to see him undone.

"Tell me how you want me, then." His fingers traced my waistband, making me arch into his touch, aching for him to slide lower. "Tell me how to break you."

Seas have mercy on me. The place between my legs was molten, and he hadn't even touched me there yet.

My mouth was dry. I moistened my lips, hot with the awareness of how Aric followed the motion, his gaze dropping to my mouth before returning to my eyes. "I want you on your knees."

Slowly, holding my gaze, Aric sank to his knees on the floor.
"I—I want you to touch me."

He splayed his hands over my thighs. His thumb moved upwards, brushing lightly across my center. Even through the layers of fabric, his touch sweetly burned. My breath quickened. I tipped my head back and braced my weight on my hands, a groan escaping my throat. I needed more.

"Tell me, Bianca." Aric brushed his thumb over me again. "Tell me what you want."

How could he expect me to form words when he was unraveling me like this? With an impatient sound, I fumbled for my waistband, trying to get my trousers down over my hips. Aric gave a startled laugh. He slid his hands beneath my thighs, lifting me up to assist me.

The motion sent a wash of dizziness through me. I winced. I'd forgotten my injuries.

Aric froze. "Did I—"

I leaned forward to meet him, tangled my hands through his hair, and kissed him again, muffling his question. He laughed into my mouth, surprised, and then his hands were on me. He eased my trousers down the rest of the way and cast them aside on the floor. His fingers traced my inner thighs, delicious heat blooming everywhere he touched.

Aric's mouth moved to my jawline. "I don't want to hurt you."

The nausea had already passed, and I'd experienced worse on countless days of my life. I could tolerate ten times that just to keep Aric pressed against me. "You won't."

I shuddered as his lips scorched a trail of kisses down my throat.

"Then keep telling me what you want. Take me with you."

I shivered again. How was he holding himself together so well? I was already close to the edge, and he'd barely even touched me.

"I want you inside me," I whispered.

A low sound escaped Aric. Maybe he was closer than I'd realized. He pushed me onto my back—gently, almost too gentle despite my injuries—and climbed onto the bed, kneeling between my thighs. He slipped a hand between my legs. His thumb circled my most sensitive spot, and I arched into him, a small, desperate cry breaking free.

"Please," I gasped.

Aric slid two fingers into me, his thumb returning to the center of my need. A shudder racked through my entire body. My hands clenched on the blankets as he found a rhythm. Seas, I was drowning. He was the one on his knees, and yet I was the one at his mercy.

It wasn't enough. I needed to break him, too.

I opened my eyes. Aric was watching me, flushed and vulnerable with his own desire, hair disheveled from where I'd run my hands through it. His eyes were like the sky; I could lose myself in them, counting stars forever.

"Not like this," I managed. "I want you closer."

I dragged the hem of his shirt free of his trousers and reached for him, my hands skating across the plane of his stomach. Aric stilled, his breath catching.

"Are you sure?" he whispered.

He really *was* going to break me. "Virtues, yes, I'm sure." I dragged in a breath, trying to collect my senses. Maybe it wasn't for my sake he was hesitant. "Unless you don't want that?"

"No, I—I do." Tentatively, Aric placed his free hand on top of mine. Pressing me against him. Accepting my touch. Both of us held still, poised on a precipice.

Aric took a breath, as if making a decision. And then he turned my hand, gently, so that my fingers slid beneath his waistline, dipping into the crease of his thigh. His hand tightened on my wrist, then released me, giving me another chance to pull away.

"Show me. Please." His words were only a breath, but I knew what he meant. *Show me that you want me. That you want* this.

I did. I had never wanted anything more. I slid my hand deeper and closed my fingers around him.

Aric's eyes fluttered, a spasm running through his entire body. "Bianca," he groaned, and then he kissed me again, his mouth hungry, desperate, as if a dam had broken and now his desire poured out in a torrent. His hand faltered in its rhythm. I needed him closer. Nearer. I gave him a long stroke that sent a tremor through him again, then released him, reaching for his hips, drawing him towards me to claim him as mine.

He paused to pull his shirt over his head. I helped him with his trousers, hurried, eager. Then he was over me on hands and knees, his hair a tangled mane around his face, his eyes like the heart of a fire. He was so beautiful it took my breath away. I'd seen him naked before, but not like this. Never like this, hard and wanting, nothing of himself hidden away.

"I want you, Aric," I told him again, and pulled him towards me, opening myself to him.

He was gentle at first, sliding into me slowly, the way made easy by my own hot want. It was my turn to tremble as he sank deep within me, his mouth lowering to claim mine. Aric moved his hips, long, slow thrusts so exquisite I could hardly bear it. Oh seas, he was going to shatter me. I would fall into a thousand pieces, completely undone. There was nothing of my walls left to hide behind.

I tilted my hips so he could take me deeper. Aric responded to my needs as readily as if we'd done this a hundred times, moving faster, harder, relinquishing my mouth and gripping my waist instead to pull me into him. I arched into the pillows with a cry. He lifted my leg over his shoulder and kissed my inner thigh as he thrust deep into me, his thumb finding my center—

Like a wave, I crested and broke. Shudders rippled through

me as I fell apart, crying his name—a plea for mercy, a surrender. Aric followed me over the edge moments later. With a deep
groan, he pulled out and spent himself over the sheets, burying
his face in the crook of my neck.

For uncounted moments we lay tangled together, both of
us breathing hard as our bodies slowly cooled. I ran my fingers
through Aric's hair, reveling in the silken feel of it. In the wonder
of having license to touch him freely.

Aric shook himself and lifted his head from my neck. He
looked dazed, as if he couldn't quite believe it, either.

"Stars, Bianca," he whispered, saying my name like a prayer.
"You're incredible."

I kissed him, deep and slow. Showing him again, with my
body as well as my words, how much I wanted him.

By the time we broke apart for air, he was hardening again. An
answering heat rekindled within my core. Perhaps it was time to
see what else his previous lovers had taught him—whether he was
as adventurous as I hoped.

I reached for him. Aric raised his head to look at me, lifting
one brow incredulously.

"Truly?" he asked. "Were you not satisfied?"

"Oh, I was satisfied." I gave him a wicked smile. "But I'm not
done. This time, I want you to tell me what *you* want."

Aric laughed helplessly, as if I'd finally bested him. And then
he obliged, whispering all the things he wanted to do to me, and
then ensuring I had ample demonstration.

His mouth, learning the shape of my body. His hands, pas-
sionate but gentle, leaving trails of fire everywhere he brushed
against my skin. Every touch a question: *Do you want this?* Every
touch an answer: *Yes, and yes, and yes.*

24

The greenwitch woke us shortly before dawn. By then Aric and I were clothed again, but we hadn't left the bed. Exhaustion had claimed us both after a while, and we'd fallen asleep side by side, our fingers interlaced.

I rubbed sleep from my eyes and nudged Aric awake as the greenwitch removed her short cape, the grey fabric spotted dark with fat raindrops, and hung it beside the door. It settled neatly into place, assuming a shape worn familiar by the passage of years. She stooped over the washbasin to clean her hands. As she rolled up her sleeves, I tried to catch another look at the tattoos twining up her arms. Today they looked like ordinary ink. Nothing magical. But I didn't quite believe their innocuous appearance.

"The rain's stopping," our host said over her shoulder. "Should be clear for travel within the hour."

I sat up eagerly. We'd wasted so much time on my account. Our chances of making it to the border and back before the coronation dwindled with each delay, and if we couldn't make it . . . I didn't want to witness the chaos that would unfold. "Am I healed enough to ride?"

The greenwitch dried her hands and crossed to the bed. Aric moved to the stool to make room. My hand felt empty without his in it, even though I'd lived that way my whole life.

Our host eyed me critically, as if I were a piece of knitting that had dropped a stitch. "Let's see the wound."

I lifted my shirt so she could unwind the bandages. The greenwitch's fingers were cool and dry against my skin.

"Hmm. Well, the rib's healed, but it will continue to ache for a while. Flesh mends fast. Bones take time." She gave me a pointed look. "But I don't expect that will stop you from doing exactly what you think is best."

I flushed, suddenly certain she knew what Aric and I had been up to.

I looked down at my side, where the bandages had been, and sucked in a startled breath. I'd expected to see an open wound, perhaps held together by stitches. Instead there was only a pink scar, tender and slightly raised, tracing across my ribs.

I lowered my shirt and looked up at the greenwitch, not quite believing my eyes. The Adept magic I was familiar with could build technological wonders, but it had little effect on the body. After the number of things they'd tried on me, I ought to know. "How did you do that?"

"Magic flows through everything. It just needs a bit of guidance." The greenwitch gathered up my blood-browned bandages, no longer needed, and tossed them into a wash basket. "You'd heal faster if you slept again. You need it badly."

I didn't have time for sleep. "Can I ride, then?" I asked, not trying to disguise my impatience.

"Another day of rest would be better. But riding won't kill you." She looked at Aric. "It's almost sunrise. The stable behind the infirmary is clean. I assume you can find your way back there."

I turned my head towards the window. The sliver of sky showing through the shutters had brightened from midnight to periwinkle: sunrise was imminent.

Aric stood. "Thank you," he told the greenwitch. He turned to me and gave me a smile so small I almost missed it. "I'll meet you outside when you're ready, Bianca."

He slipped out the door. As it closed behind him, it felt like some essential part of me had left the room, too.

The greenwitch knew of Aric's curse. A thought struck me, and with it a tentative hope.

"My husband," I said to the greenwitch. "His curse. Can you help him?"

She shook her head. "I deal in wounds and broken things. Greenwitch magic isn't like that."

"But it's still magic."

The greenwitch's lips flattened pensively. "It's more than just the flavor of the spell. The particular enchantment on your husband is unusually strong. A temporary transformation—for instance, air into light . . ." She snapped her fingers, and a pale glow appeared on her palm. A miniature star that pulsed and then winked out. "Any competent practitioner can do that. But a long-term transformation? One that persists for days, and cycles back and forth? That sounds more like blood magic."

My hand closed around the locket resting beneath my shirt. It pressed into my palm, warm from the heat of my body. I didn't understand. Tatiana's magic was wild, unpredictable—and strong. She'd once enchanted the door of the Council of Nine's meeting chamber to cackle maniacally whenever anyone passed through it, until after a week of fruitless attempts to remove the spell the Adepts had finally replaced the door entirely. It had still been chuckling gleefully to itself as it was carted away. But Tatiana couldn't have cast blood magic, not if what Aric had told me about the practice was true. Besides, I knew my sister—she wouldn't put blood into her spells.

I thought of the scars from our wedding night now crossing my palms, a gilt map of an unplanned future. The same marks

Aric had said were a sign of blood magic. A chill coursed through me, and I curled my hand tighter around the locket. Surely I hadn't inadvertently cast blood magic. If I had, wouldn't I have known?

The greenwitch had to be wrong. Tatiana would know the answer. We just had to reach her first.

"Here. This came for you." The greenwitch rummaged in her pocket. "The chicken who delivered it gave me an earful. Didn't like flying all the way from Arnhelm through the rain."

"Chickens can't fly," I protested.

"Tell that to the chicken." The greenwitch produced a small scroll and held it out to me. Another message from Evito. His delivery methods were certainly unconventional.

I read the missive twice, hoping I'd misinterpreted the ambassador's sharply slanting script. A third perusal confirmed it beyond a doubt. My heart kicked into my throat.

I pushed back the blankets and swung my legs over the side of the bed.

"I'm going to talk to my husband," I told the greenwitch.

She shrugged. "Suit yourself. I've done what I can for you."

The room swayed when I stood up, but I braced myself on the headboard until the ground steadied under me. I found my shoes and crossed the hut, my steps as cautious as a toddling child's, then stepped outside into the dawn.

Outside, the rain had stopped, leaving only a languid drip from eaves and branches; birds were trilling a chorus the finest court musicians would have envied. The trees were silhouetted against the sky, dark shapes like bristle-tipped spears. The mountains shone pale in the waxing light. I had only a few minutes before Aric transformed.

Several other buildings were set back among the trees, neat garden beds between them. A few bold shoots prodded their way loose from the dark earth, risking the teeth of another frost. Gentle puffs of smoke rose from the houses' chimneys and blended into the mist. A worn track in the muddy earth led past the dwellings to wind around the back of the infirmary. I followed it, slower than I would have liked, leaning on each tree trunk and fence rail I passed.

The trail ended at a small but serviceable stable. A piebald horse thrust its head over one of the stable doors as I approached, whickering hopefully.

I stopped in confusion. "Aric? You were white before."

"And I thought you would be able to tell your own husband from a regular horse."

I turned. Aric, still human, stood in the next stall over, resting his elbows on the half door. He'd removed his shirt, and if my breath hadn't already been short from the effort of walking, I would have lost it now. Want surged through me with the force of a tidal wave. Being with him earlier was nowhere near enough. Having him once only made me want him more, a fire that grew hotter the more it was fed.

I arched an eyebrow. "I didn't realize you made a habit of stripping naked in strangers' stables."

Aric's flush was clear to see, even from a few steps away. Red as sunset against his pale cheeks, spreading down his bare neck towards his chest.

"I'm attempting to not waste any more clothing," he said. "I've gone through several sets in the past few days."

The corner of my mouth twitched. I wasn't certain what had happened to the clothing—shredded to pieces or vanished by magic—but it was true he'd left a trail of missing trousers along our route from Arnhelm.

"Whose horse is this?" I asked.

"Ours, as of last night. We rode her here. Although I offered her to the greenwitch in exchange for supplies for the road, so now I suppose she belongs to the greenhaven."

The horse—the real one—snorted. I rubbed her velvet nose, wishing I had more to offer her in exchange for saving our lives. I had so little to offer anyone, equine or otherwise. At least here she would be in better hands than with the brigands.

"You followed me," Aric said. It was an invitation, not an accusation.

I stepped towards him, clasping my hands behind my back to prevent myself from running them over every part of his body within reach. My eyes, however, roamed lower, crossing the plane of his chest before being thwarted in their journey by the stall's closed half door.

Right. I'd come here to tell him something important. If only I could pretend the news hadn't reached me—was allowing us a moment to be happy really so much to ask?

But I had neither time nor luxury for selfishness. "I received an update from Ambassador Dapaz. They're going through with the coronation—without you." I hesitated. "They're going to crown Lord Varin."

Aric went as still as an iced-over lake.

I knew he hadn't wanted to believe his half brother was behind the assassination attempt. He'd argued that Varin didn't want him dead. But we'd hoped that leaving the castle, pretending that Aric was dead in truth, would draw out the forces responsible. And our ploy had worked—faster than either of us could have anticipated. Varin must have been making his preparations for weeks, if not months: courting factions to gather the support he needed; secretly arranging the treaty's terms to lure a likely suspect to Gildenheim; and then arguing, under the aegis of a false grief, that with the equinox so close, Gildenheim couldn't afford to risk not crowning a ruler of the proper bloodline, even an illegitimate one. It explained why I'd been framed—it took suspicion off of Varin, and cleared the way for him to inherit. We had our proof, in actions if not in writing.

"There's more," I said reluctantly. "Marya has been arrested as a murder suspect. They found a bloodstained knife in her quarters."

"That's not possible." Aric's hands whitened on the stall door. "It's a setup. How could she have murdered me? I'm not dead. And even if I were—"

"I know." I laced my fingers through his. "I know she would never betray you."

"*Everyone* should know that. The entire court knows how close we are. Who gave the order to arrest her?"

"It has to be Varin," I said. "Marya knows you're alive. She must have been causing trouble for him—she wouldn't let him take the throne from you without a fight." I thought of how Aric warned Marya to be careful before we left. How she'd shrugged it off. If she and Aric were really as close as he'd said, of course someone with her temperament wouldn't have sat safely back and watched while an enemy plotted against her king.

Aric's fingers tightened on mine. His shoulders curved as if under a massive weight.

"It isn't right," he said. "All she's done is be loyal to me."

I put my hand on his cheek, leaning closer until he met my eyes again. "I know," I said softly. With an effort, I cleared the worry from my face. I could be a shield for us both. "But we can free her and set this right. We still have time. We just need to break the spell and get back to Arnhelm before the coronation."

Which was . . . if my count was right, on the third day from now. Only two full days to get to the border and back. Only two full days to stop a usurper and avert a war. Seas, it was so little time.

I met Aric's eyes. "We'll fix this together," I promised, hoping my vow was one I could fulfill. "All of it."

Aric raised his hands to my jaw, cupped my face as if it were something precious. "If anyone can, it's you."

In the final moments before sunrise, I pulled him to me and kissed him hard, trying to bury my fear and doubt. But they lingered, bitter against the sweetness of his lips. Aric might believe I could meet my promises. But I didn't share his confidence in myself.

25

We left the greenhaven shortly after. We'd lost our belongings to the brigands, but I saddled Aric with the piebald mare's tack, and the greenwitch supplied us with a satchel of provisions, including a tincture to prevent conception. By the Virtues' mercy, I still had the dagger I'd worn strapped to my wrist. My rapier was lost somewhere on the road—not that it had done me much good against the outlaws. All my training, and yet I had proved myself as useful as a dessert fork in a naval battle. Still, I felt better having a blade, even if I'd lost confidence in my ability to use it.

As we prepared to depart, our host held me back at the threshold. She handed me a waxed cloth bag full of what felt like pebbles. "Here. For when your stomach troubles you."

I took the bag from her warily. Its contents smelled strongly of peppermint. "What do you mean?"

She waved a hand, encompassing my entire body with the gesture. "Your aches. The abdominal pain. I've seen those symptoms before."

I barely prevented myself from taking a step back. I hadn't told her about my condition. Moreover, it had never occurred to me that it might not be unique to me. I'd always thought myself alone in my affliction. Was it possible that there were others like me—each of us hiding our symptoms, not realizing there were others just as afraid of being seen and judged?

"You're poisoning yourself," the greenwitch said. "That's the root of it."

I shook my head, recovering my composure. "I have an excellent apothecary. She would never—"

"I don't mean deliberately." The greenwitch cut me off. She studied me as if I were an interesting weed in her garden. "There's something afflicting your body. Figure out what's poisoning you and your symptoms will eventually stop. It won't cure you. But you won't have to live in pain."

It was such a mirror of my earlier conversation with Aric that the world seemed to double, as if time had repeated itself. I glanced at my equine husband, who was waiting near the stables, saddled and shifting his weight impatiently. He tossed his head, snorting, as a fly circled his hindquarters.

"Do you know what it is? The thing that's poisoning me?"

"No. There can be different causes for different people." She nodded at Aric, following my gaze. "But that husband of yours is clever, even if he was foolish enough to get himself horsified. He can help you figure it out."

I remembered all the questions Aric asked me when he learned of my condition. Not what was wrong with me. Not what I couldn't do. No, he wanted to understand the shape of my pain—studying it as an abstract problem, not the personal failing I'd always understood it to be. He was already seeking the answer, and he didn't even have a greenwitch's magical intuition. It was suddenly hard to breathe, and not because of my healing rib.

I turned back to the greenwitch. She was watching me with arms crossed, her eyes knowing. The tattoos were hidden again, folded beneath her sleeves.

"The peppermints should help," she said. "Use them sparingly. I put a little power into them."

I tucked the bag into the pocket of my coat.

"I don't know why you're helping us," I said. "But thank you."

The greenwitch smiled, sharp as a scalpel. "The Lady of the Wilds has her plans," she said. "Occasionally they involve we who serve her. Take care of the king. Be careful with your blood."

"What do you—"

My words cut short: she'd closed the door in my face.

A shiver ran down my spine like a cold drop of water. We'd never told her Aric was royal. I might have spoken his name in her presence—I wasn't certain now—but it was a common one in Gildenheim. It shouldn't have been enough to betray us. Or . . . had she recognized the blood magic scars on my hands and realized what they meant?

I forced myself to turn away from the door. The greenwitch had proved herself no threat to us, and we had many miles to cover. We needed to make up for lost time if we had any chance of returning to Arnhelm before the coronation.

I went to Aric and got up on his back with the help of a mounting stool.

"How far are we from the border?" I asked him. I'd lost any sense I had of Gilden geography, disoriented by the twists our route had taken.

He flicked his tail, considering. *-If we ride hard, I think we can make it to the inn by sunset.-*

I gripped the pommel and settled myself in the saddle, ensuring our satchel of provisions was secured.

"Then let's ride hard." Tatiana would be waiting for us by now, and she wouldn't let me down—she never had, no matter how often we fought or how deeply we disagreed. The sooner we reached her, the sooner we could repair everything I'd broken. The more chance we had to build something better in its stead.

I just hoped we weren't too late.

We rode hard. From the greenhaven, we emerged onto the main road earlier than I expected and were soon flying south. Aric's hooves tattooed a steady drumbeat on the thoroughfare. After the brigands, I tensed at every village we passed, fear needling an anxious line down my back.

But no one looked twice at us. In my common clothes, I was just an ordinary traveler on horseback. I had shed the bright trappings of my life, sloughed them away like a bird's molted feathers, and without them I was anonymous. It was surprisingly freeing to not be recognized for who I was. Not a duchess. Not an heir. Not anybody, except what I made of myself.

We passed through the village without incident and continued on. As we rejoined the main road, mist curled around the trees and obscured the mountaintops, slimming the world down to only Aric, and me, and the way forwards. As the day wore on and our elevation increased, the fog broke, surrendering to the clearest day I'd seen in Gildenheim—the sky as blue as ice.

But I was in little state to enjoy the day's beauty. As Aric's hooves ate away the miles, every one of my fears spoke up, each trying to make itself heard over the rest: My guilt over abandoning my retinue. Aric's curse. The impending coronation. The fear that now that I had gained Aric for my own, I was about to lose him for good.

All my life I'd hidden my heart, guarded myself with meaningless words and empty smiles, pretending that concealing my pain was the same as never feeling it. Under my parents' tutelage, I'd even learned to hide my condition—in their eyes, the worst of my flaws: a weakness I couldn't carve away through training or prac-

tice or sheer force of will. My parents had been forced to acknowledge, eventually, that my flares were unavoidable, but that didn't
mean they were acceptable. And they'd made it clear: I wasn't allowed failure in any other aspect. I had to be flawless. I had to be
a weapon, wielded for the advancement of my House and country.

Riding towards the border astride the husband I'd accidentally
cursed, I felt the farthest thing from flawless. I wasn't a weapon. I
was a hairpin, easily bent and readily discarded.

Yet Aric hadn't discarded me when he saw my flaws. Instead,
he'd seen a different sort of strength in me, one I'd never realized
I possessed. And his acceptance disarmed me more than any op-
position could. He'd reached past my defenses, and I had let him,
welcomed him, against the logic of everything I'd been taught. I
knew that wanting him was a blade that could be turned against
me. To love someone was to throw down your shields, lay your
heart bare, and watch as it was cut in two.

Love. The word stopped my thoughts short.

I hadn't allowed myself to consider whether I was falling in
love with Aric—but the possibility alone was dizzying. I had been
walking blithely along a trail I thought was certain, only to come
abruptly to a precipice. Now the drop plunged at my feet. Another step and I would fall.

But . . . surely this was different from what had happened with
Catalina. Aric was my husband. I'd married him out of duty; I
wasn't acting on a selfish impulse. I was strengthening our countries' ties, not jeopardizing Damaria's future.

Surely, in this case, it was all right to let myself want him. To
allow myself to memorize the sensation of his hand against my
palm, my neck, my hip. To lose myself momentarily in the warmth
of his lips and the depths of his eyes. Duty had bound us together,
and duty was safe.

There was no reason to feel this inkling of doubt. No reason to be afraid of what was happening between us. I wouldn't fall. I wouldn't drown.

But though I tried, I couldn't cast that feeling off. Not entirely. It spiraled through my core, a dark thread winding tighter and tighter around my all-too-open heart.

Meanwhile, oblivious to the bleak turn of my thoughts, the road unwound beneath us like a spool of pale ribbon. I'd expected we would need to rest frequently, but Aric, stronger and more confident now that he'd had time to adjust to his equine form, was determined to eke the use out of every moment of daylight. Halfway through the afternoon, my stomach began to cramp. I dug out one of the greenwitch's peppermints and ate it without saying anything to Aric; we couldn't afford to stop. The cool, sweet taste carried the bite of something more powerful, and to my relief, my nausea abated—though it didn't vanish entirely.

The land blurred by, town after forest after mountain pass. As we approached afternoon, I realized something subtle had shifted in the landscape: evergreen forests giving way to newly budding leaves, the land sloping gently downwards, the fresh taste of spring in the air. We'd crossed the bulk of the mountains and were rapidly approaching the border of Damaria.

As the sun brushed the horizon, the road rose upwards again towards a final mountain pass. In the valley before its crest, a well-maintained two-story inn waited by the roadside. A flagpole jutted from its eaves, bearing two crisp banners: the blue ninefold star of Damaria and the winged white horse of Gildenheim.

I swung down from the saddle, my legs trembling with fatigue, my stomach in knots.

We had made it. We had reached the border, and—assuming Tatiana was here—the answer to my husband's curse.

26

As it was already nearly sunset, we took the precaution of retreating a short distance into the trees so Aric wouldn't transform in front of inquiring eyes. A few minutes later, as the colors of dusk were bruising the horizon, we crossed the road and headed for the inn.

The building's courtyard was quiet, no other travelers in sight. A girl emerged to take our horses: a hostler, though she couldn't have been more than fourteen. She looked confused at the sight of Aric carrying a saddle with no steed in sight, but took it from him without question and promised to store it with the rest of the guests' tack.

I stopped her with a touch to the shoulder as she started to leave. "Are there any guests here from Damaria? A young woman, about my age and build?"

The girl's expression lit with recognition. "Oh yes. The lady said she was expecting a visitor. She was right—you *do* look like her. Though I expected someone more . . ."

Her voice faded, her cheeks flushing dark. I became suddenly, critically aware of the state of my clothes. Travel had done me no favors. My hair was a bird's nest, and I'd acquired a layer of grime that felt as indelible as varnish. The hostler didn't need to finish her sentence. I might share Tatiana's face, but I didn't look like a noble.

It didn't matter. My sister was here; that was the important part. She would plot a way out of this mess, just as she'd schemed her way into mischief dozens of times when we were younger. And despite my exhaustion and the nausea lapping at the periphery of my awareness, I felt lighter just at the thought of seeing her.

"Where can I find her?" I asked.

"She's staying on the second floor."

I left the girl to her duties and started towards the inn's front door. Halfway across the courtyard, I realized Aric hadn't followed.

I turned back to face him. "Aren't you coming?"

He cast a dubious look at the sky, where the first stars were brightening the vault. "Considering what happened the last time I entered an inn, I'm not sure that's wise."

"Tatiana's here," I said. "She can fix this before sunrise. Come with me."

I took his hand. Aric was resistant at first, but then wrapped his fingers around mine and let me draw him after me. The warmth of his palm was as welcome as a fire on a cold night.

The inn was clean, bright, lit by both the hearth and a host of pewter-backed candles lining the walls. It was early to light so many tapers, but as the glass-paned windows indicated, the place was doing well for itself. As the only inn at one of the few border crossings between Damaria and Gildenheim, they must pull in plenty of business from wealthy travelers. Like Tatiana.

The main room wasn't as busy as I'd feared; but again, it was barely after sunset. More travelers would probably file in with the arrival of proper darkness. Still, I held Aric's hand more tightly and headed towards the stairs, eager to be out of sight. I couldn't forget how we'd been targeted the last time we stayed at an inn—although, small mercy, we looked decidedly less royal now: Aric in his homespun from the greenwitch and I in garments so be-grimed they might have been brown to begin with.

At the top of the stairs, I hesitated, surveying a hallway lined with identical doors. I should have asked the hostler which room was Tatiana's.

But I didn't wonder for long. The next instant the door at the end of the hall flew open and my sister hurtled down the corridor towards us, a whirlwind of diaphanous skirts.

"Little bee!"

She flung her arms around me so hard the air whooshed out of my chest. My ribcage shrieked with agony.

"Tatiana," I wheezed. "Too tight."

She bounced back on her heels, holding me at arm's length. "Is it your condition? You *are* looking a little green—" Her eyes traveled over my shoulder and found Aric. They widened, then abruptly narrowed into what I knew from experience was Tatia-na's most baleful stare.

"Your Majesty." Her tone had cooled at least ten degrees. "I wasn't expecting the pleasure."

"Yes, I told you I would explain in my letter," I said hurriedly. I cast a nervous glance over my shoulder. How far did sound carry in these halls? "Could we please go to your room, so I can fill you in and we can set things straight before my husband turns into a horse in the middle of the hallway?"

To her credit, my sister didn't question. She merely turned on her heel and led us to her chamber, where she closed the door be-hind us with a definitive *click*. Then she spun to face me, her com-posed expression dissolving into a private look of concern.

"Thank the seas you're all right. Do you have any idea how worried I've been? I've been pacing this room for two days straight, ready to pull my nails out. When you sent me that *extremely* cryp-tic message via barnacle goose—"

I couldn't spare the energy to wonder why of all the birds in existence, Evito had chosen a barnacle goose as his first messenger. I sank down on the settee, my head spinning. "Wait. Two days? How did you get here so early? And where are your guards, for that matter?"

I'd sent my message—apparently, entrusted to the delivery skills of barnyard fowl—the day before Tatiana arrived here, if my count was right. I wasn't certain of the traveling speed of a goose, but it should have taken at least a day for the letter to reach Tatiana, and another three or so for her to travel to the border.

My sister's entire expression lit up. I braced myself.

"You recall the legend of the seven-league boots?"

"Yes?" I said warily. Tatiana had always been particularly fond of that tale—traveling seven leagues from our parents in a single step had an undeniable appeal, especially when we were younger.

"Well, I was tinkering around and decided to put my own spin on them." Tatiana rummaged in one of her satchels and emerged triumphantly holding what appeared to be a chamber pot. If, that is, a chamber pot were made of brass, encrusted with enamel, and clearly fashioned for public display.

"Tatiana," I said. "That is a spittoon."

"I know!" she said brightly. "It has a nice ring to it, doesn't it? Seven-league spittoon? Don't worry, it's been thoroughly cleaned." She frowned pensively at the enchanted cuspidor. "Although it does have quite a kick to it. Threw off my entire retinue in the palace courtyard. They didn't even make it a single step, poor souls. Perhaps that's for the best—I'd hate for them to be strewn across the road to Gildenheim like a string of sausages. Or maybe like breadcrumbs? That's a much nicer thought . . . although I suppose it implies that they would be broken up into little pieces?"

Virtue of Patience. Under normal circumstances I was happy

to listen to my sister's rambling theories about her various magical mishaps, but now was not the moment.

"Never mind the spittoon," I said. "We don't have much time. At sunrise, my husband is going to turn back into a horse. A very large horse with a propensity for breaking bed frames."

Tatiana arched a brow at me. "Breaking bed frames? Really, Bianca?"

Heat rushed to my face. "It's not like that—"

"Agreed," Aric put in hastily, spots of color flaring in his own cheeks, "it would be ideal to end the curse before I risk losing another pair of clothes."

"Another—" Tatiana began.

"*Anyway,*" I forged on, my cheeks on fire, "the relevant point is that we need you to undo your enchantment before Aric turns back into a horse."

Tatiana looked at me, for once without a ready response. Then she set the spittoon carefully on the bed and folded her arms across her chest.

"Explain. From the very beginning."

I did, as fast as I was able—Aric offering the occasional quiet addition, Tatiana pacing the floor as if determined to wear a hole through the boards. I left out the part about sleeping with Aric, my words faltering over the gap in my tale, and Tatiana's eyes flickered between us in a way that told me she missed nothing. I continued, blushing, and related the rest as clearly as I could.

By the time I was done, the sky was spangled with stars and my tongue was dry as beach sand.

"—and that's the sum of it," I finished. "Now you just need to undo the spell so we can get back to Arnhelm before Varin takes the crown."

I fished the empty locket from where it hung below my neckline, drew the chain over my head, and held it out to my sister.

Tatiana, most unlike herself, had fallen silent. She looked at me, her lower lip caught between her teeth.

I braced myself. I knew that expression—it was the same she'd worn when she accidentally turned our mother's favorite diadem into a puddle of very liquid gold.

"I'm sorry," Tatiana said. "I can't."

27

Blackness lapped at the edges of my vision, as it did on the days my condition flared its worst.

"What." The word came out like a blow.

Tatiana threw up her hands. "I'm sorry, little bee. I would if I could. But what you've described—that's not the spell I made."

A faint roaring had started in my ears. "I think you should explain exactly what your spell was meant to do."

"Like I told you, it was a protection charm. It was supposed to turn an attacker into a horse so you had a chance to escape. But just for a few hours. No more." My sister shook her head, chewing her lip again. "It shouldn't have lasted this long. That's far stronger magic than I've ever cast."

I couldn't muster the energy to ask why she had thought turning an attacker into a massive *horse* was a good idea. The room swung beneath me. "Then how is Aric still cursed?"

Tatiana spread her hands helplessly. "I don't know. You know I'm not even a proper Adept—I only dabble."

But even as she answered, a sick realization spread through me, as nauseating as one of my flares. The greenwitch's words came back to me—her warning when I'd asked her about Aric's curse. *A long-term transformation . . . One that persists for days . . . That sounds more like blood magic.*

I opened my palms, now crossed by gleaming gold scars. It

was fortunate I was already seated, for a chasm seemed to open beneath my feet.

"Bianca?" Aric asked. "What is it?"

"I think I know what happened." Each word was bile on my tongue. "When the assassin attacked, and I cut myself . . ."

Aric's eyes lit with understanding. "Blood magic. It must have combined with your sister's original enchantment."

Tatiana perked up immediately, as if she'd spotted a particularly enticing pastry. "Blood magic? So it isn't just a rumor?"

"Not a rumor," my husband confirmed. "Though I almost wish it were." He studied the gilt scars at his own fingertips with a wry expression.

Tatiana leaned forward eagerly. "Wait, are those blood magic marks? On both of you? How does it work? What exactly are the—"

"Tatiana," I cut in. "Not now. Can you think of any possible way to undo the spell?"

My sister's face fell. "I can try a few things now that Aric is here. But . . . I can't guarantee anything, little bee. Transformations are tricky, and that's without the complication of whatever the blood magic did."

Aric cleared his throat. "In theory, it could be reversed with a spell of equal power. An enchantment of similar strength would provide an opportunity to reset the enchantment's parameters."

Tatiana spun to face him, her entire face glowing with excitement. "You've studied magical theory?"

"A little," Aric confessed. "I've read all the books on it in the castle library."

"I would *kill* to get my hands on those." Tatiana's expression was an alarming mix of hunger and yearning. "Did you know that they're entirely out of print in Damaria? They used to be more widely circulated, but the Adept Guild refuses to admit any theories that could conflict with—"

Aric leaned forward. From the looks of it, my husband and my sister were fully prepared to launch into an hours-long discussion on the minute points of Gilden versus Damarian magical practice.

"Not to interrupt this fascinating thaumaturgical conversation," I broke in, "but I'm exhausted, at least one of my ribs was recently broken, I'm having a flare, and the coronation is the day after tomorrow. Could this wait until we've figured out how to stop Varin from being crowned?"

Aric and Tatiana shared a mutual expression of sheepishness.

"Getting back to Arnhelm is straightforward enough," Aric said after a moment. "I can use my authority to commandeer a mail coach. If we leave at sunrise and change the horses at courier stations, we can reach the castle by dawn tomorrow."

Tatiana bounced to her feet. "Well, that's settled, then. I'll go see if the inn has another room available."

I closed my eyes as she bustled out the door. Tatiana's assessment was rather optimistic—as was Aric's, for that matter. Hadn't we just established that he would become a horse again at dawn? The last I'd heard, horses didn't ride in carriages.

But I was too exhausted to argue logistics—let my husband and my sister figure out how they would fit a stallion into a mail coach. They seemed eager enough to discuss it.

Aric turned to me, his brow furrowing with concern. "I'm sorry—I should have thought of your injuries. I know we pushed hard today."

I put a hand to my ribs. An ache lingered there, but it was only painful when I moved at certain angles. No worse than a pulled muscle.

"I'm exhausted. But I think the healing held."

"And your condition?"

I hesitated, thinking of the peppermints the greenwitch had

given me. The one I'd taken earlier had helped more than I'd expected—my nausea was nearly gone, though it had been replaced with knots of hunger.

You're poisoning yourself. That's the root of it.

If there was a chance she was right . . . that there might be a way to if not prevent my flares altogether, at least to manage them . . . It was the smallest of our concerns at the moment, but I couldn't help but hope.

"It's not troubling me much now," I said. "But Aric, the green-witch told me there's something causing my symptoms. Something that's poisoning me. She said she's seen people with my condition before. Have you ever heard of this?"

He shook his head, thoughtful. "Never. But that agrees with what you told me about your flares, and I would trust a green-witch's intuition. Their magic is closely tied to living things. Did she tell you what the poison was?"

"No. But she said you and I could figure it out."

Aric reached for my hand. "Then we will. It might take time. But I promise we'll find the answer."

He met my eyes, his gaze warm enough to melt me. He lifted his free hand to my cheek, his thumb brushing aside a loose strand of hair. I closed my eyes and leaned into him.

It was a softer kiss than our first. Gentle, deliberate, as if this were something delicate, a growing tendril that needed to be protected. My pulse fluttered in my ears, as if my heart had darted free of my chest.

"Ahem."

Aric and I broke apart. Tatiana, with uncharacteristic stealth, had reappeared in the doorway. Her gaze danced between us again, and her eyebrow lifted.

I straightened, my face hot. "Did you secure a room?"

A devious gleam brightened my sister's eyes. "Unfortunately, no. They're all out of rooms. But I did reserve a nice stable for the two of you to share. It even comes equipped with leather tack, in case you feel like getting adventurous."

I looked at her, stone-faced.

Tatiana broke. She slapped her thigh, spluttering with hysterical laughter. "Oh, the look on your face," she wheezed. "Of course they had another room. And they'll be bringing up a hot meal shortly."

I rose, still vexed. Virtues guide me, I loved my sister dearly and was grateful she'd come. But right now, if I'd had another locket handy, I would gladly have used it on her.

"Save the tack for your own bed partners. I'm going to lie down until dinner." I truly was exhausted. My legs had turned to lead.

"I'll show you where your room is," Tatiana said cheerfully, undeterred by my annoyance.

I looked at Aric questioningly. He'd been arrested by the sight of books poking out from one of Tatiana's satchels and was eyeing them with undisguised yearning.

"I'll follow you later, Bianca," he said. "I'd like to further discuss the spell with your sister. Perhaps we can decide on a few things to try at sunrise?" This last was directed at Tatiana, who lit up with eagerness.

"Oh yes. There are *galleons* of experiments I'd like to try."

Virtue of Mercy. I suspected Aric wasn't prepared for what he'd just agreed to.

"Come along, little bee," Tatiana trilled, and steered me forcibly out the door. I heard the rustling of turning pages as the door closed behind us.

The moment it was shut, my sister whirled to face me with an impish grin on her face. "So, which is better: riding him as a horse, or as a man?"

I reeled back from her, my face hot. "Tatiana! This is a serious matter."

"More serious for you than I anticipated, it seems." She tilted her head, examining me shrewdly. "How scandalous of you, little bee. I never expected you to actually fall in love with your husband. Our parents would be appalled."

Every defense, every resistance to showing vulnerability that I'd spent years building came charging out at full defensive. Tatiana's teasing was a reminder of what I'd heard all my life: love was a weakness that anyone could exploit, one I had to hide at all costs. Even from my sister.

"I don't—" I started reflexively. Tatiana raised her brows, as if daring me to deny it.

I swallowed. *Did* I love Aric? I'd barely allowed the idea into my reach, keeping it at bay with all the mental weaponry at my disposal. I'd learned from my mistakes with Catalina that letting my heart take the reins steered me down a painful path. But with Aric . . . it felt different. My feelings for him were a vulnerability, yes, but they also made me stronger in ways I'd never expected. Was that what love meant: knowing a chink in my armor existed, yet believing, however recklessly, that no blade could find the gap?

I looked away from Tatiana so she wouldn't read the turmoil in my eyes. "I don't know what you're talking about," I finished wanly.

My sister looked at me with her mouth quirked, every inch of her radiating skepticism. I kept my eyes fixed on the wall, refusing to meet her gaze. It had taken me years to admit the totality of what had happened with Catalina to my sister, even though of course she'd heard the rumors. I wasn't about to discuss matters of the heart with her now, when I was exhausted from travel, recovering from injury, and barely understood what I felt myself.

Besides, it wasn't important. What mattered at this moment was breaking Aric's curse before our time ran out. Fulfilling my duty to my family and my people—the only thing I could do right.

"All this distance, and you're still doing exactly what our parents would want," Tatiana said after a moment, her voice wry. She started down the hall, leaving me to trail in her wake as usual. "I used to envy you for that."

I stared at her, utterly taken aback. "What?" Why would she possibly envy me, when she was the one with everything? Despite my best efforts, I had *never* been what our parents wanted, and not a day passed that I wasn't reminded of the fact.

Tatiana shrugged. The movement was casual, but I knew her well enough to see the brittleness the gesture hid. "You've always been so committed to your duty. To House Liliana. Our parents expect things of you they never would of me."

Because I had nothing to offer them but duty. Because I could never measure up to my older sister. Not because they were *proud*. "But you've never wanted to do what they expect. And you have magic—that's what our parents value. Not . . ." Not a sick daughter. I didn't need to say it: Tatiana knew.

"Magic?" Tatiana snorted. "I can't even do that right. I'd never make the cut as an Adept, and when I tried to protect you I ended up cursing your husband."

I'd always thought Tatiana relished her freedom, disdained the dogmatic Adept Guild—not that she felt as inadequate as I always had. It had never occurred to me that both could be true.

I reached for her hand, stopping her. "It wasn't your fault. And you'll break the curse—I know you can. You're brilliant, Tatiana. If anyone can fix this, it's you."

Tatiana squeezed my hand in return.

"I'll do my best," she said. "I promise." She gave a dry laugh. "It's twisted, isn't it? The way our parents hold us against each other like distorted mirrors? I'm glad you're far away from them, little bee. Even though I've missed you terribly."

I swallowed. "I've missed you, too."

I let her pull me into her arms and rested my cheek on her shoulder. She smelled of lavender and bergamot, the scents of home. The softness of her embrace was a familiar comfort. My sister, trying to care for me as always, in whatever chaotic way she could manage.

"I really am sorry about the curse," she said into my hair. "I only wanted to protect you." She drew away to inspect me more thoroughly. "Though perhaps you don't need my protection as much as I thought. Look at you. You're hardly a little bee anymore. You're a queen."

My throat felt uncomfortably tight. Neither Tatiana nor I was practiced with sharing how we truly felt, especially when our emotions were delicate. Anger was so much easier than love.

"Of course I'm a queen," I said tartly. "I married a king."

Tatiana chuckled and released me. "Not a king yet."

I didn't need the reminder of how much we had at stake. I swallowed down the knot in my throat. Aric wasn't crowned yet, but we still had another full day before the coronation. That was enough time for Tatiana to figure this out. For us to stop a coup and save our friends.

It had to be.

I'd half expected Aric to be up all night talking magical theory with Tatiana, but it couldn't have been more than a few hours before I woke to feel him slipping into bed beside me.

Instead of reaching for me, or easing into sleep, he lay in the dark staring at the ceiling. His tension was palpable, even though he didn't move.

I turned onto my side to face him. "What's wrong?"

Aric didn't look at me. "Nothing worth waking you for."

Now I *was* fully awake. I raised myself onto one elbow to look at him better. The hearth had burned down to embers that flickered green in my peripheral vision—leaving just enough light to see his face, as tense and closed off as he'd been back in Arnhelm.

"Is it the curse?" I asked. "Did you and Tatiana not . . ."

"No. Not that." Aric hesitated, his misgivings clear as daybreak. A tight coil of worry twisted inside my chest in response. Perhaps he regretted *me*.

"I can't help but wonder if it's worth it," Aric said finally, his tone bleak as winter. "If there's another way to save Marya and your retinue. If I should just let Varin take the throne."

I stared at him, taken aback. *"Why?"*

Aric turned his head away from me, staring at the hearth.

"He's always been so much better suited to being a courtier. And I'm no king." His voice was acid. "I'm not good enough to rule. Not good enough to marry. Too soft. Too interested in books. Not interested enough in the maneuvering and manipulations that make a powerful ruler. All in all: a worthless heir."

My fist clenched on the sheets. I'd heard such sentiments enough to be certain the words were not his own. He was repeating what someone else had told him.

"Who said those things to you?" I demanded. If they'd been in the room, I would have challenged them to a duel.

A muscle in Aric's jaw feathered. "A woman who knew what it meant to rule."

I remembered how Aric had drawn back from the topic of the late queen. How shadows had circled his eyes back at the castle. I'd thought he was in mourning, but it was more than that, and worse. "Your mother."

Aric nodded, his gaze distant. "She was a good ruler and a hard woman. She wanted an heir like her—bold, fearless, a commander born. Someone who could hold an entire room in his grasp and wind courtiers around his finger as effortlessly as a spider on its web. Someone who always had the right words and wasn't afraid to use them."

He didn't need to say it: someone who wasn't like Aric. Who wasn't gentle, thoughtful, reserved. Someone who loved being the center of attention. It must have been difficult to be the son of a woman like that, a woman he hadn't even referred to as his own mother.

Anger flowed through me, bitter as vinegar. And with my outrage for Aric—I tasted anger on my own behalf, too. I knew all too well what it was like to grow up under the eye of parents who deemed you inadequate, unworthy, *wrong*. I had experienced all the subtle ways that twisted love could hurt.

"She was right," Aric said flatly. "Gildenheim deserves a different ruler. I never wanted to be king." His mouth quirked, a contortion as sharp as a lance. "My ambition was to hide myself away among my books, see the queen live to a ripe old age, and pass the throne to the next person in line without ever having to sit upon it myself. I've never wanted to be responsible for an entire country."

"Neither have I."

My own admission startled me. The words slipped out without consideration, startled forth like a flushed bird. I opened my mouth to swallow them back—but they were true. I'd never acknowledged them before, but seas, they were true.

I allowed myself to imagine it for a moment: what would unfold if we broke the curse but abandoned the throne. Gildenheim's magic would no longer be our responsibility. We could leave, Aric and I. Go anywhere. Be whoever we wanted. Claim a life for ourselves, free of a noble's duties.

And meanwhile, Varin would use his newfound power to

wreak destruction on his own land. Expanding the iron mines. Logging the forests, decimating whatever magical creatures remained in these wild woods. Using those resources to build an army. It had all been spelled out in the treaty. With the terms broken, and apparently by a Damarian hand, Varin would have an excuse to demand recompense—even go to war.

The notion of running away with Aric was a dream as insubstantial as clouds. There was nowhere to run when the world was a battleground. And more than that, I knew my responsibilities' weight as intimately as a mantle over my shoulders. Just as it had been my duty to marry Aric, it was my duty to break the curse, free my retinue, and set this all to rights. Monarchy might be a flawed system, but if anyone could change it for the better, it wouldn't be Varin. It would be Aric.

I laid a hand on my husband's jaw, turning him to face me. "Aric. The queen was wrong."

He allowed me to move him, though I felt the tension in his muscles, his desire to hide himself away again. I kept my eyes fixed on his. I wasn't so certain about my own parents' judgments, but in Aric's case, the queen had undoubtedly been mistaken.

"At the castle, you left me a book," I said. "A history of Damarian wars."

A wry smile. "I did. I couldn't find very many texts in your language that might interest you on short notice."

So it hadn't been an insult after all, but another instance of kindness. He was so much more than he gave himself credit for. "My point is, we both know our countries' histories. Years of conflict, spurred by the desire for control. Craving power—*killing* for power—doesn't make you a good ruler. It makes you a tyrant." I ran my thumb along his jaw. "You're not like that. And you are a better man for it."

Aric's eyes were shadowed. Tentatively, he caught my hand in his, interlacing our fingers. I could tell he didn't believe me. Not fully. Not yet.

"It isn't always easy to choose our duty," I said, my voice low. "But it's a choice we have to make. For the people we . . ."

Love. I faltered on the word. Tatiana might have seen that delicate truth, but I couldn't admit it yet. Couldn't lay down the final, feeble shield I held against the world.

"For the people who depend on us," I finished instead. "And whatever you've been told, you *are* worthy. Even if you don't believe it yourself."

Finally, infinitesimally, Aric softened. He turned onto his side to face me. Whatever subtle duel we'd been fighting, I had won.

"You're the one who's worthy," he murmured, his fingers tracing the curve of my spine. "You deserve so much more than me. So much more than I can give you."

My eyes fluttered closed as his hand found the hem of my shirt, scattering my thoughts. "I'm not so sure of that. You gave me quite a lot the other night."

Aric's breath quickened as I reached for him. He was already hardening as my hand skimmed across his stomach. I found the tie of his trousers.

"Perhaps," I whispered, "you'd be willing to show me exactly how much you can give me."

Aric touched his brow to mine, his fingers twining in my hair.

"Bianca," he said, his voice rough with want, "I'd give you everything."

It was my turn for my breath to catch. The way he said my name sounded like love. It sounded final.

But I could save such fears, such revelations, for the morning. Tonight I was eager to lose myself, even just for this moment, in the feel of my husband's arms around me and the surety of our mutual desire.

"Please," I whispered.

This time, when Aric kissed me, it was hard and breathless, so deep it almost hurt. But his hands were gentle as he pulled my shirt over my head. As they slipped lower, his fingers finding my center so that I shuddered and arched into him.

I pulled away long enough for us to shed the rest of our clothes. We undressed hurriedly this time, both of us impatient. Aric gripped my hips and pulled me on top of him so that I straddled his waist, bracing myself on his bare chest. Asking me what I wanted in a different way. Letting me take what I needed.

I rose up onto my knees and reached between us to position him. Aric's eyes closed and he released a raw sound as my fingers curled around his hardness, as his length nudged my opening. I held us like that for a moment, drinking in the way his lashes fluttered and his lips parted with want. Then I sank onto him, inch by sweetly aching inch.

Aric's hands found my waist, pinning my hips to his. He bucked into me, taking me as deep as I could bear. I matched his movements, my hair spilling loose around my shoulders. This was what I needed. This, and nothing more—no thoughts, no fears, only the sensation of him driving into me. I rocked my hips, a cry escaping as we found our rhythm.

This time there was nothing slow or hesitant about our lovemaking. We met each other hard and fast, using our bodies to drive away our doubts. I lost myself to the thrust of Aric's hips against mine, the way he found a place deep inside me that banished the possibility of anything but this moment. Let myself be conscious of nothing but this, and him, until I could forget that we were running out of time.

We woke before dawn and met Tatiana at the top of the stairs before heading outside in the twilight of early morning. No other guests were up, though I heard the sounds of breakfast being prepared as we passed the kitchen and made our way out to the stables. A dozen hopeful equine heads poked over stall doors. Tatiana woke the startled hostler, who was asleep on a pile of hay, and shooed her out. I saw the flash of coin changing hands, which assuaged my guilt about interfering with the girl's duties.

Aric let himself into an empty stall to disrobe, using the half door for privacy. Meanwhile Tatiana sat on the ground and fussed with a collection of wires and notions, muttering obliquely to herself while twisting them together.

Suspicious, I stepped closer to look at what she was up to. "What are you planning to do with all those?"

"Make a spell, of course," Tatiana said breezily. "You never know when you'll need a good button."

A decidedly unhelpful answer—not that I'd really expected a proper explanation from her. Tatiana had been building eccentric contraptions since she first manifested the ability to channel magic, much to our parents' dismay.

"Tatiana," I said sternly. "Tell me what you intend to do to my husband."

My sister looked up from her fiddling. "Well," she said in a conspiratorial tone, "have you ever heard of a *miniature* horse?"

"I—what? Tatiana, are you planning to *shrink my husband*?"

Tatiana clutched her sides, falling over herself with laughter.

"Tatiana!"

Behind us, Aric cleared his throat. "I'm ready."

I looked up, and my heart forgot a beat. Though the half door of the stall hid everything below the waist, Aric was unmistakably unclothed. The shadows picked out the hollow of his throat, making my fingers yearn to trace his collarbones and pull him close. If we didn't have company . . .

"Please don't let my sister shrink you," I implored. "I like the size you are."

Tatiana cackled. Aric turned red.

I flushed. "I—never mind. Size doesn't matter. Are you sure you agree to this, Aric?"

He smiled faintly, but the expression hid a thought I couldn't parse. "It will be all right, Bianca."

He hadn't answered my question. My heart dipped towards my stomach.

"How long until sunrise?" Tatiana asked.

I looked out the stable door, trying to dispel the visions of a palm-sized Aric impinging on my attempt at calm. The courtyard blocked my view of the horizon itself, but from the periwinkle glow of the cloudless sky, sunrise was imminent. "Any minute now."

Movement flickered in the courtyard. I narrowed my eyes, straining to see. It was nothing, surely—a departing guest, or one of the inn's staff attending their duties—but for some reason, tension gripped the back of my neck.

"—whether it's the moment the sun touches the horizon, or the moment it clears it," Tatiana was saying. "What defines sunrise, anyway? I've never really given it much thought—"

"Tatiana," I said, my voice low.

My sister knew every pattern of my speech. She looked up, her words cutting off mid-syllable.

At that moment, the sun rose.

A flash of light. A sound like an explosion heard through muffled ears. A heavy thud from the stall behind me, and then a white horse rose to all four legs, vigorously shaking his mane.

For a moment, I thought the shadow filling the stable door

was some new effect of the spell. Then the shadow split into two, then three, then more, and as the afterimage of the enchantment's flash cleared from my vision, the truth became clear: five strangers dressed in knee-length black coats in the Gilden style, each bearing a saber at their hip.

An iron fist squeezed my heart, tight with dread.

The centermost stranger, a woman around my mother's age, leaned forward to peer into the stable. As Tatiana and I stared back, her gaze cut across us like a knife.

"That's her," the woman said. "The king's wife. Seize her."

28

atiana and I both moved at once. I stepped forward—or rather, I tried to. She, anticipating my
move, bolted to her feet, scattering buttons and
wires, and practically threw me behind her.

"Run," she ordered.

"I'm not—"

The strangers didn't wait for our argument to conclude. They
charged into the stable, straight towards me and my sister.

Tatiana flung a contraption of wires in their direction. With
a bang, acrid purple smoke began to pour into their faces. At the
same time, Aric reared, screaming a stallion's war cry that split my
ears. With a crash of splintering wood, he battered through the
stall door. The stable's other occupants whinnied and shied, adding to the chaos. Confronted by flailing hooves and unexpected
magic, our assailants retreated, coughing and choking.

Tatiana dragged me away from the fray, towards the back of
the stable. "You have to get out of here. Run. They won't dare
follow you across the border."

I wrenched my arm out of her grip. "I'm not abandoning you!
Either of you!"

-Listen to her,- Aric broke in. -It's you they're after.-

"But I—"

-Rot it, Bianca, save yourself and GO!-

Tatiana kicked open a door I hadn't noticed—a back exit—and shoved me out. I tripped over the lintel and pitched onto hands and knees in the courtyard, the hard-packed earth stinging my palms. I struggled to my feet and whirled, but Tatiana was blocking the door with a resolution I knew all too well.

"Your duty is to save yourself," she snapped. "Make the right choice. *Go.*"

She slammed the stable door in my face.

Choice. Duty. Responsibility.

Curse her—curse both of them—they were right. We were unarmed and badly outnumbered, and I was still recovering from my earlier injuries. I would accomplish nothing by getting myself arrested. Nothing except delivering the throne directly into Varin's hands.

With a wordless sob of rage, I turned my back and fled towards the Damarian border. Doing my duty, just like always.

I didn't run far. My resolution, and my strength, took me only to the edge of town before I stopped. Even had I wanted to keep running, I couldn't. Every ragged breath was a lance in my side, spearing me through where my rib was still mending.

I ducked into an alleyway, holding my arms tight to my sides as if my own embrace were the only thing keeping me from falling apart. I sank to the ground and leaned against the wall, my coat dragging across the plaster. The earth was cold beneath me, damp seeping through the fabric of my trousers. Every breath was a gasp. My heart beat at my chest as if trying to batter its way out.

Breathe. Just breathe. If I treated this like one of my flares—a pain to be endured, nothing more—it would pass. It had to.

Slowly, my breathing steadied, my heart stopped hammering.

I became gradually aware of the noises around me. The rumble of cart wheels on the road. The disgruntled clucking of a nearby flock of hens. Voices in both Gilden and Damarian, chiding and bartering and laughing and shouting.

The ordinary sounds of a border town just after dawn. No cries of alarm. No clanking of weaponry. It made no sense, but it was clear enough: no one was chasing me. The strangers hadn't followed me from the inn.

I crept forward until I could see out of the alleyway. People passed on the street, headed to work or to market, none of them so much as glancing in my direction. The town was readying itself for a bright new day. And here I was, the flower of Damaria, huddling in a dank alleyway while my sister and husband were attacked and I did nothing to defend them. Guilt churned within me, as nauseating as one of my flares.

I couldn't stay here. I stood, bracing myself against the wall as my knees trembled beneath me, and limped on towards the border. Trying to drown out the voice in my head telling me to stop. That I was going the wrong direction.

I wasn't sure how long I forged on, each footfall sounding a reproach. My sense of time was warped by fear and fatigue, and the village hadn't bothered with a public clock. I recalled that something about being on the border affected Adept devices.

Aric probably could have told me why. Or at least discussed theories about it for hours. The thought was a punch to my gut, doubling me over.

It didn't last long. I was practiced at fighting through pain. I straightened, gritting my teeth, and continued.

Finally, seas only knew how much time later, I was in view of the mountain pass marking the border. Only yards from Damarian soil. A guard hut squatted on each side: the one nearer me flying the flag of Gildenheim, the farther the banner of my country.

I was almost home. Almost safe. A hundred more paces, and I would be back in Damaria, ready to be whisked off to the palace.

I stopped, staring at the watershed point of the pass.

It was too easy. Something about this didn't feel right.

No one had pursued me from the inn. No one had tried to stop me, and I didn't understand why. Furthermore . . . the attack hadn't been random. They were looking for me.

But how had our attackers known I would be there? It was possible Aric had been recognized at the inn where we'd stayed the first night—but how would anyone have known where we were headed? Somehow, Varin must have intercepted my message to Tatiana and set a trap.

Or else Evito had betrayed us. Varin couldn't have pulled this off alone—how much of the court had he rallied to his side?

I pulled my coat tighter against a gust of wind, staring at the dual flags as they cracked in the crisp breeze.

If Tatiana and Aric had been taken captive or, drown the thought, killed, there was nothing more I could do for them. I wasn't foolish enough to think I could outfight five trained guards with nothing more than a dagger. But surely not even my parents could fault me for gathering more intelligence before I returned home, especially since I hadn't even crossed the border yet. Surely learning as much as possible before I left could be considered part of my duty.

I set my jaw. I would return to the inn, just briefly, and garner what news I could. Perhaps it would ameliorate nothing except my conscience, but at least I would know what had happened to my husband and my sister.

I pulled up my hood, more grateful than ever for the generous cut of Gilden military coats, and turned back the way I'd come, telling myself that this decision was the intelligent one. The one called for by duty, not by selfish desire.

It took me longer than I expected to reach the inn—desperation must have sped my flight more than I realized. By the time the inn was in sight again, the sun was already high overhead. The guards—and with them, Tatiana and Aric—would be long gone. Still, I walked towards the building with all my senses prickling, prepared to dive back into the shadows at any moment.

The inn looked disarmingly tranquil. Sunlight reflected on the fresh paint of its sign as it swayed in the slight breeze. From within came the hum of voices, the clink of cutlery. The remaining guests were enjoying an ordinary luncheon, oblivious to the incident only hours before.

I pulled my hood up more snugly and slipped around the back of the inn towards the stable. If there was any sign of what had happened to Aric and Tatiana, that was where I would find it.

The courtyard was unnervingly quiet. No one stopped me as I crept to the stable entrance, clinging to the shadows. I paused, listening. From the darkness within the structure came the grinding sounds of contented chewing. A horse softly whickered. Another stamped its hoof.

"Aric?" I whispered.

"Can I help you?"

My heart jolted into my throat. My hand dove for my rapier before I remembered I no longer had one. I turned and found myself facing the hostler who had met us on arrival. Her braid hung over her shoulder, a few wisps of hay clinging to its dark strands. She hadn't recognized me in turn, and her expression was wary. Most likely, she thought I was here to steal her charges.

I eyed the courtyard behind her and considered bolting. But that would only confirm her suspicions, and if she called for reinforcements, I was in no state to outrun them.

I lifted my hands to my hood, hesitated, then pushed it back so she could see my face. "I'm looking for a white stallion."

The hostler's eyes widened. She lowered her voice. "It's you! I thought you'd been taken with the lady."

I shook my head. "What happened to her? And the horse—where are they? Who were those people?"

The hostler darted a furtive glance towards the inn's back door, then took a step closer. "That lot arrived yesterday—I heard one of them say they'd come from Arnhelm. They had a warrant from the castle. They didn't tell me anything, not that it would be my place to ask, but I saw them put the lady in a carriage and take the northbound road."

So they were taking Tatiana to Arnhelm. I bit the inside of my cheek, hard enough that I tasted the bitter tang of my own blood. I was right: the attack wasn't random. Those were royal guards, and they'd been lying in wait.

"But why?" I asked, thinking aloud. It still didn't make sense. It was me they wanted, not Tatiana.

The girl lowered her voice again. "I overheard them say the lady was the new queen—the Damarian duchess who married King Aric a few days ago."

Understanding slid into place like a rapier into its sheath. They had mistaken Tatiana for me. We shared similar enough features that we could pass as one another, to those who didn't know us well. The guards wouldn't have been looking closely at her eyes in the struggle, and of the two of us, she was the one dressed like a noble. The mistake would be clear enough once they reached the castle, but for now—they thought they had *me* in their grasp.

Thank the seas I hadn't mentioned Aric in my letter to Tatiana. At least the guards wouldn't know to look for a white horse. Not unless they'd interrogated Marya. And even then, I felt sure she would give them nothing.

"And the horse?" I asked, trying to contain my desperation.

My composed mask had never been so difficult to keep in place. "Did they take the white horse, too?"

The hostler's face twisted with disgust. "They sold the stallion to a merchant. Name of Pranto." She made a gesture that must be Gilden superstition, as if to ward off the thought. "Despicable man. He doesn't deserve to call himself a horse trader."

It took everything I had to keep my legs from folding. I braced myself on the wall, sick with despair.

"Are you unwell?" The hostler was peering at me, her face concerned. "Were you injured?"

I shook my head. I was, but not in the way she meant. "It's just—a heavy blow," I managed. "I don't know what to do."

I hadn't meant to say the last, but it slipped out, a truth that slid between my ribs like a dagger. The girl's face softened with curiosity.

"Who are you, anyway?" she asked. "You look a great deal like the other lady and you share her accent, but . . ." She gestured vaguely at the state of my clothes.

I realized, belatedly, that we'd been speaking in Damarian. So much for subterfuge.

"You're right—she *is* the new queen. I'm her bastard sister," I said, improvising. "I was meeting her here in secret. She sent me away when the guards arrived so they wouldn't take me, too."

My story wouldn't hold up under scrutiny, especially not to anyone who knew my parents and how duty was the byword of House Liliana. But the girl was only a hostler, and a young one at that. She nodded in understanding, and her eyes lit with keen interest.

"Is it true?" she asked. "That the king is . . ."

I wasn't sure what she thought the king was, but I was certain the answer wasn't *an enchanted horse*. I didn't give her the chance to finish—I knew an opening when I saw one. I leaned closer to her, and she responded like a flower to the sun, tilting her head to hear my whispered words.

"King Aric is alive," I said. "But there's a conspiracy to kill him, and he's in terrible danger. Only the queen can save him."

The girl's eyes widened. "But the queen is . . ."

"Exactly," I said, again rerouting her conclusions. "I was looking for something to help her. A possession of hers. I thought maybe she had dropped it in the stable."

The hostler shook her head, and my heart slipped towards my toes. I shot a hopeless glance into the stable, even though I hadn't actually been looking for any possessions of Tatiana's. Only for an explanation of what had happened. A chance, however slim, that this could still be salvaged.

I'd gotten my answer. There was nothing here for me. I'd waited too long already; I needed to make my way to the Council and admit my failure to my parents.

"Not in the stable," the hostler said. "I would have noticed if they'd dropped anything here. But . . . there may be something left behind in the lady's rooms."

My gaze snapped back to hers. "They weren't searched?"

"Well, they were," the girl admitted. "But the cleaning boy's my older brother, and from what he told me, the soldiers just threw things around. They hardly took anything with them. He hasn't cleared out her possessions yet, just in case . . ."

It took hardly any persuasion after that for the hostler to let me in the back door of the inn. Minutes later we were creeping up the servants' stairs, she so wide-eyed with excitement I feared she would faint away, me with my hand drifting towards the dagger at my wrist. The door to Tatiana's chamber was locked, but the hostler produced a key from a ring at her waist, turned it, and stood aside so I could look.

It was as she'd said: possessions thrown everywhere, the place ransacked. If Tatiana had brought any jewelry or coins, they were gone, but the rest was still there. I walked through the chaos slowly, lifting the filmy skirts of a discarded gown to look beneath, stepping over the glittering shards of a shattered looking glass. Her satchels were thrown on the settee, turned inside out.

A metal hilt poked out from under the bed, nearly hidden by a pile of crumpled sheets. A rapier. I stooped eagerly to pick it up, pushing the bedding aside.

No, not a rapier. Only the fire poker. Despair roiled in my stomach, more debilitating than any of my flares.

The hostler leaned in to look, her voice bright with curiosity. "What is it? Did you find something useful?"

"No," I said, barely able to force the words out. "There's nothing useful here at all."

29

My shoulders slumped. I didn't know what I'd hoped to find—a message, maybe. Something I could use. Some reassurance that I'd done the right thing.

"I'm sorry." The hostler plucked at her cuffs. "I don't know what you're looking for, but . . . you look like you've lost something important."

In my despair, I'd nearly forgotten she was in the room with me. I forced myself to look up at her, to clear the utter dejection from my voice. "What's your name?"

Her brows lifted in surprise, and she stood straighter. "Alicia. Not that anyone usually asks. I'm only a servant."

"Alicia," I repeated. "Thank you, Alicia. I'll remember."

She laughed, as if my remembering was an amusing thought, then caught the laughter behind her hand—swiftly, as if she expected to be slapped for impertinence.

"Is there anything else you need in here?" she asked.

"A little time, if it won't get you in trouble. I won't disturb anything. I just need to think."

I must have spoken more like a noble than I intended, for Alicia's posture abruptly changed. She dipped her head and retreated a step.

"Of course, milady," she said, her tone suddenly deferential. "And . . ."

I waited, an invitation.

"I do hope you can save them," she said in a rush. "Your sister and the king."

Suddenly, tears pressed hot behind my eyes. It was all I could do to prevent them from flowing.

"Thank you," I managed, and then the door clicked shut and I was alone.

For an endless moment, I didn't move. Then I slumped onto the settee, staring fruitlessly at the useless poker. Despite my best efforts, tears burned my eyes again. This time, I didn't try to hold them back. I let them tremble and fall.

Some scion of House Liliana I was now. Racked by tears in a roadside inn, dressed in tattered, travel-stained clothing without a coin in my purse. And worse than my ignoble appearance, I'd dropped my shields. My despair, my weakness, my vulnerability, all were there for anyone to see and exploit. Everything my parents had feared had proved true: I wasn't strong enough, and I had failed. The only blessing was that no one was here to witness the wreckage I'd become. I was, for the first time in my life, well and truly on my own.

I dragged my sleeve across my eyes. My sister was a captive. My husband was sold as horseflesh. A usurper was poised to take the throne of Gildenheim, and war hovered on the horizon. I'd failed at every last thing I'd come here to accomplish. The only thing left to do was return to Damaria in defeat. Whatever my parents thought of my failures, they would have agreed: better to lose one daughter than two, even if the second was a disappointment. Even Aric would agree I should run. He'd told me so himself.

The road lay plain before me. I would leave this inn; drag myself the last few miles across the border; use my rank to commandeer aid; and return to the palace, where my parents would use the full political might of the Council of Nine to negotiate a truce with Varin and free Tatiana. There wasn't a hope of stopping Varin from being crowned or restoring the original treaty. But my sister, at least, I could fight for.

It was the right choice. The clear one. The choice defined by duty. I'd been born and raised to make decisions like this, sacrificing my own desires to save the lives of many.

Sacrificing my retinue. Sacrificing Aric.

My nails dug into the blood magic scars on my palms. I sucked in a shuddering breath.

As much as I wished I could ignore it, this was part of my duty, too: acknowledging the consequences and following them to their conclusion, however painful. I could picture all too well what would happen next. My guards would be executed, Julieta along with them. As for Aric, he might survive whatever mistreatment the trader he'd been sold to doled out today—but when dusk came and he turned back into a man . . . From his name, the merchant was Damarian, and my people didn't take well to wild magic. It wasn't difficult to imagine how a superstitious man would react when his new horse suddenly turned human before his eyes.

Aric had frozen when we were attacked before; he wouldn't do any better against a different assailant, especially not immediately after transforming. And even if he escaped, he had nowhere to go. He couldn't return to Arnhelm. I knew the fate of rightful heirs when a usurper seized the throne. And what other options did he have? He'd be naked, alone, destitute. He hadn't even managed to steal a pair of shoes on his own. If the merchant or more outlaws didn't kill him, the cold would do the job.

The conclusion was inevitable. Saving myself, following my duty, would mean losing Aric forever.

Despair, clear and cold as a midwinter night, settled around me. It was almost a relief. It finally numbed the pain.

I never expected you to actually fall in love with your husband.

Tatiana's words, spoken only hours ago, echoed chidingly in my mind. Now, too late, I could admit the reason they'd struck so hard: they were true. I *had* fallen in love with Aric. It had never been physical want alone that drew me to him, never just a truce that kept us together, and somewhere, deep down, I'd known. I had never desired someone solely because I found them beautiful. Beauty was hollow. It was Aric's inner life that I loved. The way he'd been gentle and patient, never guilting me when my body needed rest. The way he glowed with passion when he talked about the things he loved. The way he'd opened his heart to me, showed me his scars, the words that had made him bleed—even though I could have used his trust to hurt him more.

I thought of the warmth of Aric's hand in mine, the cautious smile that lit his face with the hope of a new dawn. His eyes, deep with trust. Trust in *me.* Aric believed in me, even when I didn't.

Caring means you're strong. It means you're brave enough to let yourself feel, even though it puts your heart at risk. And you are *strong, Bianca. Stronger than I think you know.*

I wasn't brave. I wasn't strong. But Aric was. And if that was true—that his vulnerability made him strong—then opening my heart wasn't a weakness at all, but a step of courage I hadn't dared to take.

Maybe I wasn't following my duty because it was right. Maybe I was following my duty because I was a coward, afraid of my own vulnerability.

Maybe what I'd thought was the right choice wasn't right at all.

The thought was as startling and sure as a rapier driving home into its target. Logic and duty defined what I was meant to do: abandon my sister, my retinue, and my husband to save myself and salvage the treaty. But my heart told me otherwise, and for the first time, I was listening.

All my life, I'd done exactly as expected. I'd followed my head and ignored the shallow beating of my heart. I'd tried so hard to be the daughter my parents wanted, craving their approval. And look where it had brought me.

Maybe it was time to stop thinking with my head and start thinking with my heart.

I thought of the arboretum where I'd fled with Aric. The green shoots of flowers reaching through the snow. Another hard frost would kill them. But if they didn't take the risk, they lost their chance at any life at all.

And wasn't it better to take the chance to live than to hide underground forever, waiting for a certainty the world could never promise?

Slowly, I raised my head. I took in my surroundings: the ransacked room, the embers going dark in the hearth. If this was where duty brought me, if this was what my parents' approval looked like, I no longer wanted it.

I stood up, done with this room and its reminders of my mistakes.

Something glinted, catching my eye: enameled brass. The seven-league spittoon, half hidden under Tatiana's abandoned gown.

Stooping, I picked it up and turned the enchanted cuspidor over in my hands.

Tatiana had always charted her own path, regardless of our parents' approval. It was time for me to do the same. To choose what I wanted—not for anyone else, but for myself. To show that Aric's faith in me was founded after all. To fight for the people who loved me for who I was, instead of those who told me I was never enough. To take my fear and turn it into my strength.

I had abandoned the person I loved once. I would not do it again.

My hands closed into fists: not of despair this time, but anger. Mine, to use as I wished.

"I'm coming for you, Aric," I whispered. "And seas help anyone who stands in my way."

30

The Virtues smiled upon me: the horse trader was still in town. I gathered up everything from our rooms that seemed like it might be useful—including, to my immense relief, the greenwitch's peppermints—planted a few questions in fruitful locations, and an hour later was striding across town with all the force of my anger propelling me.

The tavern looked like any other on an ordinary afternoon: well lit, the noise of its customers spilling out into the otherwise quiet street along with the stink of overly crowded bodies and spilled fluids. I curled my fingers around the fireplace poker and yanked the door open. I had only a few hours until sunset, and I intended to waste none of them on hesitation.

A few people looked up as I entered, their eyes glazed with drink even though it was early afternoon. They turned away quickly at the expression on my face. I strode past them and headed straight for a table at the back.

The merchant, Pranto, was easy to recognize. The description I'd gotten from the hostler was a clear match: salt-and-pepper hair, a mouth as cruelly curved as a meat hook. He hunkered over a ceramic tankard, deep in argument with two companions.

I stopped a pace away from the table. Waited.

Pranto's companions glanced up at me, then away. The merchant himself didn't acknowledge my presence, though he must know I was there. I knew what a snub looked like: I'd seen it hundreds of times at court.

Very well. I was conversant in five spoken tongues and basic sign. I could speak a language he understood.

I raised the poker and slammed it down on the table, inches away from Pranto's face.

Ceramic shattered. Beer sprayed, soaking the merchant's beard and doublet. His companions made themselves scarce, their expressions avowing that they wanted no part of this. Pranto himself roared with anger and started to his feet, his face purpling.

I lifted the poker to point at his throat.

"I wouldn't," I said in Damarian, my voice like flint.

The tavern had fallen silent. All eyes were on us now. I sensed curiosity more than hostility, but my back still prickled a warning.

Pranto's eyes flicked down to the poker, up to my face. He sneered. "That's a fire iron."

"Exactly," I said. "If I'm unreasonable enough to confront you with a poker, just imagine how much damage I'm willing to do with it." I flicked a shard of tankard towards his face, and he flinched.

Pranto swallowed and eased back into his seat. "What do you want? Be quick about it, before I call the town guard." Despite the bluster in his voice, his brow shone with sweat. And maybe a few wayward drops of alcohol, thanks to my enthusiasm with the poker.

"You bought a horse of mine this morning," I said. "A white stallion, sold to you at the inn. You will take me to him. *Now*."

I followed Pranto out of the tavern. The afternoon sun was momentarily blinding after the darkness inside, but I kept the poker aimed between his shoulder blades. A cascade of whispers followed us. But no one made a motion to pursue us or raised their voices for the town guard. Either they were all too drunk, or the merchant was even less popular than I'd expected.

Pranto led me through the center of town to a large wooden building that smelled strongly of horses. As we approached, a steady thud like a battering ram reached my ears. Along with it came a muffled equine scream.

Aric. My heartbeat quickened.

"Open the door," I said to Pranto.

I kept the poker ready while he fumbled out his keys and unlocked the door to the stables. The door swung outwards, releasing the heavy scent of manure, the dry sweetness of hay, and the continuous thud of hooves against wooden planks. Pranto stood aside, waiting for me to enter. His lip was curled with scorn, his eyes echoing the sentiment.

I hesitated. I couldn't turn my back to him or risk him locking me inside, and walking past him put me uncomfortably close to his meaty hands—

Pranto lunged.

I had just enough time to step back and bring the poker up. He swatted it aside and kept coming. I was good with a sword, but this wasn't a rapier—it wouldn't cut him; there was nothing preventing him from simply wrenching it away from me. Another breath, and he would have his hands on my throat. Panicked, I swung the fire iron like a bludgeon.

Just as Pranto reached for me. The poker slammed into his thick wrist with a sickening *crack* of iron on flesh.

The merchant howled, clutching his arm. His hand hung from his wrist at a nauseating angle. My stomach lurched, but I didn't have time to dwell on what I'd done. Pranto glared down at me, teeth bared, face livid.

"You'll pay for this," he roared. "You and that stallion both—"

He lunged at me again.

This time I didn't hesitate. I brought the poker down on his skull.

The merchant collapsed with a grunt, his eyes rolling up. Breathing hard, I prodded him once to make sure he was truly unconscious. Then I scooped the keys from his hand and stepped over his supine form into the building, holding the poker before me like a sword.

Inside, I paused to let my eyes adjust. My gaze ran over rows of stalls with curious heads poking over them. Horse ears swiveled towards me, some nervous, some eager. Dark and dun and piebald. None of them white.

Fear stoked my anger, turning it white-hot. If Pranto had lied to me about where he was keeping Aric, by the sea's endless depths, he would think my first blow with the poker had been a mere tickle.

"Aric?" I called.

The thudding abruptly ceased, leaving a silence punctuated by the nervous shuffle of hooves.

-Bianca? What are you doing here?-

Relief extinguished my rage, leaving me weak-kneed. I shoved the poker through my belt and ventured deeper into the barn, equine heads turning to follow me. A few nosed hopefully at my elbows.

When I finally saw Aric, I almost wished for darkness. The white stallion was in a stall at the end of the barn, a space too small for him to even turn around. His eyes were wild, his sides sweat-streaked and swollen with welts. Even worse, a length of rope was tied around his muzzle, clamping his mouth shut and cutting into his jaw.

My vision went red. I'd rarely wished to murder someone, but now I burned with the need to not only kill the man who had done this, but then to resurrect him so I could do it again.

I ran to Aric. My hands shook with anger as I worked the rope free from his muzzle.

-You're supposed to be safe in Damaria,- Aric said. He flinched as my fingers touched a tender point, and my ire flared again.

"The ocean can take Damaria. I'm here for you." I flung open the stall door and threw my arms around his neck.

Aric shuddered. I pressed my brow to his neck, breathing in the scents of sweat and sawdust. His emotions washed over me—confusion, fear, but overall a bone-deep relief that made me want to weep. To think I had almost abandoned him. I truly was a coward.

Outside the barn, I heard the distant sound of raised voices. Blast it. Someone had called the town guard after all, and I was on the wrong side of the border for my rank to be an asset.

I disentangled my arms from Aric's neck. "We have to get out of here. Are you well enough for me to ride you?"

-You're here,- Aric said. *-I'm well enough for anything. Once these hobbles are off, at least.-*

I looked down. His ankles had been wrapped in leather hobbles, limiting his movements. Now I understood the source of the thudding I'd heard earlier: despite the muzzle, despite being bound, he'd tried to batter his way out of confinement.

My heart twisted. My poor, gentle husband.

My rage was incandescent, but I couldn't afford to act on it now. The sound of voices drew nearer, and a groan notified me that Pranto was regaining consciousness. I knelt and unfastened the hobbles, throwing them aside, then looked for a stool to help myself climb onto Aric's back.

A dozen pairs of eyes met my searching gaze: the ordinary horses, watching intently. I saw the hollowness of their faces, the welts on their flanks from relentless application of the crop.

A man like Pranto didn't deserve to profit from their pain.

"A moment," I said to Aric, and strode towards the nearest stall.

One by one I freed them. The first hung back in its stall, eyes wide with fear, but the second bolted towards the open stable door with a relieved snort. The rest followed. Someone else would pick them up before long—hopefully, someone more worthy than the merchant. Either way, I promised myself I'd return after this was through and personally ensure that Pranto never touched a horse again.

I returned to Aric and pulled myself onto his back. Moments later, we were riding hard towards Arnhelm.

We were miles from the village before I dared to slow. The escape of the other horses should have obscured our tracks, and I doubted the town guard would pursue us far, but I was taking no more chances. I had already lost enough in a single day.

Finally, Aric stopped, shuddering with exhaustion. I slid from his back, my knees nearly giving way as I hit the earth. I gripped Aric's mane for balance as we stumbled off the path and into the trees. Then, when the road was out of sight, I turned to face him and assess our situation.

Aric's eyes were wild and glazed. He was trembling, his sides damp with sweat and flecked with mud. Steam rose from his flanks, twisting into the shadows between the conifers where the late afternoon sun didn't reach.

Worry soured my tongue. I didn't know as much as I should about horses—I'd ridden plenty, but the details of their care had always been left to the palace hostlers. But anyone could see Aric's condition was poor. And I knew that horses, despite their size, were delicate creatures: massive statues made of glass, breaking at the wrong touch.

Once again, I cursed Pranto. Being bashed over the head with a poker was better than he deserved. Even if Aric hadn't been human—if he'd been a stallion in truth—what sort of man called himself a horse trader and treated an animal this way?

-*I'm fine,*- Aric said, catching the gist of my thoughts, or perhaps reading the murder in my expression. But even his words sounded dazed.

"You're absolutely not." I pointed to the ground. "Lie down. I'm not the only one who needs rest."

I dumped out the contents of the satchel I'd taken from Tatiana's chambers, not waiting for Aric to comply. A small tin rattled free, and I snatched it up. A tinderbox—I'd decided the inn wouldn't miss it. If this succeeded, I would send them a replacement from Arnhelm, along with enough funds for Alicia and her brother to buy the inn themselves if they so chose. I set to work building a fire and within minutes had a small blaze going.

-*It's too visible,*- Aric protested weakly. -*It will be dark in less than an hour. Someone could see it.*-

"Stop arguing and lie down. I already almost lost you once today. I'm not letting the cold finish the job." I prodded the now-crackling fire with the tip of the poker.

I felt Aric's hesitation give way to surrender. He settled to the ground beside me, legs folding under him, for once heedless of the mud. I kept working on the fire, building it hotter and higher. Once it had stabilized, I shucked off my coat and used it to rub Aric down as best I could. He flinched under my touch when I ran over the welts, though I tried my best to avoid them.

When I'd finished, quiet dropped over us along with the lengthening shadows. The fire crackled and spat as it devoured branches. The wind whispered rumors to the pines, and in the distance, the river murmured a reply. Aric's head drooped as he slipped into exhaustion.

I fed more wood to the hungry blaze; the pine branches were mercifully dry, but they didn't last long. At least I knew how to build a fire and keep it going, thanks to childhood lessons from Catalina. It was one of the things that would have been useful had I ever joined the royal guard alongside her as I'd once naively dreamed.

A needle of guilt pricked my heart. Julieta, Catalina, the rest of my retinue—they were still locked up in Aric's dungeons. Soon to be Varin's dungeons, if we couldn't fix this by . . . seas have mercy, the coronation was at dawn. And now I had Tatiana to worry about, too. By now she would be well on her way to Arnhelm; we didn't stand a chance of catching up before she reached the city. I had to believe that Varin wouldn't dare harm her—she was too valuable a hostage—but he wouldn't be pleased when he learned his soldiers had captured the wrong sister. And I could only imagine how he would express his anger.

An owl's call jolted me out of my brooding. I looked up and discovered the sky was beginning to darken, the western horizon a syrupy honey-gold hue. Sunset was imminent.

"Aric," I said.

Aric lifted his head. Seeing the colorful sky, he staggered to his feet—

And the sun set. With a flash of white and a sensation like silent thunder, the horse was gone and my husband had returned.

He stumbled, his face pale and drawn, but I was there to catch him. I wrapped my coat around his shoulders and pulled him close. Relief settled over me like a warm jacket of my own. I had my husband back.

Aric's arm slipped out from beneath the coat and wrapped around my waist. I let out a startled breath as he pulled me against him, hard and vulnerable and shaking, and then I put my arms around him and held him close. My chin rested on his shoulder, his breath stirring my hair.

"Bianca," Aric said hoarsely. "You came back."

I opened my mouth—to protest, to deny, to excuse—but what was the point? Here I was, confirming his words with my presence. I nodded into his neck.

He drew back a few inches—just enough to look me in the eye, still holding me close. "Why? You were safe. You were supposed to escape, not run back into danger." His throat worked. "I thought I'd never see you again."

I allowed myself to fall into his gaze. His eyes were a summer afternoon after a heavy storm.

Because I love you.

I opened my mouth to say it. Then pressed my lips together, hesitating, as the cautions I'd heard a thousand times crowded my mind. I had never told someone else I loved them—not like this. I knew Aric wanted me, cared for me, but was it too soon to offer him the entirety of my heart?

I'd been silent too long. Aric drew back, his expression dimming. Resignation settled across his features, reverting him to the distant man I'd first met. "You came back for your sister."

I shook my head. "No, Aric. I came back for *you*."

His eyes clouded with confusion. "But why? I'm . . . I'm not worth it. I've never been worth it. I only proved that to you again this morning."

My hands curled tight around his collar, as if I could keep him from distancing himself that way. "I don't know what you mean."

"I'm weak, Bianca," Aric said, his voice bitter. "I can barely hold a sword the right way. I'm not fit to rule. Your life was in danger, and there was nothing I could do to save you. You could do anything, *be* anything you put your mind to. Why would you want to give the world up for me?"

"Listen to me, Aric." I pressed my brow to his, meeting his eyes. "You've been cursed and threatened. You were nearly killed thrice over. You've risked your life for a crown you don't even want, all to keep your country safe. Most people would simply give up, yet you've never wavered." I traced his jaw with my thumb. "There's more than one way of being strong—you've shown me that. And how is it giving up the world to choose the one thing in it I want most?"

Instead of answering, Aric's arm tightened around my waist, crushing me to him. I tangled my fingers in his hair and dragged him down to me, meeting him in kind. He kissed me hard and desperate, his heat against the length of my body melting me at the knees. I kissed him like a fire, devouring whatever I could take, until I was forced to gasp for breath, only to surge into him again.

When we finally broke apart, both of us were flushed and breathless, Aric's hair tousled thanks to my enthusiasm. Unable to keep my hands away from him, I reached to brush a lock out of his eyes.

He caught my hand and pressed his mouth to my palm, sending a dart of heat up my arm. It sorely tested my resolve to not rip the coat away from his shoulders and bear him to the ground.

"So," Aric said. "What now?"

"We set things right," I said. "We rescue my sister, stop the coronation, and undo the curse."

"About that last one," Aric said. "I think I have an idea."

My hand tightened on his. "Tell me."

Aric's thumb traced pensive circles around my knuckles. "Tatiana and I discussed it at length, and . . . I don't want to falsely raise your hopes, but we think she could use the coronation to undo the curse."

Despite his caveat, hope immediately flared sun-bright in my chest. "How?"

"The crown itself is a powerful magical artifact. During the coronation ritual, it's activated using blood magic—similar to what

happened when you accidentally combined your blood with Tatiana's enchantment. I won't go into the theoretical details, but if
Tatiana crowns me, she should be able to use my blood and the
crown's power to unravel the curse." He saw the eagerness on my
face and held up a finger in warning. "But it's only a chance. And a
slim one. And it would have to happen exactly at sunrise."

"Then we'll make it happen at sunrise." It didn't matter how
small the chance was. It existed. We would have to somehow return to the castle—a journey that had taken us days—in a matter
of hours, but . . .

"Wait!" I dove for the satchel I'd taken from Tatiana's chambers. In it, I'd hastily packed anything I'd thought might be useful: the greenwitch's tincture and bag of peppermints; a set of
travel clothes I'd found in Tatiana's luggage; the poker—and an
enameled, enchanted cuspidor.

I held up the seven-league spittoon.

"Aric. How many leagues is it to Arnhelm?"

31

Fifty leagues to Arnhelm, Aric had estimated. Approximately seven magical steps. This was probably a terrible idea, the kind Tatiana loved best.

I picked up the spittoon and turned it in my hands, examining the enamel embellishments. It had gotten Tatiana here safely, and her magical devices, while erratic, were strong. There was no reason to think it couldn't get us to Arnhelm now. If only I could get images of sausage links and breadcrumbs out of my head.

"This will work," I said, as much for my own benefit as for Aric's. "We just need to get to the castle before sunrise. We'll figure the rest out from there."

Aric still looked dubious, but I didn't let it sway me. I had to be certain for both of us.

I tightened the strap of the satchel hung over my shoulder, adjusted the poker shoved through my belt, and picked up the spittoon. Its polished surface returned a warped moonlit image of my face, stretching my features so that my reflection leered back at me mockingly. "Ready?"

"Not really," Aric admitted, tugging at his cuffs. He'd donned Tatiana's set of travel clothes, and they were too small and too tight for him—though better than wearing nothing but a jacket. "My prior experience with your sister's magic doesn't make me eager to try it again."

I lowered the spittoon and looked at him more seriously. "If you don't want to do this, you don't have to. It would be safer if you didn't, come to think of it. You could wait here while I retrieve the crown and—"

"Bianca. I may be fairly useless outside of a library, but I would never abandon you to fight my battles for me."

"You're not useless. And I'm trained in weaponry. You're not."

"The latter is definitely true." He stepped closer to me, the back of his hand tracing my cheek in a manner that seriously tested my self-restraint. "But whether or not I know how to brandish a fire iron properly, we're married. That means we do this together."

I leaned into his warmth, allowing myself this brief indulgence. His palm cupped my cheek.

"Besides," Aric said, his voice low, "I already thought I lost you once. Losing you again would break me."

I met his eyes, wishing we had time for more. Leading him into the jaws of danger was probably a terrible idea after all. But I was selfish. Leaving him twice would break me, too.

I took a deep breath. "All right. Together."

We both looked down at the spittoon. Each of us gripped the rim with one hand, and Aric slid his free arm around my waist. I did the same, holding myself tight against him.

"Seven steps," Aric said. "We count together. We don't stop until we're done."

I gripped the polished brass so hard its edge bit my palm. "Seven," I agreed.

We faced northwest—hopefully, as Aric had calculated, towards Arnhelm. Aric's arm cinched more firmly around my waist.

"Ready?" he asked.

I wasn't. I nodded. "One, two—"

The first step felt like being thrown from a balcony: a shocking lurch that jolted my stomach into my throat. The landscape whizzed by, trees and rocks and *seas have mercy entire mountain peaks* hurtling towards my face. Tatiana had said the spittoon had a bit of a kick, but I hadn't anticipated meeting my demise by mountaintop—

My foot landed on solid ground—on the crest of a boulder, in the midst of a pine grove whose trees we had somehow managed to miss. My sole slipped on the mossy granite. Before I could think I took an unbalanced step backwards, bearing Aric with me—

"Wrong way!" he gasped, but too late. Now we were zooming in reverse, the road shrieking past underfoot, foraging deer a startled blur as we hurtled by. My stomach threatened to eject itself from my mouth.

"Get ready!" Aric shouted.

Our feet landed with a jolt, this time on soft pine needles. Before I could stumble again, Aric tightened his arm around my waist and practically shoved me forward.

"One!"

This time we landed on the crumbling talus slope of a mountain flank.

"Two—" Aric said, and we stepped again, my knuckles bone-white on the edge of the spittoon.

Virtue of Mercy. Another five to go.

The world dissolved into a nauseating blur, punctuated by the jolt of each step. A village square. A road. Forest again. The icy slope of a glacier, which would have sent us careening backwards to only the seas knew where if Aric hadn't hastily tipped us forward into the next step. I focused on maintaining my grip on both Aric's waist and the rim of the spittoon with every shred of attention I could spare. It was all too easy to picture myself strung out over a half-dozen waypoints—as Tatiana had said, exactly like breadcrumbs or sausage links—

"Seven," Aric gasped, and released the spittoon.

I pried my fingers loose. The enchanted object fell at my feet with a resounding clang.

We were surrounded by stacks of houses crammed side by side, shingle roofed and built of the same grey stone as the castle. The fresh salt scent of the sea filled the air, along with the riper odors of a city's heart and the cold patter of rain. Above the houses, not far in the distance, jutted the castle's crenelations.

"Arnhelm," I said dazedly. "We made it."

Then I turned and vomited into the gutter.

32

ehind me, I heard Aric doing the same. When I finished emptying my guts into the capital's streets and turned around, he was wiping his mouth with the back of his wrist and looking queasy.

"Archives and indices." His voice even sounded green. "Please, let's never do that again."

I shuddered. "Not if I can help it." *A bit of a kick,* Tatiana had said. Being crushed by a battering ram would have been a more accurate description.

I took in our surroundings. It was raining. Thin, cold drops darkened the shoulders of my coat and splotched like fallen tears on my sleeves. The weather explained the empty streets, and why no one was calling the city guard to complain that two disheveled nobles had plummeted out of the nighttime air with an enchanted spittoon in hand. I was suddenly grateful for Gildenheim's gloomy climes.

The buildings lining the narrow street, crammed together like a mouth of bad teeth, could have used a fresh coat of paint. A few sported window boxes bristling with last year's dead herbs. The overripe odor of the flowing gutters was notable, but not unbearable. Most significantly, the street was paved. We weren't in the city's nicest district, but we had by no means landed in its worst, either.

The spittoon, entirely unaffected, had rolled into the gutter. Raindrops pinged on its shining sides with incongruously cheerful notes. I picked it up—carefully, so that I didn't accidentally find myself careening across Gildenheim again—and stuffed it into my satchel.

I wiped my hands dry on my coat, then tucked them into my pockets. The rain might be helping to hide our arrival, but there its advantages ended. Aric, barefoot on the cold stones, was already shivering.

"Are you sure you don't want me to steal you another pair of shoes?" I offered.

"While I appreciate your dedication to stealing from my subjects on my behalf, I must refuse." Aric looked over his shoulder as if he expected an assassin to jump out of the nearest window. Which, to be fair, was possible. "It's more important to reach the castle while we still have time."

Before sunrise. He didn't need to elaborate.

I glanced at the sky. Grey sheets of clouds obscured the stars. No trace of sunset colors remained. Surely it couldn't be more than an hour after dark, but we couldn't chance running out of time. Not when so much needed to be accomplished before dawn.

I settled the satchel higher on my shoulder. "Lead the way."

We set off along the street, heading uphill towards the wealthier districts—and the castle, perched above the city like a bird of prey.

It took us another hour to pass through the common districts. I'd expected Aric to lead us straight to the castle gates, but instead, as we neared the noble district where the houses bloated, we veered off. I was too out of breath to ask him where we were going. Exhaustion was catching up with me and the climb was precipitous enough to be challenging, especially with my healing rib.

Finally, Aric stopped at a building that smelled strongly of hay and manure. An equine snort came from inside.

"A stable," I said. "Of course."

Aric gave me a wry look. We slipped through the stable door. The interior was lit by the steady, clear glow of an Adept lantern. Unlike Pranto's charges, the occupants here appeared well cared for. A dozen pink noses pushed eagerly over stall doors as Aric and I stepped inside, hoping for treats. I rubbed a chestnut's nose as I followed Aric down the aisle, and it snorted out a warm puff of hay-scented air and attempted to sample my sleeve.

Aric went to an unoccupied stall at the end and swept aside hay with his bare foot, revealing a trapdoor. The winged horse of Gildenheim was burned into the wood.

"Ah," I said. "A trapdoor with the royal emblem. This doesn't at all suggest a secret way into the castle."

"It won't work for anyone who isn't royal," Aric said, but he sounded amused. "May I borrow the dagger you insist on hiding up your sleeve?"

I slid my knife from its wrist sheath. Had he known it was there the entire time? "Are you planning to stab your way through? That seems more like Marya's style."

"Not exactly." Aric took the knife from me and held his free hand over the trapdoor, grimacing in anticipation.

"Don't—" I started.

Before I could snatch the knife back, he pressed the blade to the tip of his smallest finger until a tiny drop of blood beaded, then handed the dagger back to me.

"There. Unpleasant, but no dramatic blood loss necessary." He crouched and smeared the blood along the trapdoor's wood. "My ancestors have always been practical. It's hard to wield a saber with a gash across your palm."

I wiped the blade clean on my thigh and returned it to its

sheath. I looked down just as the blood vanished into the wood, and a soft flare of light illuminated the edges of the trapdoor.

"More blood magic?"

"Keyed to the royal family's blood." Aric heaved the door open, revealing a drop into darkness. "After you, your Grace. You're the one with the poker."

Drawing the poker, I stepped past him and peered down into the tunnel. I was greeted by a wash of cool air that smelled of earth and damp.

I sat and slid my legs over the edge. The darkness was oppressive, a moist, crushing black that made me think of being smothered. I hesitated. Fighting my way through the castle's main gates suddenly seemed a more appealing option.

Tatiana wouldn't have hesitated. She would have charged into the tunnel like the hero of a folktale, doing whatever it took to rescue me. I'd never shared her boldness, but I couldn't balk now. If this was the way in, I had to take it. For my husband. For my retinue. For my sister.

I held my breath and dropped into the darkness.

"I don't see why Marya didn't just take me this way before," I muttered sometime later.

"Because she didn't trust you," Aric said. "Which, I might remind you, was mutual. But we had better keep quiet. The walls are thin here."

I closed my mouth and breathed carefully so I didn't inhale too much of the tunnel's dusty air and give us away by sneezing.

The trapdoor in the stables, as it turned out, led into a network of spyways—including one that took us straight to the castle's heart. This passage proved narrower, dustier, and far more disused than the route Marya had taken me in the ambassadorial wing. The neglect only served to deepen a fear I hadn't known I possessed.

Darkness lay heavy over us; we made our way by feel, a slow and painful progression. I pressed close behind Aric, who had taken the lead when we reached the first branch in the passages, clutching the poker and trying not to let it rasp against the walls or floor. My chest squeezed tight, my breath coming sharp. The weight of the castle's stones felt palpable above us.

I adjusted my grip on the poker and swallowed down my nerves. Somewhere nearby, down in the black and damp, were Julieta, Catalina, and the rest of my retinue. For their sake, and Tatiana's, I could at least pretend at bravery.

At last, just as I thought I could stand the heavy darkness no longer, I saw it: a rectangle of pale light, glimmering as faint as the stars on a full moon night. The doorway out.

I reached for Aric's arm in warning at the same time he reached for mine, so that our hands crossed paths and then met in the middle. Now I could see his profile, ever so faintly outlined. We crept the last few steps together with hands clasped, the poker cradled against my ribs, my breath sounding too loud to my own ears.

Silence greeted us at the portal. We waited a full minute, then another. Then, cautiously, Aric turned a hidden latch, his hands faintly gilded by the trickle of light, and pushed the door open.

Over his shoulder, I saw a stone hallway lit by Adept lanterns. The place was much brighter than I'd expected, given how far we were belowground.

"Let's go," Aric whispered. "Before anyone comes." We weren't sure how often the guards patrolled, or when they changed the watch. It wasn't the sort of detail that kings typically needed to be informed of.

I moved in front of Aric, poker at the ready, and started down the hallway. The lanterns' light passed over us with a quality like water. Behind me, Aric's bare feet were quiet on the floor. I thought about what substances might be darkening the stones we trod and suppressed a shudder.

We reached the first cell—a three-sided stone chamber fronted with iron bars, each as thick as my fist. Empty. The door hung ajar, gaping like a dead man's mouth. I grimaced, thinking of Tatiana—thank the seas she and her captors hadn't reached Arnhelm yet. The thought of my sister being locked in one of these cells sent oil slicking through my blood.

We moved on. Three more empty cells. Apparently Gildenheim didn't keep many prisoners. Either that, or the people we sought had been moved somewhere else. Or—

No. I couldn't let myself consider that possibility. My retinue was fine. They had to be.

As I reached the next cell, the light caught a group of figures against the far wall. It gleamed on a muscled shoulder, a drawn-up knee, a head of dark hair. Tailored fabric in bright colors, now muted by grime.

I snatched the nearest lantern from its sconce and held it close to the bars. "Catalina? Julieta?"

Heads raised, turning towards me. One of the figures scrambled to her feet.

"Your Grace!"

Catalina's voice sent a thrill of recognition through my entire body. She was at the bars in an instant, her hands reaching through to grip mine. Her face was drawn, her hair matted with what I prayed wasn't blood. Anger burned in my throat. If my people had been harmed, I would make Varin pay for every ounce of pain with three times his own.

"Your Grace, thank the seas you're all right. But what are you doing here? I thought—"

I could explain everything later, when we had more time. I cut her off. "Are you all right? Is anyone hurt? Is Julieta—"

"Your Grace." Something about Catalina's tone stopped me short. "We're all right—the six of us. But Julieta . . ."

A coil of dread tightened around my heart. "Say it."

"We don't know where she is. None of us have seen her since your wedding night."

I forced myself to keep breathing. Julieta's absence didn't mean she was dead. She was talented, and clever, and she could take care of herself. She might be hiding out in the castle, or even in the city. There was no reason to think she hadn't survived.

I would find her. But right now, I had to focus on the task at hand.

"We need to get you out of here."

I turned to Aric, who stepped forward to join me.

Catalina's eyes widened. "They told us your Majesty was dead."

"Fortunately for all of us," I said, "he's very much alive."

"Thanks to Bianca." Aric looked at me. "I'm going to need that knife of yours again."

I slid it from my wrist sheath. "Please tell me this isn't more blood magic."

Aric took the knife. "It's more blood magic."

"Step back, Catalina." I watched with resignation as Aric pricked his finger again, reopening the first cut. "I'm beginning to think this entire castle is drenched in royal blood."

"It probably is," Aric replied, dry as old bone, and squeezed a drop of blood into the keyhole. I couldn't decide whether he was joking or not. Gildenheim's monarchy seemed alarmingly comfortable with spilling its own blood.

Light flared from within the lock. A click, and the cell door swung inwards.

Aric was already moving down the corridor. "Get them out. I need to find Marya."

I hesitated, looking between him and Catalina. The rest of my guards were helping each other up, moving towards the open cell door as quietly as they could.

Catalina nudged me. "Go with him. He needs you."

"But you—"

"Your Grace, the man isn't even wearing shoes. He may be king, but from the looks of it, he needs you more than we do." She gave me a smile that, though strained, was genuine. "We've already been in this cell for a week. Another few minutes isn't going to end us."

I swallowed, tasting the familiar tang of guilt. "Cata," I whispered, "I'm so, so sorry."

"This is my duty, your Grace. I knew the risks when I volunteered."

I shook my head. "Not for that. For abandoning you."

I met her eyes, choked by my own regret. Hoping she knew what I meant. That my inadequate apology wasn't just for the catastrophe of this journey, but for all the ways I had let her down. All the times I'd chosen cowardice and called it duty.

Catalina held my gaze. Despite all the pain I'd caused her, there was no trace of anger in her eyes. She took my hand and pressed it between her own.

"Go after him, Bianca," she said softly. "We'll have time later."

I squeezed her hand in return before letting go. My chest felt lighter, my breathing easier. There was no undoing the hurt I'd inflicted on her in our youth, and I had much to account for from the years between. But maybe, going forward, we could try again after all—not as lovers, but more importantly, as friends.

Recovering my composure, I broke away from Catalina and turned to find Aric.

He'd stopped outside another cell door, not far down the hall.

Behind the bars, her black hair coming loose from its knot, was Marya. She turned from Aric to me and raised one eyebrow.

"Well, this *is* a night full of surprises. I can truthfully say I never expected to be rescued by a barefoot king and his poker-wielding wife."

"Heir apparent," Aric muttered. "Not king yet." He squeezed his finger again, milking out another drop of blood.

"Coronation's at dawn," Marya said sardonically. "You could still be fashionably late."

I was starting to like her now that she didn't have a sword pointed at my neck. "Actually, we're hoping to be right on time."

The lock clicked. The door swung open, and Marya stepped into the corridor. She crushed Aric into a sudden hug, nearly impaling herself on the knife he held. He let out a startled wheeze.

"You muckhead," Marya muttered into his chest. "You could have gotten yourself killed."

"Nearly did," Aric choked. "That's why I'm here."

A step in the hall behind me. I turned, my hand tightening on the poker, then relaxed. My guards had caught up to us—looking somewhat the worse for wear, but all on their feet and apparently uninjured.

Marya released Aric, who was out of breath but smiling wider than I'd ever seen. She cracked her knuckles and switched to Damarian.

"Well, it looks like the crew's all here. What do you say we run some people through?"

33

So," I finished, "now we just need to rescue my sister, stop Varin from taking the throne, and make sure Tatiana crowns Aric exactly at sunrise. Any questions?"

My guards and Marya exchanged a skeptical glance.

We were seated around a dusty wooden table, helping ourselves to midnight rations: a veritable mountain of pastries that Marya had somehow managed to abscond with from the kitchens. My guards ate eagerly while I filled them in, making up for the shortages of the past week. I'd forced myself to eat a few bites, knowing it was far too long since I'd had a proper meal, but the food sat poorly on a stomach twisted with nerves.

We hadn't headed to the building in the arboretum as I'd thought we might. Instead, after making our crowded way through the tunnels as silently as possible—a difficult feat with nine people—we'd emerged into a disused storage room. Gildenheim's castle was apparently packed with secrets.

"We'll need reinforcements," Catalina said finally. "Your Grace, we would fight to the death for you, but there are only six of us—"

"Seven," Marya interjected. "Ten, if you count me properly."

"—only seven of us. And we're not in our best condition."

"Fighting to the death sounds counterproductive," Aric said dryly. "I'd prefer you didn't attempt it."

Catalina gave my husband a dark look. I had the impression she might do just that for the sake of spiting Aric. After a week of being imprisoned by his guards, my retinue hadn't quite had time to revise their assessment of his character.

"Nobody is fighting to the death," I cut in hastily. "We'll gather more support. Somehow."

"What about Ambassador Dapaz?" Catalina asked. "Could he rally reinforcements if we get a message to him?"

I shook my head. Evito had been critical in setting up the rendezvous with Tatiana, and he had kept us informed along the way—not the actions of a man under Varin's influence, or so I'd thought. But someone had betrayed us. The guards waiting at the border inn were proof. Even if Evito wasn't directly involved with Tatiana's capture, he'd been compromised.

"The ambassador's messages are not secure," I said. I would wait to share my suspicions until I had more evidence, but I wasn't going to give him more ammunition to potentially turn against us now.

"What about my personal guard?" Aric asked Marya. "Do you think they're loyal?"

Marya turned a pastry in her fingers. Judging by her expression, she was considering its potential uses as a weapon. "Your personal guard, yes. As for the general castle guard . . . I can think of a few I trust, but it would be hard to draw them away from the rest without attracting notice." She grimaced. "From what I gathered before Varin decided to toss me in prison, someone has been distributing a steady stream of bribes over the past few months, starting before the queen passed away. And to be blunt, Aric, you have been . . . less than present at court. They don't have much reason to ally with you. Not when they're being paid handsomely to look away."

Aric's jaw tightened. I pressed his hand under the table.

"I understand," he said. "I intend to do better."

He didn't say the rest, but we all heard it: *If I get the chance.* I ran my thumb over his knuckles, and this time he returned the pressure.

"How many soldiers are in the king's personal guard?" Catalina asked.

Marya answered through a mouthful of crumbs. "A dozen."

Catalina drummed her fingers on the table. "That nearly triples our forces. If we can get word to them, we can ask them to gather as many firearms as possible. That should give us something of an advantage, since my people regularly train with explosives. If we split up, one group can intercept the guards who have Duchess Tatiana before they reach the castle while the other storms the throne room—"

"If I may make a suggestion." Aric's voice was low but cutting. "There's a critical point you're all forgetting. We don't actually need to kill anyone. We just need to get the crown and Tatiana, and give her the opportunity to crown me, before Varin can go through with the coronation."

I exchanged a sheepish look with Catalina. Here we were focused on how to spill the most blood, missing the point entirely.

"Please," I said. "Continue."

"The coronation ceremony has two parts," Aric said. "It ends with the monarch entering the throne room to be formally recognized by the court. But before that, there's a private ritual in the council chamber, where the new monarch takes an oath to protect the realm and its wild places. A dignitary then brings in the crown and facilitates the blood magic ritual—but only after the monarch has taken their vows."

We were all leaning eagerly forward, following the implications, but it was Catalina who said it. "So the crown won't be in the room with Varin. Not at first."

Aric nodded. "And Varin won't be in the throne room, where there are more guards. So we'll have a short gap before dawn where the crown is unwatched."

A beat, while we all processed what that meant.

"We could get the crown before Varin does," I said. "And Aric could meet Tatiana and undo the curse without having to fight Varin at all." Showing up already crowned before the entire court, instead of confronting Varin in a more private setting, would be a much stronger—and safer—tactic.

It was a desperate shot, and the timing was tight. But if we played it out precisely . . .

"We're going to need to stop that carriage before Duchess Tatiana reaches the castle," Marya said. "And we'll need a distraction to keep Varin busy until after dawn. If he realizes the crown is missing, he'll summon the guards in full force."

"I have an idea." Aric looked at me. "But I don't think any of us are going to like it."

Several hours later, I stood in the darkness of another spyway, facing down a door I didn't want to enter. On the door's other side lay the council chamber where Varin would be crowned at dawn. Unless I was strong enough to stop him. Unless Aric, Catalina, and Marya all pulled off their pieces of the plan.

I pressed my eye to the door's peephole, the wood cold against my cheek. The view revealed an oval chamber ringed by six ornate chairs, tall windows set between them with an overlook of the still-sleeping city. A seventh throne-like seat squatted at the apex, directly across from the set of double doors.

Outside the windows, the clouds were lifting. The dusky sky had brightened to a deep plum hue, almost ripe for the picking.

Not much longer until sunrise. Any moment now, Varin would

arrive to begin the private coronation ritual, not suspecting that Aric and Catalina were making their way out of the castle with the crown to rendezvous with Marya, my guards, and my sister. All of them relying on me to keep Varin occupied until Tatiana had broken Aric's curse.

A twist of nausea burned its way through my stomach. I drew back from the peephole and closed my eyes against the pain. Dizziness washed over me, and I concentrated on the sting of my nails biting into my palms to drown it out. Seas have mercy. This was the worst time for my condition to flare.

On the other side of the door came the tramp of footsteps. The courtiers were arriving.

Another wave of pain clawed at the inside of my ribs. I pressed my fist to my stomach, working to keep my breathing steady, and leaned back against the wall. Something crunched in my clothing.

The peppermints.

I fumbled for the bag, my fingers shaking. I popped one into my mouth and bit down on the cool mint, then hesitated. The greenwitch had said to use them sparingly, but . . .

I pulled out a second mint. Whatever consequences overusing them brought couldn't be worse than what would happen if I failed to keep Varin and his allies distracted. Taking care of myself would have to wait for later.

I swallowed both mints as fast as I could, feeling the cool burn and the tingle of magic. The fire in my stomach abated slightly. If we pulled this off, I was going to have a serious discussion with my parents about where my family's portion of the Adepts' funding was directed. Relieving pain seemed a much more worthy use of magic than inventing new ways to kill people.

Another breath. The pain ebbed a little more. I took a final breath for good measure, then pressed my eye to the peephole again.

Just in time. The courtroom doors swung open. Lord Varin

stepped into the room, followed by six courtiers draped in the finest fabrics.

Varin stalked down the center of the deep green carpet towards the end of the room where I stood hidden. The courtiers fanned out behind him, each taking their place in one of the chairs. The two nearest to me—a stout man with warm brown skin, and a woman with white hair and the fair complexion of Gildenheim— sat to Varin's right and left. Their expressions were flat as mirrors, ready to reflect whatever image they deemed most advantageous. It was impossible to tell what they thought of Varin's ploy for the throne.

My eyes swept the room, looking for allies. I recognized only Evito, stoic in a lapis doublet. His expression was as inscrutable as any other courtier's.

The last of the procession entered the room. Behind them—my heart stuttered at the sight—a double line of guards filed into the chamber. A dozen soldiers, outnumbering the nobles two to one. The guards were dressed in forest green as usual, but wore their finest attire, threads of silver embroidery dazzling at the collar and neck. Sabers hung at their hips, hilts gleaming. They placed themselves between the chairs, halberds gripped firmly. The last two framed the door. Blocking an easy escape.

Aric hadn't mentioned any guards. My pulse fluttered in my throat. This was an unexpected complication.

Varin was close enough now that I could pick out the glitter of each individual jewel sewn into his shirt, the flash of every ring on his fingers. Almost where I needed him.

A hot wave of pain surged through my core. I bit down on a gasp and braced myself against the wall. The most critical mo-ment, and my weakness threatened to undo me. My parents had been right after all. I wasn't good enough, wasn't strong enough, simply wasn't *enough* of anything I was meant to be—

You are *strong, Bianca. Stronger than I think you know.*

Aric's words. Aric, who had seen me at my weakest and called me strong. Not because I pretended to be. Because I already was.

It was time to prove him right.

I drew in a steadying breath. Then I lifted my head, set my shoulders, and cleared the pain from my face as I had a thousand times before. Not hiding my weakness, but revealing the strength that burned within my core.

I reached for the door and flung it open.

"Stop." My words, spoken in Gilden, rang through the shocked courtroom. "I am Duchess Bianca Liliana, flower of Damaria, and this coronation must not proceed."

34

Every head in the room snapped towards me. Whispers rolled through the chamber like ripples from a stone thrown into a pond. I knew how I must look: emerging from the wall in mud-stained clothes, hair tangled, dust and cobwebs streaking my face and attire from my earlier trips through the tunnels. Enough to cause a stir even if I wasn't wanted for murder. I could hear the gossip I'd always tried to avoid forming around me with every step I took.

But for once I welcomed the whispers. This time my goal was not to keep them at bay, but to bring them howling in—focusing Varin and the courtiers' attention on me so they wouldn't notice the crown was missing until it was too late.

I kept moving forwards, driving towards Varin like a lance. "This man is a usurper." I raised my voice so that it echoed through the entire room. "This isn't a coronation—this is theft."

Varin gestured. Two guards stepped forward, their crossed halberds blocking my path. I halted, lifting my chin.

"I am the representative of Damaria's Council of Nine and wife of Aric of Gildenheim. Step aside and let me pass."

It was a gamble—one I didn't think would succeed, but it was keeping all eyes on me. And my purpose here wasn't to win. It was to distract.

The guards flicked uneasy glances at Varin, but didn't move.

Varin's gaze was cold and heavy as a boulder as it landed on me. "While I regret your loss, your Grace, Aric is dead."

"No," I parried, "he's not—despite your attempt to have him assassinated on our wedding night."

A gasp ran through the courtiers. I kept my expression neutral, but a satisfied smile hid at the corner of my mouth. The Gilden court would be talking of little else for days.

Varin's brows drew together, ominous as thunder. I braced myself to be seized. Then, to my surprise, he flicked his hand, calling the guards off.

Varin rose from his seat and walked towards me with measured paces. I held my ground and thought of the dagger in my sleeve as he bent to murmur into my ear. "I advise you to consider your words carefully, your Grace. A certain Damarian guest was admitted to the castle a short while ago. You want to make sure she's well cared for, don't you?"

Tatiana. I forced myself not to visibly react, but my nails bit into my palms. This wasn't how our plan was meant to unfold. Marya and her guards should have intercepted my sister before she reached the castle.

They must have been too late. My mind raced, searching for a way out of this trap. If Marya hadn't managed to rescue Tatiana, where were the captain and her guards now? And if Varin had Tatiana, what would Aric do with the crown?

Varin's eyes burned into mine. Like any capable politician, he recognized victory when he was on its cusp.

"Well?" he asked, interrupting the scurry of my thoughts. "I'm willing to accept a public statement acknowledging my right to the throne, after which we can negotiate a new treaty between our countries. If you insist on being difficult, however, I'll have you arrested for murdering your husband instead."

Nausea curdled my stomach. I fought it down. I didn't need

to agree to this in truth. Varin might have Tatiana, but he didn't have the crown. And Marya wouldn't have given up on freeing my sister so easily, not when breaking Aric's curse depended on it. I just needed to give her enough time to rescue Tatiana and rendezvous with Aric.

A public statement. I could draw that out until I bored his advisors to tears, stalling Varin while letting him think he had won. I gave Varin a brittle smile, wishing I could strangle him instead.

"It would be my honor to make such a statement, your *Majesty*," I said, sweet as poisoned wine.

Varin returned to his seat and gestured for me to step forwards. I turned to face the room, and the whispers fell silent.

I hadn't planned to make a speech—I'd planned to make a spectacle of myself. My role was to make a dramatic entrance, spout accusations to the court, and keep all eyes on me while Tatiana crowned Aric in secret—stalling the official coronation until Aric, curse broken, could make an entrance of his own.

But now Varin had invited, or rather ordered, me to address the courtiers. I could twist that to my original purpose if I was careful. Words were like swords: they could be sharp on both sides.

"Nobles of Gildenheim," I began.

But before I could get any further, tramping feet and rattling metal turned all heads to the courtroom doors.

"Out of the way!" A woman dressed in the uniform of the royal guard pushed past the soldiers at the door. The crowd parted to make way. Behind her, a pair of guards appeared in the entrance, flanking two people with hands bound behind their backs: one a dark-haired woman, eyes flashing as she struggled against her captors. The other a man pale as a winter morning, offering no resistance as the soldiers hauled him forwards.

Aric and Catalina.

My heart dropped to the floor and shattered. *No*—they weren't meant to be here. Not like this, uncrowned and captive. I fought to keep the horror from my face as the guards dragged Aric and Catalina the length of the courtroom and threw them to their knees before Varin. Whispers exploded around us like gunshots. *Is that—surely it couldn't—the heir apparent is—*

Varin stood abruptly. Lightning crackled through his voice. "Why have you brought them here?"

"We found them in your personal chambers, my lord." The soldier who had entered first spoke again. "Just as you anticipated. They were trying to steal the crown."

Varin's expression flashed from fury to cold calculation. The guard swayed back on her heels, realizing her mistake—Varin hadn't intended the court to know of Aric's capture.

My head spun, bile rising as I realized the flaw in our plan. Varin had expected this. He'd anticipated that Aric would attempt to stop the coronation and had laid plans of his own. Our only advantage now was that he hadn't meant for his guards to bring Aric into this room, where all of the court's highest ranking nobles could see that he was alive.

Catalina met my eyes, her gaze an apology. She'd taken a beating and looked even worse than before. One eye was swollen; a crimson trickle ran from her nose. Guilt threatened to choke me.

Aric didn't look at me. He stared straight ahead, as if he'd been turned to stone. A drop of blood beaded from a cut on his temple and tracked towards the stubble on his jaw. I bit down on my tongue so hard I tasted iron.

Varin stared at his half brother for a long moment, a vein pulsing in his temple. Then, without looking up, he pointed at the door.

"Get out." The words filled the room. "All of you except the guards. Out now."

The whispers rose to a frenetic roar, but the courtiers filed out, looking over their shoulders so dedicatedly I was shocked that no one tripped. The closest duo of advisors hesitated, looking at Varin.

"You two as well," he snapped. "This is a personal matter."

The white-haired woman's mouth pinched in disapproval, but she took the man's arm and headed towards the door.

"My lord Varin." A man's smooth tones, accented with the lingering syllables of the Damarian tongue. I knew that voice. Both Varin and I looked up as Evito Dapaz walked towards us. His hands were easy at his sides, his eyes bright and calculating. "Perhaps I can be of service in this discussion."

A look passed between him and Varin that I couldn't read. Apprehension stirred in my stomach as I recalled my earlier doubts about the ambassador.

Varin nodded curtly. "You may stay."

The rest of the courtiers filed out. Within moments the only people left in the courtroom besides Varin and Evito were me, my husband, and Catalina—and over a dozen soldiers, all under Varin's command. The doors slammed shut, sealing us in. I could still hear voices on the other side; the nobles were clearly not dispersing. But now we were out of their sight.

Which meant that other than the guards, there were no witnesses. No one impartial. A shiver ran like sleet down my spine. Our plan had crumbled at the foundations, plunging us into an abyss from which there was no escape. Tatiana was still a captive; now my husband and Marya had been taken prisoner as well; we'd failed to steal the crown. And judging by how bright the eastern horizon was, we had only minutes until sunrise.

Varin turned to me, his eyes cold. "Your Grace. Have a seat."

I hesitated, my gaze flicking around the room. But the guards stood threateningly close to Catalina and Aric, and I hadn't a chance of fighting my way through them. If I ran, they'd only catch me, too. Stiffly, I sat in the chair the white-haired noble-woman had vacated. It was still warm.

Varin resumed his seat at the head of the room. His fingers splayed over the chair's armrests, gripping them possessively.

"This is what will happen." His voice was sharp, the crack of steel on stone. "In a few minutes, I'm going to summon my advisors back into this room. When they arrive, you, Aric, will confess to murdering our dearest mother. You will formally and totally renounce your claim to the throne and give your blessing to my coronation. Tomorrow, you will be executed for regicide and treason."

My breath came short and sharp. Varin's eyes swung towards me, flat as slate.

"And you, Bianca Liliana. Flower of Damaria." A sneer twisted his lip. "You will sign a revised version of the treaty on behalf of the Council of Nine, binding our nations together and expanding trade for a mutually successful alliance—as per the original terms, a treaty sealed by your marriage to the new king of Gildenheim."

It was fortunate I was already seated. The ground gave way beneath me, a faint whine singing in my ears.

"No. She won't."

Aric's voice was a lightning strike, drawing all eyes towards him. His gaze was locked on Varin. Sharp and clear and more certain that I'd ever seen him.

Varin arched an eyebrow. "And why is that?"

"Because if those are your terms, I'll agree to none of your conditions." The set of Aric's shoulders was resolute. "I'll die denouncing you as stridently as I can. People will believe me. Perhaps not all of them, but enough to undermine your claim to the throne. You might have supporters now, but will they still support a bastard who murdered his own kin to clear the way to power?"

A muscle worked in Varin's jaw. "You speak as if you have a choice. I could simply have you killed right now, in the privacy of this room."

My hands fisted in my lap, my teeth clenching so tight it hurt. I wanted to scream, and drown courtly manners to the ocean's depths. But playing the part I'd been taught was the only way out.

Aric's gaze didn't waver. "Your closest advisors all saw me taken in. The rumors will have reached half the court by now. Without my public confession, your word is worthless."

Varin drummed his fingers on the armrests. "What does it matter to you what happens to Bianca? You'll be executed either way. Cooperating will spare you a good deal of unnecessary pain."

"Because I love her," Aric said quietly. He turned to me, seeking my gaze. "And I will do anything it takes to protect her from you, even if it means facing whatever tortures you contrive."

I stared at him, too shocked to hide my surprise. My lips parted, but only silence emerged.

Aric's eyes were locked on mine, a silent prayer. I didn't need a magical bond to know what was in his thoughts. His fear—not for himself, but for me—cut deep into my chest.

"Let Bianca go," Aric said. "Let her return safely to Damaria, and I'll do whatever you ask."

My heart soared and plunged at the same time. Aric loved me. Even knowing me at my weakest and worst, he loved me. He had given me everything in the end, just as he'd sworn—even his heart, laid out bare and bleeding. And his love was worth everything to me in return.

My only regret now was that I hadn't been brave enough to tell him what was in my own heart when I had the chance.

I stood—careful, measured, to keep my nausea at bay. Two guards moved towards me at once, halberds raised. I didn't even look in their direction. I was the image of poise. A daughter of

House Liliana, as flawless and untouchable as my parents had always wanted.

Aric wasn't going to die. Not for my sake. Not if I could help it. I was a duchess of Damaria and queen of Gildenheim, and I'd had enough of others deciding my duty and my fate.

"Your Majesty," I said, deliberately looking at Varin. "I request a private word with Ambassador Dapaz."

Another look passed between Varin and Evito. Then, curtly, Varin nodded.

"You have five minutes."

The guards stood back as I walked towards Evito. I gave him a pointed look, and he followed me to the far end of the room. I lowered my voice, switching to Damarian.

"You are the Council's ambassador to Gildenheim." I kept my tone flat, armoring myself with my words. "And you have failed abominably at your role. Tell me exactly what you and Lord Varin are playing at before I cut you a new mouth—one that can negotiate better than your current orifice."

"Your Grace." Evito's eyes met mine, earnest and dark. "I understand your anger. I deeply regret that you were held responsible for the attack on the heir apparent, and the difficulties you have faced since. Had I known that Lord Varin would publicly blame you, I would have ensured that our operative waited for a better moment. I assure you of my deepest loyalty and commitment to the Council and House Liliana."

I drew back, my anger turning into icy shock. "*You* sent the assassin?"

Evito's eyes crinkled with confusion, but his voice remained composed. A courtier born and trained. "Of course, your Grace. As per House Liliana's orders."

The ice grew, sending shards through my veins. I'd thought that Varin had arranged the assassin to frame Damaria and take the throne. But I should have guessed from the terms of the treaty that it was crafted in part by a Damarian hand. The same trade that had lifted my country to power was always hungry for wood and iron—for ships, for fuel for the Adepts' newest weapons. Varin was part of the plot, and he'd been all too happy to take up the crown, but he hadn't worked alone. The irony—Damaria and Gildenheim truly had been partners in this, all too willing to sacrifice Aric and me to their ploy.

My parents had always been fond of efficiency. Eliminate a queen who had long refused to compromise; improve the trade agreements in Damaria's favor; put a daughter on the Gilden throne; remove me from the scrutiny of their rivals; depose an heir who would have had qualms about the new trade terms while making a new ally of Lord Varin—all accomplished in the same maneuver. It would have been admirable, if it weren't so sickening. All of it—the treaty, the marriage, the assassination attempt—had been a plot from the first, a web of strings slowly tightening around me to shape my life to someone else's design.

"You didn't know I would be framed for the attempt on Aric's life," I clarified, staring at Evito with barely disguised loathing.

"Of course not, your Grace," Evito assured me. His polite facade was slipping, showing the self-interested worry beneath as my anger deepened. "It was meant to be blamed on Countess Signa—the Council obtained evidence that she was considering instigating a coup after the queen's death. But Lord Varin is more . . . impulsive than we had realized, and matters got out of hand. I am certain, however, that your Grace is more than capable of keeping him in check in the future, especially with my expertise at your disposal. I assure you, there will be no further such mistakes."

My anger turned to resolve and settled along my bones like armor.

"You're correct," I said. "There won't. Consider yourself formally relieved of your duties, Ambassador Dapaz. And get out of my sight."

I turned my back on Evito, not waiting to watch the shock cross his face, and walked towards Varin with measured strides. As I went, I straightened my shoulders, held my head high, and settled my features into the gilded mask I'd worn all my life.

My parents had been right. A danger lay in forging my own path. In choosing what I wanted, instead of a life defined by duty. I had followed my heart, and now it was being slashed to pieces in my chest. Even worse, it was my own hand that held the blade.

My parents had been right. But they were also entirely wrong. It had been worth it—every moment, every vulnerability. Hearing Aric say he loved me. Knowing I loved him back. I was prepared to don my mask again, wear it the rest of my life to save the man I loved. And doing so would hurt me. But if I was going to bury my heart, at least I'd known the sun. At least I had its memory to warm me.

There would be no war, and Aric would live. That was all that mattered now.

"My lord Varin." My words came out as smooth and polished as steel. "I propose an alternative solution. Release my guards, beginning with Captain Catalina Espada. They cannot be faulted for following my orders. They will be sent back to Damaria, as will my sister, and treated with dignity. Aric will make his confession as you wish. But instead of execution, he will go into exile and quietly live out his days." I lifted my chin. "In return, I will remain in Gildenheim to renegotiate the treaty between our countries and see its provisions through."

Catalina started to protest. I managed not to react as she grunted, one of the guards kicking her to make her be silent. I kept my eyes on Varin instead, not daring to look at my captain or my husband lest my face betray my feelings.

Varin studied me in return, his eyes calculating. "And what do I gain from this alternative solution? I have no guarantee the Council will see things the same way you do."

"You will be known as a just and merciful king. The sort of monarch the Council of Nine would be pleased to call an ally." I hardened my voice ever so slightly. A subtle threat. "I might remind you that the Council's agreement is necessary for the treaty to be ratified. And, as noted, I represent the Council."

Varin stood and approached me. His eyes, the color of Aric's but so much colder, narrowed on mine. "I'll need more guarantee than that, I'm afraid. The original treaty was sealed with a marriage."

Catalina gave a sharp intake of breath. Every muscle in Aric's body tensed.

I kept my breath steady. Inhale. Exhale. I had hoped it wouldn't come to this, but Varin's face held no softness, no room for argument.

Very well. I had come to Gildenheim for a political marriage. My future, in exchange for peace—and now for the life of the man I loved.

My voice betrayed none of my inner turmoil. "Accept my terms, and I will divorce Aric and marry you instead."

Aric finally struggled against the guards. "Bianca, *no*. You can't—" His words cut off in a gasp as one of the guards silenced him. I bit down hard on the inside of my cheek to prevent myself from reacting. If Varin believed I cared for my husband, my bargain would fall apart. He had to believe I was like my parents— that my actions aligned with theirs.

Varin's eyes narrowed. "Aric says he loves you. Do you not return the sentiment?"

"It's touching, but I've always known that love is a weakness." I dredged up every ounce of bitterness I'd allowed to fester throughout my life, letting it drip from my words. "Like the Council, I recognize the right alliance when I see it. I've studied my history, Lord Varin. I know what kind of man makes a good king. And I know exactly what kind of man my husband is."

Aric couldn't hear my thoughts. But I sent them towards him anyway, hoping he would understand. *Please hear what I truly mean.* I couldn't look at him or my defenses would shatter, but I felt my husband's eyes on me. *Please know what's in my heart, even though I never told you when I had the chance. I need you to live. For both of us.*

I lifted my chin, meeting Varin's eyes. "I'll sign the papers as soon as the coronation is over. Do we have an agreement?"

A beat of tension while he studied me, his suspicions playing out behind his eyes. My fists were tight at my sides. It was the only thing that betrayed me.

"We do."

Varin held out his hand. I put my fingers in his, the barest touch.

Varin brushed his lips to my knuckles, his eyes not leaving mine. "I look forward to a fruitful union."

I smiled at him, the expression hurting my face. *I look forward to making your life a waking nightmare.* "I share your sentiments."

Behind me, Aric made a soft and broken sound. I couldn't bear to look at him. I'd done what I had to. The people I loved would be safe. That was all that mattered.

"As my future queen, you will stay here to witness the coronation and formally acknowledge the legitimacy of my rule." Varin dropped my hand as if it were a piece of carrion and turned to the guards. "Take the prisoners away. I'll deal with them later. And call the courtiers back. We've had enough delays in this coronation."

"A coronation," a voice cut in from behind us. "Don't you need a crown for that?"

The guards' hands sprang to their weapons. The entire room turned to look in unison.

Standing beside the spyway entrance were a dozen soldiers in full armor. Aric's personal guard. In their midst stood Marya, saber drawn, her expression promising a painful death to anyone who opposed her.

And beside her—my sister, beaming as brightly as if she'd just arrived at her own birthday celebration, twirling an ornate golden crown from the tip of her finger.

The crown of Gildenheim.

35

Tatiana waved cheerily at Varin, dangling the crown from her fingertip. "Looking for this?"

And then she wobbled. Hiccuped. And dropped the crown, which bounced on the carpet and rolled across the floor towards Varin.

I stared, torn between relief and horror. Was my sister *drunk*?

"Seize them," Varin snapped. "And get that crown!"

I just had time to see Marya grab my sister by the waist and shove Tatiana safely behind her. Then Varin's guards were closing around me, reaching for my arms. I moved faster. I ducked out of their grasp and ran for Aric and Catalina, drawing the dagger from my sleeve as I went.

"Charge!" Marya roared, with a fervor that suggested she was enjoying herself. Aric's personal guards rushed forward. In an instant I was in the midst of a melee. Sabers flashed, halberds thrust. I couldn't help but sense that Varin's soldiers were not terribly enthusiastic about performing their duties.

Two guards remained watching my husband and Catalina, gripping their halberds uncertainly. I brandished my dagger at them.

"Beware the wrath of House Liliana!" I shouted in Damarian, stabbing at the air for good measure.

The guards exchanged a glance, and then sidled out of my way.

They weren't exactly vanquished, but it felt like an acceptable compromise. I slipped behind Catalina and sliced through her bonds. She was on her feet immediately, snatching up a fallen halberd and turning to cover my back. I turned to Aric and cut him free, the ropes falling to the floor. A bright slash of blood welled along his thumb where I hadn't been careful enough. Guilt coiled in my chest, constricting my breath. I would apologize later. For that, and for so much more.

But right now, we didn't have time. Light was spilling red through the chamber's high windows, at an angle that painted the roof's arches in blood. The sun pushed at the horizon like a bubble ready to pop.

I gripped my husband's elbow. "Quickly! We have to get the crown."

Aric stumbled to his feet, bracing himself on my shoulder. He cast a glance out the window, his face pale. "There's no time to break the curse now. It's almost sunrise."

"You're still human. That means there's time. *Hurry.*"

I seized his wrist and pulled him after me: weaving around clusters of dueling guards, brandishing my dagger at anyone who looked like they were considering stopping us. Catalina followed, covering our backs. I caught a glimpse of Marya as we ran past— she was in the thick of it, happily stabbing and hacking. She didn't seem to have actually run anyone through yet, but Varin's guards lay crumpled on the floor around her like discarded garments, groaning and clutching assorted body parts.

I pulled Aric past them, scanning the floor. Where was the crown?

"Little bee! Here!"

A flash of rose-colored skirts caught my eye. Tatiana. She had circled around the melee and was running towards me, the crown clutched in both her hands. It was a wobbly run, more stumble than sprint, but she was closing the distance. I sheathed my dagger, reaching to meet her.

A blur of motion to my right. Varin had evaded the dueling guards and was racing towards Tatiana, hands outstretched for the crown. She veered away from him, skirts flaring. He tackled her from behind and they both went sprawling on the floor, grappling for the crown.

"Tatiana!" I skidded to a halt, reaching for my knife again.

"Get off me, you usurping frog of a man!" Tatiana shrieked. She scrabbled in her sleeve and flung something small, shiny, and suspiciously button-shaped at Varin.

A burst of light exploded from the contraption. Varin flopped onto his back, clutching his throat and looking like he'd been punched in the gut. A half dozen guards closed in around them.

Tatiana sat up, her hair wild, her dress hanging off one shoulder. "Bianca! *Catch!*"

She hurled the crown in my direction. It spun through the air, a blur like a golden arrow—

I dropped Aric's wrist, lunged, and caught the crown in both hands. It was heavy, a mass of golden bands twisted together to look like vines. A shock of power ran up my arm—the enchantment was eager to come to life. I gripped the crown in one hand and seized Aric with the other. We ran towards Tatiana, Catalina guarding our backs—only to stop short again as Varin's guards dragged my sister away from us, her heels kicking on the deep green carpet as she spat and twisted in their grip.

I wavered, the crown biting into my palm.

The sun reached the sky.

A burst of white light shook the courtroom like a thunderclap, and Aric's hand was suddenly no longer in mine.

I turned, though I already knew what I would see.

A white stallion stood beside me, dark eyes wide and wild. The sun had risen, and we had failed to break the curse.

Around us, the fighting had stopped. Everyone was staring at Aric, weapons loose in shocked hands.

"Did the heir apparent just turn into a horse?" someone whispered. A second person hastily hushed the speaker.

Varin sat up, looking dazed. He took in the startled guards, the stallion standing in the midst of it all, me beside Aric with the crown now useless in my hand. With admittedly admirable composure, Varin rose, holding his hand out imperiously.

"Give me the—" He stopped, looking puzzled, and put a hand to his throat. Coughed and tried again. "Give me the cr— *crrrrrkkk*."

Behind him, held between two guards, Tatiana giggled.

Varin scowled, opened his mouth, and released a loud and distinctive *croak*. He turned on my sister, his eyes wide with horror. "What did you—*crroooak*—do to—*crrriiiick*—"

"I *said* you were a horrible frog of a man," Tatiana smirked, and waggled her fingers suggestively.

Varin's face purpled with rage. He rushed at Tatiana, only for Marya to block his way. She raised her saber, resting its tip on Varin's nose.

"Touch her," she said, "and I'll happily run you through." She nodded at the guards holding my sister. "And you two sorry excuses for soldiers. Let her go or I'll make your thumbs into earrings."

Tatiana beamed at Marya. "Ooh, please do. I would wear them every day." She wrinkled her nose. "Until they started to smell, at least."

-Bianca.-

I turned back to Aric, my heart sinking towards my feet. He was watching me, his gaze heavy with regret.

-It's too late. Varin should take the crown.-

My entire body rebelled against the idea. "But you're the king. You're my *husband*."

His sorrow dragged on me like an ebbing tide. *-I'm only the heir apparent. I haven't been crowned. And I won't be your husband much longer.-*

"Aric, *no*." The words came out as a sob. I was done with hiding. Done with pretending I didn't care. "I don't want to divorce you, and I certainly don't want to marry Varin instead. I never have. I agreed to those terms to *save* you, not because I wanted you gone."

I stepped closer to him. Put my arms around his neck and pressed my face into his shoulder, not caring that everyone could see my vulnerability.

"I love you, Aric," I said. "I didn't come back because of duty. I came back for you. Because I choose you. Exactly as you are."

Aric's pulse beat against my ear. *-But we might never break the curse now.-*

"Do you think I care?" I cried. My hand tightened on the crown. "Of course I want you as a man. Of course I want the curse broken. But I know how it feels to have a part of yourself that you can't control. If that doesn't stop you from loving me, why should it lessen my love for you?"

I felt Aric's love wash through me, filling my heart. Bright and certain as the sun breaking from night to dawn. As if in response, the crown warmed in my hand. A pulse of magic rolled through me, lifting the hairs on the back of my neck.

Behind me, Marya cleared her throat. "Your Majesty. The sun is almost above the horizon."

Wait. I lifted my head from Aric's neck, and hope flickered bright and devastating in my chest.

Marya was right. The courtroom afforded an unbroken view of the eastern horizon. Beyond the walls of Arnhelm, below the cloud line, a thin golden sliver of sun still gleamed against the mountains. Just on the verge of lifting free of their peaks.

Which meant, even though Aric had already transformed, that sunrise wasn't over. Not quite yet.

Thoughts began to tumble through my mind, an avalanche set into motion.

A spell of equal power . . .
Keyed to the royal family's blood . . .
I seal these vows with my blood . . .

The crown pulsed in my hand, glowing with latent power. A drop of blood in a chalice. A drop of blood on a fingertip. Through our marriage, I shared Aric's blood—blood I'd already used once to alter a spell. I might not be an Adept, but my marriage linked me to a different sort of magic. And the curse hadn't been Tatiana's alone. It was also mine.

I drew the knife from my wrist sheath. In a sharp motion, I slashed it across my palm, parting the golden lines from our wedding night. Blood flowered immediately, spattering onto the floor. I ran my hand along the crown, painting it red, and lifted it high.

"By the royal blood I share through our marriage vows, I crown you king of Gildenheim!"

I brought the crown down on Aric's head.

The entire courtroom froze, as if the castle were holding its breath.

Then the world exploded into blazing white light.

A gust of wind nearly bowled me over. Someone screamed. I narrowed my eyes against the brightness, shielding my face with one hand. The light pulsed once, then faded.

The shape of a horse was imprinted on my vision. I blinked away the afterimage, and in its place was a man. A man with gold-bright

hair, a bloody crown crooked on his head, and a tenuous smile forming on his lips.

"*Aric,*" I breathed. I flung myself at him and crushed my
mouth to his.

His arms went around me, holding me so tight I could barely
breathe. His hands were on my back, my hips, my hair, his mouth
covering mine, kissing me with desperate relief until we broke
away gasping for air. I dragged in a breath and kissed him again,
my hands in his hair, holding him against me as if I could sub-
sume him. As if I could imprint the feel of him onto my skin and
never lose him again.

Behind me, someone cleared their throat. We broke apart,
breathless and dizzy.

"I hate to interrupt," Marya said pointedly, "but the advisors are
clamoring at the door and your Majesty isn't wearing any clothes."

Tatiana whispered something I didn't catch. A muffled laugh
ran through the guards, Aric's and Varin's alike. All of them were
staring, though most were making a valiant effort to keep a straight
face.

Aric's cheeks turned red as dawn. He held me closer, one arm
wrapped around my waist, using me as both shield and support.

"As my first order as king," he said to the room at large, "I
command someone to bring me a set of clothes. Something suitable for a coronation, please."

"And shoes," I added.

"And shoes. And while I'm waiting—"

Aric turned back to me and cupped my face in his hands. His
fingers traced my mouth, following the curve of my lips as if they
were more precious than any crown.

"While I'm waiting," Aric whispered, for my ears alone, "I'm
going to kiss my wife."

And, certain as a vow, he did just that.

36

The throne of Gildenheim was more comfortable than I'd expected. I tipped my head against the high back, grateful for its support, as I watched the last of the courtiers file out of the throne room.

Aric and I sat on the dais of the marble-floored chamber where we'd first met. Neither of us was dancing today—we were both exhausted, and my stomach still pulsed with faint waves of pain. I'd had worse flares, but even mild nausea quelled my desire to move. I didn't try to force past it. Taking care of my body's needs was also a form of strength.

After Aric's unorthodox coronation, we'd permitted the advisors back into the council chamber—except for Evito, who had been caught attempting to flee the castle and escorted to the dungeons along with Varin and the guards who'd fought for him. The courtiers were surprised by the circumstances greeting them, to say the least, and their questions threatened to take up the entire morning. In the end, though, they couldn't ignore the facts: Aric was alive, he wore the crown, and I was here beside him. The reign of a new king had begun.

To the rest of the court, we said nothing and let them draw their own conclusions. A wave of gossip had flashed through the entire throne room like a riptide when Aric and I appeared in the doorway, but the courtiers were appeased soon enough by music to dance to and freely flowing wine.

And if rumors whispered through the court like wind in the pines—stories of the king turning into a horse and back again, of a legend come to life and reinvented—well, Aric might hate it, but I suspected that the element of mystery would only enhance his rule.

And now, finally, the day was over, and with it the celebrations. Aric, seated at my left on the second throne, removed the crown and rubbed his temples.

"Thank the Lady that's done," he muttered.

"Not quite done." Marya fiddled with the hilt of her saber, as if she thought it hadn't gotten enough use today. "You still have Varin to deal with."

"I know." Aric sighed. "But I'll think about that tomorrow. At the moment, my most pressing duties lie elsewhere." He looked at me and smiled.

Tatiana sashayed up to me, her steps a touch too breezy. She leaned on the arm of the throne so she could whisper into my ear.

"The captain of the guard. Marya." She suppressed a giggle. "Do you think she likes women?"

I looked at my sister skeptically. "You *are* drunk. I thought so earlier."

"I'm not!" She shook her head so hard she almost lost her balance. "The guards drugged me. They thought it would make me cooperate."

They clearly didn't know my sister. "And did it?"

Tatiana gave me a conspiratorial smile. I suddenly wondered what exactly *had* happened to my sister's captors. I knew by now that Marya had intercepted Tatiana as planned after all, and Aric's guards had taken the place of Varin's to sneak her into the castle in plain sight—pretending they were delivering her to the dungeons. But it occurred to me that Marya might have had a bit more help than she'd bargained for. My sister was undeniably talented at enchantments, and she'd evidently had at least one magical device literally stashed up her sleeve.

Tatiana nudged my elbow. "Well?"

I looked at Marya, remembering how ardently she'd defended my sister during the fight. Even now, while arguing with Aric over whether she could run Varin through, the captain of the guard was eyeing Tatiana with an interest impossible to miss.

"Yes," I said dryly. "I assure you she most definitely does."

This conversation was giving me another idea. The role of monarch had been filled, but we were unexpectedly in need of someone to negotiate a new treaty and stabilize relations with Damaria. Someone who wouldn't think assassination attempts were an acceptable form of diplomacy.

"Tatiana," I said, drawing her attention away from Marya, "how would you feel about becoming the new ambassador to Gildenheim?"

Tatiana beamed and hiccuped. "I would love to ambass the door. Especially if it has biceps like Marya's."

I patted her gently on the arm. "We can discuss details once you're no longer drunk. Or drugged. Whichever it is."

The appointment would need to be officially approved by the Council, but there was no reason Tatiana shouldn't have the role—not once she was sober. She spoke Gilden more fluently than I did. She adored social events. She had no attachments at home. And, apparently, she was already getting along just fine with the locals.

It would make me happy, too, to have my sister close at hand—and away from our parents' influence. We would both be the better for it. If our parents objected, they could find themselves another heir as they'd threatened to do for years, and we'd both finally be free of contorting ourselves to suit their machinations. I was certain Tatiana wouldn't mind.

Another brief wave of nausea rolled through me, and I pressed my arm to my stomach. Tatiana's eyes narrowed in concern, and she lowered her voice.

"Your condition?"

I nodded. The greenwitch's peppermints had gotten me through the worst of it, but they couldn't negate the basic need to rest.

I rose, smoothing my skirts. "If the decision about Varin can wait, I would like to go to bed. I don't think I've slept in the past twenty-four hours."

Aric rose immediately. "Of course."

He held out his hand to me. I gave him mine—the left, with its new golden scar. The wound from the coronation had closed quickly, but not without a signature. Wounds—like words, like magic—always left a mark.

When we reached our adjoining chambers, Aric hesitated. I didn't need a magical bond to guess why. Surely by now the glass had been repaired, the traces of blood removed, but I had no more desire than he did to sleep in the place he'd almost died.

I tugged him by the hand. "My bed has plenty of room for us both."

I sat on the edge of the bed, watching Aric as he undressed. The soft lamplight gilded the planes of his body, and I traced every inch of him with my eyes. I had never had the chance to savor him like this. Our previous times had always possessed a sense of urgency.

Now the room was warm, the night was soft. And my husband was here, beside me. Human. For good. I wasn't certain I fully believed it yet, but daybreak would help my conviction.

Aric dropped his shirt to the floor and turned to face me. His brows drew together in concern. "You're still dressed. Are you well? Is your condition . . ."

I started to shake my head, then stopped myself. I had nothing to hide from him. "It's bothering me a little," I admitted. "But it's tolerable."

Aric still looked troubled. "I don't know what's causing it yet," he said, his voice soft. "But I'll find it. I promise."

"I know." I trusted him. It might take time, but whatever the source of my illness, we would root it out together.

But that could wait for another day. Right now, I had my husband alone, in a bed with ample space for exploration, and I intended to waste no more time on misunderstandings. I lightened my tone. "My condition isn't why I haven't undressed."

He arched his brow, and desire curled low in my stomach, overriding the nausea. "Oh?"

I ran my eyes over him, all of him, allowing him to see my open want. "I thought perhaps you could help me with the fastenings."

Aric walked over to me. Slowly. Deliberately. I turned to give him access, and his fingers brushed the back of my neck, sending a shiver down my spine.

Cool air caressed my skin as he worked the laces open. His lips followed, dropping a kiss to every place he exposed. I closed my eyes, need stirring between my legs. Every part of me yearned to melt into his touch, lose myself in the feel of his hands on my body and his mouth on mine.

But there was something I had to tell him first. I'd made a wound, and I couldn't let it fester.

"Aric." With my back to him, I felt braver, better able to say the words. "In the council chamber, when I . . . when I said those things about you . . ."

I faltered. Aric's hands stilled on my back, his palms warm against my bare shoulder blades.

"I remember." His voice was like music. "Your exact words. *I know what kind of man makes a good king.*"

Despite myself, I flinched, hearing my own words turned back on me. I'd wielded them as weapons against Varin, but they'd cut me, too.

"I'm sorry," I whispered. "I couldn't think of any other way to save you. I meant—"

"I know. I remember your words because I knew exactly what they meant."

His hands on my shoulders, Aric gently turned me to face him. The expression in his eyes made my breath catch.

"You don't need to apologize for doing what it takes to survive," he told me gently. "I understand you, Bianca. And I love you—including the parts of you that you don't love yourself. I will love them for you, if you'll let me."

My heart was too large for my chest. Aric's thumb brushed my cheek. His eyes drank me in as if I were something wondrous.

"I love you, Bianca Liliana, flower of Damaria." A laugh lurked in his words, making them bright as sunrise. "I choose you as my wife, queen, and love. For as long as you will have me."

I lifted my face to him. "Always," I whispered.

Our mouths met—a choice, a promise—and he laid me back onto the bed.

That night we renewed our marriage vows with every inch of our bodies. Whispered them against each other's bare skin. Elicited them with gasps when we came together. And when we were spent, lying tangled together with our scarred fingers entwined, no wound remained between us. We were husband and wife, a duty of our own making, and we would choose each other to the end of our days.

37

Sometime late in the night I woke to a soft sound in my suite. My mind was instantly alert, my senses tingling. A shadow flickered across the window, a form momentarily silhouetted against the glass.

My heart pounded like a horse's hooves. Someone was in the room—someone other than Aric, who was fast asleep beside me, his breathing soft and steady.

My hand crept towards the knife on the nightstand.

Paper rustled, followed by the scratch of a metal nib. Glass clinked faintly as the midnight scribe dipped their pen. The intruder was taking pains to be quiet, but letter writing was not a silent pursuit.

It was also, to my knowledge, not the typical pastime of would-be assassins. They tended to complete their business and leave without signing off on their work. Which meant that whoever had entered my chambers was not here for blood.

I closed my hand around the knife's hilt and sat up quietly, not wanting to wake my husband. "Who's there?"

The pen's scratching abruptly ceased. As my eyes adjusted, I picked out the outline of a figure stooped over my bureau, quill in hand. A faint sigh, and then the person straightened into a familiar silhouette.

"My apologies, your Grace." The voice brushed my ears, as

light as the touch of a feather. A familiar voice. One I'd heard nearly every day for the past decade of my life. "I didn't mean to wake you."

"Julieta." The word hissed out as a sigh. Relief loosened my fingers around the dagger hilt. But I didn't release it entirely. "What are you doing?"

"I was writing my letter of resignation, my lady."

I sat up, frowning. I'd been worried about my apothecary's safety for days. The last thing I'd expected was for her to show up in the dead of night, safe, but with the intent to quit.

Aric stirred in his sleep. I flashed a look at him to make sure he hadn't woken, then slipped my legs out from under the covers and stood, leaving the knife on the nightstand. I crossed the room to Julieta and took her by the elbow.

"Come with me, please. I want a proper explanation, not a letter."

My attendant allowed me to steer her out of the bedchamber, into my personal washroom. I shut the door behind us and whispered the command to illuminate the chamber's Adept-forged lanterns.

They flickered to life, revealing my apothecary. Julieta was dressed entirely in close-fitting black, a hood pushed back from her face. Shadows highlighted the guilt on her face.

"Explain," I said, keeping my voice low. "You told me before that your home is where I am. What caused this change of heart?"

"My heart is the same, my lady." Julieta's lips pressed together into a thin line. "But a would-be assassin has no place in your retinue, however devoted she might be to you."

For a moment, shock cast me in stone. *Julieta* was the assassin? I would never have believed it, but—my thoughts raced, tying the loose threads together. The way the attacker had come through my rooms without alerting my guards. The knife of Damarian make found in Aric's bedchamber. How the assassin hadn't attacked me—only Aric; I'd only been injured because I'd put myself in the way. The mystery of why Julieta hadn't been imprisoned with the rest of my retinue, and why no one had heard from her since my wedding night.

"I see," I said slowly. "But why?"

Julieta looked down at the tiled floor. "I was planning to confess everything in the letter."

"Well, here we are. Now's your opportunity." I folded my arms. "I've cared for you like family for many years. You at least owe me an explanation."

Julieta sighed. She ran a hand through her hair, disrupting its sleek coif.

"Please believe me, your Grace, I never intended to put you in any danger. Some months ago, your parents gave me a commission for a very particular poison. I was reluctant to make it, especially without knowing its intended use, but they made it clear that my continued employment was contingent upon agreeing. I hoped it was merely one of their precautions, that nothing would come of it. But when the Gilden queen unexpectedly fell ill . . . well, I knew the symptoms of my own poison, even if I'd never expected it to be used in such a way.

"By the time I learned the rest of the plan, it was too late to back out. They had the evidence to lay the queen's death at my feet."

Anger glowed in my chest, a hot coal of old resentment. "Blackmail."

Julieta nodded, shamefaced. "I didn't want to kill again, but I told myself that at least I was serving your Grace. Everything I knew about Aric suggested he would be a cruel husband to you."

To be fair, Aric hadn't given either of us a good initial impression—though that was hardly an excuse for murder.

"They ordered you to kill him," I confirmed. "And you agreed."

Julieta nodded, guilt torquing her mouth. "But I swear, your Grace—had I known it would endanger you, I would never have gone along with the plan. I had no inkling of Varin's machinations. I never suspected that you would be framed, or that you would be coerced into marrying *him* instead. I never once intended to harm you."

I believed her. I could see how the situation had spiraled: Julieta had told Evito what happened in the bedchamber; Evito had relayed it to Varin; and Varin had seized the opportunity and sent guards to intercept me at the border, not knowing his half brother's curse was cyclical. Julieta couldn't have predicted that course of events—even Evito hadn't anticipated Varin twisting the failed assassination attempt to his advantage.

"And since then?" I asked. "Where have you been? Did Evito harm you?"

Surprise flickered behind Julieta's eyes, followed by caution. "No, my lady. I've been in hiding. First in the ambassadorial wing, and then, after I learned of Varin's plans and argued with Dapaz over them, in the city." She looked away from me, her shoulders bowed. "And now you know everything, so there's no need to finish writing my resignation letter."

"No," I agreed, "there isn't."

Julieta nodded, with the face of a prisoner who had just received confirmation of her own execution. "I'm glad you've found a happy marriage after all, my lady. And . . . I'm sorry. I know you might never forgive me, but . . . I'll always remember you fondly."

She made to move past me, to slip through the washroom door and out of my life. I laid a hand over the latch, stopping her.

Julieta looked up, her expression melding regret and resolve. "I'm sorry, your Grace, but I do value my life. I have no wish to fight you, but I won't stay to be executed."

"Julieta," I said firmly. "I haven't accepted your resignation."

Her eyes widened in surprise. "Your Grace?"

"You're the best attendant I could ask for, an excellent apothe-cary, and a dear friend." I reached for her hand and took it in both of mine. "I forgive you, Julieta. And I want you to stay."

Julieta's eyes widened further. "Even though . . ."

"Yes," I said firmly. "Even though. I need people I can trust beside me." I gave her a wry smile. "And besides . . . knowing I have a skilled assassin at my disposal isn't the worst thing, either."

Julieta choked out a laugh. "Not so skilled, considering I failed at my only assassination attempt to date. And I'm not entirely sure your husband would agree."

"Perhaps not yet. But I'm sure it won't take long for him to trust you like I do once he hears the whole story."

The corners of Julieta's eyes were glinting in the lantern light. "Thank you, my lady. I won't prove you wrong."

I squeezed her hand. "If that's settled, I would very much like to get back to bed. I'll expect a full supply of your tonics by the end of the day tomorrow."

"Of course, my lady." A smile flitted across her face. It suited her much better than regret.

As we returned to the bedchamber, Julieta brushed her hand beneath her eyes. Quickly enough that both of us could pretend I didn't notice.

Three days later, I stood beside Aric in the arboretum, accompa-nied by a dozen guards. Marya stood at my husband's right hand, Tatiana beside her, a touch closer than necessary given the space available. My sister hadn't been officially confirmed as ambas-sador yet—the Council liked arguing far too much to come to quick resolutions on anything, even simple matters—but I had the impression she was staying no matter what their decision. Tatiana wasn't in the habit of changing her mind once she had made it up. I hoped Marya was prepared.

In front of us, flanked by guards, stood Varin. His hands were free, but soldiers surrounded him on all sides, and the arboretum, while large, was walled. Moreover, Tatiana hadn't disguised her interest in additional experiments, and Marya's hand was blatantly close to her saber's hilt.

We had come to an agreement about Varin's fate. It was unclear whether Varin also agreed, since all that came out of his mouth when he tried to speak was a series of undignified croaks; whatever Tatiana had done to him seemed to be sticking. But since he hadn't contributed any viable alternatives, we'd decided to proceed.

Aric stepped forward to face his half brother.

"Varin of Gildenheim," he said, "I formally sentence you to exile. You are to leave Gildenheim in peace and never return, on pain of immediate arrest and execution. If you ever conspire against this realm or my reign"—unlikely, I thought, given Varin's current vocabulary—"I will make it known you are wanted with a generous bounty, dead or alive. Do we have an agreement?"

Varin said nothing, but he glowered at Aric in a manner that suggested otherwise.

"If you don't accept the terms," Marya put in, "I'd be more than happy to run you through right now."

Varin hastily backed away from her, raising his hands with a pacifying croak.

"Excellent," Aric said. "I'll take that as agreement." He nodded to one of his guards, who stepped forward. An enameled brass spittoon gleamed in her hands. Aric was taking no chances on his half brother having a final dagger up his sleeve: one of his most trusted guards would be personally seeing Varin as far as Damaria, where his exile would formally begin. My parents had a hand in creating this mess—it was only fair that they dealt with the consequences.

"It's a seven-league spittoon," Tatiana explained cheerfully, as Varin gave the cuspidor a wary look. "Works just like the legendary boots. All you have to do is hold the rim and take a step in any direction."

The guard stepped beside Varin and held the spittoon towards him, ready to grip together. Varin regarded it with obvious reluctance.

"If you'd prefer—" Marya offered, starting to draw her saber.

She didn't get the chance to finish. Varin emitted a bilious croak, wrenched the seven-league spittoon out of the startled guard's hands, and was gone in a single step before anyone could react.

For a moment, appalled silence fell over the assembly. Then an entire chorus broke out at once: the appointed guard apologizing profusely, Tatiana irate over the loss of her spittoon, half the soldiers zealously offering to track Varin down.

Aric raised a hand, and everyone fell silent.

"Let it be," he said, his voice quiet but firm. "His sentence of exile stands. If he turns up croaking around the borders with that spittoon . . ." He sighed, rubbing his forehead. "Well, we'll deal with it then."

Marya slid her sword back into its sheath with a disappointed huff. "I knew I should have run him through when I had the chance."

Tatiana tapped a thoughtful finger to her chin. "Do you think he realized he was aiming for the sea?"

Aric opened his mouth, looking distressed, then shut it again. He stared towards the horizon for a long moment, his thoughts unreadable.

I touched his hand. Aric shook himself and turned to me, offering his arm.

"Walk with me?"

"With pleasure." I hooked my arm through his. A few guards trailed us at a respectable distance, far enough back to afford our conversation privacy.

Aric led me deep into the arboretum. Flowers were starting to open in the places where sunlight fell between the evergreens: crocuses blooming purple and gold, spots of color as bright as jewels against the rich dark earth.

Aric was quiet for a while, and I let him ponder. Being around him had taught me to wait for his answers. They were there if I was patient, emerging like stars in the evening sky.

"I know this isn't how you think," I said eventually, "but he was going to kill you, one way or another. You're offering him more than anyone else thinks he deserves."

Aric sighed. "I know. But this wasn't what I wanted. I never saw Varin as an enemy. I never wished him harm."

I squeezed his arm. "I know."

"I keep wondering . . ." Aric's face was troubled. "Maybe if I'd been a better brother, if I'd tried to reach out to him instead of hiding myself away . . ."

I stopped and waited for him to face me. "He made his own decisions, Aric. You did what was necessary to protect yourself and your people. You can't blame yourself for the choices Varin made."

"Maybe," Aric said. But I could see he didn't fully agree, even if he wished he could. Knowing something was true didn't equate to believing it. This was a knot that could only be untangled with time.

Aric shook his head. "Never mind Varin. We can speak of him some other day. That wasn't why I wanted you to walk with me."

I tilted my head to look up at him. "Oh?"

Spots of color brightened Aric's cheeks. "Actually, there was something I wanted to ask you."

He drew away from me, far enough to fumble in the pocket of his coat. "In Gildenheim, we have a tradition. When two people are to be wed, one gifts the other with a token to display their intentions."

I didn't try to hide my smile. "Aric, we're already married, in every sense of the word. I would say your intentions are clear."

"I know that." He was blushing harder now, which made me want to interrupt his words with my lips. "But the circumstances of our engagement were . . . less than ideal. And I would like to make up for that. To formally offer you the choice of being my wife."

He opened his hand. On his palm, gleaming in the morning light, was a familiar silver locket.

"Bianca Liliana, flower of Damaria. Will you choose me as your husband, as I choose you to be my wife?"

Now I was smiling so hard it threatened to hurt. "Aric of Gildenheim. Did you just propose to me with the same locket that turned you into a horse?"

His mouth quirked into a wry smile. "You haven't given me an answer."

I plucked the locket from his hand and closed the distance between us with a single step. I hooked my arms around his neck and pressed my brow to his, looking into his eyes.

"Yes," I said simply. "I choose you with all my heart."

Choosing what I wanted was a risk. Discarding my armor and revealing my heart was a danger. But as Aric kissed me in the spring sunshine, I was finally ready to be brave. I would no longer take the safe road that behooved me, but run instead along whichever path led to the man I loved.

It was worth the risk, for now and always.

AUTHOR'S NOTE

When I was a small child, I stopped growing.

For two years—between when I was two and four years old—I didn't gain weight or get taller. I had incessant stomach pains and was constantly cranky. When I was older, I spent days curled on the couch holding my stomach, unable to summon the energy to move.

Fortunately, doctors identified the cause of my symptoms while I was still quite young. I have celiac disease—an autoimmune disorder that affects approximately one in one hundred people worldwide, although it frequently goes undiagnosed. When celiacs ingest even trace amounts of gluten—a protein found in wheat and other grains—the immune system perceives it as an attack, causing damage to the body. Celiac most commonly affects the small intestine but can harm any organ, including the brain. There is no cure, and the only treatment is a completely gluten-free diet for life.

Bianca's "condition" represents some of the symptoms of celiac disease. As a child, I devoured fantasy novels—but always in the back of my head was the knowledge that someone like me had no place in those books, where I wouldn't be able to survive on the classic fantasy fare of bread and cheese and no one would have the words to understand what was making me sick. So much of traditional fantasy implicitly tells us that people with disabilities, invisible and otherwise, don't belong.

As an adult, I thought: But what if they did?

In *Behooved*, I wanted to show a fantasy heroine who has symptoms like me—and who still gets to have epic adventures and a happy ending. Disabled people belong in fantasy, just as much as we belong in the real world.

If you see anything of yourself in Bianca, I hope this book brings you some measure of joy.

—Marina

ACKNOWLEDGMENTS

Getting a book published has been a long ride, but not a lonely one. I have the following people to thank for getting me across the finish line:

My incredible agent, Maddy Belton, an absolute powerhouse of a literary champion. Thank you for your enthusiasm for Bianca and Aric and for making my author dreams come true! A heartfelt thanks also to the entire MM team, especially Valentina Paulmichl and Hannah Kettles, for advocating for *Behooved* abroad.

My peerless editors, Lindsey Hall and Calah Singleton, for wholeheartedly embracing this book and steering it into becoming the best version of itself. And to Aislyn Fredsall and Hannah Smoot, for taking the reins in Lindsey's absence and for everything else you do behind the scenes!

The rest of the team at Tor, for your unbridled enthusiasm for *Behooved*: Isa Caban, Laura Etzkorn, Christine Foltzer, Devan Norman (those interior details make my heart sing), Rafal Gibek, Megan Kiddoo, Jacqueline Huber-Rodriguez, Sheryl Rapee-Adams, Susan Redington Bobby, Melissa Frain, Eileen Lawrence, Sarah Reidy, Michelle Foytek, Alex Cameron, Lizzy Hosty, Erin Robinson, Alexa Best, Monique Patterson, Lucille Rettino, and Devi Pillai. An especial thanks to Sheryl for saving me from embarrassing math errors in this book's single instance of arithmetic, and to cover designer Christine Foltzer and artist Kelly

Chong for creating a truly stunning cover. I'm honored to have so many talented people working behind the scenes to usher this book into the world.

The rest of the Hodderscape herd, *Behooved*'s wonderful home across the pond: Molly Powell, Sophie Judge, Marina Dominguez-Salgado, Laura Bartholomew, Kate Keehan, George Biggs, Daisy Woods, Natalie Chen, Bethany Lee, Katy Aries, and Claudette Morris. *Behooved* couldn't be in better hands (or hooves) with you!

It's an unreal feeling to read words of praise from writers you've looked up to for years, and I'm so grateful to the authors who blurbed this book for your time and kind words. Thank you also to Jasmine Skye, who gave me guidance when I needed it most.

The fellow writers who read various versions of *Behooved* in its entirety: Amanda Adgate, Finn DeLuca, Michaela Cunningham, O.K. Inneh, Hannah Loraine, Sabina Nordqvist, and C. J. Subko. An extra heartfelt thanks goes to Amanda for reading so many of my manuscripts and still asking for more, as well as for being a genuine and supportive friend for multiple years. I can't wait to have our books on the shelf together!

For support, friendship, and keyboard smashing at all hours: the Sub Slog Comrades, the Inklings, the Wildborn Writers, the Unicorn Vibes Only group chat, Jess V. Aragon, Jules Arbeaux, Po Bhattacharyya, Lindsey Byrd, Erica Rose Eberhart, Amalie Frederikson, Leilani Lin Lamb, Erin Luken, Steffi Nellen, Kate Shay, and Isabel Sterling. I am endlessly grateful for your insight and kind words as well as for fielding my pterodactyl screeches.

My family, who read this book despite my warnings about certain scenes. My dad for typing up some of my earliest manuscripts, and my mom for encouraging my author dreams since before I could write them down for myself.

My husband, for too many things to name here, including the

conversation that sparked the idea for this book and for reminding me to pause to celebrate.

You, the reader, for picking up this book. Your support means the world to this debut author. I hope *Behooved* has brought you what you needed.

Finally, if you, as I was not that long ago, are a not-yet-published author reading the acknowledgments in search of a sign: this is it. Keep going. The world needs your stories.

ABOUT THE AUTHOR

Anna Simonak

M. STEVENSON is a writer, educator, and naturalist with degrees from Brown University (BA, Geology-Biology) and the University of Idaho (MEd, Environmental Education). An avid swing dancer, she's often found dancing Lindy Hop or wandering the woods talking to birds and plants. She is a dual US/Irish citizen and is based in the Finger Lakes region of New York.

WANT MORE?

If you enjoyed this and would like to find out about similar books we publish, we'd love you to join our online Sci-Fi, Fantasy and Horror community, Hodderscape.

Visit hodderscape.co.uk for exclusive content from our authors, news, competitions and general musings, and feel free to comment, contribute or just keep an eye on what we are up to.

See you there!

HODDERSCAPE

NEVER AFRAID TO BE OUT OF THIS WORLD